What Reviewers Say About BOLD STROKES Authors

KIM BALDWIN

"Her...crisply written action scenes, juxtaposition of plotlines, and smart dialogue make this a story the reader will absolutely enjoy and long remember." – **Arlene Germain**, book reviewer for the *Lambda Book Report* and the *Midwest Book Review*

Hunter's Pursuit is a "...fierce first novel, an action-packed thriller pitting deadly professional killers against each other. Baldwin's fast-paced plot comes...leavened, as every intelligent adventure novel's excesses ought to be, with some lovin'. Even as she fends off her killers,...the heroine...finds the woman she wants by her side — and in her bed." – **Richard Labonte**, Book Marks, *Q Syndicate*, May 2005

ROSE BEECHAM

"...a mystery writer with a delightful sense of humor, as well as an eye for an interesting array of characters..." – *MegaScene*

"...her characters seem fully capable of walking away from the particulars of whodunit and engaging the reader in other aspects of their lives." – *Lambda Book Report*

JANE FLETCHER

"...a natural gift for rich storytelling and world-building...one of the best fantasy writers at work today." – **Jean Stewart**, author of the *Isis* series

"In *The Walls of Westernfort*, Fletcher spins a captivating story about youthful idealism, honor, and courage. The action is fast paced and the characters are compelling in this gripping sci-fi adventure." – **Reader Raves**, BookWoman 2005

RADCLY*f*FE

"Powerful characters, engrossing plot, and intelligent writing..." – **Cameron Abbott,** author of *To the Edge* and *An Inexpressible State of Grace*

"...well-honed storytelling skills...solid prose and sure-handedness of the narrative..." – **Elizabeth Flynn**, *Lambda Book Report*

"...well-plotted...lovely romance...I couldn't turn the pages fast enough!" – **Ann Bannon**, author of *The Beebo Brinker Chronicles*

THE TEMPLE AT LANDFALL

ISBN 1-933110-27-9
THIS TRADE PAPERBACK ORIGINAL IS PUBLISHED BY
BOLD STROKES BOOKS, INC.,
PHILADELPHIA, PA, USA

FIRST US EDITION OCTOBER 2005
PUBLISHED IN THE UK AS *THE WORLD CELAENO CHOSE*, DIMSDALE PRESS, 2001

CREDITS
EDITORS: CINDY CRESAP AND STACIA SEAMAN
PRODUCTION DESIGN: J. BARRE GREYSTONE
COVER IMAGE: TOBIAS BRENNER (http://www.tobiasbrenner.de/)
COVER DESIGN: JULIA GREYSTONE

The Temple at Landfall

by

Jane Fletcher

2005

Acknowledgments

I'd like to start by thanking all the usual suspects - Rad, Cindy, and everyone else from Bold Strokes Books, who have provided such fantastic support. My thanks also go to Pauline from the Dimsdale Press for first demonstrating faith in my writing.

Additionally I would thank the members of the Gay Authors Workshop, who patiently listened to sections of this being read out at the monthly meetings, gave support and encouragement, and a very nice round of applause when I was finally able to announce that it was going to be published.

DEDICATION

For Lizzy
always

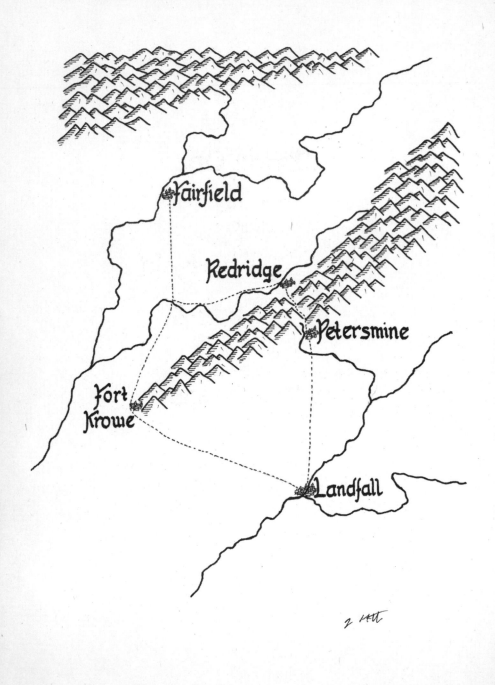

PART ONE

From Fairfield
to Landfall

1 March 536

CHAPTER ONE—THE CHOSEN OF THE GODDESS

From the steps of the temple at Fairfield, you could look out over the bowed heads of the assembled pilgrims and supplicants, over the thatched roofs of the houses and shops, over the broad meadow where they held the twice-yearly fair that gave the town its name, and see the distant mountains far to the north. The boundary of the known world. The line of high peaks glinted, a white so pure as to catch the breath in your throat, even under the sullen gray March sky. Looking at them, you could almost hear the rustle of the fir trees, smell the clean mountain air.

The corner of Lynn's lips twitched. Well, maybe that was straining the imagination too much, especially with the winds that day coming from the cattle market on the east of town, and she did not really have the time to enjoy the view. All eyes were on her. The constant flow of women up and down the temple steps was halted, held expectantly behind the line of red-and-gold-clad Guards. A few steps away stood the senior Sister, looking at her quizzically. Not much of the Sister's expression was visible, just her eyes showing in the gap between the bottom of her cowl and the top of the thin gauze mask covering her lower face, but the faint furrowing of her forehead managed to convey the first hint of impatience. There were prayers to be sung.

Lynn turned her back on the mountains. Between the open twin doors of the temple stood the tall statue of Himoti, the carved stone face staring down blindly on all those who would come in to entreat with her divine mistress, seeking consolation, a blessing, or a child. But today, as always on the first day of the month, the prayers were for Himoti herself, greatest of the Elder-Ones, Celaeno's favorite, the patron of Imprinters. Lynn lifted her voice in the song of praise.

Blessed Himoti,
Favored of Celaeno,
Life bringer, law giver,
Heed our prayers…

The pure notes were clear and strong, but even if Lynn had crooned tunelessly, she would have been listened to with entranced awe. The Guards stood impassive in their bright uniforms. The rows of Sisters lined the sides of the steps, hidden beneath their masks and white robes. The statue of Himoti towered over everyone, yet the crowds spared hardly a glance for any of them. Wide-eyed, they watched the young singer dressed in a simple suit of blue, a plain-cut tunic reaching to mid-thigh and loose leggings, no gold braid, ornament or mask. Just brilliant blue. Imprinter blue.

But for all their attention, it is likely that few really noted the details of Lynn's appearance, that she was a little below average height, in early to mid-twenties, fine-boned. Like all Imprinters, her uncut hair was plaited straight down her back, but a few stray wisps revealed a natural tendency to waves. Her mouth was wide, which combined with large eyes, had earned her the nickname "Frog" as a child, though none would presume to call her so now, even if the name had truly been deserved. For she was an Imprinter, the chosen of Celaeno, and it would surely be verging on a sin to think of her so disrespectfully. She was the living embodiment of Himoti's gift to the world. Which was why it was fitting that once a month an Imprinter should step outside the temple, into the view of all, and lead the prayer of thanks in her patron's honor.

The rituals were slightly longer than usual, with a few extra prayers added in recognition of the fact that March was the month of the festival of Landfall, the month Himoti had first set foot on the world Celaeno had chosen for her daughters. Lynn's clear singing filled the forecourt of the temple. The Sisters and crowd joined in at the appropriate places, incense was burned on cue, and the senior Sister read extracts from the book of the Elder-Ones, but all too soon the ceremony was over and the last note faded.

For a moment, the silence held, and then a faint rustling began at the rear of the crowd, the first murmurs and whispers, although still subdued and respectful. Lynn let her head fall back so that she looked up into the sky at the circling black specks of birds wheeling under the rolling blanket of gray. She knew she was fortunate in her singing ability. It meant she was nearly always the Imprinter chosen to lead the prayers to Himoti, the one who got the chance to stand outside for a few minutes each month, in the open air under Celaeno's wide skies.

Lynn's thoughts shifted briefly to the other five Imprinters in the temple at Fairfield. Did they get as much enjoyment from this brief excursion as she did, or were they more content in the confines of the temple? They certainly did not appear to show any signs of resentment or disappointment when they were not selected for the ceremony. Lynn was not sure if she could survive without it. Her eyes returned to the statue and she offered her own silent prayer. *Please, Himoti, help me grow to like this life you have chosen for me.* Lynn's lips tightened in a line as she fought back a sigh. Maybe someday it would work itself out.

On either side, the Sisters began to file into the temple, but the senior Sister left her subordinates and came to stand beside Lynn while waiting for the Guards to advance up the stairs and form an escort around them. The eyes above the gauze mask regarded the younger woman with approval. "You sang well today, Imprinter."

"Thank you, Sister."

"Indeed, with your gift of imprinting and your singing, you have been doubly blessed by the Goddess."

"That was more or less what I was just telling myself." Lynn was adept at keeping any trace of irony from her voice. Over the years, she had found it a valuable skill.

The Guards surrounded them in a phalanx, fending off the waves of worshippers who, now that the ceremony had finished, were surging up the steps and into the temple. Although even without the soldiers' armed presence, it was doubtful that anyone would have dared barge into an Imprinter. Certainly not on purpose. The Guard captain surveyed the scene, making sure her troops were ready, then she snapped an order and the small entourage marched through the great doors. The crowds slipped aside around them. Lynn took one last deep breath of crisp air before the daylight was lost.

Inside the great hall of the temple, the mood was dim and oppressive. Mean shafts of watery light fell from slits high beneath the ceiling, lost in the thick pall of incense and candle smoke. The sweet smell of the fumes mingled with that of the bodies pressed around her.

The hall was high and wide, yet it seemed to close in about Lynn. She felt as if she were buried in the heavy, choking atmosphere of the public temple, sight and sound smothered by the constant murmur of voices in darkness dotted with flickering candles.

And despite the poor light, Lynn could still feel herself to be the focus of attention. She was aware of the eyes peering through the gloom, watching her progress across the hall, even though she was hidden between the ranks of her escort. She looked at the Guard walking beside her, a tall woman whose face, framed by her helmet, was set in a blank military stare. Light from candles rippled like flame over her red tunic and glinted off golden braid, buckles, and the long sword hanging from her belt. The effect was intimidating, which was the intention. The Guards demanded respect. *But are they to protect me or to stop me from running away?* The thought leaped unbidden into Lynn's mind, although neither case required such a strong display of force. Surely no one would dream of harming an Imprinter, and there was nowhere for her to run.

The entrance to the sanctum came into view, its mysteries concealed behind the heavy drapes hanging to one side of the main altar. Within was the private inner world of the temple where the Sisters and Imprinters lived out their daily lives, hidden from the gaze of the public. As they reached the curtains, the ranks of Guards parted, some taking their posts on either side, some returning to the main door, allowing Lynn and the senior Sister to enter alone.

The two women separated just inside the entrance, Lynn to rest in preparation for her next appointment in the imprinting chapel, the Sister no doubt to talk to someone about somebody else. The air inside the sanctum was far cleaner than in the main temple and the light brighter, sufficient to pick out details on the carved wooden panels with their inset illustrations of scenes from the book of the Elder-Ones, gilt-leaf giving a hint of luxury. Lynn spared a last, cynical look at the senior Sister as she disappeared from view. It was a fair bet that life in the sanctum was less austere than most of the outside world would guess, and it was a dead certainty that it was far less holy.

However, Lynn was not involved in the intrigue, backstabbing, and political maneuverings of the Sisters. An Imprinter was an Imprinter. There was no chance of promotion or power or any hope of leaving the temple. Lynn's shoulders slumped as she walked. She tried to tell herself that it was wrong to think of the temple as a prison. She was privileged, gifted by Himoti. Perhaps she should try to be more grateful. But the only thought that rose in her mind was, *Well, that's my outing for the month over. Back to the grindstone.*

❖

The swirling streams of DNA spun around Lynn as she worked. It was a dance with the essence of life, imprinting patterns on the strands, teaching them how to link, making something unique, creating a new soul. Like jewels on a necklace, she strung the sequences together and tucked them up neatly within cell walls. A spark of life that would bud, split, and grow. A new human being. A daughter.

For a while, Lynn considered her handiwork, content. But the task was over and it was time to retreat. Her focus expanded, stepping back from the spiraling double helix to the level of cells where she watched the small egg drifting toward its safe home on the walls of the womb, beginning its journey through life. Then she became aware of blood and warmth and the layers of flesh. Again she heard the pounding of two heartbeats, the constant background rhythm, forgotten while she worked. The two women. And another step back.

In a sudden onslaught of light and sound, Lynn's ordinary senses returned. Her eyes watered at the attack, even in the dim imprinting chapel. It was followed by a second, even less pleasant burst of sensation as her legs and arms made their tingling cramps felt. She was back in the everyday world. A woman lay before her on the altar, the mother-to-be. One of Lynn's hands lay over her womb; her other rested on the head of a second woman kneeling beside her. The mother's partner, whose genes Lynn had mingled and imprinted on the embryo. Their child.

Still, Lynn was sensitized to their bodies, the blood in their veins, the air in their lungs, and the new spark of life inside the woman on the altar. But her own body's demands began to lever her away from the bond. From the shadows on the wall, Lynn knew she had taken less than two hours to complete her work. Even so, she could feel the cricks in her neck and joints, the stiff, exhausted ache in her back, and it was not yet time for her to rest.

Two Sisters had been watching from either end of the altar. Seeing

Lynn come out of the imprinting trance, they stepped forward, and at Lynn's tired nod that all was well, they prompted the woman to get off the altar and kneel beside her partner to join in with the formal prayer of thanks, their words echoed by the small family group who had been allowed to witness the imprinting. The prayer was short, but in Lynn's state of tiredness, it seemed, as always, to drag on and on.

> *...Guide us in Celaeno's path.*
> *Praised be the Goddess,*
> *And keep us ever in her grace.*
> *Praised be the Goddess.*

The last paired lines of the litany finished, and Lynn was finally free to leave the chapel. *Just as long as I can summon the energy to walk*, Lynn thought grimly. She turned around, intending to make her escape with as little fuss as possible, but halted abruptly at the sight of the couple's family.

An elderly woman knelt in the stalls, tears trickling down her smiling face. A soon-to-be grandmother, no doubt. The five or six other witnesses showed a similar, solemn depth of emotion, except for one woman whose face was split in a broad grin. Lynn followed the direction of her gaze and looked back to see the two women by the altar shyly, tentatively reach out to take each other's hand, wonder on their faces, their eyes locked together. A lump rose in Lynn's throat. *How long before I become immune to this?* she asked herself. Because surely one day the repetition and exhaustion would grind away the sense of awe, and she would become as deadened to the marvel of life as the other Imprinters in the temple who viewed creating each new child as a burdensome drudge to be gotten through with as little effort as possible.

However, Lynn could not stay to share the moment with the family. Her body was shaking with exhaustion as she left the chapel, moving as quickly as her leaden legs would allow and oblivious to the Guards who slipped into place around her, but she heard someone whisper, "That was quick."

And it was. Lynn knew that she was by far the most talented of the Imprinters at Fairfield. Then she thought of how tired she was, and wondered how the others coped. Elspeth frequently took up to seven hours to create a new soul. *It will kill Elspeth in the end,* Lynn thought. Small wonder the elderly Imprinter could be so bitter about her calling.

Even now, the demands on Lynn's endurance were not finished. She must go to Himoti's oratory and give thanks again for the gift the Elder-One had bestowed upon her. Only then would she be free to rest until she was called to the imprinting chapel once more. She was the only Imprinter to regularly create three new embryos a day and had heard the Sisters wonder if four might be possible. A worthwhile question had it been inspired by the people's need for children rather than thoughts of extra imprinting fees for the temple. For all their talk of theology, some Sisters could be more materialistic and greedy than the sharpest market trader.

Lynn's expression grew bleak. *It will kill me too, in the end.*

❖

The window was not much to get excited about, scarcely twenty centimeters square. Its purpose was to let a little light in, not to provide a view, but if Lynn pulled the small wooden altar over and stood on it, she could just rest her chin on the sill and peer out. The room was on the south side of the temple, so Lynn could not see the mountains. In fact, with the angle of sight, she could not even see the ground, but she had a fair expanse of evening sky to watch. The solid blanket of cloud that had hung over the morning's ceremony had started to break up, and streaks of washed blue showed through ragged gaps. A noisy flock of birds was coming home to roost. Lynn's eyes followed their flight until they slipped from view. There was certainly nothing in the room worth looking at. Its bare plaster walls were two meters wide by three meters long. The only items in it were the altar, two candles, a small statue of Himoti, and the thin blue prayer mat.

Lynn allowed her thoughts to drift idly, trying to recapture childhood memories of running under the open sky in the days before she had been taken to the temple. She had only been twelve years old at the time. At first, she had cried herself to sleep each night, wanting her parents. Now she could not even recall with certainty what they looked like. Neither could she remember saying goodbye to them for the last time the day she went to the temple to be tested. Her parents must have been so worried when they left her at the door of the assessment room. They must have known she was exceptionally talented with the healer sense, but perhaps they had convinced themselves that their daughter would be a Cloner, able to do no more than induce the farm animals to replicate themselves. It was a good profession to have. Cloners were trained by the Sisters, but were then free to travel from farm to farm, bringing about new animals, each one identical to its mother.

Lynn's eyes were no longer focused on the scene outside the window as she wondered about her parents. Surely they must have known that there was a good chance she exceeded the level of ability needed to induce cloning? That rather than simply transplant a complete cell nucleus, she would be able to step inside and manipulate the strings of DNA. That she would be an Imprinter. Someone able to imprint genetic information and thereby create a human being with a unique soul.

Lynn's face was grim. Her parents must have worked so hard to hide their fears from her, so as not to alarm her. Lynn wished that they had not. She wished they had sobbed and shouted and that she had been dragged from their arms. Then at least the parting might have made a strong enough impression for her to remember it. But she did remember the Sister telling her that she would not be going home. Lynn could still hear the Sister's syrupy voice as she explained how lucky Lynn was to be able to live in the temple. That Himoti was the greatest of Celaeno's disciples and that the Goddess only chose the best little girls to receive Himoti's gift. That Celaeno's chosen should not cry.

Lynn was so lost in the old memories that when the door to the meditation room opened without warning, she jumped and almost fell. Two of the altar's stubby legs lurched into the air, waved around drunkenly, and thumped back on the ground. Lynn's arms flailed for balance, then one hand managed to catch hold of the window, and she twisted around, half hanging, to meet the surprised eyes of the Sister standing in the doorway. For a confused moment, the two regarded each other in silence, wondering who was the more out of place. Surely the Sister had no business to interrupt her? Lynn was supposed to be meditating, and it was completely against temple rules to disturb an Imprinter at this task. But equally, she was supposed to be meditating, not looking out the window.

It would be awkward to explain, even though temple discipline had become somewhat lax under the administration of Consultant Hoy.

Lynn looked at the woman in the doorway, noting the absence of lines around the eyes staring over the mask. She was one of the new batch of novices whom Lynn had not yet learned to distinguish by outline, and maybe just young and inexperienced enough not to challenge the actions of an Imprinter, particularly if she had entered the meditation room by mistake. It was certainly worth an attempt to bluff it out.

Lynn tried to look as confidently serene as her position allowed and asked, "Can I help you, Sister?"

"Er...yes. I think so. You are the Imprinter called Lynn, aren't you?"

Damn, she isn't in the wrong place, Lynn thought, although out loud she restrained herself to a simple, "Yes."

The silence returned for a few more seconds, but then the junior Sister apparently decided it would be easiest if she pretended that nothing untoward had happened. Her eyes dropped to her feet and she cleared her throat while Lynn got down from her precarious balance. When Lynn was standing before her the Sister spoke again. "You must come to Consultant Hoy's rooms at once. You have permission to conclude your...um...meditation."

"Yes, Sister."

Lynn slipped past the white-clad woman, breathing a faint sigh of relief, but while she hurried through the corridors of the sanctum, her mind whirled as fresh fears surfaced. She searched her conscience for any misdemeanor that might have come to light, but could think of nothing even remotely serious enough to justify interrupting her meditation. By the time she reached her destination, Lynn's stomach was a sick knot and her palms felt sticky.

The consultant's study was large and very well appointed. The room had been designed for comfort, and it was clear from the rich furnishings where a fair slice of the imprinting fees went. The only thing marring its usual air of serenity was the consultant herself, who sat beside the fire, hands clasped tightly in her lap and eyebrows drawn together in a furious scowl. The sight of the consultant brought Lynn to a halt, wondering what could have so provoked the normally complacent Hoy. To her relief, though, it was immediately apparent that the force of Hoy's anger was directed toward three Sisters standing at the other side of the fireplace. The atmosphere in the room was crackling with tension. Lynn was so confused that a few seconds passed before she realized that the three were strangers to Fairfield. After an awkward pause, she managed to gather her wits enough to say demurely, "You wished to see me, Consultant?"

"Yes, Imprinter. Please come in and shut the door."

Lynn complied and then stood uncertainly while Hoy and the oldest of the three strange Sisters engaged in some sort of glaring competition. Just as Lynn was starting to think she would not be getting any explanations, Consultant Hoy drew in a deep breath so that her gauze mask was sucked back against her nostrils, and then turned away from her opponent.

"We have been graced to receive a delegation of our beloved Sisters from the temple at Landfall." Despite her words, Hoy's clipped tones held very little in the way of love. "These are Sister Smith"—the oldest of the visitors gave a faint nod—"and her colleagues, Sisters Quento and Ubbi. It would appear that reports of your talent have reached as far as Landfall."

Lynn's bewilderment grew. Especially since reports had gone both ways and, even at Fairfield, they had heard the name of Smith. The Sister's career had been controversial, but her rise through the temple hierarchy had been unstoppable, if not always steady. Word now was that she had her rivals in retreat, and it was predicted she would take the Chief Consultant's chair within the decade. From what she had heard, Lynn could say with certainty that the Sister's visit to Fairfield would be for political rather than religious purposes. Although if it had been hoped to gain Hoy's support for some venture, it had obviously badly misfired. However, Lynn's main thought was, *What does she want with me?*

Hoy looked as if she was gathering herself to say more, but Sister Smith stepped in first. She faced Lynn while, as if coincidentally, turning her back on Hoy. "Indeed. Even at Landfall we have rejoiced in the good news that you have been gifted to an unprecedented degree. And we have considered how to best show our appreciation of the blessing the Goddess has given to the world. And given through you. For while we are all daughters of the Goddess and equal in her sight, it cannot be denied that some are called to a higher destiny than others." There was something in her tone that implied Sister Smith included herself among these fortunate individuals. "When someone has been favored by Celaeno, as you have been, it would be an affront to her beneficence to leave her to languish in a minor temple."

Lynn could almost hear the sound of Consultant Hoy biting her tongue at the words, but Smith went on smoothly. "The temple at Landfall is where the Elder-Ones first set foot in the world, where the blessed Himoti first instructed Celaeno's children in the mysteries of life, where her mortal remains are buried. And surely it is clear to all, your place is there. In this, the Chief Consultant has agreed with me, and I come with her full authorization to escort you to Landfall with all possible speed."

Consultant Hoy could keep silent no longer. Her voice snapped out, "But it has always been the custom that Imprinters do not leave a temple once they have been taken into its sanctuary."

"Customary, true. But precedents exist," Smith countered. "In the words of Himoti herself..."

Lynn fixed her eyes on the fire and switched out of the argument. Whatever she might want was irrelevant, as it had been since the day she had been declared an Imprinter and taken away from her parents' farm. Now she belonged to the temple, and it was no comfort to know that, in this matter, Consultant Hoy was as powerless as Lynn. No doubt Hoy would draw on the finer points of scripture to support her argument, but it would all be wasted against the supremacy of the Chief Consultant's warrant.

Of course money would not be mentioned, but it would be of prime importance, at least as far as Consultant Hoy was concerned. Lynn's work contributed a quarter of all the imprinting fees taken at Fairfield. But Sister Smith's motives might be more complicated. While waiting for the inevitable conclusion, Lynn did a quick calculation. Landfall was fourteen to fifteen day's journey, which would give plenty of time to reach there for the big festival on the twenty-third of March. Celebrating Landfall at Landfall, and Smith's chance to present her new acquisition for the temple. It would be a few plus points for Sister Smith's tally. Her name would get mentioned in the right places; the Chief Consultant would be pleased. All of which could be turned into a step up onto the next rung in the ladder for Smith.

The sudden onset of silence recalled Lynn from her reflection as the heated debate spluttered to a halt. Even had the outcome been in doubt, Lynn could have deduced her fate from the body language before her. The visiting Sisters were triumphant and Consultant Hoy was disgusted. It was a serious matter for the consultant, Lynn thought wryly. With the loss of income, Hoy might be forced to limit her appreciation of the heavy southern wines to the less expensive vintages.

But Lynn did not have long to consider Hoy's misfortune. Sister Smith came to stand in front of Lynn, claiming her attention and placing a hand upon her head. Smith raised her eyes to the ceiling and spoke in a voice resonate with the fire of piety. "May the love of Celaeno bring an end to contention and guide us all in the wisdom of her will." Smith's gaze dropped to rest on Lynn's forehead. "Truly, my child, you are the chosen of the Goddess."

With effort, Lynn kept her face blank. But had it not been blasphemy to think it, she might have wished that the Goddess had chosen someone else.

CHAPTER TWO—DELAYS ON THE ROAD

The next day was spent in preparations for departure. These consisted almost entirely, in Sister Smith's view, of prayers for a safe and speedy journey. After hours spent on her knees in Himoti's oratory, Lynn was almost left with the impression that Smith expected the Goddess to personally pack the luggage for them. The day after dawned mild and wet. A steady drizzle began before sunrise and was still falling when Lynn was escorted into the stable yard at the rear of the temple. It was a dreary way to start the journey. The damp, lazy wind swept ripples across the surface of puddles and snatched volleys of drips from the eaves of buildings.

As Lynn emerged into the courtyard, she was greeted by a confusion of activity. Four cart horses were being harnessed to the carriage that would carry her and the three Sisters. Adding further to the commotion was the escort of a dozen Guards. The soldiers were milling back and forth, mounting, dismounting, and adjusting buckles and packs in a seemingly haphazard fashion. The cart horses were matching the weather in a mood of sullen intractability, and it required the attention of the civilian driver, her second, and three grooms to get them into the harness. Other temple servants dithered at the sidelines, unsure whether their help was needed, but unwilling to step out into the rain to volunteer. A group of Sisters huddled in the shelter of a porch, and the faces of several of the kitchen staff peered through an open doorway.

For the journey, Lynn's plain suit of blue had been supplemented by a thick cloak, gloves, hat, and boots. They were slightly too warm for the weather that day but might well prove invaluable later, since it was too soon in the year to be sure that they had seen the last of winter. But even with her Imprinter's clothes hidden, everyone recognized her. The familiar sensation of knowing that all eyes were on her swept over Lynn as she stepped into the courtyard. The chaos, if not actually abating, flowed away from the spot where she was.

Consultant Hoy accompanied her across the cobbles to the carriage—a gesture possibly intended as a mark of respect, but more likely prompted by the consultant's desire not to relinquish control of her most valuable asset until the last possible moment. Once she was inside, Lynn removed the cloak to keep from overheating. The rain was more of a nuisance. The damp seeped into everything, and her braid was a clammy weight on the back of her neck. Yet despite the weather, Lynn was hard put to hide her excitement. Not that she had any illusions of the temple at Landfall being any better than the one at Fairfield. If Smith was anything to go by, the reverse seemed far more likely. But the journey to Landfall gave her fifteen days outside the confinement of the temple, the opportunity to see a little of the countryside, perhaps even one last close look at some mountains. It was quite literally the chance of a lifetime.

The door of the carriage opened again and Sisters Quento and Ubbi climbed in, fussing about the mud splattering the hems of their long white robes. They were shortly followed by Smith, and in an instant, the fidgeting stopped and they had taken their seats in dour silence. When the door was finally shut, the senior Sister sent a withering glare through the small window at the ragtag group assembling to watch the departure and let out a snort of disgust. "How have they got time to dawdle around? It's not as if they are even offering prayers for our safe journey. Consultant Hoy should be directing them to some worthwhile employment."

"Yes, Sister," Quento and Ubbi agreed in unison. Agreeing with Smith appeared to be their main function in the proceedings.

"The Goddess has not called them to her temple for the sake of their amusement. Her will is that they devote themselves only to pious endeavor," Smith said firmly.

Already in their acquaintance, Lynn had come to recognize the style of Sister Smith's pronouncements, the self-righteous certainty with which she would announce the Goddess's inner thoughts. It did not bode well for life at Landfall. Lynn suspected she would come to look back with fondness on Hoy's easygoing incompetence, but she forced herself to push her uneasiness aside. She did not want to spoil the journey with useless worries about the future.

The carriage shook abruptly as the driver and her second climbed onto the box, and then with a shout and the creak of axles, the vehicle started to roll out of the temple courtyard and through the gates, flanked on either side by a line of mounted Guards. Lynn stared out the window, taking her last sight of the temple. A sudden unexpected feeling of loneliness washed over her. She was not leaving behind anyone in particular that she would miss—the isolation and punishing schedule of an Imprinter's life did not allow room for making close friends—but the temple had been her home for eleven years. It was familiar and safe. Lynn sank down in her seat, blinking back the tears. When she next looked out, the temple was gone, replaced by a row of houses.

To the eyes of most, the town of Fairfield was uninteresting at the best of times, a product of indifferent craftsmanship, not overly well maintained, and the rain effectively washed away what little charm the place might have held. Even so, Lynn's sense of excitement returned at the sight. So long had passed since she had been anywhere outside the temple. Between the horses of her escort, she caught brief glimpses of alleyways and shop fronts, the mayor's house, and the edge of the cattle market. People on the street stepped aside to make way for the cavalcade, their faces holding expressions of bitterness verging on hostility, due either to resentment of the imperious temple Guards, or possibly to rumors that their Imprinter was being taken. It was a safe bet that once the news got out, Sister Smith's name would not be popular in Fairfield.

Before long, the town came to an end and the road became a muddy track through the open countryside heading due south. The air was heavy with the smell of wet grass and soil. The absence of crowds to push aside meant the pace picked up considerably, and the line of Guards was more strung out, giving Lynn a good view of fields already plowed for planting. Collections of shacks dotted the distance, surrounded by the familiar stumpy outlines of pigs. Lynn watched the changing scenery eagerly, while at the same time trying to appear as disinterested as possible, since she was sure Sister Smith would disapprove of her curiosity and might even order the curtains closed.

After a kilometer or so, the carriage slowed to ford a shallow stream. By its banks stood an old woman, clad in layers of rain-soaked rags. Mud was ingrained in the deep lines on her face, and her back was bent from a lifetime's toil on the land. She looked a hundred, though she was probably closer to fifty. It did not require the healer sense to tell that the elderly peasant was not in good health. Yet she still held a long hoe in her hand and had obviously only paused her work for a moment to watch the cavalcade pass. Lynn's eyes lost their focus on the landscape. *Lots of people have to work hard,* she told herself, *and get little reward to show for it.* No matter how cheerless life might be in the temple, at least as an Imprinter, there was no risk she would ever go hungry or be without a roof over her head. There were worse things to be than an Imprinter. There had to be. Yet Lynn still envied the peasant. The old woman had lived her own life and made her own choices.

"Imprinter?" Sister Smith's querying voice interrupted Lynn's reflections.

"Er...yes, Sister?" Lynn floundered. Inside the carriage, three pairs of eyes were looking at her expectantly. Smith had been maintaining a constant monologue of moralizing ever since the carriage had left the temple. She had obviously now gotten as far as requiring some response, but there was no hint of what that might be. Lynn swallowed. She was going to have to admit her lack of attention. "I beg your pardon. I missed what you said."

"I asked if you could start the reading from the book of the Elder-Ones," Smith said with a cold emphasis on each word.

"Oh...yes, Sister. Any chapter in particular?"

Smith settled back. "This will be a long journey. Start at the beginning."

The well-thumbed volume was placed into Lynn's hands, and she opened it on the first page, although the words were so familiar that she could have recited them from memory. She began to read.

"At the start of time, there was only Unsa, the spirit of life, who called the stars into being and cast them into the dark void and named them. Then, so she might better know her creation, Unsa took form and made of herself Celaeno, the mother, that Unsa might have material presence in her universe. For ten thousand years, Celaeno searched the depths of space, seeking a home for her children, and in her belly slept the Elder-Ones, who were not born of this world, who would arrange all things according to her design..."

❖

The rain splattered softly against the thick green glass of the window. Lynn wiped away the mist of condensation on the inside and rested her shoulder on the wooden frame. The upstairs room of the inn provided a reasonable view of the thickly mired street below. Not that there was much to see. Opposite, three ramshackle buildings leaned against each other, as if for support. The tops of trees showed above their thatched roofs, stretching away until they were lost in the low clouds. If Lynn twisted her neck and pressed her face against the cold glass, she could just catch sight of the river and the jumble of broken, half-submerged timber that was all that remained of the bridge. A small group of women stood at the site of the wreckage, Sister Smith's white robes clearly visible among them.

For the four days since they had left Fairfield, the rain had fallen continuously. So far it had only hampered their progress a little, but now the weather threatened to cause serious delays. They had arrived at the small village to be told that two days ago, the heavy spring rains, combined with melting snow from the uplands, had swept away the bridge, and despite Smith's anger, there was no chance that the bridge could be repaired or that anyone could cross the river until the floods subsided. With the grace of the Goddess, the group of locals was persuading Smith of this fact, and she was not browbeating someone into building a raft.

Lynn raised her gaze to the skies. It was getting brighter, the clouds thinning. Even as she realized this, the rain began to ease and the suspicion of watery sunlight touched the window. But no matter what happened, they would go no farther that day. In less than an hour, it would be dusk. She shifted away from the window and looked around the room. Quento and Ubbi had been sent on an errand, so for once, she was on her own. Something that had become a rare luxury. Smith had suggested, in her usual dictatorial manner, that Lynn could make use of the time reading a book of prayers, but she was already familiar with them. Certainly well enough to answer questions should she be asked.

The place they were halted was hardly big enough to call a village: five houses, a blacksmith's, and the inn, set in a clearing by the river. Nothing more than a way stop in the middle of the forest. Lynn left the window and began pacing the room, remembering the ranks of dark trees she had seen from the carriage and the sweet, clean smell of the wet foliage. Her footsteps paused again by the window. The rain had stopped, she was alone, and the forest was only a few meters away. This might be the very last chance she would ever have to actually touch a tree. Even before Lynn had properly considered the idea, the door was open and she had stepped into the hallway.

The murmur of voices came from the taproom of the inn below. Slipping out unnoticed by that route would be impossible. However, the back stairs were to her left, leading out onto the stable yard. Lynn crept silently along the hallway and cautiously began to descend. There was no sound of anyone nearby, but just as she got within three steps of the bottom, she saw the outside door begin to swing open.

Lynn froze. Trying to dash back to the room was pointless. She would certainly be seen, and fleeing would be an admission that she knew she was in the wrong. Lynn cursed herself. Sneaking outside had been a silly idea from the start. To Lynn's relief, the person who stepped into view turned out to be a very junior member of the inn staff.

The girl blushed nervously when she saw Lynn in her blue Imprinter's garb, standing on the stairs. The inn maid's eyes dropped to the ground, and she made an odd movement that might have been intended as a curtsey, or might have been an aborted attempt to run away. There was certainly no risk of the girl challenging Lynn's right to be there. As confidently as she could, Lynn continued walking down the stairs and reached for the handle of the door.

"Please, ma'am," the girl's voice squeaked.

"Yes." Lynn paused and smiled in a friendly fashion, though it seemed to have little calming effect on the child.

"Could you bless me?"

Now it was Lynn's turn to feel herself blushing. She had never felt herself to be very holy. The expectations of others only sharpened her awareness of her own imperfections, but she could hardly explain this to the child. Lynn groped around vaguely for a general blessing.

> *Eternal Celaeno, who hangs above us all,*
> *May you watch over this child and guide her actions.*
> *And when her life is done, hold her safe forever,*
> *To dream of paradise in your chambers of sleep.*

The blessing was neither particularly profound nor appropriate, but the girl seemed delighted with it and skipped away happily. Lynn watched her go and then again reached for the handle of the door.

"Imprinter, where are you going?" Sister Smith's voice was quiet. There was no need for her to shout.

Lynn stopped as if she had hit a wall. It took all her composure to look up the stairs to where the senior Sister stood and keep her voice even as she said, "I thought I might have left my hat in the carriage."

"Why would you want it now?"

"Well, I don't. Not right now. But I wouldn't want to lose it."

The excuse was decidedly weak. And the set of Sister Smith's eyes made it clear that she thought so too, although she was not about to dispute it aloud when others might be listening. With a sharp gesture, Lynn was beckoned up the stairs and back into the room.

"Did you read the prayers?" Smith snapped once the door was shut.

"Yes, Sister."

"And what did you think of the eighth one?"

Smith's tone made it obvious the question was a test, but Lynn was hard put to keep the smile from her face. The prayer was one that she was very familiar with. She hesitated for a second, as if thinking seriously, and then said, "About Himoti's sacred petri dish? It was... uplifting. And the part in the fifth line about in vitro..."

Smith cut off her words, clearly displeased and only slightly placated. "I fear you have been allowed to develop some dangerously lax ways at Fairfield."

As the Sister paced the length of the room, Lynn stood in silence, fearing what might come next. Fortunately, Smith's wrath fixed on another target, and when she spoke again her tones were less harsh. "But perhaps it is more to your credit that you have been able to perform the Goddess's work so well with such poor supervision. I am sure that once you are better instructed in the true love of Celaeno, you will achieve even greater things for her glory."

"That is my most devout hope," Lynn said calmly, although she felt her spirits drop still further. Sister Smith used the word "love" a lot, but seemed to have her own private meaning for the term.

"It was evident to me that Consultant Hoy lacked rigor in enforcing the will of the Goddess. I formed grave doubts about the strength of her devotion. The prayers were performed appallingly. When we get back to Landfall, I think I will have to prepare a report on the regime at Fairfield."

And you won't get the half of it, Lynn thought. As long as things gave the appearance of piety, Consultant Hoy never bothered herself with what was actually happening in the temple. She even turned a blind eye to affairs between the Sisters, in disregard of all the rules about celibacy. Rumor was that she frequently lapsed herself. She might have been equally unbothered if the Imprinters engaged in similar indiscretions were it not that loss of virginity would destroy the ability to imprint. The risk of losing the imprinting fees was the only thing that could guarantee Hoy would stir herself enough to intervene.

On the other side of the room, the senior Sister was also deep in thought, probably considering the possibilities of having Hoy replaced by someone more favorably inclined to herself. But any further remarks Smith might have made were interrupted by the return of Quento and Ubbi.

"Oh, Sister. Have you any news about the bridge?" Ubbi fluttered.

"Yes. I'm afraid it will not be repaired before the end of the month."

Lynn was surprised by the tone of the announcement. The delay put a definite block on any plans Smith had of getting to Landfall for the festival, yet the Sister did not seem bothered.

"Are we going to be trapped here until then?" Ubbi asked.

"Of course not. We will head east. One of the crossings upstream will surely be passable. Do not worry. The Goddess will guide our steps."

The confidence in Smith's voice was tangible, the utter conviction that the Goddess would exert her powers to aid them. Lynn's eyes fixed on the floor. It must be nice for Sister Smith to know that Celaeno took such an active interest in her political career.

❖

"Then Celaeno gathered all the Elder-Ones before her and said to them, 'To each of you I have given a skill.

*That you may instruct my children in their chosen trade,
so their lives may be fruitful...'"*

"Excuse me, ma'am." The head of a Guardswoman appeared at the window of the carriage, interrupting Quento's reading.

"Yes," Smith answered.

"The town of Redridge is just up ahead. And Major Machovi thought you'd be pleased to know that even from here, we can see the bridge is open and there is traffic going across."

"Praised be the Goddess." Smith paused piously then said, "Please convey my gratitude for the news to the major."

"Yes, ma'am." The Guardswoman disappeared.

"Shall I continue reading?" Quento asked.

"No. I think this would be a good time for silent prayer," Smith replied, bowing her head. The other two Sisters copied her action.

While pretending to join in, Lynn studied Smith surreptitiously, wondering if the Sister's faith in the Goddess's aid might be ever so slightly wavering. The journey from the destroyed bridge had not been easy. For five days the route had climbed steadily, taking them on poorly maintained back roads where the wheels of the carriage had frequently become stuck, requiring that the Guards dismount to push it free. Before the end of the first day, the red and gold of their uniforms was lost beneath a layer of mud. Even the horses seemed downcast; their heads drooped as they plodded over the rough farm tracks. Twice they had reached the site of bridges only to find them swept away by the exceptional weather. Now at last, they would be able to cross the river, but the delays on the road surely meant there was no chance they would reach Landfall by the twenty-third.

Lynn shifted her head slightly so she could catch a glimpse of the scene outside the window, and restrained a smile. Maybe Celaeno had chosen to answer her prayers rather than Smith's. The detour had taken them toward the mountains, and whenever she was able, Lynn had feasted her eyes on the jagged spires of high peaks drawing ever nearer. Mountains had become a symbol of her childhood to Lynn, a reminder of her parents' farm in the enclosed valley to the north of Fairfield. A time when she had felt happy, loved, and free. Perhaps the Goddess, in her mercy, had granted one last close look.

The midday bells were ringing out as they stopped in the main square at Redridge. The town clung right on the northern flanks of the mountain range that divided the plain around Landfall from that around Fairfield. Getting out of the carriage, Lynn cast her eyes up to the nearby peaks. The tops were lost in clouds, but that served only to emphasize their scale, though she was not given long to admire them. The three Sisters soon bustled her into the large inn opening onto the square, which was by far the most prestigious building they had seen since leaving Fairfield. Redridge was clearly small but wealthy.

The proprietor of the inn rushed about, bullying her staff into making their best effort for the important guests. Food and accommodation were promised, and the spirits of the entire party began to rise visibly, particularly when Smith announced they would wait until the next morning before continuing their journey. This would give time for a visit to the town baths, a chance for the Guards to groom their horses and polish their uniforms, and an opportunity for everyone to rest. The Guards jostled each other in play as they dismounted, laughing. And for once, the rowdiness went unrebuked by either Smith or the Guard major.

Lynn and Sisters Quento and Ubbi were shown to the inn's most elegant suite of rooms where already the staff was laying a table for lunch. The senior Sister joined them just as the preparations were complete. Immediately, Lynn could tell that Smith was ecstatically triumphant. Her shoulders were thrown back and her eyes swept the room as if she were already ruler of the world, although nothing was said until the four were seated at the table.

"Surely the hand of the Goddess is guiding our venture," Smith declared.

"You have good news?" Ubbi asked, stating the obvious.

"I've been informed that the pass above Redridge is open. In three days, we can be at Petersmine, and then it will be only another six days' travel before we reach Landfall."

Quento and Ubbi immediately began counting days on their fingers. Lynn's only thought was that she would not merely get to see a mountain range; she would actually travel through it. She joined in the thanksgiving prayers with a fervor that almost matched Smith's. The three Sisters were buoyant, slipping the food under their loosened masks with apparent relish, although the atmosphere at the dining table was not relaxed. Lynn doubted whether anywhere within a hundred paces of Sister Smith could ever truly be described in that way.

When the meal was finished, Smith began making plans. "Imprinter, it would not be suitable for you to visit the public baths, but I have arranged for a tub of hot water to be made ready for you. Afterward, there is a small local shrine that I—"

Smith's words were interrupted by a knock. The door opened and the proprietor stuck her head around. "Excuse me, ma'am, but the town mayor is here to see you."

"Please, show her up."

Smith's tone was gracious, doubtless taking the visit as a tribute to her importance. But from one look at the expression on the face of the elderly, dignified woman who was led in, Lynn knew the mayor had not come to flatter the Sister's ego. After the most cursory of introductions, the mayor and Sister Smith disappeared into a nearby room. Lynn was grimly certain that it was bad news, although Quento and Ubbi seemed oblivious of any potential difficulty.

The anxiety made it hard for Lynn to settle, even though the bath helped to relax her after days of being shaken around in the carriage. When she was dried and dressed again, Lynn attempted to see if anything had been learned but was unable to speak to anyone apart from Quento and Ubbi, both of whom were totally lacking in curiosity. They always let Smith do their thinking for them, and they would not start worrying until she told them to. From the window of the room, Lynn looked down on the courtyard. Several of the Guards were in sight, grooming their horses and talking quietly to each other. Their expressions were grim, and any trace of the high spirits that had accompanied their arrival at the inn had gone. Clearly, some rumor of the mayor's news had already reached them.

Nearly an hour passed before the mayor of Redridge left, looking even less happy than she had when she entered. Immediately, Lynn and the other two Sisters were summoned by Smith. Before she said a word, the glitter in her eyes made it obvious that the senior Sister was furious.

"That mayor is a fool. A faithless fool, with no trust in the Goddess." Smith spat the words out.

"What did she say?" Lynn asked the question, since neither Quento nor Ubbi seemed about to open their mouths.

"She said it was not safe to go over the pass. There was some nonsense about a pride of snow lions in the mountains."

A faint sound, suspiciously like a squeak, came from Quento's direction, but apart from that, utter silence filled the room for the space of a dozen heartbeats.

"Snow lions are hardly nonsense," Lynn said eventually, shocked enough to risk disagreeing with Smith.

Smith glared at the Imprinter. "Oh, I don't dispute that there may have been a few somewhere to give rise to the rumor. But this far south, so late in the year, it is unheard of. Even if the lions did get as far as here, they would have moved back north weeks ago."

"The mayor must have had some evidence," Lynn persisted.

"Do you argue with the will of the Goddess?" Smith's voice snapped in anger.

Lynn swallowed. "No, I don't. But snow lions are dangerous."

"No doubt they are. But Celaeno is powerful over all, and with her love to protect us we need have no fear of any wild beast."

Try telling my aunt that, Lynn thought, but left the words unsaid.

"What are we going to do?" Ubbi found the courage to ask.

Smith hesitated for a second and then pulled herself up straight. "We will pray. We will ask Celaeno to guard us and bring us safe to Petersmine."

"You are not thinking of going over?" Lynn blurted out.

"Yes, I am. The only other option is what the mayor suggested. She wanted us to go around the mountains, heading west, and join back up with our original route, but that will put days on the journey. We wouldn't reach Landfall until April. Now, we will all get our prayer books. Have faith, and Celaeno will keep us safe."

Lynn followed the instructions in a daze, appalled by the realization that Smith would risk all their lives just to get her into Landfall in time for the festival.

CHAPTER THREE—

THE 23RD SQUADRON OF RANGERS

The rest of the afternoon passed for Lynn in rising fear and despair, a mood that was apparently shared by no one else in the entire party. After their initial faltering, the Guards had rallied with a show of bravado, and the three Sisters were united in Smith's certainty of the Goddess's protection, none of which eased Lynn's sickening dread, especially when she realized that she was the only one who had ever seen a live snow lion.

She had been nine or ten at the time, in the hard winter that had forced one semi-senile snow lion down from the heights. No one in the district had dared venture abroad once its presence had been confirmed. Confirmed when the shredded corpse of Lynn's young aunt had been found, her blood staining the churned snow in an outlying paddock. For days, all had stayed inside, doors barred. Then one night, they had heard sounds outside the farmhouse, sounds of a large animal, blundering around the yard and low, growling calls. The adults had taken what weapons were to hand, mainly pitchforks and staves, and the children were sent upstairs. But Lynn and her young cousin had crept to a window and peered out. She would never forget the huge, prowling shape, padding around the pig sheds in the moonlight, not that there was anything there the snow lion could have eaten, but the starved animal was not to know that. The next day, a patrol of Rangers had arrived in the district and hunted down the beast. Lynn had suffered from nightmares for weeks after, panic-filled dreams that she felt sure would return that night.

The room at Redridge felt like a condemned woman's cell, despite its cozy furnishing and the roaring fire in the hearth. Lynn's appetite for her evening meal was poor. She picked at a little of the food and tried to shut out the sound of Smith's sanctimonious platitudes. No one seemed to even consider the idea that the journey over the pass could be death for them all.

The hour for sleep was approaching when another knock came at the door and the proprietor trotted in. Sister Smith put aside her book and ushered the woman to a corner of the room where they exchanged a few words, their voices too low for Lynn to catch anything said. It was probably no more than the order for breakfast. *Maybe the last meal I will ever eat,* Lynn thought miserably. Neither Smith's eyes nor the proprietor's deferential expression gave away any clues, but after the bustling innkeeper had left, Smith returned to her chair and announced, "Already Celaeno has answered our prayers."

Lynn averted her eyes and stared at the burning logs in the fireplace. The only way her prayers could have been answered was if Smith had abandoned the idea of going over the pass, but the senior Sister's exultant tone made that eventuality seem most unlikely. No other explanation was forthcoming, but within a few seconds, the door reopened and the town mayor entered again, followed by Major Machovi of the Guards and two officers from the Rangers in their uniforms of gray and green. Lynn looked at the newcomers with the first spark of hope. The Rangers protected the borderlands, tracking down and removing any dangers that threatened. Perhaps they brought good news. Maybe they had already dispatched the snow lions.

"Ma'am?" the mayor said hesitantly.

Sister Smith inclined her head graciously, granting her permission for the town leader to continue.

The mayor cleared her throat and said, "The 23rd Squadron of Rangers has just arrived in Redridge. They've been sent from Fort Krowe to deal with the snow lions. This is Captain LeCoup and her deputy, Lieutenant Ramon. I've brought them here so they can tell you a little more about the nature of the threat the pride poses to travelers."

The mayor's tone made it clear that she expected the Rangers' advice to dissuade the Sister from her folly. Lynn wondered how the woman could be so naively optimistic after an hour of talking to Smith. If the mayor had the political drive to reach her current status, then surely she could recognize similar ambition in others? Or perhaps she thought the holy Sisters were above such things. Lynn managed to restrain a wry grimace. Three days in a temple sanctum would teach the mayor otherwise.

All eyes in the room were on the Rangers. Captain LeCoup was a thickset woman of about forty, with a tired, dogged expression and a manner that implied she had little time for fools. Lieutenant Ramon was younger, probably in her mid-twenties, tall and lean. She stood half a step behind her captain while her level gaze surveyed the room, as if assessing it for hidden dangers. Both had the close-cropped hair of soldiers, in Captain LeCoup's case graying slightly at the temples. Short Rangers' swords hung by their sides. They still wore spurs, and their uniforms bore the stains and grime of a long journey. They had obviously been dragged over to meet with Smith the instant they arrived in Redridge.

LeCoup took the mayor's introduction as her cue. She nodded respectfully to Sister Smith and started speaking. "Yes. On the way over here the mayor was telling us that you were hoping to go over the pass. She felt you might be...underestimating the danger."

The captain's words were probably intended as a tactful beginning. Even so, Smith let her go no further. "No. I was not underestimating the danger, but neither was I underestimating the power of the Goddess. It is clear to me that the workings of her will are visible, even in the fact of your arrival in Redridge. You have been sent by Celaeno to guide us safely over the pass."

The room was in silence while the captain considered how to respond. At last she said, "Excuse me, ma'am, but we were sent by the Ranger Command in Fort Krowe to clear the snow lions from the area."

"The Goddess is the higher authority."

"My orders were quite explicit. I am to hunt down these animals as quickly as possible, before someone gets killed." LeCoup's tone was polite, but every bit as implacable as Smith's.

The senior Sister paused for a second, and then softened her tone, as if explaining something obvious to a child. "All things work to the will of the Goddess. Whether you know it or not, her hand was responsible for bringing you here. It was by her design that the Ranger Command sent you."

"Then she should have made her intentions a little clearer when I was given my orders." The sarcastic edge in LeCoup's voice was apparent to all, as was the immediate outrage it provoked in the Sister.

"How dare you be so flippant when you refer to the Goddess? Do not forget you are in the presence of one of her chosen ones."

LeCoup's eyes dropped from the combative stare, but the set of her jaw showed that she was not yet ready to give way. At her shoulder, Lieutenant Ramon looked grimly concerned. Lynn half opened her mouth, trying to summon the courage to say that the Goddess's chosen one had no wish to go over the pass, but it was Major Machovi who now stepped into the debate.

"Surely the two courses of action are not irreconcilable? The Rangers can come with us over the pass; it will take no more than three days. Then they will be free to hunt down the snow lions, and the journey over the pass will give them a chance to make an initial reconnaissance of the area." Machovi looked to Smith and was rewarded with a nod of approval.

LeCoup was unmoved. "Escorting a carriage is not a viable method of reconnaissance, and even if it were, it would still not be safe for you to—"

"What!" Smith broke back in, loudly. "You have a full squadron of Rangers, thirty-four armed women, plus twelve Guards, and you think you can not keep us safe from a few half-starved animals?"

LeCoup's chin went up. "No. I don't. Hunting snow lions is a dangerous job. You have to move slowly, pick your route and your time. Make sure you're tracking them, not them tracking you. With a carriage, we'd be forced to stay on the road, strung out and vulnerable to ambush. On top of that, our horses are trained for this sort of work, trained not to bolt. The cart horses would be unpredictable in an emergency, putting everyone in the carriage at risk." LeCoup was obviously only controlling her anger with effort.

"You have no faith in the Goddess," Smith said savagely.

Lynn knew that in the Sister's reckoning, it was the worst accusation possible, but anyone could see that it was having little effect on the stubborn Ranger captain. Smith spun around to face the fire, while the rest of the assembled group exchanged anxious glances. Things could get very nasty, very quickly if Smith were to make it an issue of religious dissent. However, when she turned back to the room, she moved to a different line of attack.

"Major Machovi, who is the senior officer here?"

The question was not completely straightforward. The Rangers, the Guards, and the Militia all had nominally independent chains of command, but in the final analysis, they were all part of the same organization and were supposed to work together when necessary. The major's right to pull rank was open to dispute, but one did not get far in the Guards by ignoring such a blatant appeal from a senior Sister. Machovi hesitated for only the barest instant before turning to the Rangers.

"Er, yes...Captain LeCoup. Having listened to both sides, I've decided that the best course is for you to delay your hunt for the snow lions until after you've escorted Sister Smith and the Imprinter safely to Petersmine. As superior officer, I will countersign your orders, unless you wish to refer it to higher authorities."

Of course the Rangers could do that, although it would mean sending a messenger all the way to Fort Krowe, and it was in no way certain that the Ranger Command would choose to defy the wishes of a Sister, particularly one with Smith's reputation. LeCoup looked as if she were about to explode, and Ramon's eyes glinted with anger. The Rangers had little option other than to fall in line, but it was clear they were both furious at the decision.

The meeting was over. The Rangers, with their anger only partially hidden behind the blank faces of professional soldiers, saluted and left the room. The mayor and the major followed after, neither looking totally convinced that the best possible outcome had been reached. But no such doubts troubled Sister Smith. As soon as the door was shut, she faced Quento, Ubbi, and Lynn.

"It is a sign from the Goddess. The 23rd Squadron will get us to Landfall for the twenty-third of March. Come now, we must offer our thanks to Celaeno and then go to our beds. Tomorrow will be a long day."

If we get to see it out, Lynn could not help thinking.

When she was dismissed to her room, Lynn lay awake a long time staring at the darkened ceiling. She had played no part in the meeting, but she was not sure if there was anything she could have said. While the argument had been in progress, the eyes of the Rangers had occasionally flicked in her direction, showing the combination of awe and curiosity that Imprinters always provoked in ordinary folk. But for all the veneration they received, the Imprinters had no power. The temple existed for the glory of the Goddess and to provide sanctuary for her chosen ones. The Sisterhood existed to administer the temple, and to train and care for the Imprinters in the same way that you train and care for children. Sister Smith had no hesitation in making all the decisions for Lynn. Decisions such as whether or not she wanted to be bitten in half by a snow lion.

Lynn found herself praying from the heart that the Goddess would not desert them. The words of the mantra rolled round and round her head until she fell at last into an uneasy sleep.

❖

Lynn was woken at first light by Sister Ubbi. She dressed and gathered her few belongings and made an attempt on breakfast that was, if anything, even less successful than the evening meal of the previous night. The inn was full of commotion, people rushing back and forth, preparing for the journey. Lynn felt herself superfluous, even though she was, in theory, the whole reason for the expedition. She managed to find a quiet corner in the inn's taproom, deserted at the early hour, and sat down to wait until it was time to go. For once, she was on her own. The three Sisters were concluding their business with the innkeeper and the mayor. Lynn thought bitterly that it was typical that she had solitude only when she would have been grateful for any company to distract her thoughts from the journey ahead.

The hectic activity in the inn was just starting to slow when sounds of a fresh disturbance came from the courtyard outside. Lynn twisted on her seat and knelt to look out the window. Judging by the noise, the entire squadron of Rangers had arrived in the street beyond with their horses. As there was not room for them in the tiny courtyard, after a moment of bustle, several of them dismounted and strolled toward the entrance of the inn. Lynn recognized the sturdy form of Captain LeCoup as she disappeared through a doorway, presumably in search of Sister Smith. A few seconds later, Lieutenant Ramon flitted past the windows of the taproom, heading in the other direction, to the inn's stables.

In haste, Lynn scrambled to negotiate the tables and benches and leaped to the side door of the inn, emerging into the narrow alley between the taproom and the kitchens just in time to see the tall Ranger walk past, a few meters away.

"Excuse me. Lieutenant Ramon." Lynn called as softly as she could while maintaining a reasonable hope she would be heard.

Ramon backtracked and reappeared at the end of the alley, her expression changing from uncertainty to stern reserve when she saw the Imprinter. "You want something, ma'am?" she asked icily.

The Ranger was clearly not pleased to see her, but Lynn's state of anxiety would not let her be put off. She took a couple of steps closer and said, "Last night at the meeting, there were some things that didn't get mentioned."

"And things that were mentioned that weren't listened to." Ramon was evidently not in the mood to be tactful even though she was talking to an Imprinter.

"Yes, I know, and for what it's worth, I'm sorry. But how good is your information that the snow lions are in this area?"

"We didn't ride 240 kilometers in two days for the sake of exercising the horses."

Lynn was too worried to take offense at the brusque retort, even though the anger in the Ranger's voice implied that playing nursemaid to a group of suicidal idiots had also not been on their agenda.

"How many lions are there in the pride?"

"Reports range from ten to twenty-five." The lieutenant shrugged. "Best guess is twelve to fifteen."

The cold knot in Lynn's stomach tightened still further. "Are you sure? That's a very large pride."

"Well, maybe on the way over the pass, you'll get the chance to count them yourself."

Ramon's tone was clipped, barely polite, and at last the sarcasm drew a reaction from Lynn. She flushed slightly and looked up to meet the Ranger's eyes. "I've got no wish to get that close. I know about snow lions."

"And I'm sure if we're attacked, your advice will be most valuable. Or it might prove a learning experience for us all."

Now it was Lynn's turn to be sharp. "I was born in the marchlands, north of Fairfield. Snow lions came to the mountains above my parents' farm most winters. One of them killed my aunt when I was ten, and I saw some of the bits that were left of her. What more do you think I need to know?"

The vehemence in Lynn's voice clearly caught Lieutenant Ramon by surprise. Her eyes dropped, and when she next spoke, her voice was less biting, although no less pointed. "Then can't you talk sense into your reverend Sister?"

"If she won't listen to Rangers about snow lions, why do you think she'll listen to me? My grandmother used to say that only fools and Rangers go out when snow lions are around. I know it might seem obvious to you which of those two categories I belong in, but believe me, I have even less choice in this than you do." Lynn turned sharply and stormed back into the inn.

❖

As the door slammed shut, Lieutenant Ramon pursed her lips ruefully, already regretting that she had been quite so blunt. A second Ranger appeared at her shoulder, a sergeant with shrewd eyes and an easygoing smile.

"Was that the Imprinter I saw you talking to?"

Ramon sighed. "Yes. And I think I may have compromised my immortal soul."

The sergeant laughed. "And not for the first time. What did you do?"

"I antagonized her."

"Ooh. Definitely tricky theological ground."

Ramon grinned at the bantering tone, but then her expression became more serious. "At first I thought she was asking pointless questions out of childish curiosity. But I've just realized she was frightened."

"Oh well," the sergeant said with a sniff. "At least she has that much sense."

CHAPTER FOUR—OVER THE PASS

The snow had melted in the lowlands below Redridge, leaving no more than the occasional icy crusting at the bottom of sheltered hollows, but it still lay thick on the high mountains, and by midmorning, the steeply rising trail was taking the carriage and its escort through a landscape of white. Lynn was grateful for her fleece-lined cloak and gloves. The road was well marked and firm underfoot, although the carriage was frequently jolted by potholes and loose rocks, displaced by bad weather during the winter. Presumably, someone had ridden over not so long before to take word to Redridge that the route was open, but blown snow had erased all sign of her passage.

The Guards still rode at either side of the carriage, but the Rangers had split up. LeCoup was in the rear with a half dozen of her troops, while Ramon commanded a similar number, riding a hundred meters ahead. The remaining Rangers were skirmishers, traveling wide of the road to check the surrounding hills for signs of the snow lions. The rough terrain meant they traveled on foot, slowing down the speed of the whole party. Lynn could see Sister Smith getting more and more impatient each time the carriage was called to a halt while the skirmishers negotiated some hazard on the hillside. A heated three-way argument took place between Smith, LeCoup, and Major Machovi when they stopped for the midday meal. Lynn was not close enough to hear what was said, but when the journey resumed, she noted that the skirmishers had been called in and now rode with LeCoup at the rear.

The Guards had also noticed the change in strategy. Lynn overheard two exchanging remarks.

"Looks like the girls have been told they can't play hide-and-seek in the bushes."

"Typical Rangers. Never take the road if they can scramble through the undergrowth instead."

"It explains why their uniforms get in the state they do."

"Is that it? I thought they played mud fights in their spare time."

The Guards did not mention that their own appearance when they arrived in Redridge had not been quite so pristine, but a traditional rivalry existed between the two elite services, which must have only added to the rancor when Machovi had pulled rank at the meeting the night before. Fortunately, the differing duties of the temple Guards and the border Rangers rarely brought them into close cooperation. When it came to opinions about military matters, the only thing they were agreed on was a common disdain for the ordinary Militia who policed the towns and countryside.

Lynn's gaze slipped past the line of red and gold riders and up to the mountains. The lower slopes were covered with wide sweeps of tall firs, while above them hung dark faces of sheer rock, slashed with snow-filled crevasses. The peaks cut a jagged line against the clear blue spring sky. Ahead of the carriage, the road over the pass rolled across the softer folds of the valleys. These were clear of trees and probably used for grazing sheep in the summer, though now they were deserted.

The sight of the open fields of white set Lynn thinking of her childhood, memories of playing snowball fights with her sisters and making snow women. Her mind turned to another clear recollection of one winter's day, climbing to the high pastures with her teenage aunt and looking down on the whole farm laid out below her, toy-like in the snow. Her mother had been furious when they returned. Her aunt always had been a touch indifferent to the dangers of snow lions on the uplands.

The bump as a wheel bounced over a pothole jolted Lynn back to the present, jarring her neck and making her stomach lurch. It would have been much more comfortable for them if they had all been on horseback. *Or then again, maybe not*, Lynn told herself. She had not ridden since she had entered the temple, and by now her muscles would have completely lost their tone. After the first couple of hours, riding would not be fun at all.

"Imprinter. Could you lead us in a hymn?" Sister Smith's voice completed Lynn's return to the here and now.

"Certainly, Sister. Is there any one in particular you think appropriate?"

"Yes. I think 'When First the Elder-Ones Set Foot' would be suitable."

The thoughts occupying Sister Smith were not hard to guess. Lynn raised her voice in song as the carriage rolled on over the snow-covered hills.

❖

By dusk, they reached a staging post one-third of the way over the pass and on schedule to be in Landfall before the twenty-third of the month. Sister Smith's mouth was hidden under her mask, but Lynn was certain it held a triumphant smile. There had been no sign of the snow lions all day, and even the Rangers seemed a little more at ease once the last of the riders had entered the wooden stockade and the gates were shut and barred.

The staging post was like a small fort, set in the middle of a long valley. Its stout timber walls were three times the height of a woman, high enough to keep out any snow lion. Within these defenses, the sides were lined with buildings: stables, stores, and barrack rooms. Latrines were situated in one corner and a tall watchtower in another. It would provide a safe resting place for the night, although a little cramped, and the squeezing of Guards and Rangers into such close association could well give rise to friction.

Captain LeCoup appeared to be well aware of the possibility, and she acted quickly to keep a firm hand on things. While stabling the horses and preparing for the evening meal, she and Lieutenant Ramon moved continuously among their troops, stamping on any injudicious attempts of humor at the Guards' expense. Unfortunately, the captain's attempt to instruct the Guards in methods of dealing with snow lions was less well judged. From her seat beside a fire, Lynn overheard part of one such conversation.

"You can't fight lions from horseback. The tops of their skulls are solid bone and their pelts act like cushions. If you try swinging your sword down on them you'll only cause superficial wounds that will just make them mad," LeCoup explained.

"That may be true for the short swords you Rangers have." The Guard was disdainful.

"A meat cleaver wouldn't go through. The pelt is like matted rope.

You have to use the point of your sword in a straight thrust, preferably at the throat or chest where the fur is thinner. Get down and under when they pounce."

"I think I'd prefer my chances on horseback," a second, bored Guard chipped in.

"But your horse hasn't been trained to deal with them." LeCoup's voice held a touch of impatience.

"*My* horse has been trained to deal with everything," the Guardswoman snapped back.

Lynn glanced around. Five Guards were listening to the captain with expressions ranging from hostility to amusement, while LeCoup looked as if she was fighting a battle to control her temper, and only just succeeding. It was doing nothing to soothe relations between the Guards and the Rangers and LeCoup appeared, at last, to realize this. She started to rise, in search of a more receptive audience, when Major Machovi joined the small group.

The captain sank back onto her seat. "Ah, Major. I was talking about snow lions."

LeCoup's voice made it clear that she hoped the major might force her women to take the advice more seriously. Lynn could have warned the Ranger against such optimism. The Guards were selected for their doctrinal orthodoxy. The only way to get promoted was to make a show of doing and believing everything a Sister told you. Maybe tall Guards looked more impressive in their uniforms, but physical strength and fighting ability came poor seconds to piety in terms of desirable qualities, and intelligence could be a positive handicap to an ambitious Guard. It was very unlikely that Machovi had reached her rank by thinking for herself. However, LeCoup seemed unaware of this and returned to her lesson.

"Snow lions often work in teams to make ambushes. A couple will get behind their prey and try to stampede it toward where the others are lying in wait."

"You make them sound intelligent," Machovi said skeptically.

"Not intelligent, but cunning. Whatever you do, you mustn't run the way they are guiding you—"

"Guards don't run."

The arrogant assertion stopped LeCoup cold. Another of the Guards stepped into the silence. "The Ranger captain has been telling us to dismount if the snow lions attack. She says that swords are no good against lions when you're on horseback."

Major Machovi smiled patronizingly. "Well, maybe the short swords that you Rangers carry, but I think you might be surprised at what a Guard's sword can do."

LeCoup's face froze in a stony glare. Lynn suspected she was silently counting to ten. Then the captain got to her feet, bid the Guards a formal good night, and stomped off to where the Rangers were starting their preparations for sleep, spreading blankets over piles of fresh straw. Lynn felt all her fears of the previous two days return in a rush. Even after eleven years in the temple, she could still be amazed by the obstinate stupidity of the Guards. The Sisters were imaginative radicals by comparison.

The time to sleep was approaching. Lynn slipped outside to visit the latrine block. On the way back, she stopped in the middle of the square. The air was cold, but the skies were clear. Laurel, the smaller of the two moons, had just edged its way above the mountains. Its light reflecting off the snow was enough for Lynn to see her surroundings but not enough to diminish the brilliant intensity of the stars. At the corner of the stockade, the watchtower was a black silhouette against the glittering backdrop. A few more minutes would pass before her absence attracted comment. After a moment's thought, Lynn wandered over to the ladder and began to climb, soon reaching the flat platform at the top.

Immediately, she saw that she was not alone. The tall figure of Lieutenant Ramon was leaning on the railing and looking out over the winter landscape. Lynn hesitated, one foot on the ladder and one on the observation platform, then mumbled, "Excuse me," wondering if she could climb back down without it seeming too much like running away.

The lieutenant glanced over her shoulder, her peaceful expression changing to one of surprise. She had obviously expected the sound of footsteps on the ladder to belong to another Ranger, but she recovered quickly and spoke before Lynn could decide what to do.

"Please, ma'am. If I may take this chance, I...I would like to apologize for being rude this morning. I was angry at the way Sister Smith..." Ramon's voice trailed away, although judging from her expression, she would have liked to say something very unflattering about the Sister.

Lynn paused then smiled and stepped onto the platform. Being angry at Smith was definitely a reaction she could identify with. "That's okay. I wasn't in a good mood myself this morning."

"Have you come up here for a reason? Do you want to pray in private or...?" Ramon stopped, looking uncertain.

"Oh, no. I just wanted to admire the view. Are you on sentry duty?"

Ramon matched Lynn's smile. "No. Like you, I'm just here for the view. We aren't bothering with sentries tonight. The snow lions won't be able to get in, and with them on the prowl, we'd probably even take pity on a bunch of bandits and let them in. If they knocked on the door and asked nicely."

"Do you really think the snow lions are around here?" Lynn asked anxiously, hoping to have her fears allayed.

The Ranger sighed. "I don't know. The year is getting on. They might be moving back north, but if they're really hungry, they might be desperate. I'm afraid I can't be as certain as Sister Smith."

"I don't think anyone could be that certain," Lynn said with feeling.

"She does seem very"—Ramon paused as if hunting for a word—"sure of herself."

"You must remember Himoti whispers directly into her ear."

Lynn could tell that Ramon was unsure whether to take her statement literally. "And she doesn't talk to you, an Imprinter?"

"Oh, on occasion. Four times a year we have a fast day when we aren't allowed to eat anything after sunrise and have to spend the whole day on our knees, praying. It's supposed to be a spiritual experience, and by the end of the day, Himoti's statue often talks to me."

"Really?"

Lynn grinned. "Yes. Mind you, I'd have more confidence in it as a religious miracle if it didn't usually start right after I'd seen little pink fairies dancing on the altar and just before one of the reverent Sisters turns into a flying pig and flaps her way out the window."

For a second, the lieutenant was silent, clearly startled to realize that a blessed Imprinter could joke so irreverently, but then she joined in the laughter. They leaned against the railing and surveyed the bleak winter scenery together.

After a short while longer, Ramon asked, "How are things going in the barracks? I was wondering if I should go back and support the captain."

"There have been no fights yet, and now people are more or less settling down for the night. Your captain was having a hard job explaining to the Guards how to deal with snow lions, but I doubt there was anything you could have done."

"Didn't she make any impression on them at all?"

Lynn's nose wrinkled. "Not so as you'd notice. They seem to think they can cut the lions down in their tracks and that you have problems because your swords are too short."

"Their swords are longer, true enough, but they are also lighter. Like the uniforms, they're mainly for show. They'll just bounce off the lions' heads." She reached to her waist and half drew her own sword. "This sword is more like a Ranger herself: short, ugly, and very efficient."

Lynn laughed at the analogy. "I can't see that all three apply in your case." She looked up pointedly; Lieutenant Ramon was a clear twenty centimeters taller than she was. For the first time, Lynn studied the Ranger's face. The moonlight enhanced the clean lines of Ramon's high cheekbones and well-formed lips. *In fact*, the thought shot through Lynn's mind, *there's only one of the adjectives that's in with a chance.* Aloud she said, "I mean, how efficient are you?"

"I can make a jar of boot polish last a whole year," Ramon retorted quickly.

"Don't let one of the Guards hear you say that. They'd have a fit."

"Do you think so?" Ramon bit her lip mischievously. "I might make a point of repeating the line just to see the reaction."

Lynn grinned then turned to look into the fort below and sighed. "I'd better go back before Smith starts to wonder where I am."

She started to climb down the ladder, but as her foot touched the third step, a long, desolate howl echoed over the mountains. Lynn froze and looked back to where Ramon was standing.

"It might just be the wind." The Ranger's voice held little confidence.

Lynn shook her head, either in denial or to loosen the sudden tightening in her neck and shoulders, then continued her descent. Ramon came to stand at the head of the ladder and looked down at her. "Ma'am."

Lynn stopped and glanced up.

"If things do turn nasty, remember, you're the important one, not Sister Smith. You are the one we'll protect. And if it comes to it, there isn't a Ranger or Guard who won't willingly give her life to keep you safe."

The assertion was nothing less than the truth, and both of them knew it. Lynn's face was sober as she made her way to the ground and back into the barrack hall. She could not help wondering if Smith had included that in her calculations.

CHAPTER FIVE— SNOW LIONS

The sun had not yet cleared the tops of the mountains when they left the staging post. The cavalcade filed out between the large wooden gates and headed south toward Petersmine. At first, the journey was much like the day before, but while the morning wore on, the road became bumpier as they reached the high point of the pass. Here the effects of frost and wind had done the most damage. The landscape was also colder and bleaker. In places, the firs extended down to the roadside so that the route wound between the dark columns of tree trunks. Elsewhere were fields of broken rock where the sharp contours were softened only by the covering of snow. The hooves of the horses slipped on the ice, and Lynn twice bit her tongue when the carriage wheels hit large stones.

Despite the poor state of the road, the party made good time, and as the route began to fall again, the scenery softened. The afternoon was drawing to a close when they caught the first glimpse of the next staging post, their destination for that day. The wooden fort was perched atop a distant ridge, its tall watchtower outlined against the soft evening sky. Although still some way off, the sight of it encouraged everyone with thoughts of a hot meal and a rest, and the speed picked up noticeably. Lynn felt herself begin to relax and enjoy the panoramic view. This was the last time she would ever see mountains, or any sort of countryside. When she entered the temple at Landfall, she knew she would never again leave its walls.

The road dropped down into a basin-like depression hollowed between high mountains on either side. Ahead of them, a saddle ridge shielded the staging post from view, but it could be no more than three kilometers away, barely a quarter of an hour. The hope of getting out of the bone-jarring carriage even put a temporary stop to Sister Smith's constant stream of theological discourse. In the welcome silence,

Lynn's gaze settled on the distant peaks. Her thoughts were drifting away to where the serrated ranges began to fade into the purple of twilight, when the peace of the evening was torn apart by a sudden fury of howling from behind.

Sister Ubbi screamed. Lynn leaped up and stuck her head out the carriage window in time to see the nightmare forms of three snow lions break from cover on the hillside and charge down toward the riders on the road, lunging and bounding in an avalanche of white fur. At once, the Rangers' rear guard swung around. Before Lynn was able to register what was happening, some were dismounted, their horses shooed back to safety behind the growing line of drawn swords. But Lynn did not have long to observe the action.

Major Machovi's voice rang out wildly. "Quick! Get to the fort!"

From the driver's box came a sharp cry and the crack of a whip. The carriage leaped forward, urged on by shouts from the line of Guards at the side.

"No! Slow down. There'll be more ahead!" But Lynn's words were lost in the rush of wind and the pounding of hooves. The jolt when the wheels hit another pothole threatened to send her sprawling across the carriage floor, but she clawed onto the rim of the window, pulled herself back, and was again able to get her head out.

The carriage was racing up the slope toward the top of the ridge. Ahead, Lieutenant Ramon and the advance party of Rangers were already dismounted and standing in the road, waving their arms in an attempt to halt the headlong rush of the carriage and its escort. Their action had no effect on the resolute Guardswomen, and at the last moment, the Rangers were forced to jump aside, letting the onrushing cortege through.

"You deal with the lions; we'll see the Imprinter safe to the fort!" one of the Guards shouted as they passed.

In despair, Lynn saw the faces of the Rangers flash by, a montage of disbelief and anger. Lieutenant Ramon's mouth was open in reply, although nothing could be heard over the thunder of hooves and wheels. Then the carriage reached the top of the ridge, surged over, and the Rangers were lost from view behind the crest of the hill.

As they began to descend, Lynn looked ahead, dreading the sight of more snow lions, lying in wait. This valley was more rugged than the last, scooped from the side of a mountain and rising steeply on the far side. Across its middle was scored the gash of a ravine, widening into a precipitous gorge to the west. The landscape was devoid of trees, but dense clumps of bushes were strewn on both sides of the road in an uneven patchwork. Tauntingly close, the staging post stood high on the opposite hillside, but it would be a longer ride than Lynn had anticipated. The road swung out wide and looped around the valley floor to cross the ravine by a wooden bridge where it was narrowest, on the eastern flank.

Lynn ducked her head back into the carriage, screaming her words so loudly her voice cracked with the effort. "Smith! Make them stop. They're driving us into an ambush!" But for once, Smith was speechless, frozen in the corner like a tableau of horror, with Quento and Ubbi as attendant wailers. All Lynn could do was return to watching through the window and pray they could outrun the ambush when it came.

The carriage was halfway down the valley, hurtling toward the bridge, when Lynn saw the first motion in the undergrowth beside the road, and then the explosion of teeth and claws as the snow lions erupted from the depths of the bushes. Even before there was time to react or change course, the first Guard went down, her horse disemboweled. The Guard following was able to avoid the mound of flailing hooves and claws, but a second lion charged toward her, causing her horse to rear in panic and unseat her. Lynn had a flashed vision of blood spurting onto the pure white snow, a lion with its jaws locked on the throat of a horse, and then the carriage was past, careening on in its desperate race for the bridge. As she looked back, Lynn saw that already four of the Guards had been lost to the first assault. In horror, Lynn watched as three other Guards wheeled about in an attempt to rescue their comrades and deter the lions from chasing after the carriage. They struck out with their swords, slashing wildly while fighting to control their panicked steeds, until they too went down under the onslaught.

Lynn tore her eyes away from the doomed battle. The bridge was getting nearer, less than three hundred meters. "Please, Celaeno, help us," she whispered, her gaze fixed on the staging post on the hilltop above, the promise of sanctuary. It seemed too much to hope that they were past the danger, and then she caught sight of motion out of the corner of her eye. Three more lions had burst into view, charging forward over the snow to intercept the path of the carriage.

The bridge was close, but the lions were closer still. In a state beyond terror, Lynn watched the three huge beasts, seeming to bound in slow motion, yet moving so quickly, converging on the carriage. Then, without warning, another lion appeared from nowhere, rising out of the snow and taking down the Guardswoman in the lead. Now there were only four of the escort left, and the bridge was still a hundred meters away. It was by no means certain they would be safe if they got across, but their deaths were surely inevitable if they did not.

The lions put on a final spurt, lengthening their gait to swallow more ground with each bound, and Lynn realized the race to the bridge was going to be lost. But one of the Guards peeled away from the carriage, spurring her horse into the path of the charging beasts. Her voice lifted in a shrieked battle cry, claiming the beasts' attention as her sword lifted high and fell upon the head of the first lion. The animal howled in pain and dropped back, but the other two snow lions leaped onto the woman, tearing her from the saddle. Somehow, the Guard regained her feet, swinging her sword in a desperate two-handed grip until a second attack sent her sprawling. But her action had bought the carriage time, and while the snow lions ripped at the fallen woman, Lynn heard the sound of the wheels change to a hollow rumble as the carriage jolted over the wooden slats of the bridge.

Lynn looked down. Five meters below, a frozen river glittered at the bottom of the narrow chasm. She had a brief impression of sheer rock walls on either side, the dark shadows obscuring the depths, and then they were across.

One of the Guards shouted, "Hold the bridge!" and the last three riders spun away from the carriage, circling back to try to defend the crossing against pursuit.

The carriage did not slow as it swung around a large curve and began its hectic ascent. The gradient was steeper on this side and the road was cut into the hillside, its path a diagonal scar around the valley walls, sweeping upward. As they got higher, Lynn was given a better view of the carnage below, a sight she had no wish to see, yet she could not pull her eyes away. Already the three Guards at the bridge had fallen, but the snow lions had given up the chase and were turning back to investigate the spoils of battle. One of the beasts raised its head to follow the flight of the carriage, its eyes seeming to meet with Lynn's, then it lowered its jaws to the carcass at its feet.

Both the junior Sisters were screaming. For the first time since the lions appeared, Lynn became aware of the noise, and then of other sounds—the creaks and groans from the wood around her, the dull knocking of the axles. The carriage had not been intended for this treatment. It had never been built to race over rough roads. The whole frame jumped and shuddered as the wheels thumped from stone to stone.

"Driver! Slow down!" Lynn hung half out the window, shouting to the woman on the box above her head, but it was doubtful if she was heard, and even more doubtful if there was anything the driver could do. One glance showed that the horses were bolting, fighting for their heads. The driver was as helpless a passenger as those inside.

Lynn looked back down to the valley floor. The road up the hillside had curved around so they were now directly above the site of the first ambush. The steep slope led down to the brink of the widening ravine, and on the other side were the snow lions, squabbling angrily over their victims. In horror, Lynn realized that not all of the Guards were dead. One blood-soaked woman was trying to crawl away until a lion dragged her back. Lynn averted her eyes and tried to concentrate on the road ahead. The staging post at the top of the hill was less than a half a kilometer away. Safety. If they could make it.

The carriage seemed about to burst apart from the shaking, but there was nothing Lynn could do. Then a wheel smashed down into a larger pothole and ricocheted up and out. The carriage veered wildly to one side, crashing against the rock face where the road was cut into the hillside. There was the screech of tearing wood. For a second, two wheels left the ground before keeling back and pitching the vehicle, equally violently, against the low embankment that marked the other side of the road. The retort as the rear axle snapped echoed around the hills. The chassis of the carriage hit the ground, sheering sideways and splintering from the force of the impact. It began to topple over, still dragged forward by the panicked horses, but the shock had burst the door open, throwing Lynn clear before the carriage completed its disintegration into a tangle of shattered timber.

Lynn hit the ground hard; the impact almost knocked her senseless. She was aware of sliding, rolling down the snow-covered slope, out of control. Her braided hair whipped about her face. Frantically, she clawed at the ground, trying to slow her descent, but the snow was powder under her hands. Her sense of up and down was lost in the confusion of white. There was a slap as her leg crashed into a bush and then nothing as she tumbled into free space. She hit ground again, softer this time, the fall cushioned by a deep drift of snow, and was still.

For a moment, Lynn lay on her back, stunned and breathless, then she opened her eyes and looked up. The sunlight had gone and the blue sky was a ragged-edged band between two black planes of rock. The remains of the small avalanche caused by her slide fluttered down about her in a dancing snowfall. In her shaken state, it took a while for Lynn to realize she had fallen into the ravine.

Every bone in her body felt jarred, but nothing was broken, of that she was sure, but even serious injury would not have been her main concern. Roars and the screams of women and horses came from immediately overhead. Even as Lynn lay recovering her wits, she saw the head of a snow lion swing into view over the top of the ravine, the white fur of its muzzle stained red with blood. Luckily, the beast was intent on the ruins of the carriage. It appeared to be considering crossing the ravine to investigate and did not notice the woman lying below. The animal was close enough for Lynn to see the heavy, bony ridges over its eyes, the saber-like fangs, and the powerful muscles bunching in its jaws, but after an eternity of dread, the snow lion turned away and withdrew from view.

Lynn forced herself to move, to creep, one step at a time across the frozen river, and get to the side of the ravine under the lions, searching for an overhang to shield her from view in case another of the beasts should chance to peer down. At last, she found a shallow niche, the best cover available, and flattened herself against the rock. Then she pressed her hands over her ears and tried, desperately, to block out the sounds from above.

❖

Lieutenant Ramon watched in disbelief as the carriage and its escort crested the ridge and disappeared over.

"The idiots! The stupid fucking idiots," Sergeant Coppelli shouted over her shoulder.

It was an understatement; however, hurling insults would achieve nothing. Ramon looked back down the road. As expected, Captain LeCoup already had the situation well under control. The three snow lions were at bay, snarling at the closing line of Rangers. Even as she watched, one of the beasts leaped forward, claws outstretched. The nearest woman ducked and struck out with her sword, sinking it deep into the vulnerable throat. More Rangers stepped up to assist in dispatching the wounded animal. The other two lions would not be long in following their pack mate.

"Come on. The Imprinter!" Ramon shouted the order and set off running up the hill, hoping the Guards would have come to their senses and stopped, but by the time she reached the brow, the carriage was far ahead, speeding toward the bridge.

"Look at them. They haven't got a brain cell between them." Again Coppelli expressed her contempt of the Guards.

Ramon nodded her agreement. Helplessly, the Rangers stood on the hilltop, knowing what was going to happen, but unable to do anything about it. They saw the sudden motion in the bushes and the snow lions charge, and looked on, appalled, as the Guards fell one by one. They saw the carriage's frantic race for the bridge and the Guard's suicide attack that paid for the crossing.

Coppelli sank down to a crouch, staring at the snow and then looking up. "I said they were idiots, not cowards."

"As brave a bunch of dead fools as you could hope for," Ramon agreed, sickened. Her eyes fixed on the carriage as it began to climb the opposite hillside. Against all the odds, it seemed as if the passengers would escape and reach the staging post in safety, as long as the driver could bring the bolting horses under control. But even as she was starting to hope, Ramon saw the crash and Lynn's tumbling slither into the ravine. A stunned silence claimed the watchers on the hilltop.

"Was that the Imprinter?" one Ranger asked.

"Yes." Ramon had seen the flash of blue as Lynn fell.

"Do you think she's okay?"

"I don't know. But I'm going to find out. The rest of you stay here until the captain finishes with the ones back there. Tell her where I've gone."

"Shall I come with you?" Coppelli offered.

"No. One is enough to see if she's unharmed. And if not..." Ramon shrugged and did not finish the sentence.

The bushes were thick on the lower reaches of the valley. The Ranger set off, slipping from cover to cover as she headed straight for the ravine. Within a few minutes, she stood by the jagged edge, her position downstream from the bridge and well away from where the snow lions were congregating around the fallen bodies. At this point, the ravine was wider and deeper. Luckily, the sides were cracked and eroded, giving plenty of footholds. After a last check on the snow lions, Ramon lowered herself over the side and began to climb down to the frozen river.

❖

Lynn hugged herself against the rock face, eyes squeezed shut, trying to make herself as small as possible. Never had she felt so alone. The noise from above quieted for a moment, and in the silence, she heard the sound of a soft footfall, the faint clink of a stone shifting, no more than five steps away. Her heart leaped to her throat, her eyes flew open, and she saw Lieutenant Ramon, like a gift from the Goddess, cautiously negotiate the last few meters and crouch down beside her.

"Hi. I thought you might like some company," Ramon whispered very quietly, smiling.

In wordless gratitude, Lynn reached out and grabbed her hand.

"Can I take that as a yes?"

"Yes, please, thank you." Lynn was inarticulate with relief.

"Anything broken?"

"No...I can walk. Do you know how to get out?"

Ramon hesitated thoughtfully then said, "I know it's not easy, but we're probably best waiting here. Once Captain LeCoup has had a chance to evaluate the lay of the land, she'll launch an attack. We don't know what plans she'll have, and if we move, we run the risk of getting caught up in the middle of something nasty. There'll be snow lions rushing left, right, and center once it starts. But since she knows we're here, she'll try to keep them away from us."

The whispered words were confident. Lynn took reassurance just from the impression that the Ranger knew what was happening. The tension in her stomach eased a little and she nodded. "I'm sure you know best. At least I'm not alone."

"No, you're not, and don't worry, we'll soon be safe in the fort, Madam Imprinter."

Lynn swallowed. "Given the circumstances, I won't consider it an affront to my dignity if you call me Lynn." She squeezed the Ranger's hand as she spoke.

"Okay. Lynn. My first name's Kim, by the way. Short for Kimberly."

"Kim." For the first time Lynn managed a weak smile. "Thank you for coming for me."

The lieutenant pulled a lopsided grin. "Well, I did promise we'd keep you safe."

A sudden burst of enraged snarling broke out above. Lynn shrank closer to the other woman. "You'd think they'd be quiet while they're eating." She tried to make her voice light though still keeping to a low whisper.

"Ah, but they won't be. Having killed everything, they'll now be discovering they don't much like the taste of people or horses. They are probably going from body to body, taking a bite out of everything, trying to find out which one is best and getting very frustrated. If they're hungry enough, they might force something down. In which case, by tomorrow, their hair will be falling out in clumps, and they'll have the most horrendous case of diarrhea. And you won't believe how easy that makes them to track."

Abruptly, the sounds changed; high shouts were answered by a renewed frenzy of roars from the snow lions. The Rangers were attacking. Lynn flinched at the sound, scrunching her eyes closed in a grimace of fear. It seemed as if the battle was about to spill over on top of them.

"It will be finished soon." Lynn could tell that Ramon was trying to sound as reassuring as possible. After a second's hesitation, the Ranger's arm slipped gently around her shoulders. Lynn did not mind admitting that she was terrified, and she leaned into the other woman's body, trying to draw strength from her. Whatever happened, she did not want to draw attention to their position by screaming.

The battle raged on above. Ramon was listening intently to the sounds, as if trying to judge the flow of events from them. All Lynn could tell was that the center of the action seemed to be moving down the valley, when a fresh outbreak of shouting erupted. Voices yelled commands, coming closer. Lynn opened her eyes, just as a shadow was cast on the opposite wall of the ravine, and then a snow lion appeared above, gathering itself for a leap.

The beast sprang. Its front paws landed on the far side, but the jump was not quite enough. Its hindquarters hit the rock wall, and after wild scrabbling, the lion tumbled back and crashed down, landing not thirty meters away from where they stood.

Wide-eyed, Lynn stared at the unmoving form of the beast. "Please, Celaeno, please. Let it be dead," she prayed silently. And for long seconds, it seemed as if the Goddess would grant her request. But then a paw twitched, the shoulders jerked around, and the snow lion struggled to its feet. It shook its head, still dazed from the fall, but then its enraged glare fixed on the two women, and with a snarl, the snow lion advanced.

The Ranger's sword was drawn in an instant, and Ramon rushed forward, putting herself between Lynn and the lion. A low rumble began in the beast's throat, growing to a full roar as it surged forward, launching itself into a charge. To Lynn, it looked as if Ramon were frozen to the spot. What chance did the Ranger stand with no comrades at hand to come to her aid? Lynn took a half step forward just as the lion leaped for the Ranger's throat. And then Ramon moved in a blur and dived under the deadly claws.

With lightning-quick reactions, the lion began to twist in midjump, swiping down at its intended prey, but Lynn realized that the Ranger's aim and timing had been exact. The point of the blade sank between the bones of the lion's chest. The force of the animal's momentum drove the sword in to the hilt, slicing through the vital organs encased within. Lynn did not need her knowledge of anatomy to know that the snow lion was already dead as it continued to plunge forward, crashing down and bearing the Ranger to the ground. The large frame shuddered convulsively and then was still, a lifeless heap of white fur on the floor of the ravine.

Lynn took a hesitant step forward. Then she saw the first signs of movement as the Ranger began to squirm from under the carcass. Lynn hurried to her side, lending a hand to roll the dead lion away. Ramon braced herself up on her elbows, breathing heavily.

"Are you all right?" Lynn asked.

Ramon grinned. "Better than the lion." She made as if to stand, but gasped and fell back.

Immediately, Lynn placed her hand over the Ranger's forehead, exerting the healer sense. White-hot fire was shooting up the Ranger's leg. Gently Lynn swept it away, but her intervention had only eased the pain, not cured its source. Nothing but time would do that.

"Is it broken?" Ramon asked.

"No. But your knee is very badly sprained," Lynn said. "You'll have to take it easy for a while."

Ramon pursed her lips thoughtfully, then raised her eyes to the top of the ravine and back to Lynn. "In that case, you'll have to deal with the next lion that drops down here."

Lynn smiled, happy that she was being teased. The sounds of battle had faded, the snow lions presumably either killed or fled. Lynn helped Ramon to her feet. Climbing out of the chasm would not be easy, but with the fighting over, there should soon be others to help. Just as the thought went through Lynn's mind, a head appeared over the top of the ravine. The initial anxiety on this new Ranger's face changed to a cheery grin as she saw the body of the snow lion.

"Ah, Kim. I see you sorted out the one we sent down to you. Thought we'd better share it. I knew you wouldn't have wanted to miss out on all the fun."

From the way the Ranger's expression had changed to relief, Lynn was sure the banter masked real concern. Lieutenant Ramon clearly took it in good humor. She looked up and answered in kind.

"Thank you, Sergeant Coppelli. Now do you think your spirit of generosity would extend to a rope to help us get out?"

CHAPTER SIX—THE AFTERMATH OF BATTLE

Someone was lighting lamps in the main barrack room of the staging post. One by one, they blossomed into existence— steady, unwavering circles of light to supplement the manic flickering of the fires. Some people sat in pensive silence in the gentle glow, while elsewhere in the hall, there was talking and nervous laughter and the occasional stifled groan. Then from outside came grim shouts and the sound of horses as more bodies were brought up from the valley below. Captain LeCoup strode through the center of the room, her crisp orders imposing a sense of purpose on the activity as the living and the dead were separated.

Lynn knelt in one corner of the room, surrounded by the worst of the wounded. In front of her lay a blood-soaked Guard who somehow had survived the mauling she had received, though she would never wield a sword again, even if she made it through the night. Her right arm had been torn from its socket, and only the freezing of the snow had stopped her from bleeding to death before she could be brought to the fort. Blocking out the activity around her, Lynn called on the healer sense, reaching out to seal the ruptured veins, ease the trauma of wrecked flesh, and strengthen the pulse of life that beat within the woman's breast. Then finally, she bestowed the gentlest of healing sleeps.

When she had finished, Lynn sat back on her heels and examined the woman's face, noting the shallow breath and deadly pallor of the skin, but there was no more she could do. Now it was in the hands of the Goddess.

A Ranger came and knelt beside her. "If you please, Madam Imprinter. I have a little of the healer sense. Not much, I'm afraid. The best healer in the squadron is Carma, and she is..." The woman broke off and pointed to one of the two injured Rangers who lay close at hand, awaiting Lynn's attention. "But if I can be of any use..."

"You can stanch bleeding? Ease pain and inflammation?"

The Ranger nodded. "Yes, a little. You tend to get quite a lot of practice at it in the Rangers. But usually Carma takes care of such things. I'm definitely the woman for minor injuries."

"Okay." Lynn met the Ranger's earnest expression. "If you do what you can, and make sure no one is more seriously injured than they realize, it will be a help. And if there's anyone who's not immediately critical but beyond your skill, sedate them if they're in pain, and I'll get to them when I've finished with these women here."

"Yes, ma'am." The Ranger nodded again and set off to the task.

Lynn moved on to the next of her patients, taking them in order of seriousness. The responsibility was daunting—lives depended upon the decisions she made—but she had no time to waste in worrying. When the final reckoning was taken after the fighting, it was found that three of the Guards were still alive, although only one stood any chance of ever returning to active duty. In addition, two Rangers had suffered serious wounds. However, their cases were better. At least they both had all their limbs intact.

The last of the women who had been brought to Lynn's corner of the room was Sister Smith, dragged unconscious from the ruins of the carriage, blood oozing from a deep gash at the back of her head, but seemingly otherwise unharmed. Yet forcing herself to be honest, Lynn had left the comatose Sister until last not just because of her appraisal of the level of injury. Nine Guards had been killed, and while Lynn had seen the civilian driver and one junior Sister walking through the hall, stunned, there had been no sign of the driver's young second or the other Sister. It was only to be feared that they had died in the crash and now lay among the dead. And the blame for it all lay with Smith and her absurd, arrogant ambition.

Lynn paused for a moment, looking down at the unconscious woman. The thin gauze mask lay flat, revealing the contours of the Sister's lower face for the first time. Smith's chin was nondescript, but her mouth was surprisingly full. A mirthless smile twisted Lynn's own lips. She would have laid a wager on them being thin and tight. Lynn shook her head, trying to dismiss her feelings of anger. Celaeno was the one who would judge them all some day. In the meantime, she had a job to do.

Lynn laid her hand on Smith's brow, letting her senses flow into the woman, tracing the electric pulses of nerves to read the state of the body. There was a large lump at the back of the skull, but no bleeding in the brain, at least not yet, and it was the work of minutes for Lynn to dispel the swelling that might put pressure on the delicate tissues. Then Lynn probed into the bones, searching for fractures in the skull. It was whole, but a faint dissonance twanged on Lynn's consciousness. She followed the tingling trail, like a fisherwoman reeling in a line, and reached the fine, hairline crack at the base of the spine, little more than the suggestion of a flaw. No harm had been caused yet, but...

Lynn looked again at Smith's unconscious face. The weakness in the spine was a lottery. Maybe Smith could ride all the way to the western border on horseback without coming to harm, or maybe she might roll over too quickly in bed and the bone would snap, paralyzing her for life. Was it what she deserved? That also was a question for the Goddess. Lynn redoubled her effort into bonding the bone. She would do her best, but whichever way it went, it would be weeks before Smith could safely be moved from the staging post. Landfall at Landfall was out of the question.

❖

Midnight was drawing close before Lynn had finished tending to everyone who needed her care. In a haze of tiredness, she wandered over to where LeCoup and Ramon sat by the fire to give her final report on the wounded. The sergeants, including Coppelli and the Ranger with healer skills, were also called in for the briefing. Three lions had broken out of the Rangers' cordon that afternoon and would now be in full flight, although still together with any luck. It would be a long hard ride to track them down before they set upon some unfortunate hill farmer, but with Smith's injury, there was no argument about delaying the Rangers from their work. While the main section of the squadron was away, Lynn could remain in safety at the staging post with the wounded.

"Do you know how many Rangers will not be fit to ride tomorrow?" LeCoup asked Lynn.

"There's the two you sent to me, plus one with a broken arm and one with a deep cut. I've stitched it up, but she should go carefully for a while or it might rip open again." Lynn counted the women off on her fingers, and then turned to the other healer. "Do you know of any more?"

"Only the lieutenant."

"I'll be fine by morning," Ramon snapped out immediately.

Lynn was not put off. "Oh yes, your knee. How is it?"

"Like I said, it will be fine by morning."

The Ranger healer shook her head in denial but said nothing. Ramon glared in response. Captain LeCoup's eyes shifted between the two stubborn faces and then settled on Lynn. "Madam Imprinter. Would you be able to give your assessment of the state of the lieutenant's health?"

Ramon's lips drew together in a tight line, but she obligingly stuck her leg out for Lynn to examine. It did not take long. The healer had dispersed the swelling, but only time would mend the torn ligaments.

Lynn met Ramon's eyes slightly apologetically and said, "I think the lieutenant will be lucky if she can stand on her leg tomorrow, let alone walk."

"I'll be able to ride," Ramon asserted.

"But you can't fight snow lions on horseback. Ask the Guards," Coppelli said in firm tones, attracting a glare from her friend.

In the end, the decision was left until the morning. If Ramon was able to walk, she would go with the rest; if not, she would be left in command of the fort. In her own mind, Lynn had no doubt of what the outcome would be.

❖

One of the injured Guards did not survive the night, dying in the hard, cold hours just before dawn, but the rest of the patients did well. A succession of Rangers took nurse duty, waking Lynn only when some crisis appeared imminent and allowing her to catch a few hours of interrupted sleep. She was yawning conspicuously when she joined Lieutenant Ramon outside the barrack room to watch the rest of the squadron assemble in the central square soon after breakfast.

Lynn had been unsurprised to learn that the lieutenant was unable to put any weight on her leg, but Ramon had found two sticks to use as crutches. Now she stood leaning on them heavily. Her tight scowl showed that she was resigned to staying behind but not happy about it. Lynn hovered close by.

Sergeant Coppelli urged her horse over to where the two women stood. "Hey, Kim. Don't look so sour, or I'll come over and kick your sticks away."

The gibe succeeded in putting a defiant grin on Ramon's face. "You want to give it a try?"

"I might be forced to. Purely for your own good, to remind you that you're only human, like the rest of us. You don't want to risk becoming vain and conceited, because then no one will love you anymore."

At that, Ramon gave a full laugh, but she had no chance to make a further retort. Captain LeCoup's voice rang out, calling the Rangers to order. The squadron members formed themselves into a disciplined column, and then, two abreast, they filed out through the gates of the fort. The clink of the horse harnesses blended with the thud of hooves in the crisp morning air.

Sister Ubbi, the driver, and the two less seriously injured Rangers also came out to watch them go. Once the last of the riders had left the fort, the driver and Rangers went to push the gates shut, dropping the bar into place. Lynn had already seen that the second staging post was an identical copy of the first, even to the position of the watchtower in the corner.

As the sound of the riders faded away, the two injured Rangers went inside in search of warmth, and the driver, Jeanne, picked up an axe and headed toward a pile of logs stacked against the side of the stables, walking in a purposeful manner that declared she had appointed herself odd-job-woman for the small group left behind.

Sister Ubbi fluttered to one side, pitiful in her confusion now that she was without Smith to obey or Quento to confide in. The eyes above the mask were red-rimmed and swollen. It had been small consolation for her that Quento's broken neck had been a quicker death than those of the Guards. And Lynn had learned the driver's second had also been killed by the snow lions. The jolt from a pothole had knocked her from the top of the carriage before the bridge had been reached. Hers was the loss that had touched Lynn the keenest. The girl had been sixteen at the most, an ordinary temple employee. If anything, her death was even more senseless than the rest, and it was somehow more terrible that her life had been taken unnoticed by any at the time.

"Is there...Is there anything I c-c-can do?" Sister Ubbi was in desperate need of direction. However, it was not totally compassion that prompted Lynn's reply, which was spoken very slowly and clearly, as if to an anxious child.

"You know that Sister Smith must stay still. I have put her into a very deep sleep to aid the healing so she will not move and harm herself by accident. It would be helpful if you went and kept watch over her, and if she seems to be stirring, come and get me at once." Actually, Smith was so deeply out that the end of the world wouldn't wake her, but Ubbi was not to know.

The junior Sister looked at Lynn as if she had been thrown a lifeline. "Would it help if I read prayers over her?"

"Prayers are never in vain." It took all her years of training at the temple for Lynn to keep a straight face as she quoted one of Smith's own favorite clichés. Out of the corner of her eye, she saw that Ramon was not coping quite so well, but Ubbi departed, unaware that any humor was being had at her expense.

"How long will Smith have to stay asleep?" Ramon's tone was deliberately innocent.

"It might be...beneficial if she remains out for"—Lynn pursed her lips—"maybe two weeks."

"Beneficial?" Ramon deliberately did not ask for whom, but the glint in her eye made it clear she had taken Lynn's meaning. "We are lucky to have such a competent healer at hand, Madam Imprinter."

Lynn bit her lip to hide her smile. "Actually, I'd prefer it if we stuck with Lynn and Kim. At least when Sister Ubbi is not around."

"That's fine by me. I've never been too keen on formality."

"I've noticed. I heard what Sergeant Coppelli said to you. I think if a sergeant in the Guards spoke to a lieutenant like that she'd be in front of a court-martial before the words had left her mouth."

Ramon laughed. "Which is one very good reason for not being in the Guards."

"So you weren't tempted to join them?" Lynn's question was not totally serious.

"Not for a second. I've wanted to be a Ranger ever since..." Ramon paused, as a shadow crossed her face. "Well, for quite some time. I joined the Militia when I was sixteen. We all have to start there. As soon as I'd completed my two years' probation, I applied to take the entrance tests for the Rangers. But the Guards...” She gave a scornful snort. “I feel sorry for them. The snow lions weren’t impressed by the pretty uniforms, and the Guards don’t have a lot else going for them.”

Lynn tilted her head to one side and observed, “I know the Guards, the Rangers, and the Militia don’t have much in the way of compliments for each other.”

Ramon laughed in acknowledgment. “Well, I know a lot of Rangers look down on the Militia, but personally, I have more respect for them than I do for the Guards. They may not be the world’s best soldiers, but at least they do a worthwhile job, rounding up drunks and street thieves. And there are some good women in the Militia who stay there because they have family ties that don’t leave them free to join the Rangers.” Again, Ramon’s face grew solemn. There were clearly other memories at play, and then she turned and began to hobble toward the entrance to the barrack room. Lynn kept pace beside her.

“But you’re right about us not standing on our rank like the Guards.” Ramon reverted to the previous subject, though Lynn had the feeling it was a deliberate shift of conversation. “Our work can be dangerous. Like yesterday. Our lives depend on each other. If someone has just saved your neck, you aren’t going to throw the book at them if they forget to call you ma’am, and over the years I’ve lost count of how many holes Chip and I have pulled each other out of.”

“Chip?” Lynn queried.

“Sergeant Coppelli.”

“Why is she called Chip?”

“An old joke, and not one that is funny enough to be worth repeating,” Ramon said, smiling. “We’re good friends, and I don’t count myself as particularly senior to her. Chip has been in the Rangers a few years more than me. When I joined, she was my patrol corporal. I caught up with her on the promotion ladder, so for some time we were both sergeants together. Then three months ago, Lieutenant Ritche had an accident, and I got the commission. But between Chip and me, it could only have come down to a toss of a coin.”

They had reached the door of the barrack room. Lynn raised her hand to push, when it was wrenched open. Sister Ubbi stood on the other side, her eyes wide with fright. “Please, Imprinter, could you come? I think I saw Sister Smith’s finger move.”

Only with great effort did Lynn stop her own eyes from rolling to the skies in despair, and as she accompanied the agitated Sister, she thought she heard the faint sound of Lieutenant Ramon's chuckle follow her down the barrack room.

CHAPTER SEVEN—PLAYING WITH FIRE

The horse made a huffing sound and shuffled its hooves restlessly. Lynn patted its neck to comfort it and then examined the raw lines of the parallel slashes on its side, her healer sense probing beneath the visible layers to feel out the extent of the damage and recovery.

"That lion nearly did for you, didn't it?" she said aloud.

The horse turned its head to look at her, its eyes rolling wide, for all the world as if facing for the first time a worrying and hitherto unconsidered possibility.

"It's all right. You're going to be fine."

And it would be. Again she patted the horse. The cuts were healing cleanly and there was no permanent injury to the muscle underneath. Within days, it would be fit and eager for exercise. Lynn's face grew thoughtful as an idea occurred to her. Maybe she could take the chance to ride the horse a few times, tell Sister Ubbi that it was necessary for her to monitor the animal's recovery. Of course, Sister Smith would not accept the statement without detailed questions, but Smith was in no condition to ask them.

Lynn lay the palms of both hands against the flanks of the horse and let her senses sink in. She could feel the glory of the animal, the strength, the power of its muscles, the long limbs meant to run, and also something else—the horse was more than a little hungry. A quick glance confirmed that the manger was empty. Food for the animals was stored next door to the stables. Lynn trotted into the barn and was picking up a suitably sized bale when a shadow fell across her.

"Icy, you shouldn't be doing that."

Lynn looked over her shoulder to see Kim standing in the open doorway. *And yes, I'm definitely starting to think of her as Kim.* The words danced through Lynn's mind while a broad grin spread across her lips. In fact, over the previous two days, Lynn was aware her feelings about the Ranger were starting to shift in all sorts of ways.

"And why not?"

"You're an Imprinter."

"And I'm also one of the few able-bodied people around here. I mean, you're hardly in a state to lug bales of hay around." Lynn looked pointedly at the two sticks in Kim's hands.

"You could get Jeanne to do it."

"She's quite busy enough, and I don't mind. It's nice to get the chance to feel really useful for once." Lynn heaved up the bale and began stepping toward the door. Kim shuffled aside awkwardly to let her out. She was clearly finding sideways the hardest direction to manage with her injured knee, but had little trouble keeping pace with Lynn as they walked along to the stable.

"What's more useful than being an Imprinter?" Kim asked, her voice completely serious for once.

Lynn sighed. "I suppose in theory, not much, but in practice it doesn't always feel like it. I think it's that we never get to see the results of what we do. Our work is supposed to be a tribute to life, but everything about the temple seems designed to alienate us from it. We don't see the children we create; we don't know the world they live in; we hardly even see the sky they walk under. We're supposed to be the chosen of Celaeno, but we're kept isolated from the world she chose for us."

Lynn realized her tone had grown vehement, more bitter than she had intended. She put a clamp on her train of rhetoric and forced herself to relax before concluding. "After a while we turn into miserable old crones who just complain about our lot whenever we find a fool gullible enough to listen." She dropped the bale into the horse's manger and turned to grin at the other woman.

Kim returned her smile but did not look convinced by the change in tack. "Aren't you happy in the temple?"

"Would you be?" The reply shot out before Lynn had time to think.

Abruptly, tears burned behind her eyes. Her emotions were definitely getting more volatile whenever Kim was around. A bad sign. She turned back to the horse, stroking its neck while she regained her composure, then walked to the stable door and leaned her shoulder on the jamb. Her gaze lifted above the walls of the stockade and rested on the high peaks beyond. Evening was close at hand, the snow was tinged softest pink in the fading light. The peace of the mountains slowly washed into her, easing the frown from her face and the lump from her throat.

"Now you're looking more cheerful." Kim had watched her in silent concern.

"I like mountains," Lynn said softly.

"There's a lot of them around here."

"True." Lynn sighed, and a wistful smile touched her face. The mountains had worked their magic upon her. She had found her emotional balance again, enough to regain her sense of fun. "You asked if I'm happy in the temple? No, I'm not. Maybe some day I'll get to like it better. If not, at least the Goddess has given me a chance here to experience a little freedom, and I really shouldn't waste her gift in useless brooding." The smile shifted to a grin of pure mischief, and Lynn bent down to take a scoop of snow, quickly shaping it into a fair sized snowball. She turned her eyes to Kim, clearly sizing her up as a target.

"Not fair, I can't retaliate." Despite the words, there was laughter in Kim's voice.

"Damn, you're right. I'll have to wait until your knee is better."

"Even then. Isn't it a mortal sin to throw a snowball at an Imprinter?"

"Only if Sister Smith finds out." Lynn spun about and launched the snowball at the wall of the main hall, making a fair guess at the spot behind which the Sister lay in a private anteroom off the barracks. The snowball exploded against the timbers, leaving a small circle of white behind. "And I suppose I had better go and see how she is before Ubbi comes and grabs me." Lynn begun to trudge toward the doorway. Kim swung along on her crutches beside her.

"You know, you're not at all what I thought an Imprinter would be like."

"Sorry, I'll try and be more holy in future." But there was nothing of piety in Lynn's grin.

Laughing, they entered the light and warmth of the barrack room, their paths separating by the round, central hearth with its heap of burning logs. Close by were two Rangers and the driver with a set of dice before them. The lieutenant was eagerly hailed by the players, but before she went to join them, Kim stood and watched Lynn head down the hall toward her patients, and the words rose softly to her lips, "No, don't change. You're fine just as you are."

❖

Seven days passed before news from the rest of the squadron arrived. Just after noon, shouts outside the stockade proclaimed the arrival of two Rangers with word that the rest of the snow lions had been tracked down and killed. By now, all of the wounded except for Smith were able to hobble to the fireside and sit to listen to the messenger's account of the hunt. In the relaxed atmosphere of the barrack room, the telling drifted away from a formal military dispatch, aided by many interjections and questions from the listeners, but at last it drew to a close.

"And so Captain LeCoup has taken the rest of the squadron on to Petersmine. She's going to send word to Landfall to explain what has happened and why Sister Smith and the Imprinter have been delayed."

The speaker seemed unaware of any hidden implications to her words, but Lynn felt the corners of her lips twitch. Smith might have some awkward explaining to do now that her version of events would not be the first to reach the Chief Consultant's ear. With twelve dead and the supporting evidence from the mayor in Redridge, it would be a nasty hiccup in Smith's career. Insurmountable, if there was any justice in the world. And no matter how high Smith's star might rise, it would always be tarnished by rumors and questions muttered behind her back.

The Ranger continued speaking. "The captain will also arrange for more supplies to be sent up here, and we will remain with you so we're on hand to carry messages down to Petersmine if there's need."

"Any other instructions from LeCoup?" Kim asked, reverting to her role of lieutenant.

"No, ma'am. Apart from the hope that your knee's feeling better."

"It is. I can now walk with just one stick."

"Oh yes." One of the messengers held up a hand. "Sergeant Coppelli sent a private message for you."

"It's repeatable?" Kim sounded surprised.

"Probably not. She put it in writing."

The scrap of paper was handed over. It was not sealed. Presumably, the Rangers took it for granted that neither messenger would disgrace their trust by opening it. Kim read the words, her eyebrows rising slightly and a laugh shaking her shoulders, and then she folded the paper and dropped it in the fire. Lynn felt a twinge of something that could only be jealousy—absurd as it was.

The mood of the two Guards was more vengeful. "That was definitely the last of the snow lions you killed?"

"Yes," one of the messengers replied.

"So how many were in the pride in total?"

"Fourteen."

"I hope Celaeno lets them burn in hell forever."

"They were only animals," Kim said evenly.

"But my comrades weren't." The Guard spat out the words.

Wisely, Kim let the conversation drop.

❖

Some time later, Lynn found a chance to talk to her in private, when the pair sat by the glowing embers of the fire after the others had gone to their beds.

"You didn't seem to take much satisfaction from hearing about the end of the snow lions."

"Oh, I'm pleased enough," Kim replied. "I've seen the remains of too many women to be happy with the thought of a pride roaming the farmlands. But I couldn't join the Guards in their talk of revenge. The snow lions weren't being evil, they were just hungry and following their nature. You can't expect them to know any better."

"Unlike gangs of bandits." Lynn finished the sentence for Kim.

"No." It was just one word, but it held a bleak intensity that made Lynn glance across.

Kim was staring into the hearth, jaw clenched and lips pressed shut. Her eyes seemed to be looking on other scenes, and not pleasant ones. Along with wild beasts, the murderous gangs who scavenged at the edges of the civilized land were the main responsibility of the Rangers. Kim had never spoken of them before. Lynn realized it was a deliberate omission, and painful memories were obviously involved.

Uncertainly, Lynn asked, "Bandits have killed comrades of yours?"

Kim drew a breath. "Since I've joined the Rangers? Yes, a few. But before that a gang murdered my family."

"Oh, I...I'm sorry." Lynn heard the pitiful inadequacy of her own words.

"It was years back. I was only fourteen or so. Old enough to be sent into town to get supplies. When I got back that night, I found everyone dead with their throats slit...even my baby sister. They'd taken everything of value that could be picked up and carried." Kim's eyes were hard, her voice tight. "And yes, I did join the Rangers looking for revenge."

"I can understand that."

Kim rubbed her face with her hands and then raked her fingers back through her cropped hair as if trying to scrub the memories away. She pulled a bitter, lopsided grimace. "You'd think by now I'd be able to put it behind me."

"No," Lynn said quietly.

"But it doesn't get me anywhere. Though Chip says remembering makes me nasty, mean, and vindictive, and therefore ideal material to become a Ranger captain." Kim's expression shifted to a soft, sad smile. "I think if it hadn't been for Chip, I'd have gotten myself killed the first time I went into action against bandits. I was so eaten up with lust for vengeance I wanted to take on the whole lot single-handed. It's taken her the best part of the last eight years to talk some sense into me. The Goddess knows what I'd be like without her."

"You're very close."

"Very." Kim paused, then a genuine smile formed on her lips. "Despite what she wrote in her letter."

Lynn hesitated. No point was served by probing into Kim's pain, and the letter was something that had pricked her curiosity. "I suppose it was too personal to repeat what was in the letter?" she said cautiously, unsure if Kim would be willing to answer, but the Ranger's smile grew even broader.

"I don't know about personal, and certainly not verbatim. But Chip implied that I am addicted to certain immoral practices, involving sheep, turnips, and swinging from trees, and commiserated that I wouldn't be able to satisfy my urges again until my knee was better."

Lynn stifled her laughter with one hand. When she had herself back under control, she said in mock seriousness, "Perhaps when Sister Smith is awake again, you should ask her for guidance in this matter."

"Guidance? You mean like, left a bit, right a bit?"

Lynn creased forward, unable to reply.

Kim laughed as well, her humor fully restored. "No. Chip is the one who needs help. Believe me, I know."

Lynn sat up again and then surprised herself by blurting out, "Are you lovers?" She was not certain if she even wanted to know the answer, but Kim shook her head.

"We considered it years back, mainly when we were drunk, but decided we did better as friends. And since Chip met Katryn I don't think she's even noticed anyone else."

"Katryn?"

"Corporal Nagata. She transferred into our squadron a couple of years ago. Steady relationships between Rangers aren't approved of. They can get in the way in a crisis. But Chip and Katryn have an understanding. It's one of the reasons Chip wasn't bothered when I became lieutenant rather than her. She's a few years older than me, her term of duty expires next year, and she won't re-enlist. Katryn will be out of the Rangers the year after. They'll both have their de-mob payments, and they won't be too old to think about children."

"But you don't have any similar plans?"

"No. I made it to lieutenant when I was still twenty-five, by the space of two weeks. I would like to be a captain before I'm thirty."

"A career soldier."

"Oh yes. The outlaws took my family. The Rangers are my life now."

Only the faintest trace of the former pain remained in Kim's voice, but when they bid each other good night and parted, the thought shot through Lynn's mind that the temple had stripped her of her family as surely as the bandits had taken Kim's.

❖

The vertebrae in Smith's back got stronger with each passing day, eventually reaching the point where Lynn could no longer pretend that total sedation was necessary. The Smith who woke up was a changed woman. But not changed by much. Less domineering and arrogant, but no less sanctimonious or meddlesome. She spent her time in quiet but fervent prayer, as if waiting for the Goddess to tell her who was to blame for her misfortunes. The prayers, of course, required constant attendance from Lynn and Ubbi. The only release was the hour before sleep, which Smith spent in private meditation. By the fourth evening, Lynn was eager to be out of the staging post, except that it brought partings nearer.

At the end of another tedious day of prayers and hymns, Lynn was finally dismissed from Smith's room. Ubbi trotted to where her own possessions lay and pulled out her copy of the book of the Elder-Ones, obviously intending to spend the time in quiet reading. Possibly Smith took it for granted that Lynn would undertake a similar occupation and thought it unnecessary to give instructions, but Lynn took advantage of the oversight to wander down the barrack room and join the group of soldiers sitting around the central hearth.

She was greeted by a ring of smiles, and a mug of hot tea was pressed into her hands. During the twenty-one days in the fort, a camaraderie had grown up, the rivalry between the Rangers and the Guards replaced by a gentle teasing, and Lynn had become an accepted member of the group, happier than at any time since she had entered the temple at Fairfield. Her singing ability had been seized on enthusiastically, and the soldiers had taught her several songs that would never form part of any service in the temple.

As much as anything, Lynn enjoyed the honest, open banter. Although the jokes were frequently bawdy, to Lynn's mind they were far less offensive than the conversation of the Sisters: the intimidation by pious quotes, the political backstabbing disguised in religious platitudes. The soldiers spoke of a world Lynn would never know, but it did not matter. Their stories were like breathing fresh air after years of choking in incense. When Lynn sat down, they were in the middle of an innocuous debate about the quality of merchandise available in the inns of a certain town, but the subject soon took an abrupt turn.

One of the Rangers was speaking, "And it's not just the beer there that's for sale. You can get the barmaids as well."

"In what way?"

"Horizontal. I was there once and this barmaid was giving me the come-on. Sat down beside me, hand on my leg. Well...she was nice;

I had some spare time and...okay..." The woman shrugged. "I was a little drunk. But I thought *'Why not?'* The next thing, she's quoting a price."

"Maybe she assumed that with a face like yours you couldn't get it for free." The gibe raised a general howl of laughter around the fire.

Carma, one of the Rangers, turned to the Guard beside her and said in semi-serious tones, "You won't be at all surprised to learn that's a problem our lieutenant has never suffered from. One smile and she has them falling at her feet."

"Oh, it's her *feet* they're aiming at," a second Ranger said, feigning innocent enlightenment.

"I think some would be happy with any part they could grab."

"Then it's fortunate Kim is so easygoing about women grabbing her parts." More laughter followed.

"Hey." Kim kicked the Ranger's shin gently, with no deterrent value at all.

Carma's voice was dryly ironic as she carried on talking to the Guard. "Now you might think the rest of us would be resentful of the easy way Kim avoids being lonely in bed, but we've also seen the problems that go with it. For instance, there was this blacksmith's apprentice in Northcamp who, I'm afraid, was a bit cracked."

"Couldn't see it from where I was standing," someone cut in.

The laughter had risen to screeches; the story was obviously well known. Kim's expression was one of resigned good humor, although even in the firelight it was possible to see a faint blush touch her cheeks.

Carma continued with the tale. "There was this woman, totally obsessed with our lieutenant, except she was a sergeant then. Anyway, one day the woman breaks into Kim's quarters, strips all her clothes off and poses on the bed waiting for Kim to come in, flaunting her..."

Suddenly, Lynn knew she had no wish to hear the end of the story. Trying to cause the minimum disturbance, she slipped out of the circle, but her departure was noticed and the recounting faltered. She met Carma's abashed look with a reassuring smile, mimed "It's okay" and fled toward the outside door, pausing only to grab her cloak and hat.

The fort was peaceful in the moonlight, snuggled in the protective ring of mountains. Stars were splashed across the velvet darkness overhead and snow lay on the ground, but the covering was patchy now that the spring thaw was setting in. Lynn crossed the square and climbed the ladder to the watchtower. The high platform had become a refuge for her, especially once she learned that Sister Ubbi suffered from vertigo. She leaned against the railing, resting her folded arms on the rough wooden bar and looking out over the dark hillside, while trying to work out whether it was jealousy of, or sympathy for, the blacksmith's apprentice that had prompted her to leave the fireside.

The sound of feet on the ladder caused Lynn to glance over her shoulder. Kim climbed up onto the platform.

"I'm sorry about that back there. I should have put a stop to it," Kim apologized at once.

"It's all right."

"Carma was just getting carried away at my expense. She forgot that you're an Imprinter and you don't..." Kim's sentence trailed away.

Lynn returned to the panorama of mountains, her gaze fixing on the distance. "No. I don't." She mouthed the words too softly for Kim to hear.

"It's just, you don't normally seem to mind and...no one meant to embarrass you."

"I wasn't embarrassed. Just because I have to be celibate doesn't mean I'm under some delusion that everyone else is too."

Kim came and stood beside her, leaning on the railing. Lynn was painfully aware of every millimeter that separated their two elbows. Silence followed while she waited for Kim to frame her next sentence. "But there was something you couldn't cope with."

"The envy."

"Pardon?"

"I have no option about being a virgin. But it doesn't mean I like it."

Lynn turned her head. Now Kim's eyes were fixed on the horizon, but at last the Ranger said, "I suppose, for the work you do, you need to keep your mind clear of such distractions. Free your thoughts for higher things and all that."

Lynn laughed cynically. "When you're forced to be celibate you don't think about sex, in the same way that you don't think about food when you're starving. There's probably nothing on earth more depraved than the dreams of a twenty-three-year-old Imprinter, except maybe those of a forty-year-old Imprinter. I could let you know in a few years' time." She glanced across again. Kim's expression was unreadable, beyond a fair degree of confusion and distress. Lynn knew she had gone too far. She rested her forehead on her folded arms. "Now I've embarrassed you."

"No. You..." Kim swallowed the rest of her words.

"Perhaps you should go back to the barrack room," Lynn suggested softly.

"It's cold out here."

"I won't stay long. But I need a little time alone."

Without saying anything more, Kim walked across to the top of the ladder. The sound of her footsteps on the rungs faded away.

"Oh, mother of us all, I've been stupid. How did I let myself fall for her so hard?" Lynn whispered the words to herself, while the tears began to flow. The moonlight was smeared across the scene before her eyes. "Why didn't I realize I was playing with fire?"

But perhaps being burned might not be so bad. In the years to come, in the monotony of the temple, she could poke at the heartache, like flexing a pulled muscle to feel the extent of the strain. It hurt but let you know you were still alive. Or had been once. When the exhaustion of an Imprinter's life had drained her of all feeling, perhaps the pain of remembering Kim might breathe a little life into the memory of her weeks at the fort in the mountains.

❖

Two days later, Lynn declared Smith well enough to travel, and messengers were dispatched to Petersmine to summon a carriage.

Chapter Eight—A Buckle out of Place

The town of Petersmine sprawled across the southern foothills of the mountains. Most of the space was given to foundries, blacksmiths, and the homes of workers, each building adorned with small shrines to Peter, the Elder-One who was patron of miners, along with her friend Cedric, the patron of blacksmiths. The heavy industry occupied the center of Petersmine, making the town prosperous but not picturesque. It was therefore, presumably, with aesthetics in mind that the proprietor of the largest inn had dispensed with tradition and situated her establishment at the edge of town. The hostel consisted of a row of loosely connected buildings stretched along the side of the road to Landfall, surrounded on both sides by dusty orchards where sheep grazed between the knurled trunks of apple trees.

Lynn stood at the front of the inn with Smith and Ubbi close by. The day was chill with skies gray and dismal enough to match her mood, and the wind sweeping down from the mountains snatched at her clothes with fingers of ice. Off to one side stood the new consignment of Guards who had arrived from Landfall the day before. Their commanding officer had introduced herself at dinner as Major Rozek and Lynn had taken an instant dislike to the woman, a feeling that she sensed was shared by Kim and Captain LeCoup, who had also been present at the meal.

It had been apparent immediately that Rozek was not a typical Guard officer. She was too sharp and too well informed. She maintained a front of crisply formal politeness, but it only served to emphasize an underlying malevolence. But neither Lynn nor the Rangers were her targets. Smith had recognized Rozek and had seemed displeased, even uneasy. Lynn guessed that Rozek was the protégé of one of Smith's enemies in the Sisterhood. Someone who had seized on the disaster on the pass and set her pet hound on Smith's trail. Not that Rozek would harm Smith, but she was a warning that things in Landfall were not going Smith's way.

Rozek's troops also appeared handpicked. They had treated the Rangers with more arrogant disdain than usual, and even by the standards of the Guards, their uniforms and horse harnesses were immaculate. They now stood at attention, not moving a muscle, their line as straight as if it had been drawn with a ruler.

Doubtless with the intention of irritating the Guards, the Rangers were making a display of casual high spirits. They flaunted their battle-worn green and gray uniforms in marked contrast to the Guard's polish and lounged against walls or talked loudly in boisterous groups. It was true that Captain LeCoup was conducting herself with quiet dignity, but she made no attempt to control her troops and seemed to be enjoying the expression of pique on Rozek's face.

While they waited for the carriage, Lynn scanned the crowd of Rangers, finally spotting Kim right at the back of one group. For a heartbeat, their eyes met. Kim nodded her head in the faintest of bows, held Lynn's gaze for a second more, and then turned and walked away, rounding the corner of the inn in the direction of the stables. It cut Lynn like a knife to realize the lieutenant would not stay to watch her departure. Without thinking, she took a half step as if to follow, but just as Kim disappeared from sight, Lynn heard the sound of wheels, and the carriage drew up outside the inn. As it came to a stop, Sister Smith began to march forward, but the driver held up a restraining hand and leaped down.

"What's wrong?" Smith asked.

"It's not pulling right. I think one of the straps has split, ma'am," the driver said, slightly distracted.

"So what does that mean?"

"I'll have to replace the harness. Lucky I've got a spare on top."

"Will it take long?"

"Fifteen minutes, twenty at tops."

Sister Smith snorted. There was nothing she could do apart from glare at the driver. However, standing and glaring was one of the things Smith did best.

The strain was more than Lynn could bear. She did not want to go, but the delay was only making things worse. Reaching out, she tapped Sister Smith lightly on the arm. "Excuse me, Sister. I'm getting cold out here. I'll go inside until the carriage is ready."

"All right, you could read while waiting."

"Yes, Sister."

Lynn had no intention of complying with the suggestion. All she wanted was to hide from public view and contend with the pain she was feeling, rather than try to mask it with a show of serenity. But tears could not be allowed, not until she was alone in her bed that night.

A small private parlor lay just inside the main entrance of the inn. Lynn's hand was reaching for the doorknob when a cold draft rushed past, making her shiver. At the end of the corridor was a second door to the outside that someone must have left unbolted and the wind had snatched open. As Lynn looked at it, another icy gust slammed it shut before pulling it wide again. Her state of tension was such that the loud crash made Lynn flinch, and the thought of sitting for fifteen minutes listening to the repeated bangs set her teeth on edge. In a dozen steps, Lynn had reached the doorway and was searching for its bolt.

Lynn glanced outside. The door gave onto the courtyard behind the inn. Opposite her was the stable block. The bolt was forgotten as Lynn stood and stared at the low wooden building. Kim had headed in its direction. There was no certainty she had gone in, but she might have. A quick check left and right confirmed that no one was in sight. The entertainment value of watching the driver replace the horse harness must have proved too much, even for the inn staff. Lynn leaped down the steps, crossed the muddy cobbles, and slipped in through the stable doors.

Inside the building was very dark and heavy with the smell of hay and horses. Lynn stood for a moment letting her eyes adjust to the gloom, but already she could hear the sounds of someone moving near the back beyond the rows of empty stalls with their half-height walls.

"Kim?" Lynn called out softly.

"What's up?" The tall Ranger strode into view.

"There's been a short delay with the carriage and I just wanted to say goodbye."

"We said goodbye last night after dinner."

"Yes, but..." Lynn pressed her hand against her forehead.

"But..." Kim prompted.

Lynn's hand fell. "It's really struck me that I'll never see you again."

"No. I...I know that too. If ever I'm in Landfall, I'll come to the temple...though of course I won't be able to talk to you."

"And I suppose, even with the grace of the Goddess, there's little chance of me picking your face out of the crowds." Lynn felt her composure slipping. She walked past Kim and down the row of stalls toward where the saddles and harness hung on the back wall and then turned and faced the Ranger. "Promise you won't forget me."

"How could I?"

"I don't know how I'm going to bear it." The tears were coming. Lynn tried to fight them back, but the battle was lost before it was started. "I don't want to go to the temple. I don't want to be an Imprinter. I don't want to leave you..." Lynn knew she was whining like a child. Her head fell forward as the first sob shook her.

Kim was by her in an instant, wrapping an arm around her shoulders, stroking her, trying to rally her. "Lynn. Come on, Lynn. I can't promise it will be fun. We both know it won't. But you'll cope. I know you will. And despite all the shit you get from the Sisters, being an Imprinter is the most important thing in the world, and deep down you know that as well as me." Kim gave a last hug and let her arm drop.

Lynn choked on a stifled sob and managed to get herself back under control, fighting with the muscles in her face. She wiped her eyes and swallowed. "I'd better go back. I've made enough of a scene here."

"That's all right." Kim stepped away, leaving the path to the door clear.

Lynn began to take a step forward and then stopped. Suddenly, she knew it was very important to say something, that if she walked out of the stable without letting her heart speak, she would regret her cowardice for the rest of her life. Not that it would do any good. Kim would probably be mortified, but some truths had to be spoken.

"What is it?" Kim must have seen the change of expression on her face.

"I..." Again her voice failed her.

"Lynn?"

Lynn stared at the doors and then said in a rush, "I know it's stupid, but somehow I've let myself develop a really adolescent crush on you. I love you."

Kim froze and then slowly, very slowly, she raised her hand to Lynn's chin and turned her face so their eyes met. "Oh, that's too cruel. Because somehow, I've let myself come to feel the same way about you."

Time stopped. In Lynn's sight, the stable, the whole world, seemed to fade away, leaving only Kim and her. She would have found it impossible to say who moved first, but without any conscious thought, their arms went around each other, holding each other close. Lynn felt herself clasped tight against the thudding of Kim's heart, heard the ragged breath whisper between Kim's lips, smelled the faint, warm scent of sweat and leather on Kim's skin. She tilted her head back and looked up into the Ranger's eyes, watching the face get slowly closer until all other senses were blotted out by touch as their lips met in a soft kiss.

Never had anything felt so right as to stand in Kim's arms. Never had her own arms felt so worthwhile as they did in holding onto Kim. *This was why the Goddess made me. This is where I'm supposed to be.* The words rose in Lynn's mind with the force of absolute certainty while their kiss deepened. Lynn felt as if her body was melting into Kim's, flowing with the force of her desire. Nothing else existed.

Lynn's eyes were shut, but through the closed lids, she saw the increase in light, even as she recognized the soft scraping sound of the stable door opening. It took a second for her to return to earth, to realize what was happening, where she was, and then she broke from Kim's grasp, stepping off, ducking and twisting away, and diving into the nearest stall. She ended up sitting on the straw on the ground, her back pressed hard against the wooden slats of the partition and wondering just how deep in trouble she was.

❖

Kim's back had been to the door and the change in light less noticeable, so she required a moment longer to realize that they were no longer alone. Slowly she turned around to see Chip Coppelli standing just inside the entrance to the stable, grinning broadly, and behind her the far less welcome figures of Sister Smith and Major Rozek. These two had expressions of sour disapproval on their faces, but not outrage. In a flash, Kim realized that with dimness obscuring the stable depths, they had seen what she had been doing but had not recognized Lynn. A conjecture immediately confirmed when Chip met her eyes and mimed the word, "Who?"

Kim ignored her friend and looked to the white-robed woman at the door. "Can I help you, ma'am?"

"We are looking for Madam Imprinter. Do you know where she is?"

"She was standing at the front of the inn when I came in here. Is she not still there?" Kim prayed no one would notice that she had not answered the question.

"She's gone missing. The driver thought the whole harness needed replacing, but when she looked, she found there was just a buckle out of place. So now we're ready to go, but Madam Imprinter has disappeared." Smith's voice snapped with irritation.

"I'll help you find her." Kim strode up the stable, anxious to shepherd everyone out. If she could clear the way, maybe Lynn would be able to slip back into the inn unnoticed.

Smith and Rozek were already leaving, but Chip was not so easily out-maneuvered, and Kim knew the expression of amused curiosity on her friend's face all too well. Of course, Chip would want to know who the other woman was and would recognize that it was something Kim was trying to conceal. Most likely, Chip would assume she had made a conquest of a member of the inn staff and deduce some cause of embarrassment was mixed in. Good-natured teasing was all part of their friendship. Kim set her own face into a hard glare, praying Chip would sense that this was not a time to play games.

But as she reached the door, Chip whispered from the side of her mouth, "Who was it?"

Smith and Rozek were too close to risk even a whispered explanation. Kim fixed on her friend's face, silently pleading with her to let the matter drop, but the eyes that met hers were dancing with mischief.

Chip raised her voice and said, "Perhaps your...ahem...friend might know where Madam Imprinter is. Is there a reason why you can't call her out here and ask her?"

Kim hesitated for a moment before replying, "I can guarantee that she has as much idea as I do."

This time Smith must have heard the equivocation, her ear trained by a lifetime's experience in prying out the sins of others. Yet still there was no outrage. Smith could not suspect the whole truth, but the hint of a guilty secret was enough. She stepped back into the stable and called out, "Who is it down there? Come out and show yourself."

Kim's jaw clenched while her mind raced, but no easy words of evasion came. Why did Smith have to waste her time on what could only seem a trivial matter? Surely she had more urgent concerns? But even from their short acquaintance, Kim knew that the Sister would feel that she was failing in her duty to the Goddess if she did not hunt down and punish every transgression. She would probably even take it as a personal insult that Kim had tried to avoid detection.

Smith called out again, "You. Hiding at the back. Have you seen Madam Imprinter?"

Despairingly, Kim slumped back against the doorframe, shoulders sagging, not bothering to maintain the pointless pretence of innocence. Chip's expression changed as well. She seemed to realize that she had made a bad mistake, but it was too late to recall the words. The senior Sister was already pacing down the stable.

"Answer me!" Smith shouted in annoyance.

❖

In the stall, Lynn looked about desperately, searching for a place to hide, a way of escape. Too late, she thought to try to disguise her voice and shout a reply. Smith would take it as insolence that she had not responded immediately. There was no way to evade discovery—only the choice of waiting to be dragged out or to go and meet her fate.

Smith was only a few steps away, still barking her questions. "When did you last see Madam Imprinter?"

Lynn stood up and stepped out into the passage to meet the Sister's incredulous eyes with her answer. "The last time I looked in a mirror."

CHAPTER NINE—COURT-MARTIAL

The Petersminc jail was small and squalid but not overcrowded. Kim sat alone in the cell. Two miserable bunks lined either side. Light from the tiny, barred window fell on the stout ironclad door and the square-cut stones of the walls. At a guess, it was midafternoon outside.

Tentatively, Kim felt the bruises down her side. She had not put up any resistance, but the Guards who brought her to the jail, in their religious indignation, had not let that deter them from a little rough handling on the way. The corners of Kim's lips turned down. It would be unbelievably good luck if she did not have more to complain about before the affair was finished.

The noise of the key turning in the lock sounded loud in the confined space. Kim looked up and saw the door open slightly and Chip slip sideways into the room, acting as if she feared imminent attack. They stared at each other in silence while the door shut again and the key turned, followed by the soft sound of the jailer's footsteps walking away.

Chip took a half pace forward nervously, but then she broke into disjointed speech. "Himoti's tits, Kim. I'm sorry. Why didn't you warn me? If you'd just said some—"

"It wasn't planned," Kim cut her off bluntly.

"If I'd have known...they'd have gotten into the stable over my dead body." Chip took another few indecisive steps forward, then threw herself down on the bunk opposite and looked at Kim in desolate anguish. "Oh shit, Kim. I'm sorry. I'm really, really sorry. I..."

Chip's voice choked off. She turned her face toward the tiny window. Kim looked at her friend, torn by conflicting emotions, but the sincerity was unmistakable, as were the tears in Chip's eyes. Kim felt her anger fade. She sighed and slouched back against the wall behind her.

"You weren't to know. I hardly knew myself," Kim said softly.

"I'm sorry." Chip sounded like a lost child.

"It's all right. I don't blame you."

"I'm sorry."

"I accept your apology."

"I'm just really—"

"Say you're sorry one more time and I'll throw something at you." Something of humor had returned to Kim's voice.

Chip bit back her words, but her face was a picture of shamefaced remorse. For a long while, the only sound was the clanging of a door in the distance and faint shouts from outside the window. Chip's mouth opened and closed a few times as she tried to frame her next question. "So, back in the fort, you and the Imprinter were..." She broke off with a vaguely suggestive wave of the hand.

"No, nothing happened between us in the fort. But in the stables, we just..." Kim shrugged. "You saw about all there was to see."

"Oh. Not very good timing on your part."

"Chip, you've got a wonderful way with understatement." Kim studied her friend's doleful expression and then asked, "How did you get permission to come and see me?"

"I'm supposed to be getting inventory details from you."

"It's all in the books. They're up to date."

"Oh, I know. But it wasn't hard persuading the Guards that we're not very well organized. And they trust me, as I'm the one who dropped you in it." Chip's voice faded away over the last few words and she swallowed visibly.

"So why are you really here?"

"I had to see you and apologize, but I've also got a message for you from the Imprinter...Lynn."

Kim bounced forward on the bunk. "How is she? She hasn't been...harmed at all?"

"No, of course not. No one is going to touch an Imprinter." Chip stopped as if reconsidering her words and then glanced at Kim apologetically. "Well, you know what I mean. They've got her under guard at the inn, but like I said, I'm trusted, so I was able to talk to her briefly. She's fine, but a tad less forgiving than you. She's given me a really tough penance."

"Which is?"

"I've got to try and talk you into letting her take all the blame for what happened."

"No." Kim's rejection of the suggestion was absolute.

Chip pursed her lips. "That's what we both thought you'd say."

"I'm not going to save my skin by sacrificing hers."

"But it isn't like that. Lynn wants me to convince you that she's safe. You must believe that, no matter what happens, she's safe." Chip paused for a second and looked at Kim uneasily. "They're going to court-martial you. Tomorrow, we're all heading off to Landfall. The whole squadron is going, to act as witnesses or something. One of the charges against you will be sacrilege, so the Guards will have their paws all over the trial. But Lynn will be dealt with by the Sisters, and she's worth money to them in imprinting fees. Lots and lots of money. They won't do anything that might risk damaging her value. But with you..." Again she paused. "Lynn thinks it is all going to get caught up in temple politics. Some Sisters will want to play up the scandal, in the hope that some of the shit sticks to Smith. They'd like to have you found guilty of attempting to rape an Imprinter and have you strung up by the neck in the main square in Landfall as a warning to all. And if that's what the Sisters want, then that's what the Guards will be aiming for too."

"But if Lynn takes all the blame—" Kim tried to interrupt.

"It won't make any difference to her. Even if you're found guilty of attempted rape, they'll know Lynn wasn't trying to fight you off. It's a sure bet that someone will make certain Lynn suffers what is considered to be a suitable amount of punishment. Lynn will be better off, formally brought before the Chief Consultant in an ecclesiastical court with everything out in the open."

The logic stuck in Kim's throat. She leaned forward, head in hands, elbows on knees. Without looking up she said, "How do I live with myself, hiding behind her and saying it's all her fault?"

"The other way you don't get to live at all. And from what I can see, even if you stick with the truth, there's not much you can be blamed for. But just don't start playing the hero, because if you do, there's a lot of people in Landfall who'll lap up everything you say."

"I still don't like it."

"Neither Lynn nor I thought for a second that you would." Chip sighed. "Lynn asked me to say one more thing to you. When she's in the temple, she's going to find it a lot easier to cope knowing that you're still walking the face of the world rather than lying six feet under it."

❖

"What did you say to lure Madam Imprinter into the stable?" Major Rozek repeated the question for the fifth time.

"I didn't—"

Kim was not allowed to complete her sentence. At a gesture from Rozek, a Guardswoman stepped forward. Her fist slammed hard into Kim's stomach, knocking the wind from her body. Kim doubled over, prevented from falling only by the other Guards who held her arms securely in a lock behind her. Rozek stood back, watching keenly as a succession of blows pounded into Kim. But at last, she waved the attacking Guard back and took her place in front of the battered Ranger.

A few minutes passed before Kim regained her breath and managed to lift her head enough to meet the major's eyes, to evaluate her interrogator. Rozek was tall, maybe even a centimeter taller than she was. She had a square, but finely formed face. Kim guessed that an unbiased observer would declare her good looking. The fine lines about her mouth showed her to be somewhere in her mid-thirties, while the glint in her eyes revealed more intelligence than one normally expected in a Guard officer. And something else as well. With disgust, Kim realized that the major was enjoying every second of what was happening and would probably be disappointed if Kim meekly gave in and confessed at once to everything that was suggested.

"What did you say to lure Madam Imprinter into the stable?" Rozek's voice was mild, devoid of emphasis.

"I didn't say anything."

It was a long time later when Rozek dismissed the other Guards, leaving her and Kim alone in the cell. Kim lay gasping on the floor, curled in a tight ball of pain. Rozek crouched down beside her, for a while studying her victim's battered form. Then she spoke in the same gentle tones she had used all evening.

"These are Celaeno's chosen ones, and through them shall you receive my gift of life. And you shall revere them for my sake and keep them safe from the impurity of the world, in the sanctity of Celaeno's

temple." She paused. "Are you familiar with that quote, Ranger?"

Kim made no reply.

"It's from the book of the Elder-Ones. They are the words of the blessed Himoti herself. And you have the depravity to lay your foul hands upon one of her Imprinters, to subject one of the Goddess's chosen to your miserable lust. You will die for it, Ranger. Your defiance now will not save you. You have my solemn oath as an officer in the temple Guard. You will die for it."

Rozek stood up, her eyes still fixed in contempt on Kim's huddled body, and then she turned and marched from the cell.

❖

The main headquarters of the Guards were in Landfall, directly abutting the temple grounds. But unlike the high towers of its neighbor, the headquarters were a sprawl of low buildings, strewn around the central parade ground. Kim's court-martial was held in a small room just off this open space, the charge of sacrilege ensuring that as a religious offence, it was the Guard command rather than the Rangers who had overall jurisdiction over the trial—a bias that was reflected in the composition of the adjudicating panel. Captain LeCoup, as Kim's commanding officer, could not be denied her place, but the other two seats had gone to the Guards. One was a wide-eyed captain, who was clearly having great trouble remembering her brief, and the other, the presiding officer with casting vote, was Major Rozek.

The trial did not take long. First, the cobbled-together list of charges was read out: sacrilege, attempted rape, and dishonorable conduct. Then came the evidence. Dispatches from the Rangers and the temple were read out, describing the circumstances that had brought the accused to Petersmine, followed by eyewitness reports of the stable incident. Smith's account was given by proxy, as one would not expect a Sister to make a personal appearance at such a venue.

The final part before moving on to questioning the accused was a written statement from Lynn, amounting to a full confession: that she had followed Lieutenant Ramon into the stables without any inducement, that she had accosted the Ranger, that she had been the first to speak, the first to make a move, and that the lieutenant had been too surprised to resist.

The Guard captain on the panel was clearly very confused, but then it was obvious that it would take little to confuse her. Being asked to count above twelve when she had her shoes on would probably do it. Major Rozek was far more focused.

"Do you agree with the Imprinter's account?" Rozek glared disdainfully at Kim as she spoke.

Kim hesitated for a second, out of the corner of her eye, catching Chip's impatient twitching. "Yes, ma'am."

"It is not totally in line with your first statement."

"I...I did not want to get the Imprinter into trouble."

"And you did not in any way entice the Imprinter into this rendezvous?"

"It would have been pointless to plan a meeting to take place after she was due to leave town." This time, Kim's words were more confident.

Rozek looked between her two fellow officers on the panel and tossed Lynn's statement forward onto the desk with a studied casualness. "I guess it all comes down to how much faith we can put in this."

LeCoup faced the major with an expression of deadpan seriousness. "You are surely not accusing a blessed Imprinter of lying?"

At the other end of the table, the Guard captain looked as if her brain had melted.

Rozek leaned back, her lips pursed. Then her eyes flicked sharply toward Kim, shifting her attack. "But it would seem that the Imprinter had somehow become infatuated with you. Surely you must have encouraged her in this?"

"No," Kim said firmly. "Certainly not intentionally."

LeCoup slipped in before Rozek could respond. "From my report of the encounter with the snow lions, it can be seen that Lieutenant Ramon, at considerable personal risk, saved the Imprinter's life. In fact, she would normally have been in line for a commendation. Maybe even an Imprinter might mistake gratitude for something else, without need of other encouragement?"

Rozek's face slipped into a blank stare. "Maybe. But I think we have exhausted the evidence, and all this is clearly a matter for the panel's deliberation. Fellow officers, shall we adjourn?"

The wait in the courtroom was long and hard, a full three hours wondering which way the airhead Guard captain would flutter, since the votes of the other two seemed already determined. Kim sat impassively at the front of the court, staring at the empty table. The room was packed behind her. Most of the squadron had squeezed in, and the rest were in the corridor outside. Chip had managed to get a place in the first row, just to the right of the chair for the accused, but Kim could not bring herself to turn around and meet her friend's eyes. Not until she knew her fate, not until she knew for certain whether she was bound for the gallows.

Kim's eyes lost their focus on the room as she remembered her parents, her sisters. They also had not deserved to have their lives taken. Had she not been sent into town that day, she would have died along with them. That she had lived to see the last twelve years was due solely to luck, an undeserved gift from the Goddess. What right did she have to complain if her luck had run out and the gift was being recalled? Yet it was so hard not to feel bitter. The trial had been contrived to get a guilty verdict, the charge of sacrilege a crude ploy. It had hardly been mentioned during the proceedings. No evidence had been presented, but it had ensured that the majority of the panel were officers of proven piety, which meant Guards. A panel of Rangers would have thrown the charges out, most likely without even bothering to adjourn. And someone had clearly handpicked the Guard captain, in the hope she would blindly follow Rozek's lead.

The only hiccup in the plan was Lynn's confession. Kim's expression softened as she thought of it. Obviously there had to be a statement from the victim of the alleged assault. Kim wondered whether it was principle or political maneuvering that had stopped somebody from forging one. Undoubtedly, the Sisters would have put pressure on Lynn to say what they wanted her to, or failing that, to say as little as possible. Kim shifted carefully in her chair. Underneath her uniform, she was still bruised from the beatings she had received. She had no fears that similar treatment would have been dealt out to an Imprinter, but the Sisters would have used whatever powers of coercion they had. Whichever way the verdict went, it was good to know that Lynn had held true.

The waiting dragged on. Outside the windows, the sun began to sink slowly toward the rooftops. Kim could not stop herself from wondering how many more sunsets she would see. But as soon as the three officers returned to the court, it was obvious that her neck, at least, was safe. Rozek's face held an expression of tight, bound-in fury. Excited whispers leaped from Ranger to Ranger, rising to half-cheers from outside even before the verdict was announced.

Rozek looked at Kim, holding her gaze while the courtroom settled to a muffled buzz. Only when total silence returned did she speak. "Lieutenant Ramon. This court has found you not guilty on the charges of sacrilege and attempted rape. However, the charge of dishonorable conduct has been upheld. The judgment of this court is that you be stripped of all rank, with a permanent bar on any future promotion. And as an example to others, you shall be flogged. One hundred lashes." Rozek stopped, breathing harshly through flared nostrils and then cracking the gavel down on the desk. "Court dismissed."

❖

Sometimes it seemed to Lynn that life in the temple was an unending game of one step forward, two steps back.

Smith was gone. Even before the temple authorities had decided what to do with Lynn, the ambitious Sister's fate had been decided. The events in Petersmine, following so soon after the deaths of the Guards, had handed her political opponents the very weapon they needed. Smith was not even given the chance to unpack her belongings. Within hours of arriving at Landfall, she had been dispatched again to a minor temple as far from the center of power as it was possible to go. Her chances of returning were slight; her chances of sitting in the Chief Consultant's chair were gone forever. Some small comfort could be had thinking of Sister Smith consigned to the sidelines, her dreams withering under the passage of time.

But in Smith's place had come Sister Dunsin, an acolyte of the Chief Consultant, equally as devout as Sister Smith but less arrogant and more worldly-wise. And with a sharper ear for irony. She was a large, broad-shouldered woman, but surprisingly agile, both physically and mentally. She watched Lynn with shrewd, disapproving eyes, while delivering an unrelenting discourse on the horrors of sin. She was to be Lynn's mentor: to steer her feet from the path of wickedness, to teach her humility and obedience, to instruct her in the ways of the Goddess. Within two days of getting to Landfall, Lynn began to fear she had met her match.

And still there was no word of Kim. The last news Lynn had received had been on the road to Landfall, a note smuggled via Sergeant Coppelli, and that had been vague enough to give rise to more anxiety than it alleviated. Lynn knew the Sisters were awaiting the outcome of the court-martial before they made their final judgment on her punishment. Or in Sister Dunsin's words, the chance she would be given to demonstrate her remorse. But if Kim were hanged, nothing could ever begin to match the remorse she would feel. The waiting was hell, made worse by the knowledge that if the Sisters so decided, she might never know the outcome of Kim's trial. She might take the doubt and guilt with her to the grave.

On the fourth afternoon following her arrival in Landfall, Sister Dunsin summoned Lynn from the meditation room where she was supposed to be praying to Celaeno for forgiveness. The heavy woman, with her surprisingly light footsteps, appeared without warning. Lynn was instructed to follow her though the maze of interlinked courtyards that formed the sanctum at Landfall. For once Sister Dunsin was silent and gave no sermon. Lynn took that to be a bad sign, but she did not realize quite how bad until they reached their destination.

They arrived on a narrow balcony set on the side of the building housing the Chief Consultant's apartments. Directly below was the Guards' parade ground. Presumably, the vantage point was normally used during ceremonies when the Chief Consultant and the senior Sisters could take the salute of the assembled Guards or read them suitable extracts from the book of the Elder-Ones.

Guards were assembled on the parade ground now, stretched in silent lines across the open space. Among them was a small block of Rangers, their subdued uniforms in marked contrast to the red and gold of the Guards. At their head stood the unmistakable sturdy outline of LeCoup. Lynn's heart leaped, but no tall lieutenant occupied the place at the captain's side, and in truth, that would have been more than could be hoped.

The expression on Lynn's face changed to a frown; she was unsure why she had been brought to witness the drill, or of what part she was supposed to play, since the balcony was not the focus of attention. All soldiers were facing to the side, their eyes trained on a construction of three posts formed like a doorway, but with no door, no wall.

Suddenly, comprehension dawned on Lynn. She backed off. "No. I don't want to see this."

With lightning speed, Sister Dunsin's hand shot out, grabbing Lynn's wrist and preventing her retreat. "But you will. I've read the reports of the court-martial, and I still have some doubts. Maybe this Ranger did assault you, and you've played along out of a misplaced sense of gratitude for her saving your life. In which case you have the right to see your assailant punished. Or maybe this Ranger is totally innocent. In which case you should be made to see the harm your wickedness has caused. Or maybe the truth is somewhere in the middle, so both cases apply. But whatever actually happened in that stable, you will remain here and bear witness."

There was no escape. In anguish, Lynn's eyes returned to the parade ground, in time to see the small party of prisoner and escort appear from a dark doorway and march out into the daylight. The silence of the assembled soldiers was tangible, overwhelming, as the group halted before the posts. Kim's jacket and shirt were removed, leaving her naked from the waist up. Her wrists were bound to the top bar, and then the escorting soldiers stepped back. Kim looked so very alone. Tears of desperation started in Lynn's eyes, but there was nothing she could do.

A Guard major stepped out from the group of attending officers to read out the charge and the sentence. Then she signaled to a soldier from the Militia in her black uniform who stood waiting at the side, coiled whip in hand. Lynn wondered whether it was part of the punishment, added humiliation to suffer at the hands of the ordinary Militia, like a common criminal, or whether it was just that no one else would volunteer for the job.

The Militiawoman advanced toward the posts unhurried, as if savoring her part in the gruesome drama, the only movement on the whole of the silent parade ground.

As far as could be heard from the balcony, Kim took the entire punishment with hardly a sound. Lynn was sobbing before the count reached ten.

CHAPTER TEN—
A PECULIAR ASPECT OF THE GODDESS

The solid blocks of stone under Lynn's knees felt soft, like shifting sand, but did not cushion her from the savage tingling that played along her legs, balled in the small of her back, and crawled up her spine—the ache of cramped muscles and stiff joints. She knelt before the shrine to Himoti in the dimly lit oratory, head bowed, hands clasped in supplication, exactly as she had done for the previous five days. Her track on time was slipping, but the windows of the oratory had been dark for hours. Surely it would soon be time for her to be released for the pitifully small amount of sleep that was allowed her?

The voices of the four Sisters who were also in the oratory rose and fell in unison, praying for her redemption, praying that Himoti would forgive her and not take away her powers of imprinting. *Praying that the temple doesn't lose any money.* Despite her tiredness, Lynn could still manage the cynical thought. The rhythmical chanting stopped and Sister Dunsin walked forward to stand in front of Lynn.

"Do you repent of your disobedience and fully admit to your misdeeds?"

"Yes, Sister." Lynn was far too tired to disagree, even if it had been wise to do so.

"Do you humbly beg forgiveness of the Goddess?"

"Yes, Sister."

"Do you swear to live by the rules the blessed Himoti has decreed for Celaeno's chosen ones, freely and joyfully?"

"Yes, Sister."

I don't believe you mean a word of it. Something in Dunsin's posture made the thought as clear as if she had spoken aloud. But after a long, hard stare at the kneeling Imprinter, the Sister raised her eyes and said, "We will all join in one last prayer."

The chanting began again. Lynn moved her lips in time while fighting to suppress a yawn. The spectacle she had made of herself on the balcony had more than convinced Sister Dunsin of her guilt. Lynn suspected that gauging her reaction was one of the main reasons for the Sister taking her there in the first place. But despite her aches and the bone-numbing weariness, she was not, strictly speaking, being punished. She was being shriven in the hope that a large dose of prayer might nullify any detrimental effects from her lapse in virtue.

What censure there was had been directed largely at Sister Smith. Imprinters were kept in the temples so they might be guided by the Sisters. Obviously, Lynn needed more guidance than most and Smith had not done her job. Of course, there were also technical problems in punishing an Imprinter. They had no privileges to withhold or possessions to confiscate, and any harsh treatment was likely to end up costing the temple money. Five days' imprinting fees had been lost as it was, on top of the time she had spent on the delayed journey from Fairfield.

However, Lynn was starting to find things extremely unpleasant. The cramp in her joints had long ago passed the point that might justifiably be described as painful. And she had been allowed so little sleep that there was nothing she could do about it. One irony of the healer sense was that the more in need of it you were, the less able you were to heal yourself. Using the healer sense took intense concentration. Exhaustion or pain made it impossible to reach the level of detachment necessary to step beyond the confines of your normal senses.

As an Imprinter, Lynn had the gift to an extremely high degree, but even she had limits, and five nights with only a few hours' sleep had pushed her well beyond them. Of course, it was possible to pre-empt the pain, to use the skill when you were still well enough and stop the body from imposing its limitations, but it was not wise. Pain and tiredness were important warning signs. A healer who switched them off could unwittingly and quite literally work herself to death.

The light in the oratory was dim, and Lynn's eyes were playing games with her. The flames above the candles wobbled, the walls the light fell on wobbled, and for a moment, the ground under her knees wobbled, sending a surge of nausea through her empty stomach. But she needed sleep more than food, and Lynn's hopes fixed on Dunsin's use of the phrase "one last prayer." She hoped that she would still be able to stand up when the time came to leave the oratory. Her whole body ached as if she had been kicked and beaten, although no one had laid a hand on her. It was forbidden to shed the blood of Imprinters. A protection not granted to Kim. Lynn's eyes scrunched shut as she remembered the last sight she'd had of the Ranger, half dragged, half carried from the parade ground. It was the vision Lynn called on whenever she started feeling sorry for herself.

The cycle of prayer finally came to an end. The last words echoed away into the darkness. The Sisters bowed low to the shrine of Himoti and relaxed slightly. One turned to the door, and Lynn gathered herself to rise, not sure if her legs would obey her. But before she had the chance to put them to the test, Sister Dunsin appeared before her.

"If you please, Imprinter. I have a few words I wish to share with you in private."

Lynn managed to restrain the groan of despair that rose to her lips. How much longer would the dictatorial Sister keep her from her bed?

Dunsin waited until the other three Sisters had quit the oratory before she spoke again. "I have been talking with the Chief Consultant. She has agreed we have done everything for you that we can. It now remains only to see whether you still stand in the grace of the Goddess. You will be allowed to rest tomorrow, but the day after you will be assigned to duties in the imprinting chapel. And then we shall see whether you have truly begged for forgiveness from the heart"—Dunsin paused and looked at Lynn with distaste—"which I personally have serious doubts about."

"I have listened to all that has been said—" Lynn began.

"And not paid heed to any of it." Dunsin's voice was forceful. "I wonder if you realize what might have happened to you if the Goddess had not shown her mercy and saved you from your own folly. Do not doubt it was her will that dispatched Sister Smith to your aid, for the Goddess will use even the unworthy to achieve her goals. And you are most fortunate that the Goddess did not desert you."

Lynn said nothing, though it was not quite the way she saw things.

"The blessed Himoti demands that we keep Imprinters safe within the temple, shelter you from the sins of the world, but I wonder whether we do not sometimes leave you vulnerable in your innocence. Although the circumstances you found yourself in were unique, to be virtually unchaperoned in the company of Rangers. Rangers." Dunsin spat out the word as if it was a term of abuse. "What do you know of Rangers? You became infatuated. Did you think she returned your feelings, cared for you? Rangers tally up their lovers like they do the heads of wild beasts they kill. Conquests, they call them. Trophies to their prowess. And that is all you would have been to her: a fine boast, when she was drunk enough to dare say it aloud."

No. Lynn bit her tongue, though her heart cried out against Dunsin's lies.

"And if you hadn't been rescued by the bounty of the Goddess, what would have happened? Do you imagine tender caresses? Some sweet romantic experience? Do you think Rangers make gentle lovers?" Dunsin paused for emphasis. "Fool. You had put yourself in her power. She would have taken what she wanted from you, and I can guarantee it would have been more than you wanted to give. She was taller than you, stronger than you. She would have forced you into acts that I will not mention in this holy place." Dunsin stopped, breathing harshly, and then continued in more measured tones. "You do not know in what danger you stood or how much you have to thank the Goddess for."

Kim would never have harmed me. Lynn hugged the certainty to herself.

"I think you should remain here another hour in private prayer. I will light a candle to mark the time for you. Think well on everything I have said. Open your heart to the Goddess and let her love drive away the vile baseness that has ensnared your soul." Dunsin lit the wick on an hour candle and placed it where Lynn might see, then turned and walked away. Her soft footsteps faded until there was no sound in the darkened oratory.

Once she was alone, Lynn's eyes fixed on the small shrine. Himoti, eldest of the Elder-Ones, the patron of Imprinters. Suddenly, tears began to flow down Lynn's face and after days of empty words, true prayers came to Lynn's lips, the entreaty from the core of her being. "Please, Himoti. I don't care what happens to me. I'll stay in the temple, do your work, follow all your commands. But please, look after Kim. Keep her safe. And someday, maybe, put it into her heart to forgive me."

❖

The family group was assembled in the imprinting chapel, shifting awkwardly, unsure of where they were supposed to stand. Lynn came to an abrupt halt when she saw them. During the previous days, it had been so easy to ignore Sister Dunsin's prophecies of failure, but now it had come to the test, and she was swamped by the rushing onset of fears. For the first time in her life, Lynn had doubts about her own ability. Suppose Dunsin was right? For Lynn knew there was no real repentance in her heart. Would Himoti withdraw her gift? And what happened to Imprinters who could no longer follow their calling?

The two young women at the altar looked at her with expressions of awe, seeing only the suit of brilliant blue. Lynn wondered whether she still had the right to wear it. The question nagged at her as she slowly advanced up the chapel, half in a daze. The Sisters on duty arranged the mother-to-be and directed her partner to kneel by the side of the altar. Lynn came to a stop, not daring to meet the eyes of the two Sisters. She knew they would be watching her with misgiving, which could only further undermine her confidence. Lynn's hands stretched out, moving more by habit than intention, and for a second they paused, hovering over the two women, the prospective parents. Lynn began to focus her concentration, preparing to reach inside the shells of their bodies—and wondered if she still could.

The woman on the altar had been instructed to lie still, but slightly nervously, she turned her head, rolling her neck to meet her partner's eyes. A look passed between them. The look. Something Lynn had seen hundreds of times before. Well over half of all couples would share that searching gaze. It had always seemed a minor issue before, a slight distraction, but suddenly enlightenment burst upon Lynn. The knowledge of what it meant to look into another woman's eyes and see your world reflected there. Kim's eyes in the stable.

For a second, Lynn froze, stunned, as she finally truly understood what it was to be an Imprinter. The hopes she had within her power to fulfill. The world the Sisters with their dead prayers and teachings could not begin to convey. The creation of a child could be merely the mechanical splicing of DNA, the clinical job described in the books the Elder-Ones had left for Imprinters. But the wanting of a child was a thing of love.

Carefully Lynn lowered her hands to rest on womb and head. The sense of the women's bodies flowed into her, the hot rush of blood, the sparkle of electricity, and more than that, the love between them. With absolute certainty, Lynn knew she could create this child. Never had the task been simpler, because this time she would weave not only the DNA but also the love.

As the last doubts in her mind were swept away, Lynn sank into the imprinting trance.

❖

It was a matter of tradition that Imprinters were, as far as possible, anonymous. They were the living conduits that channeled the Goddess's bounty to her children, no more than symbols of her divine will. This was why Imprinters lost their last name on the day they entered the temple. No family could claim them, and their first names were normally used only when the Sisters found the need to distinguish between them. But Lynn's exceptional ability was attracting comment, setting her apart from the other Imprinters, and not just among the Sisters. As the months passed, there were signs that even the ordinary folk outside the temple knew of the young Imprinter who performed her work with unprecedented speed and surety.

Sister Dunsin took considerable pains to ensure that Lynn did not fall victim to the sin of pride. Her daily lectures concentrated on self-sacrifice and the perils of forgetting humility. But it was obvious that whatever Lynn's mentor might personally think, other Sisters were starting to look on Lynn more favorably. The unfortunate circumstances accompanying her arrival in Landfall were if not forgotten, then at least not dwelled on.

An ancient Sister came to talk to Lynn one day, a small, round woman. Her forehead had a crisscrossed tapestry of wrinkles, yet the eyes above the mask were soft and compassionate, and her voice was cheerfully eager. She had received special permission from her superiors to talk to Lynn on matters of theology, to see if she could find out why Lynn had been so supremely blessed by the Goddess and if the lessons might be applied to others.

The Sister had some quaint theories of her own based on what was, to Lynn's mind, a rather implausible reading of one of the chapters of the book of the Elder-Ones. The superiors were obviously humoring their elderly colleague in granting her permission to investigate her unworldly ideas. But the Sister was well meaning. She used the phrase "the love of the Goddess" as if she meant it, and money was clearly not her motive. In fact she even naively suggested that if imprinting were made easier, then the fees could be reduced. A warmth filled her voice when she spoke of babies and the joy they could bring to a family. She should have been a grandmother. She had a genuine affection for the ordinary people, which Lynn cynically suspected was why a Sister of her age was not higher up the temple hierarchy.

Lynn fielded the questions as tactfully as she could, almost regretting to disappoint the Sister's hopes. It was not easy, especially when the ancient eyes met hers and the Sister asked, "Is there a peculiar aspect of the Goddess that you meditate upon?"

Lynn battled to control her face and bite back the words that threatened to let slip: *The aspect revealed to me when I had Lieutenant Kimberly Ramon's tongue in my mouth.* But it would be cruel to shock such a kind-hearted, innocent Sister.

Lynn made a vague answer, falling back on the accepted wisdom of the temple, and at last, the elderly Sister dropped her head sadly, thanked Lynn for her time, and left.

❖

Lynn still found it impossible to describe herself as happy in the temple, but she had reached a passive acceptance of her fate. Her greatest sorrow was the knowledge that Kim must blame her, even hate her, and quite justifiably curse the day they had met. Whereas Lynn's regrets were only for the day of their parting. It was she who had gone to the stable, and she who had spoken out of place. The responsibility for what happened was hers alone, and Kim was the one who had suffered for it. The sense of guilt and shame cost Lynn many hours' sleep.

At other times, the memory of Kim helped inspire her work, not just through the insight given into the love between partners. Lynn knew she would never again set foot outside the temple, but the children she made would go out into the world and walk on the same earth, under the same wide sky as Kim. And maybe one day, the squadron might pass through some outlying village, and Kim would see one of the children she had created. Of course, the Ranger would not recognize Lynn's handiwork, but it would make a bridge between their lives, a point where their worlds might touch.

Summer was fading into autumn when Sister Dunsin came to Lynn, catching her as she was about to go into a meditation cell.

"Imprinter. Some information has come my way that I think you should be made aware of."

The large Sister squeezed into the small room after Lynn and shut the door. Lynn had a nasty sinking feeling in her stomach. The things Sister Dunsin thought she should be aware of were rarely things that aided her peace of mind.

Dunsin launched into her lecture. "The justice of the Goddess will not be denied. In our weakness we might attempt to hide from her will, but she will not suffer to see her laws flouted. *I will not have my commands ignored, for in them I show my greatest care for you. They are for your protection rather than my glory.*" The Sister finished with a quote.

Lynn tried to look suitably thoughtful, but it was a rather general start and might well lead into anything. Until she knew where Dunsin was heading, the wisest course was to say the minimum possible, and so Lynn meekly mumbled, "Yes, Sister."

"I have just received news that serves to demonstrate the truth of all I have told you. Perhaps now you will pay more attention. The Goddess can see into every heart, and will judge us all accordingly. The justice of this world is flawed, but the justice of the Goddess is inescapable."

"Indeed, Sister."

"I have brought the written evidence with me, in case you think I have in some way invented facts or augmented the truth to serve my own purposes."

"I would never accuse you of falsehood," Lynn said at once. And neither would she. The Sisters might have their own strange ideas about what constituted the truth, but they never knowingly lied.

"It is a communication between the Ranger Command at Fort Krowe and the central military administration here in Landfall. The letter has been passed to me for reasons that will become clear when you read it, although it will have to be returned to the records office once we are finished. In it, we can clearly see the judgment of the Goddess. She has exacted her revenge for the sins committed against her divine will."

Dunsin held out a sheet of paper. Confusion and rising dread made Lynn hesitate for a second before she took the letter and spread it flat, twisting the paper slightly to the light so she might read. At the top was a red wax seal authenticating the dispatch, but Lynn hardly registered the details. Her eyes fixed on the few short lines of writing.

Ranger Command regrets to inform all those concerned that, while on active duty pursuing bandits in the western mountains, Ranger Kimberly Ramon of the 23rd Squadron has been killed. Please make all necessary arrangements for the standard death-in-action payment to be made to her next of kin.

⚜

PART TWO

On the Trail of Bandits

CHAPTER ELEVEN—
A JOB THE SISTERS WANT DOING

No paths led through the mountains this far west. The line of mounted soldiers had to pick their way forward as best they could, over moorlands blanketed in spiky, knee-high grass and through wooded valleys where the tangle of branches forced them to dismount and hack a way through, leading the horses on foot. July was blazing into August, summer reaching its height, hot and dry. The grass was parched yellow. The wind picked up a choking haze of dust that left the skin feeling gritty within minutes. Leaves on trees sagged limp, waiting for the relief of autumn rain, but still the mountain peaks high above glittered white with their caps of snow.

Evening was drawing near as the company traveled up a long, narrow valley beside the banks of a slow-moving river winding sinuously through the woodland. Stumpy trees overhung the water on both sides, less dense than in some other parts, but still making for difficult progress. At last, the head of the column reached a broad open tract set in a loop of the river, the largest patch of green grass they had encountered for days. Virtually the whole line was out in the open when the rider in the lead turned to confer briefly with the woman at her side. A subordinate who took her instructions wheeled her horse around and shouted, "Company, halt! Pitch camp. Officers report for briefing in an hour."

The effect of the order rippled down the line. Horses turned left and right, women slipped out of the saddle, packs were pulled down and opened, and the disciplined column drifted apart like a plume of smoke in a soft breeze, slowly spreading across the width of the open space. The motion appeared haphazard to a first glance, but patterns did emerge, most noticeable was the separation of the Guards in red and gold from the smaller, less conspicuous section of Rangers.

This latter group was definitely in the minority, outnumbered three to one. Their numbers seemed even less significant once they dispersed into the cover of trees on the edge of the clearing. The horses were unsaddled at the point where the valley walls began to rise, before being sent to graze on the green beside the river. The Guards, though, were preparing to bivouac on the open grass, on land lying a couple of meters below the site the Rangers had chosen.

Lieutenant Coppelli oversaw the setting of the Rangers' camp, although the experienced women needed little instruction, merely the detailing of a few unfortunates to the less popular tasks. She spared a cheery glance for the Guards, who were clearly far less happy with outdoor living. Their ineptitude had provided hours of amusement for the Rangers during the first days on the trail and could still raise a smile. Then she turned back, scanning the women moving under the trees until she finally spotted the person she wanted, standing shovel in hand, about to start digging the fire pit for cooking.

"Private Ramon. Leave that. Someone else can do it. I want you to come with me."

Kim paused for a moment, looking pensively at the shovel before stabbing it into the ground and walking over to join the lieutenant. The pair climbed the steep side of the valley in silence, not speaking until they stood on an outcrop of rock high above the campsite by the river where they could peer down on the activity: the grooming of horses, the setting out of bedding, the erection of Major Rozek's tent, and the first plumes of smoke from cooking fires.

At last Kim spoke. "You don't have to keep shielding me from heavy duties. My back was completely healed weeks ago."

"Yes...well. You have to allow me something for feeling guilty since I'm lieutenant and you're not. And anyway, I did have valid reasons for bringing you up here. You've got the best eye for trouble in the squadron. What do you make of the campsite?"

Kim laughed softly. "It's not the spot I'd have chosen."

"Same here, and I suspect the major is already starting to question her decision." A cheerful glint lit Chip's eyes as she looked down on the half-assembled tent. "She probably thought the Goddess had especially cleared a little picnic site for her and never stopped to think that the absence of trees might mean the ground was waterlogged. The sun has dried off the surface for now, but it will seep up at night. I'm afraid her girls are going to be soaked by morning."

"It was really mean of us to lay claim to the high ground without warning them." Despite the words, Kim's voice held not a trace of guilt.

Chip matched her grin before asking in more business-like tones, "Aside from the damp, what do you make of it defensively?"

"Pretty poor. Anyone could creep close through the undergrowth. The Guards will make wonderful targets out in the open, with their nice red tunics. Bandits could polish off a few and then slip away again. And you can work that out as easily as me."

"But what would you do about it?"

Kim studied the valley thoughtfully. "Apart from move? I'd put sentries there, there, there and there." Her finger pointed out the locations. "It would cover the most likely spots for archers, though it's nowhere close to attack-proof. In order to achieve that, you'd have to put the entire squadron on sentry duty, and we'd all be done in by morning."

Chip pulled a wry grin. "I always sleep best with the knowledge I could be murdered in my bed."

"Assuming there are actually some bandits out here," Kim said skeptically.

"You have doubts?"

"Don't you?"

"Well..." Chip's face wrinkled. "I know something doesn't hang right. I mean, when have they ever sent Guards after a bunch of outlaws? And there's nearly a hundred of them, plus our squadron, but you never get more than a dozen outlaws in a gang. I'd love to know what Captain LeCoup would say about it."

"Probably something unrepeatable."

LeCoup's presence was missed. The squadron captain had finally been promoted out of field duty. She was now at Fort Krowe, pushing the new admissions to the Rangers through their basic training. It was a fair bet the raw recruits were already cursing her name, but in years to come would praise her memory when the lessons they learned from LeCoup saved their lives.

The captain's promotion was years overdue, and there was no surprise in Chip getting the vacant post of lieutenant. More disconcerting was that the 23rd Squadron had been sent into the field without a new captain. Chip was the only senior Ranger officer. The squadron had been tagged on as auxiliaries to the Guards for their unconventional mission, supposedly hunting a band of extremely dangerous outlaws. But when had border security become the concern of the Guards? The question was one that all the Rangers were asking.

Kim had a few others. She faced Chip. "What I don't understand is, why are we here?"

"So the Guards don't get lost," Chip suggested.

"Oh, that's undoubtedly why they wanted a few Rangers along. But why out here? We've been heading due west through the wildlands for nearly three weeks. There aren't going to be bandits this far from the homelands. There is no one for them to steal from."

"They might have set up a base out here. Somewhere to hide between raids."

Kim shook her head. "It's too far to lug all the food they'd need for a long stay. It's been tight rations for us, and we're going to have to turn around in a little more than a week if we don't want to run out of food before we get back." It was an undeniable point, even though the Rangers had been able to stretch out the supplies with their knowledge of edible plants.

"Hopefully, that means our goal isn't too far off. The major knows exactly where we're going, so they ought to have worked out the provisions." Chip's tone was not quite as confident as her words.

Kim's expression grew even more perplexed. "And that's another question. Where did she get her map?"

"The Goddess only knows. I'd love to study it in more detail, but she's only let me have brief glimpses when she thinks she might be lost and wants my opinion."

"You haven't been able to work out anything from it?"

"It's just a simple drawing of the quickest way to get somewhere. But what that place is..." Chip shrugged. "I would say your guess is as good as mine, except it is usually better. So what do you think?"

Kim pursed her lips while her eyes stared down on the campsite. "I think there's a job the Sisters want doing out here, but they don't trust the Rangers to do it. Rozek is some Sister's favorite officer. Lynn thought she was in the pocket of one faction or the other. That's why the major has been trusted with this mission. She probably knows a lot of what there is to know, but she's keeping it to herself. Even the Guards are in the dark, and that's what worries me most of all. I think that when we find out what this job is we won't like it, but they're not planning on letting us know until we're not in a position to think of other options."

Chip's face was grim. "Maybe. But what worries me most is that Rozek particularly asked for the 23rd Squadron to accompany her troops. And I don't think it was because of fond memories of us. I've seen her watching you sometimes. She can't forgive you for the fact you're still breathing." Chip reached out and grabbed her friend's arm. "But just you keep doing it. And that's an order."

Kim grinned. "Yes, ma'am. But I had sort of been intending that anyway." She matched Chip's grasp on the forearm. "Come on, let's go back and see how dinner is going."

Together the two women in green and gray headed down the hillside.

❖

No attacks came during the night, and the next morning, the company continued on their way. The Guards with despondent faces and wet clothes; the Rangers with partially successful attempts to avoid looking smug. The walls on either side got closer and higher and eventually, in midmorning, the valley ended abruptly at a sheer face of white limestone where the lazy river emerged from a long, thin opening at the bottom.

Major Rozek called a halt and consulted her map, at last grudgingly requesting Chip's advice. After a short discussion, the company backtracked a couple of kilometers to where a rockslide provided a steep yet passable route out of the valley. At the top they found a wide, rolling moor, virtually treeless, burned yellow by the summer. A gentle breeze stirred the grasses in a dry rustling. Overhead, the thinnest sheet of high cloud did little to hide the glare of the sun. Due west, a line of distant mountains lifted their heads against the hazy sky. One had a distinctive double peak. Rozek spent some time looking between her map and the mountain before leading the column in a straight line toward it.

A short while later, the column passed a gaping hole in the ground, a long gash at the bottom of a steep, crater-like depression. From the black depths thundered the rushing of water. The hole was where the roof of a cavern had crumbled away and the unsupported earth slid in. Obviously, the river disappeared into a sinkhole somewhere ahead and then flowed underground along caves eroded into the limestone, until it re-emerged at the foot of the cliff they had seen. But from the sound, the river bore little resemblance to the placid waterway they had camped by the night before. Now squeezed into tunnels through the rock, its booming roar reverberated from the chasm.

The mounted women kept well back from the treacherous-looking edge and carried on across the moor. Half a kilometer farther, they passed a second hole, and then a third—a string of strange pockmarks in the otherwise even surface of the moorland that marked the path of the underground river.

At noon, they had a lengthy break to rest the horses and take lunch, a chance to talk and stretch out the cricks from hours in the saddle, and then the company went on. But it was not long before the major called another halt. The head of the column had come across yet another hole, bigger than any of the others, a full twenty meters long. From the grassy plane of the moor, steep slopes of loose gravel plunged down on either side to the ragged gash in the bedrock.

The Rangers had been riding in the middle of the column, but word arrived quickly that the major wished to speak with Lieutenant Coppelli. She spurred her horse forward and to the place where Rozek and the other Guard officers were peering into the crater.

"You wanted me, ma'am?" Chip asked as she dismounted.

"Yes, Lieutenant. There is something down there by the edge. I want you to send one of your women, Private Ramon, down to retrieve it."

Chip craned her neck to look over the edge. Some artifact, possibly made of leather, was half buried near the opening in the rock, and ten meters of loose footing at an angle of nearly 45 degrees had to be crossed before one could get to it. "But, ma'am, it's—" She did not have the chance to finish.

"That's an order," Rozek snapped.

"Yes, ma'am." Chip bit back anything else she might say and faced down the line. "Private Ramon, come here. And bring a rope with you."

"We haven't got time to waste pussyfooting about with ropes," Rozek said harshly.

Chip spun back, speechless with disbelief, but at last found her voice. "I will not order one of my women to risk her neck like that."

"Then you will find yourself removed from your post and one of my officers put in your place."

Kim arrived in time to hear the major's threat. She slipped down from her horse and walked forward, eyebrows raised in query. "Ma'am?"

"The major wants you to go down without a safety rope and collect something she's seen beside the chasm's edge. But I won't ask you to do it." Chip, in her outrage, did not bother keeping her voice low enough to prevent others from hearing.

"No. I'm going to order you to." Rozek's voice snapped out sharply from behind her.

Kim's eyes flitted between the assembled officers and then down to the fissure, evaluating the situation. She met her friend's eyes and spoke softly. "It's all right, Chip. I'll go very carefully."

"She wants you to fall."

"I know. I'll try to disappoint her. But you dare not let Rozek displace you. If I'm right, things are going to get very nasty soon, and the lives of the whole squadron might depend on having a competent officer in charge. And it won't help me anyway. If I don't do what she says, she'll hold a field court-martial and string me up for disobeying an order while on active duty."

"In these circumstances? She'd have hell to pay when the report goes back to Fort Krowe."

"The Sisters won't be upset to hear of my death. Rozek might receive a public reprimand, but she'll also get a private commendation. And we both know which is more useful to a Guardswoman's career."

A range of emotions battled for control of Chip's face, but in the end, all she said was, "It's your choice, but take care."

"I will. Just try and get the squadron back intact."

Kim stepped to the crumbling edge of the crater and looked down. She removed her spurs and sword belt, then turned around and carefully lowered herself onto the unstable slope. A small trickle of loose stones bounced down to the edge of the fissure and plummeted over, but Kim managed to get enough purchase using toes, knees, and fingers to stop herself from following.

Testing her weight at each step, she edged her way down toward the sound of furious water, a roaring that got louder and louder by the second. Her entire being became fixed on the search for secure handholds, the feel of the shifting ground under her toes, and the narrowing distance between herself and the brink of the chasm. So tight did her mental focus become that Kim was almost surprised when the object she was after appeared within arm's reach. One worn shoe, toes and heels well scuffed, half buried in the soft gravel of the slope. Kim pulled it loose and was about to stuff it inside her jacket, freeing both hands for the climb back, when she was stopped by a shout from Rozek.

"Throw it up here!"

For the first time, Kim took her eyes from the ground beneath her and looked up to the top of the slope. The entire company had dismounted and was lining the rim. The Rangers were watching her with expressions of appalled dismay. Even the Guards looked worried. Except for Major Rozek.

"I said, throw it here, Ranger."

Kim pulled back her arm and lobbed the shoe up. The action sent another small avalanche of stones tumbling over the edge and nearly unbalanced her, but after a brief struggle, Kim regained her grip on the slope. The shoe landed on the grass by Rozek's feet.

"Great, now we know the shoe size of one of the outlaws," Chip muttered to the Ranger beside her.

Kim was about to start the ascent of the slope when she was again stopped by the major. "While you're there, check that nothing is under that bush."

Kim's eyes followed the direction Rozek was pointing. The plant in question was five meters to her left, a small shrub that had somehow established a foothold on the steepest part of the slope. Its knotted branches overhung the edge. Kim looked up, meeting Rozek's eyes. For a long time, they held the contact, Rozek with an expression somewhere between expectation and triumph, Kim with resigned contempt. In Kim's head echoed the words, *You have my solemn oath as an officer in the temple Guard. You will die for it*. Rozek's intention was that she should not live to climb out of the crater, but there was a limit to how far the major could push things. Already there was muttering from above, and not just from the Rangers. No soldier liked to think her commanding officer would play games with their lives.

Kim took a quick glance down to the black emptiness opening centimeters below her feet. The thunder of the underground river boomed from the cave below. To slip would be certain death, but she had gotten this far, and a certain grim amusement arose from the thought of frustrating Rozek.

An eternity passed in the cautious sideways scramble, but at last the bush was reached and as expected, there was nothing to be found. Up above, Rozek's expression had changed to one of irritation, but she did not dare drag things out further and made no attempt to demand more exploration of the chasm, allowing Kim to begin the climb to safety.

The first meter went without a hitch, then Kim's hand fastened on a larger rock embedded in the ground. To a careful tug, it seemed securely held by the surrounding soil, but as Kim pulled on it, levering herself up the slope, it shifted, twisted, and came loose in her hand. The jolt sent the loose gravel under her toes and knees rolling, taking her with them down the slope, an unhaltable, unhurried slither. In desperation, Kim dug her fingers into the ground, trying to stop her slow slide, but the chasm's edge came ever nearer, and then her feet slipped over. A last hopeless sweep of her hands, and Kim caught hold of the bush, pulling herself to a stop. Her legs dangled in free air. Never had the torrent sounded so loud.

Helplessly, Kim looked up to the line of shocked onlookers at the top of the slope. Chip was barging her way along the rim, making for the point directly above, coiled rope in hand, but the rescue attempt was too late. Kim heard the snapping of roots as the shrub tore free, felt the world reel about her, and saw the sky spin and recede as she pitched back over the edge and tumbled into the darkness.

CHAPTER TWELVE—
A NICE NIGHT FOR A STROLL

A wave of disbelief and horror froze the row of women at the top of the crater. Only Chip's cry of "Kim!" broke the silence, and then she also stood motionless, coiled rope hanging uselessly in her hands, staring down at the tiny disturbed hollow where the roots of the bush had torn free. The last echo of the shout faded away, and then only the whisper of the wind over the moorland contended with the roar of the underground torrent.

Rozek's voice was the next to be raised. "May the Goddess treat her soul with mercy. For we are all her children and must one day stand before her to be judged."

The bland words of piety lifted the spell of inaction from the assembled women. Guards muttered to their neighbors, and Rangers slowly shook their heads in denial of what they had witnessed. Some spun away from the fissure and fixed their gaze on the horizon. Others wandered back to their horses and then stood still, as if trying to summon the enthusiasm to get back into the saddle.

Rozek turned to the junior Guard officer beside her and said, "We've wasted enough time here. Get them mounted up. I want to make a fair bit of progress by nightfall."

The Guardswoman nodded and was about to shout the command, but just as she opened her mouth, she was stopped by the sight of a furious Lieutenant Coppelli, elbowing her way through the confused line of soldiers, heading toward them, hands balled into fists.

"That was murder!" Chip screamed the words, her face only centimeters from Rozek's.

The major's eyes were contemptuous. "And *that* is gross insubordination."

A fresh circle of silence rippled out from where the two antagonists stood, eyes locked in hostility. But at last, Rozek drew in a long breath through pinched nostrils and quoted, "*The gift of life is the Goddess's alone to bestow, and hers alone to take back. At the painful parting, seek not to understand why, merely to believe that all is done according to her will.*"

"The will of the Goddess be damned! You murdered her."

The blasphemy drew gasps of shock from the Guards.

Rozek's face hardened into rigid outrage, but her voice softened to a dangerous intensity. "You have gone too far." Louder she said, "Lieutenant Coppelli is relieved of duty. Captain Ahmed, you will take temporary command of the 23rd Squadron." She glanced back at Chip. "You may rejoin the rest of the Rangers. Until further notice, you have the acting rank of private. Command headquarters in Landfall will receive my report when we get back and may make a more permanent decision."

Rozek turned on her heel and began to walk away, but she did not get far. A hand grabbed her shoulder and swung her back, then a fist smashed into the side of her head. The blow sent her reeling backward; a second sharp punch knocked her to the ground, half stunned.

Before Rozek fully realized what was happening, Chip was sitting astride her chest, thumbs pushing down hard on her windpipe. Fingers clawed into the back of her neck. The speed of the assault was such that a few moments passed before the nearest Guards gathered themselves to respond. Several grabbed hold of Chip and dragged her off the half-strangled major.

Still, an air of unreality gripped the majority of those watching. The previous few minutes had held too many shocks. They watched in dream-like confusion as Rozek rolled over and pushed herself up on one arm while the other hand massaged her throat. The major took a deep breath and rose unsteadily.

The Rangers recovered first. Even before Rozek had regained her feet, a couple were moving forward to where Chip was held, restrained by four Guards. The hands of others went to the hilts of their swords and their eyes shifted left and right as they readied themselves for action. For a moment, discipline teetered on the brink of chaos, but then Rozek's deputy stepped in, shouting commands, instilling a sense of purpose in the stunned Guards and shaking them out of their state of frozen confusion. As military order reasserted itself, the Rangers halted, reminded of the extent to which they were outnumbered. Many of the Guards looked uneasy, some looked ashamed, but there was no doubt that they would follow Rozek and the other Guard officers.

With furious impotence, the Rangers had no option but to watch as Chip's hands were tied behind her back and she was led away prisoner, to ride with an escort of Guards until Rozek should have time to consider her fate. Not that anyone had much doubt about what that would be.

Away from the hole in the ground, the soldiers reclaimed their horses and climbed back into their saddles, rapidly forming themselves into a double column. The major remained by the rim of the crater, twisting her neck experimentally from side to side, until something in the grass caught her eye. From their position in the middle of the line, the embittered Rangers watched Rozek bend down and pick up the discarded coil of rope. They were too far away to see her expression of grim satisfaction or hear the soft comment, "I guess we might have a use for this after all," but all could read her intention.

As soon as Rozek had returned to her horse, the order to ride on was called, the route still heading directly for the distant mountain. The column set off across the open moorland, but as they rode away from the chasm, hard, calculated looks passed from Ranger to Ranger. Circumstance forced them to be silent for the moment, but there was a lot they all wanted to say.

❖

Both moons floated clear in the black night sky, their brilliance diminishing the glitter of the stars and lighting the valley where the company had made the next night's stop on the other side of the moorland. Chip looked up at the shining crescents through the branches of the tree, remembering the many other occasions they had kept her company through the night on lonely sentry duties. The moons were like longtime comrades. She smiled up at the familiar sight of Hardie, now almost directly overhead. She would have one last night to watch the moons' slow progression across the sky. And bid them goodbye.

Her hands were still tied behind her securely, the rope going around the rough tree trunk that her back was propped against. Two Guards stood a little to one side talking quietly, their eyes occasionally traveling in her direction. She was being held on the edge of camp, a little apart from where the sleeping forms of Guards littered the ground. Here and there, dull red embers glowed, the remains of campfires. Then beyond them was the outline of the major's tent. Chip could not restrain the sneer that twisted her lips as she looked at it.

You did not do much for the state of your health in striking a commanding officer, let alone trying to kill her. And if you were going to do it when on active duty, the sentence was a forgone conclusion. To give Rozek her due, she had held a proper field court-martial, although Chip suspected it was only because she enjoyed the ceremonial qualities and the chance it gave to hold someone totally in her power. The gratification in the major's voice was unmistakable as she had pronounced the phrase, "hung at dawn."

But it was not in Chip's nature to waste what hours she had left brooding on someone who deserved nothing but contempt. She allowed herself a little guilt that she had not been able to save Kim, slightly more guilt that she would not be able to fulfill the promises she had made to Katryn, and some regrets that they would not be able to carry through their plans for the future, but it was better to look at the moons and let their peace and beauty flow into her.

Her contemplation was disrupted by a succession of soft sounds from the left: a thud, a muffled gasp, a dull slap. Chip turned her head. The standing silhouettes of the two Guards were gone, replaced by a confused huddle near the ground, then one dark shape broke away and scuttled to her side.

A quiet voice whispered, "Isn't that just typical of the Guards? Lying down on sentry duty."

"Katryn!"

"The one and only."

The sound of cutting followed and then the rope around Chip's hands slackened. In a few seconds, the last of the binding had been removed from her wrists.

"What are you...?" Chip's voice faded in confusion.

"I've got a message for you from the girls. We've been talking among ourselves about you and Kim. And we've been looking at the moons, and someone said, *Wouldn't it be a nice night for a stroll?* So we were all about to set off and then someone else said, *I wonder if Chip would like to come with us?* So I said I'd come and ask you, and of course a few others came with me to make sure the Guards didn't mind me talking to you."

"Katryn, stop acting the clown."

"Oh, that's a bit much, coming from you," Katryn said in mock indignation.

"I'm serious."

"So am I, my love." Abruptly, all humor left Katryn's voice. "It's bad enough we stood back and let Rozek murder Kim. There's no way we're going to form up into nice straight lines tomorrow and watch you die as well. We're deserting, every last woman in the squadron. We all know this isn't a raid on bandits. We're going to leave the Guards to sort it out for themselves. And let Rozek try and explain that when she gets back to Landfall."

"Where have we got to go?"

"You can think of somewhere worse than this? Of course, if you don't want to desert, you can wait here until morning."

Chip's head tilted back to look up at the sky, but then a grin twitched at the corner of her mouth. "Damn. Do you know I'd been looking at the moons, and I'd gotten this close"—she indicated with finger and thumb—"this close to making my peace with the Goddess."

"Good thing I came along when I did, the poor deity would never have withstood the shock."

Slipping away was absurdly easy. The term "stroll" was not misleading. Out of habit, all sentry duty, with the exception of those guarding Chip, had been assigned to the Rangers. Muffling the horses' hooves was an over-precaution. No alarm was raised as they passed up the side of the valley and assembled on the ridge at the top. Chip looked down on the peaceful campsite, then turned to meet Katryn's amused gaze.

"Do you know, I feel a bit guilty going like this?"

"Any particular reason?" Katryn asked.

"Well, I mean, how will the poor lambs find their way home without us?"

CHAPTER THIRTEEN—
SOMEONE REALLY DOESN'T LIKE YOU

Kim felt as if she fell forever into the darkness before hitting the river with a splash that was utterly insignificant in the fury of white water. Immediately, she was swept away, spinning helplessly in the torrent. Her shoulder grazed over a boulder and then she was pulled out and smashed against a rock wall. The river dragged her on through a series of jarring blows. She felt a leg rise clear of the water before she was sucked down again. Already her lungs were starting to ache, but it seemed certain she would be battered to death before she drowned. There was no light, no up or down, just the savage pounding of ice-cold water.

Once more, she crashed fully against a rock wall, leaving her semi-stunned. However, this time it was different. Still the water rushed around her, giving the sensation of motion, yet the rocks stayed in place. She was lodged in a crevice, but her lungs were burning, and she was not sure which way was up. *So it's drowning, then.* The ironic thought shot through Kim's mind, but it was still just a little too soon to give up.

The pressure of the current made movement a battle. She was pressed against the rocks like a leaf on a window in a gale, but slowly, painfully, Kim raised her arm above her head and felt it break into the air. The two sides of the crevice formed a wall on left and right, both were washed smooth, but it was just possible to brace arms, legs, and shoulders against them and propel herself upward until her face lifted above the surface of the water and she drew a deep gasp of air into her lungs, spluttering in the spray as the current hammered on her back and broke in cascades over her shoulders and head.

The cavern was pitch black, impossible to see a thing, and the roar of the water was deafening in her ears, but Kim thought she could detect a faint echo from high up, giving the hope that the roof of the tunnel was more than just a few centimeters above her head. The water surged past her in a torrent, dragging on her clothes. She was not in a dead end fissure, but a narrow channel. The current had drawn her in, but she was too large to go through. And now that her head was clearing slightly, Kim was aware of painful grazing from where she had been rammed between the two rock faces, even though both were polished smooth by the years of rushing water. Polished smooth, and therefore devoid of handholds.

Nothing Kim could feel gave even the faintest hope of a grip sufficient to pull herself out of the water, but as she had already found, it was possible to brace herself in the gap. The water was like a dead weight, trying to suck her down, and the polished rock was as slippery as glass, but slowly Kim got higher and higher, fighting to gain some purchase on the wet surfaces, not knowing where she had to go, only that she could not stay where she was. Her body was battered and bruised, but adrenaline kept her moving.

Several times, she nearly slipped back before she finally got clear of the water. The two sides of the crevice were drawing closer. Kim wedged herself in the gap and felt above her head. To her despair, she touched the roof on the tunnel, and then her exploring hand felt an opening on the sheer wall to her right and a little behind her. She had no way to tell how deep the aperture was or where it led, but it was the only way for her to go. It was a desperate struggle in the dark, to shift backward hampered by wet, clinging clothes, with the ever-present risk of falling. But eventually, Kim was able to put her arm into the empty space and feel a gently sloping ledge, maybe half a meter wide. With a hazardous kick and twist, Kim rolled onto the shelf of rock and lay on her back, gasping from the exertion of the climb.

Once she had recovered her breath, in something verging on surprise, Kim realized she could see her surroundings—very, very faintly. The darkness was no longer absolute. The space was not sufficient for Kim to sit up, so she raised herself on one elbow and looked around. The shelf she lay on was the start of another fissure in the rock, a crooked, sloping shaft, climbing upward. The faintest glint of daylight came from this opening.

Kim peered over the edge of the shelf. It was too dark to see the water below, but she could hear it roaring though the narrow channel, and other echoes of other torrents in the underground maze of caverns. She guessed that the river had divided, and by the grace of the Goddess, she had been carried away from the main channel to lodge in the cleft. Yet it was still premature to give thanks for her escape; there was no guarantee the fissure would be passable.

Kim began to squirm her way up the breach in the rock. Soon she was enclosed on all sides, and the ground beneath her had changed from a smooth, polished surface to a gritty incline, covered in loose scree. The passage was narrow, winding, and uneven. In parts it opened into small chambers. In other places, it was barely wide enough for Kim's shoulders. Once, she had to scrabble with her hands at the chippings of rock before she could continue, but she managed to force her way ever up, and the booming of the raging river faded until she emerged into the open air at the bottom of another crater on the surface of the moor, a much smaller depression than the one she had fallen into, no more than three meters deep, and a similar distance across. The hole was probably slightly off the route the company had taken over the grasslands and too small to attract attention from a distance.

The final scramble out of the crater presented few problems. Kim pulled herself over the rim and lay at last on the ground in the warm sunshine, with the wind carrying the smell of earth and grass to her, and Celaeno's sweet blue sky hanging over her. Laughter from pure joy bubbled in her throat.

A while passed before Kim gathered herself to stand and look around. With shock, she realized barely an hour had elapsed since she had fallen into the river. It had easily felt ten times as long. But the afternoon was drawing on, and the sun was well past its zenith. She shaded her eyes against the glare and looked due west. Maybe fifty meters away was the long scar of the fissure that had claimed her, and beside its rim, she could see the trampled grass and the tracks of a mounted column of soldiers. Of the horses and riders themselves, there was no sign.

Kim took a deep breath and set off toward the trail.

❖

The effort to put one foot in front of the other was becoming more and more difficult. Kim stumbled once or twice, but had to keep going. As a Ranger, she was well trained to survive in the wild, but she would require more than the clothes she stood in, especially as even these were torn from the pounding of the river. Her sword belt was no longer where she had left it. Of course, it would have been taken by the other Rangers when they moved on. Her chances would be very poor indeed, alone in the wilderness, without tools, weapons, provisions, or adequate clothing. Even worse than her chances with Rozek, since surely the Guard major would not dare make another such blatant attempt on her life.

Her only option was to try to catch up with the rest of the company. Normally this should have presented few problems, even though they were mounted and she was on foot. The horses could not be ridden non-stop; they needed a chance to rest and graze. The column would camp well before nightfall and not move on until after dawn. This would allow plenty of time for Kim to overtake them, as long as she could keep walking. But this last proviso was the issue at doubt.

The effects of adrenaline had worn off hours before, and those of cold and shock set in. The battering by the rocks had left her badly bruised and cut, and the throbbing in knee, hip, and shoulder had increased to the point of agony. The last of the sunshine had partially dried her clothing, but now the chill of evening had set in, and Kim could feel her whole body shaking. She wrapped her arms about herself as she walked, to try to hold back the tremors. The temptation was to stop and rest, but if she sat down and gave in to sleep, there was no saying when she would awake, and she might lose all chance of catching up with the others.

Dusk had faded into night. The shining crescent of Hardie was starting its journey across the sky. The other moon would not rise for some time. Yet even without small Laurel, there was easily enough light to follow the tracks of a hundred horses across the open moorland. But the contours of the land were changing, becoming more broken and scored by the paths of streams. The line of hoof marks went down into one such gully. Kim followed, taking as much care as she could, but her ankle gave way on the incline, sending her stumbling, to land in a heap at the bottom.

Once the pain of jarred bones and bruises had faded, it was so seductive, to stay where she lay, but Kim forced herself to her knees.

The small stream gurgled over its stony bed nearby. Kim splashed its cold water onto her face. The horse tracks carried on beside the banks of the stream. She stood up, turned to follow, and kept on walking.

After another fifty meters, the gully opened onto the side of a far deeper valley. Kim stood on the hillside and looked down on the sparsely wooded bottom. The trees were slightly different from those she was familiar with, or maybe they were the same species but growing in a new environment. The issue was not important to her right then. The trampled trail led off, up the valley to the northwest. Kim followed it with her eyes and saw in the distance the faint dots of red firelight, no more than another two kilometers away. Even as the wave of relief washed over her, one corner of Kim's mouth twisted in a disdainful grimace. The fires would be the Guards cooking their evening meal. No Ranger would advertise her presence so heedlessly with likely bandits about.

The sight of the camp gave fresh impetus to her footsteps. Kim left the entrance to the gully and began to make her way down the hillside. For the first time in hours, a smile lit her face and her bruises felt less unbearable. But the vegetation was rougher than on the moor, knee-high bushes and brambles that caught her feet, so it was not surprising that Kim tripped again. She fought to keep her balance, but her beaten body was slow to respond, and she tumbled down a steep slope, sliding and rolling, and ending up in a hollow at the foot of a tree.

This time it was easier to summon the enthusiasm to rise, but even before she could move, Kim heard a twig crack behind her. She froze. This far south, and at this time of year, there was no risk of snow lions, but their smaller cousins, the mountain cats, abounded, and despite their size, they could pose a severe threat, especially to a lone, unarmed woman. Slowly, so as not to provoke an attack, Kim rolled over. But instead of teeth, she was confronted by the sight of three drawn bows, the arrows trained on her heart.

The archers' expressions were impossible to read, though their eyes glinted in the moonlight. Kim raised herself on her elbows, still moving very slowly, and returned their steady gaze. For a while no one spoke, but at last Kim raised an eyebrow and said, "Good evening, ladies. Can I assume that you are the bandits?"

❖

Nearly an hour later, her captors escorted Kim into the bandit camp on horseback. Laurel was just starting to rise. They had skirted the area where the fires had been visible and were now several kilometers to the west, on hills overlooking a wide basin of grassland. The bandit camp was well concealed and they were upon it before Kim realized. Although in her battered state, she was beyond paying close attention to her surroundings. Riding required less effort than walking, but her bruises made themselves felt at every hoof fall, and maintaining her balance in the saddle was awkward with bound hands. By now, even her head was aching, and nausea gripped her stomach.

Loud shouts greeted their arrival in camp. "Hey, Cloe. We were starting to wonder what had happened to you. Did you come back by the scenic route?"

"Or did you get lost again?" another voice called.

"Of course not. We had problems," one of Kim's captors retorted, presumably Cloe.

"Problems?" an older voice spoke sharply, silencing the banter. "What are the Guards doing?"

"No, it wasn't with them. They've made camp in the valley and look set to cross the plain first thing tomorrow."

"Perfect. So what was the problem?"

"We acquired a prisoner."

"Oh? Why did you do that?" The elderly speaker was clearly exasperated.

"We didn't mean to. We waited until the Guards had settled and we were sure they weren't about to break camp and head on. Then we were just about to come back here, when she literally stumbled onto us," Cloe said apologetically.

The horses had stopped close by the campfire. In its light, Kim could pick out ten or so women, and most of them were, in turn, watching her. From the tone of the exchanges, the older woman was the leader, and she clearly had no wish whatsoever for a prisoner. To Kim's mind, this was both good and bad news. The good being that she probably was not going to be questioned to any extent. The bad that it could only be a matter of minutes before her throat was slit. The thought should have been worrying, but Kim was pretty much beyond caring.

The woman riding beside Kim slipped out of the saddle and continued with the explanation. "We think she'd gotten lost and was trying to rejoin the Guards. But she's been knocked about a bit, Gina, and not by us. Perhaps you should take a look at her."

This was Kim's cue to dismount, and when she made no attempt to do so, hands pulled her down and dragged her into the light. Kim clenched her teeth as darts of fire shot from her injured limbs, although the handling was firm, rather than rough. A white-haired woman was waiting beside the campfire, evidently the leader who had spoken before. She came forward to stand in front Kim, the few steps revealing the trace of a limp. The infirmity was reflected in one entire side of her body, the corner of her mouth sagged, and while her right eye examined Kim's face, the left one stared, disconcertingly, over Kim's shoulder. But despite the lopsided gaze, there was no doubting the intelligence in the face, or the sense of humor, and at last the leader pronounced, "Either you've been very unlucky, or someone really doesn't like you."

Kim tried to match the dry tone. "It's the latter option."

"So who doesn't like you?"

"The commanding officer."

"In which case you should have answered *both*, since you are clearly unfortunate in your choice of enemy." The one good eye took in the whole of Kim's appearance. "But I can't help wondering exactly what form your commanding officer's dislike took."

"There was a shoe at the edge of one of the holes over the underground river—" Kim was interrupted by an amused outburst from some of those listening. Apparently, the shoe had belonged to someone called Jade, but the leader silenced the quips before Kim could learn more, and signaled to continue. "The major sent me down to pick it up—"

"Was she really that interested in a shoe?" The leader interrupted with a question.

"I doubt it. What she wanted was for me to fall in."

"You're right. She doesn't like you. Can I take it you obliged her?"

"Yes."

"It would explain the state you're in. But since you obviously managed to get out alive, perhaps I should reconsider my evaluation of how lucky you are."

"Not if you want to take my current situation into account as well." Kim indicated her bound hands.

"Maybe." The leader paused for a while, then asked, "What did you do to make this major dislike you so much?"

"She caught me kissing an Imprinter."

A second of stunned silence was followed by a roar of laughter, which the leader joined in. Once a degree of calm had been re-established, she looked back to Kim. "You know, I don't like to form snap judgments about people, but you do seem to indulge in an overly dramatic lifestyle. Couldn't you have considered something more conventional, such as drunk on parade?"

Kim shrugged, but could not find the strength to say more. She was swaying on her feet, in imminent danger of collapse. The humor on the elderly woman's face faded, and she lifted a hand to Kim's forehead.

"Lay her down by the fire," the leader instructed the women at Kim's side, dispensing with any more questions. Once this was done, she settled down beside the Ranger and said, "I have some of the healer sense, and it looks to me as if you are rather in need of its assistance."

The elderly hands rested on her forehead, and Kim began to feel the familiar sense of well-being that a healer could bestow. Pain ebbed, nausea dispersed, warmth flowed out from her core, driving away the tremors, then a soft drowsiness wrapped itself around her. The behavior was highly unconventional for a bandit chief, but Kim made no complaint. Working things out would be easier when she felt better.

CHAPTER FOURTEEN—
EX-SISTER GINA RENAMED

A short time later, Kim was roused from her light doze, aware of a vast improvement in her physical state. Enough for her to look with interest at the bowl of food held out to her by the white-haired leader. Around the campfire, the other bandits were also taking a late meal before sleeping. Eating with her hands tied was a little tricky, but Kim managed well enough, and eventually put the empty bowl down while stifling a large yawn.

"I didn't know if you'd want waking for food. But I guess you did," the leader commented. Now that Kim was more alert, she also noted the lisp in the voice, the result of the elderly woman's sagging lips.

"Yes. Thank you. I'm sure I'll get back to sleep okay."

"You certainly will. I'm afraid I'm going to have to put you out cold. We can't trust those knots to hold you all night, and I don't want to have people standing watch on you, as we've got a big day planned for tomorrow. I know it's an abuse of the healer sense, and I'm sorry, but..." The leader looked at Kim apologetically.

"That's all right," Kim said, and then the irony hit her. She looked up at the elderly woman. "The Guards told us we were after dangerous bandits. But if you don't mind me saying so, you don't seem to have the game sorted out very well. Most bandits knock people out by hitting them over the head with a large blunt instrument. And they hardly ever say sorry for it."

"Really!" The woman's right hand eyebrow rose in mock surprise.

Kim was aware that other bandits were also listening. She looked at her captors thoughtfully. "It adds to some concerns I've had about your commitment to theft. You seem to have stuck yourself in a spot where there's no one to steal from."

"So putting it all together, what conclusions do you draw?"

Kim met the gaze of the one good eye and said, "That you are not bandits."

"And what do you think we might be?" The leader sounded amused.

"Some people who have seriously pissed off the Chief Consultant."

Laughter and scattered applause rang around the campsite. The leader also seemed quite pleased with Kim's assessment. "Yes, we've certainly done that. Please allow me to introduce myself. I am Gina Renamed. Ex-Sister Gina Renamed."

"Ex? I didn't know Sisters could retire."

"We're not supposed to, but it's the least of the things I've done to upset the Chief Consultant." Gina gave her an uneven smile. "And you are?"

"Ranger Private Kimberly Ramon."

"You answer to Kim?"

"Yes."

"Well, Kim, it would be best if we took a little while to digest our supper before sleeping. So how about if I tell you just what we've done to piss off the Chief Consultant?"

Kim nodded her acceptance, and the ex-Sister settled herself a little more comfortably by the fire before continuing. "I actually began my career in the temple as an Imprinter. Well...a trainee Imprinter. And that's another job you can't normally retire from. Like everyone else, I went to the temple for assessment when I was twelve years old, but I was never allowed home again. It's a terrible thing to do to a child. It leaves you with a lifelong resentment of the Sisters, which will explain a fair amount of what follows."

Kim's face grew attentive as she thought of another Imprinter with a resentment of Sisters, though she said nothing.

"I trained as an Imprinter for six years: the biology, the genetics, the lot." Gina waved her hand as she spoke. "I was a few months from starting to work in the temple, when one day, I was doing some experiments on a horse. Nothing that was going to hurt it. I don't want you getting any false sympathies, just analyzing its DNA. I was deep in a trance when some fool came charging into the stable, screaming her head off about something utterly trivial. She spooked the horse. It reared up and kicked me in the head. At least, this is what I've been told, because I was unaware of anything at the time, or for some months after. But apparently the blow cracked my skull, giving me a brain hemorrhage. Obviously, the best healers were put onto me at once. They probably saved my life. Even so, I was in a coma for fifteen weeks, and when I finally came around, I was totally paralyzed down one side. I got better slowly, but you've no doubt noticed that I never made a full recovery. At first, it was thought my mental faculties were unharmed. The Chief Consultant herself was going to lead the prayers of thanks, and then it was realized my healer sense had gone."

"You did all right by me just now."

Gina shrugged. "It returned slowly over the years, the same as my walking, but it never made anything close to a full recovery. I'm a competent healer, but I can't even force cloning, let alone imprint. So the temple had to work out what to do with me. I'd have been quite happy to go back to my parents, and I'm sure they'd have been happy to have me, but I'd been admitted into the sanctum and been privy to many great secrets of the temple. Well, that's what they said. Personally, I think they didn't want me spreading gossip about their private lives, which are nowhere near as holy as they'd like you to believe. Anyway, the end of it was they told me I had to become a Sister. Then they had the problem of knowing what to call me, since my last name had been formally annulled, so they came up with Renamed. Sister Gina Renamed. Damned stupid name."

"But it suits you," someone heckled from the other side of the fire, giving rise to more laughter.

Gina snorted, undeterred from her story. "They had one last problem. What was I actually going to do in the temple? The Sisters have an image they like to project. Aloof, spiritual workers for the Goddess. I just didn't fit in, limping around and dribbling under my mask. Plus, all you see of a Sister is her eyes, and mine didn't even point in the same direction. They decided they didn't dare let me have any contact with the general public, so they sent me off to the temple library, which is traditionally where they put the Sisters who are too dense to be trusted to perform the public ceremonies. They thought I'd fit in. It's typical. Walk with a limp, slur your words, and people think you're an idiot. It was their mistake." Gina looked at Kim. "Do you have any idea how many books are in the temple library?"

The question was clearly rhetorical, but Kim answered anyway. "No."

"Hundreds and thousands. Now, do you want to guess how many ever get read?"

"I've no idea."

"None. At least, none before I went there. It's actually forbidden. A mortal sin. Only the Chief Consultant is allowed to read them, and she never bothers. The library contains the entire wisdom of the Elder-Ones. Supposedly it's information left to assist Celaeno's children in achieving the destiny the Goddess has planned for them, and it will all be revealed, bit by bit, if and when the Sisters think the time is right."

"How will they know when to reveal the information if they don't know what it is?" Kim asked.

Gina waggled a finger. "A good question, but not a wise one to ask the Chief Consultant to her face. Anyway, these other two Sisters and I worked in the library, sweeping the floors, dusting the shelves, taking a book down, wiping the outside and putting it back. But never actually opening the cover of a single volume. The other two were hard put to read their own names, so they probably weren't tempted. Plus they believed they'd burn in hell if they did. But they'd chosen to be Sisters. I hadn't. My parents had been skeptical about religion, and they'd passed it on to me."

Gina paused for a moment in thought, as if reconsidering her last words. "Actually, all Imprinters tend to be a touch skeptical. It comes somewhere in your third year of training, when you realize that the Sisters don't understand what they're talking about. Imprinters have to be given real information. You can't be fobbed off with half-truths. Embryos can't be imprinted by faith alone, so the Sisters have no option but to let you read some of the books the Elder-Ones left. And then you realize that a lot of the prayers are...inaccurate. That's the politest word for it. Perhaps that's the really dangerous piece of information they didn't want me to take out of the temple, and why they keep the Imprinters so repressed and isolated. They might say the temple is to care for and protect the Goddess's chosen ones, but in fact, Imprinters are little more than slaves."

"Oh, I know," Kim cut in. "Remember, I said I was...acquainted with an Imprinter."

"Yes, you did." Gina frowned at her. "That was the truth? You weren't joking?"

"No."

"Umph. Perhaps we could hear your story later. Maybe tomorrow."

"Because you won't get a word in edgeways while Gina's telling hers," another voice called out cheerfully.

"Ignore them. They're just bored because they've heard it all fifty times before," Gina said to Kim after sending a dismissive gesture in the general direction of her followers. "Now, where was I? Oh, yes...in the library. I started to sneak peeks at the books. It wasn't easy, as we were never supposed to be in there alone. Still, as I've said, the other two Sisters weren't very bright, and I could wangle the odd half hour every month or so."

Gina's lips compressed in an uneven line. "And those books! They lined shelf, upon shelf, upon shelf, all looking identical from the outside. Same size, same color, and they all had the same words on the spine: *Celaeno: Encyclopedic Database Download,* and a number underneath. I'll never forget the first thing I read from them, the day I finally built up my nerve to do it. I snuck a book off the shelf, opened a page at random, my heart pounding, expecting to discover some arcane knowledge...and what I got was a section about the chemical structure of nylon. It was such a disappointment. I know I was expecting something mysterious, but not that mysterious. I still don't have a clue what nylon is. And there was lots more of the same. After two years, I was pretty disillusioned and would have given up, except that breaking the rules was the only excitement left in my life."

Kim watched Gina's face as she spoke. The ex-Sister's gaze was fixed on another time, another place, her audience temporarily forgotten.

Gina sighed and continued speaking. "But then one day, I discovered the index. That's what the numbers on the spine were. If you wanted to know about something you could look it up, and the index would tell you which book and page number to go to. It meant I could be a bit more directed in what I read. So I thought, concentrate on what I know most about—biology. Which was when I became really confused." The elderly hands waved, trying to convey the sense of the emotion. "I mean, I know human biology. I have been inside a blood cell, wandered through a central nervous system. Most of what was in the books was right on the mark, and other parts were totally surreal. Prostate glands. I read a section on human prostate glands; but humans do not have a prostate gland. So I gave up on biology." She drew a deep breath.

"Then I discovered there was a whole section on history, which threw me completely. The Elder-Ones lived at the dawn of time. What history did they have to write? So I chose a reference at random, and got the Franco-Prussian war." Gina tossed her hands into the air, miming despair. "Then I saw the date: 1870-71."

"But..." Kim's forehead knotted.

"Exactly! It's over a thousand years into the future. For a short while, my little skeptical soul was in revolt as I considered the possibility that the Elder-Ones had given a detailed breakdown of what was to come. Then I remembered prostate glands. So I picked a date I knew about: 320. Did it mention the floods in Landfall? Did it hell! *The Gupta dynasty reunites India.* That's what it talked about, and that's when I gave up with the whole thing. I decided the reason the library was out of bounds was to hide the fact that the Elder-Ones were a bunch of deranged lunatics. I would have gone back to the dusting, except that I got a kick out of imagining what the Sisters would say if they knew I was reading the books."

Kim's expression was somewhere between a smile and a frown. She was not sure where the story was going. The other women around the fire were showing only cursory interest. It was clearly a tale they were all very familiar with. Kim looked at them. Their ages varied between fifteen and sixty, with Gina the oldest by a good ten years. On the faces of the group was a familiar intensity, born of desperation, though it was well hidden beneath a show of humor. They were all armed and clearly used to living in the wildlands, but Kim was certain they were not vicious criminals. She had seen enough of that sort to know the signs. Her attention shifted back to the speaker.

"I must have been working in the library for nearly ten years when I came across something else. By then, I was the senior Sister in the library, which isn't very senior, as Sisters go. But I had more chances to read, and it was the only entertainment I got. I'd developed a liking for geology. It all seemed to make sense. There were no imaginary rocks, although most of the examples were from imaginary places. When I saw a reference to a cold place called Iceland, I thought they were being figurative, but what the hell was it supposed to imply if somewhere was a new Zealand? And what would an old one be like?" Gina raised her hands in an exaggerated shrug.

"However, there was one room of the library I'd not paid much attention to. It didn't look very impressive compared to the rest, just cabinets full of hand-written paper. And I guess I assumed that if the contents hadn't been put into the books, then they couldn't be very important. But it still needed dusting. Which is what I was doing one day, when I saw the word *Iron Pyrites* on a folder. It's a mineral formation that I'd been reading about the week before. So the next chance I got, I went back and had a look at it. They were the first reports from the Elder-One, Peter McKay."

"The patron of miners?" Kim queried.

"Yes, that one. He had been a geologist...and did you note the word I used?"

"Geologist?"

"No, *he*."

At the confused expression on Kim's face, Gina laughed. "Never mind. I scoured through the drawer of reports, and was just about to close it when I saw some other books, almost hidden, lining the bottom. The papers were all clipped into folders, but these books were the wrong size, so they had just been placed in the drawers. I took them out and found they were four volumes of Peter McKay's personal diary. And then I thought, nobody apart from me knew they were there, so nobody was going to miss them. I hid the diaries inside my robe and took them back to my room and read them at my leisure. And suddenly everything made sense."

Around the fire, other conversations had stopped. All eyes looked in Gina's direction. This, Kim realized, was the crux of the story.

"Virtually everything the Sisters tell us about Celaeno, and Himoti, and the Elder-Ones is wrong. And the parts that are true are completely distorted." Gina paused and met Kim's eyes in an intense, earnest stare. "The Elder-Ones weren't semi-divine. They were our ancestors, or at least, they came from the same place our genetic ancestors came from. They were pretty much the same as us. Nothing like the statues in the temples, just a bit more diverse in appearance. They used to live on another planet, under another sun. The original Earth, the place where humans first came into being. Their science was unimaginably more advanced than ours. I couldn't even make sense of it from the books. Particle accelerators, field-floatation tubes, nylon, and all the rest. But they were able to make ships that could travel between the stars, and that's how they got here."

"But..." Kim paused in utter confusion. "If that were true, it couldn't be kept hidden from people."

"Why not? Who, apart from the Sisters, have access to records from the Elder-Ones?"

"You think the Sisters are deliberately spreading lies and keeping everyone misinformed?" Kim was skeptical. She had no love for the Sisters but found it hard to believe they were all involved in a great conspiracy.

"It's not deliberate. Since they don't read the Elder-Ones' books, I suspect none of them, not even the Chief Consultant, actually know the truth. If they did know, I think the library would have been destroyed long ago, but the people with a stake in keeping the truth hidden no longer know what's in there to hide. Mind you, I'm not sure I'd have ever made sense of it without the diary. There is just too much information to be able to pull it together and get a sensible picture. The library was the Elder-Ones' bequest to us. It was the history of the first Earth. It described its countries, its culture. The Elder-Ones left us the information so we would know something of our true home world."

"So you don't think we were brought here by Celaeno?"

"Oh, no. In fact, I know for certain that we were. It's just that Celaeno isn't what they say she is."

"And what is she?" Kim asked.

"I've already told you. She's a ship."

"A boat?"

"A starship. The *Celaeno* was built by people on the first Earth to carry them between the stars. She's not a goddess. She's not even alive. She's a thing made out of metal and...whatever it is you build starships out of. Maybe nylon. She was named the *Celaeno* like a barge skipper calls her boat the *Daisy-lee*. Our ancestors made her to carry them to a new world, but they never intended to come here. They never intended to lose contact with the first Earth. But when traveling in the spaceship, they were all held in a sort of artificial sleep, and while they were asleep, the spaceship got lost. They were stranded here on this planet without the resources to recreate all their technology, so they did the best they could."

"The unborn Elder-Ones," Kim said in a sudden excitement. Not that she was convinced, but a quote clicked with her. *"In her belly slept the Elder-Ones, who were not born of this world."*

"Exactly. They weren't born on *this* world. But that doesn't mean they hadn't been born somewhere else."

"But don't..." Kim stopped in confusion as she tried to pull her thoughts together.

Another woman leaned forward and said, "I wouldn't bother asking too many questions now, or Gina will have you up all night. It's part of her quest to spread enlightenment through the world. She needs no encouragement at all to talk non-stop for hours and bore everyone silly." Despite the words, there was no mistaking the affection in the woman's voice when she spoke of her leader.

Gina nodded, a little sadly. "Yes, you're right. I do talk too much. And look at where it's got me." She indicated the camp. "And I'm afraid I haven't the time to finish my story properly, as we have to be up before first light tomorrow. But to put it briefly, I was still young and naive at the time. Not quite naive enough to think that if I went to the Chief Consultant with my discovery, I'd be hailed as the savior of the world, but naive enough to think I could make a difference. So carefully, very carefully, I started spreading the word. And after another twenty years I had a small network—"

"The heretics!" Kim interrupted, remembering the commotion that had only just been dying down when she first joined the Militia.

"Ah. So you have heard of us."

"I'd heard you'd all been captured and executed."

"Which is only slightly more true than the story that we used to eat babies. I'm afraid some of us were killed, but the rest of us fled west with a few sheep and plows and things, and we've been living out here ever since, trying to stay one step ahead of the Sisters. We've managed quite well up until now. But a few months back, we got word that Domia's mother was dying. We still have contacts in the homelands who pass us news about things we need to know. So Domia went back to see her mother one last time and was caught by the temple Guards." Gina's face was grim. "I know none of us want to think too much about how they did it, but somehow they forced her to tell them where we are."

"The major has a map," Kim said.

"Really? Poor Domia." Gina sighed and her head dropped. "She wouldn't have betrayed us easily. Anyway, we're stuck. We can't afford to desert the farm right now. The crops are all planted, and if we don't get to harvest them, we'll starve this winter."

Kim was staring at the ground, thinking rapidly. Regardless of whether the rest of Gina's story was true, it made sense of the way the mission had been organized. Reinforcing religious doctrine was a job for the Guards, and they would not hesitate to kill every last heretic they found. But if the Rangers had been sent alone, they would surely have thought twice when, instead of armed bandits, they met farmers in their fields.

Kim looked at the heretic leader and asked, "So what are you going to do?"

"We're going to attack the column tomorrow, before they can get to our farm."

"How many women do you have?"

"What you see here."

Kim was incredulous. "You're going to attack a hundred Guards with a mere dozen women!"

"Well, we have a plan. Actually, we have several. They all depend on circumstances, but it looks like we're going to be lucky with one of the better plans for tomorrow. And there are some more of us up ahead, with other plans, in case this one fails."

"You're hoping to inflict serious injuries?"

"Yes. I'm afraid they won't turn around if we settle for just asking them politely," Gina said ironically.

"There's a squadron of Rangers in the company."

"I know. And I don't mean it as flattery when I say that in some ways, they worry us more than the Guards."

"They are my friends."

"I'm sorry." Gina's voice made it clear that the regret was genuine. "We won't be able to distinguish between them and the Guards, and our lives are at stake. If I had the option, I wouldn't even kill the Guards. Their only crime is to believe a set of lies they've been told ever since they were babies. But we aren't going to lie down and let them butcher us."

Kim's head dropped. She looked despairingly at her bound hands. She bore the heretics no ill will, but she had to warn Chip if she could get the chance. Not that it seemed likely. Even as she sat considering her options, she saw the rest of the heretics were making their preparations to sleep. Gina came and put a hand on her head.

"Right, I'm going to send you to sleep now. Do you have any last question?"

Kim bit her lip and then shrugged, but as the waves of drowsiness swallowed her, she mumbled, half-heartedly, "You didn't explain how prostate glands fit into it."

CHAPTER FIFTEEN—CHOICES AND OPTIONS

A stiff breeze from the north sprang up overnight and was gusting over the hillside and shaking the bushes around the campsite when Kim was awakened before dawn the next day. For some reason, this seemed to please the heretics enormously, and they all offered congratulations to the weather-wise woman who had predicted it the day before. For her part, Kim would rather have done without the chill wind in the cold hour preceding daybreak.

Both moons had set, so nothing challenged the brilliance of the stars. Kim studied them as she huddled by the snapping fire, eating the hurried breakfast that was offered to her. She hardly knew what to make of Gina's story, but it was a strangely moving thought that other people might be walking on planets beneath those distant suns. Kim's gaze traveled across the glittering heavens as she tried to analyze her thoughts.

Religion had never been a major preoccupation of hers. In fact, like most Rangers, she had deliberately adopted an irreverent manner, in contrast to the Guards. If pressed, she would have said she believed the teaching of the temple. It would take a lot to accept that Celaeno was just a mechanical creation, a ship. Kim did not know if she could believe it, or if she wanted to.

The black sky to the east was showing the first signs of paling when the heretics finished their preparations and began to disperse. They headed off, in ones and twos, until only Gina, Kim, and one other were left at the camp. This third woman took a lookout post atop a nearby knoll, while Gina helped herself to an extra half-bowl of porridge and sat down beside Kim.

"How do you feel this morning?" Gina asked in her role as healer.

"A bit stiff and sore."

"But lucky to be feeling anything?"

"Definitely."

Gina took a few more mouthfuls of breakfast and said, "Just before going to sleep last night, you asked about prostate glands."

"Are they important?"

"Not to you or me. Women don't have them."

"So what does?" Kim asked, slightly confused. Something she was getting used to feeling around Gina.

"Who, not what."

"But you said..." Kim broke off and frowned.

"As a Ranger, you learn a lot about the non-domestic animals on this planet, don't you?"

"Yes," Kim agreed, though she did not see the relevance.

"And you know how they reproduce?"

"Only in general terms. You probably understand the biology of it better than I do. But I know they have males who can transmit their genetic material to the females to produce young."

"Right. Well, all the species that have males as well as females are native to this planet. And all the others were brought here by the Elder-Ones. But this is..." Gina stopped, halted by a sudden gesture from Kim. "Yes?"

"Would that explain why the two groups are poisonous to each other?"

"Yes. Our chemical makeup is, quite literally, alien."

"So that would explain the moggies." Kim's face held a thoughtful expression. "The Sisters say Celaeno had to give the wild animals a different method of reproduction, since the Cloners couldn't get near them. But that doesn't explain why you get male moggies."

Gina nodded. "Moggies are a native species that our ancestors domesticated, hence they have males. We need them to catch the indigenous vermin that would otherwise infest the grain stores. And in order to be able to eat the vermin, they have to be indigenous as well."

"But what has this to do with prostate glands?"

"Ah. Now that was what I was coming to. When the Sisters say that Himoti made the first Cloners and Imprinters, they're actually telling the truth, albeit that she made them using scientific instruments rather than prayer. Before her, there were no Imprinters."

"So how did people reproduce on the original home planet?"

"Same as the creatures here. There were two sexes. And one of the many distinguishing features was that the males had prostate glands."

"Human males!" Kim did not know whether to be amused or shocked. "But that would be..."

Gina laughed at the open-eyed astonishment on Kim's face, and almost against her will, Kim joined in until the pair were helpless with a fit of giggles.

"That can't be true. I mean, apart from anything else, why would they change if that was what they were used to?" Kim asked once she had her breath back.

"This planet was just a touch too alien for the males. The grass pollen here mimics certain hormones, which destroyed their ability to function in creating children. It was Himoti who worked out a way around the problem this caused."

Kim looked at the elderly woman. "If you make a habit of going around saying things like this, you must give the Chief Consultant nightmares."

"Oh, I do hope so."

Kim picked up a few dropped twigs with her bound hands and fed them into the fire, still shaking her head slightly. Gina watched her for a while and then said, "We won't be holding you prisoner after today. You'll be free to go back to the homelands if you want."

Gina's last three words had a querying edge, which Kim picked up on. "Do I have an option?"

"Yes."

"To stay out here with you and your followers?" Kim suggested.

"We'd be pleased to have you. You have skills we'd find very useful."

The smile on Kim's face faded as her thoughts turned to the future and to what was planned for that day. She stared bleakly at the ground. When she made no attempt to reply, Gina added, "I would have thought being nearly murdered by your commanding officer was a very strong motive for desertion."

"Oh, yes. And there's nothing else I want to go back for, but..."

"But?"

Kim took several deep breaths before speaking, her face somber. "Today you're going to try and kill some women who are my friends. I know it's not fair to blame you, but I couldn't live among you, not with my comrades' blood between us."

"Yes." Gina nodded slowly. "Yes, I can see that. We must all make our choices and live with the consequences. I am truly sorry...It wasn't quite what I was intending when I began reading the books in the library."

"And would you change things, if you had your time again?" Kim raised her head.

The elderly woman met the Ranger's earnest gaze with a rueful, crooked pout. "Some. I'd try to avoid the mistakes so a few more people would be left alive. But I couldn't ignore my curiosity, or the truth. The choices and options of our lives all come with a price attached."

Kim looked away sharply. If the heretic's plan succeeded, by nightfall, there would be an unbridgeable barrier of grief between her and Gina, which was a cause of regret in itself. Regardless of doubts concerning her sanity, there was something about the heretic leader that Kim could not help liking and respecting. In an odd way, she reminded Kim of Captain LeCoup.

Gina stood up, patted Kim on the shoulder, and hobbled a few steps away, sensing Kim's need of space. While they had been talking, the day had grown brighter. The sun was yet to make its appearance above the mountains to the east, but the sky was already pale blue, with a yellowish tinge that promised another long, hot day, despite the wind. For the first time, Kim could study the landscape before them. The camp was on the northern hills above a flat plain, where the ground sloped down gently to the south before it rose again in a long, stony ridge about three kilometers away. The wind chased waves through the dry grass covering the floor of the basin.

The second heretic left her watch post and wandered back to the fire.

"Can you see them?" Gina asked anxiously.

"Not yet, but I'd better get in position before the sun rises."

"Okay."

"What should we do about the prisoner?" Both heretics looked in Kim's direction. "You aren't going to be able to cope with her if she slips free."

"I'm going to give her a choice," Gina answered decisively. She came back to the fireside and lowered herself awkwardly, so her eyes were on a level with Kim's, then said, "And your choice is this. I can knock you out again, or you can give me your word that you won't try to escape or warn the Guards or sabotage the plan."

"You'd trust her?" The second heretic sounded slightly incredulous.

"Yes. If she gives her word." There was no doubt in Gina's voice. "I'd even untie her hands."

Kim bowed her head as she considered her options. Either way she was not going to be able to help Chip, and it would be hard to live with, but the doubts would be less if she at least knew what happened to her friends. Kim raised her eyes to meet with Gina's and said, "I'll do what you say. You have my word on it."

❖

Time passed slowly. The sun lifted clear of the distant peaks to their left, the heat began to rise, and the wind picked up a haze of dust that shimmered in the oblique morning light over the grasslands, but still there was no sign of the column of soldiers. Gina was getting increasingly nervous. She glanced back to Kim.

"What time did you normally start moving?"

"About an hour before now."

"Something's happened. Damn...damn." Gina's voice was tight, fearful.

Kim could almost feel sorry for the heretic, but her heart was cheered by the thought Chip and the other Rangers might avoid whatever had been planned for them. And then, just as she was beginning to hope some other outcome was possible, she saw at the edge of the plateau, the dark shapes of mounted soldiers riding two by two down from the eastern uplands. The dust rendered them obscure, just little black silhouettes that crawled across the landscape, devoid of detail, as insignificant as children's toys. Even their numbers seemed reduced, and the red of the Guards' uniforms was indiscernible.

Not for the first time, Kim wondered about the nature of the plan. Despite the implausibility of the small band of heretics inflicting serious damage on over a hundred trained warriors, somehow she never doubted that Gina's plan would be effective. Deadly effective. Kim watched and waited and feared the worst.

The soldiers were due south of the camp, nearly halfway across the plain when Kim saw a trail of smoke rising at the foot of the hills to the east. Then another plume appeared, and another. In less than a minute, twelve columns of smoke were reaching up to the blue sky, forming an arc to the north of the soldiers. Kim's eyes darted back to the line of mounted women. Amazingly, they were still riding in formation, as if they had not noticed the spread of the fires. Minutes passed and still the column continued, undeterred.

Chip, you clown, wake up and use your eyes. Kim almost spoke aloud. And at last, the company halted. Yet instead of an orderly response, avoiding the hazard, they milled around, some continuing to go forward, some standing still, some already heading south, away from the advancing flames. And the flames were advancing more and more quickly, as the wind did the job the heretics had obviously intended. Already, the dozen original fires had nearly joined to make a blazing semi-circle that was whipped through the tinder-dry grass by the strong gusts, its spread assisted by the heretics. Then all the soldiers at once seemed to become aware of their danger. They spun about and raced for the safety of the rocky hills on the far side of the basin.

"Fools. They've let the horses have their heads!" Kim shouted in disgust. "What's wrong with Chip today?" She came and stood by Gina's shoulder, watching the scene before her, though the wall of smoke was making it increasingly difficult. Then she looked to the woman beside her. "Okay. You'll give them a scare. Maybe a few will get caught, but most will outrun the flames."

"Actually, the fires aren't the real threat." Gina spoke almost sadly.

"Then what is?" Kim shouted.

Gina did not answer the question directly. She turned her back on the grassland and looked toward the east, her expression pained. "I don't doubt they used barbaric means to get Domia to draw them the map, before they executed her. But all they wanted, and all she'd have told them, is the shortest route to where our farm is. What we're counting on is that they don't know that the most treacherous marsh in these mountains covers the south side of this basin. It's just a mat of floating grass on a lake of mud and tar. All we needed was the luck of the wind, and we didn't need much of that. At this time of year, a strong northerly blows two days out of three."

"Chip will spot the change in vegetation. She won't let the squadron just plow into it." But Kim spoke mainly to bolster her own hopes. Chip clearly was not on form that day, and the panicked horses would be impossible to stop.

"I'm sorry, Kim. I really am." Gina's voice was raw with regret.

Kim turned horrified eyes back to the plain, but by now, there was nothing to see, just a solid wall of red flames and smoke, obscuring the soldiers, the marsh, and the hill beyond. Kim stumbled to the campfire and sat with her face buried in her hands, fighting back the tears.

❖

By midday, the last of the fires was out, halted by the wetlands, and reports began to arrive at the campsite. Kim had been through enough desperate fights to know that you never gave up hope until the final body count was made, but the waiting was hell. And, as always when bad news was expected, the old memories clawed at the edges of her mind. Her parents' farmhouse and the strange stillness when she had returned on that day, twelve years ago. Even before she pushed open the door to the kitchen, she had known something awful had happened, but she had not been prepared for what lay within. Nothing could ever have prepared her for that sight. Kim's eyes fixed, unseeing, on the distance, remembering her childish oath never to care for anyone again, so she could never be hurt by their loss. She was old enough now to know that such emotional isolation was not possible and also to know that revenge was a very poor remedy for grief.

The first news received was that several prisoners had been taken. Dragged, still breathing, from the mud. The numbers were later confirmed at twenty-seven, although there were no details of their identity. Kim tried to take encouragement from the tidings, but even if all the survivors were Rangers, it would still mean that some of the squadron had perished. However, the waiting was nearly over. Everyone who could be rescued had been, and the captives were being brought to the camp to talk to Gina. The line of prisoners and their mounted escort could be seen advancing across the blackened plain.

Throughout the long morning, the heretics had tactfully given Kim a wide berth, but now Gina came to sit beside her. "You'll be heading back to the homelands?" It was not really a question, and Gina's voice held no expectation of disagreement.

Without looking at the elderly heretic, Kim nodded her head. "Yes."

"Then it would be wisest if none of the prisoners saw you here. If the Sisters know I have had the chance to tell you my story, then it could seriously damage the chances of you seeing your next birthday, especially as you don't seem too popular with them to start off with. You could hide in the tent over there until I'm finished talking to the prisoners."

The tent in question was a makeshift affair, designed to shield the food from the worst of the sun. Kim went over and ducked inside then pulled the door flap closed, although still leaving a slight gap so she could see what happened. Soon the sounds of talking and horses' hooves announced the arrival of the captives. All the heretics were present as the sorry party was brought into the camp. They further obscured Kim's view, but not enough to stop her from counting all twenty-seven women and seeing not a Ranger among them. Most bitter of all, Rozek stood at the head of the prisoners.

The anguish hit Kim with an almost physical pain before disbelief swept in. How could the city Guards survive and not a single wilderness-trained Ranger? Some must have eluded both the mud and the heretics. Kim swore she would go to the marsh and not rest until she had searched thoroughly. But in the meantime, there was the interview with Rozek to hear, and even in her mental torment, Kim could not repress a certain satisfaction in seeing the arrogant major, hands tied, with a soot-smeared face and clothes so soaked in mud that the vibrant red had to be imagined rather than seen.

Gina was also amused, judging by her tone. "Hello, and welcome to our humble camp."

"*Doubt not that Celaeno is Goddess over all, and Himoti is her favored disciple, for all who turn their back on her law shall be eternally damned.*" Whatever else, Rozek's faith had not been shaken, not that it impressed the heretics.

"Oh dear. I hope you're going to say something a bit more sensible than just quoting fiction at us." Gina spoke as if addressing a small child.

"*The words of the Goddess shall be as a shield to the faithful.*"

"Unless I'm missing something, the words of the Goddess have been remarkably ineffective at preventing her faithful from being defeated."

The logic cut enough for Rozek to abandon her quotes. "Only because of treachery."

"And who has betrayed you?"

"As if you didn't know. Your allies, the gutless Rangers."

Kim almost leaped from her place of hiding to demand to know what was meant by the remark, but she restrained herself. Gina also seemed taken aback. "If the Rangers did something that helped us, then I'm most grateful to them. But it wasn't arranged, and to be honest, I don't even know what it was."

"They led us into this ambush, and then last night, they all ran away and deserted us."

"I thought you were led here by information you extracted from one of my followers," Gina pointed out reasonably. However, Kim did not hear the remark, or any of the next few exchanges. She was caught, uncomfortably, between laughter and tears, resulting in hiccups, which she stifled as best she could. By the time she was able to return her attention to the confrontation, it was clear that Rozek had lost her temper and Gina her patience.

"You're depraved murderers, and you will pay for it one day!" the Guard major shouted.

You'd know all about murder, Kim thought.

Gina also looked at Rozek with contempt. "We only kill in self-defense. We aren't even going to execute you, though I don't doubt you wouldn't show the same mercy to us, were our positions reversed. I estimate it will take you about thirty-five days to walk back to the Sisters' Homelands on foot, so we'll give you enough supplies and point you in the right direction." Gina paused for effect and then stuck her finger out to the east. "It's that way. Now pick up the saddlebags and start walking."

A lengthy period of complaint and muttered comments was accompanied by jeers from the heretics, but eventually the Guards were leaving the campsite, heading east, with a couple of mounted heretics monitoring their departure.

"I'll come back for you. I swear it," Rozek shouted from the distance.

"I'm sorry, pet, but we aren't going to hang around waiting for you," Gina said softly, mainly for the benefit of her followers.

Kim emerged from the tent and walked over to the heretic leader.

"You heard what Rozek said?" Gina asked when she saw Kim.

"Yes."

"Good news for you, but I'm not so certain about us. I don't know if I like the thought of a squadron of Rangers loose in the mountains."

"Maybe it could work out for us both."

"In what way?"

"Rozek accused the Rangers of desertion. I don't know why they went. There was probably more to it than just thinking I'd been killed. But whatever the reason, they can't go back to the Homelands. When Rozek makes her report, the Guards will be only too pleased for someone to blame for their losses. The Rangers will be convenient scapegoats. You said you could make use of my skills. Do you think you could make room for a whole squadron?"

Gina looked thoughtful. "Possibly...possibly. Some adjustments will be needed on both sides, but possibly." Her right eye looked appraisingly at Kim. "Find your comrades and talk to them. If they are willing to join us, bring them here, and we will discuss it further."

"How long will you stay at this camp?"

"At least five days. We must make sure the major and her women keep on walking and don't try to double back." Gina reached out and put her hand on Kim's arm. "Take a horse and anything else you need. And may the Goddess watch over you."

Kim smiled. That dawn, when the heretics were heading off, she had heard the appropriate rejoinder several times. She used it now. "And may a malfunctioning starship in geo-stationary orbit watch over you."

❖

The Rangers had made little attempt to disguise their tracks. It said much about their opinion of the Guards' abilities. Kim was able to follow the trail without dismounting. Her guess was that after deserting, the Rangers would have put ten or twelve kilometers between themselves and the Guards and then found an easily defended spot to rest out the day and following night.

Dusk was drawing close as Kim rode along the bottom of a winding valley, underneath the spreading branches of tall trees. Despite bruises that were still tender, she felt at peace for the first time in months. She had always been happiest out in the wildlands, away from the regulations, the temples, the Sisters, and the Guards. A smile crossed Kim's face as she remembered Rozek, covered in mud and soot, trying to intimidate Gina with her quotes from the book of the Elder-Ones. The image was one that she would always treasure.

The light was fading fast. Kim was starting to consider stopping her hunt and resuming the next morning, when she heard the whinny of a horse. The squadron must be encamped less than a kilometer ahead, although any sign of their presence was well disguised. Kim had no doubts that the site would be better defended than anything seen so far on the mission. Her smile broadened. The most junior Ranger could give Rozek lessons in how to be a soldier.

❖

The debate had been going around in circles all afternoon. Only two options were available, and no one was particularly happy with either. As Chip had pointed out, there was only one place to go. The Rangers, with their skills, could cope well enough in the wilds during the summer, sticking to a vegetarian diet, but the resources necessary to survive the winter could only be found in the Homelands. The issue was whether the Rangers went back to live inside or outside the law.

After a life devoted to hunting bandits, none of the Rangers was keen on the latter option, but the outcome was very chancy if they threw themselves on the mercy of the Ranger Command and surrendered. Even if they could convince the authorities at Fort Krowe that desertion had been justified, the Guards were unlikely to be so understanding, and if the Sisters got involved, the chances of a pardon became still more remote.

The whole squadron, with the exception of a few sentries, was gathered around the fire. Most were sitting on the ground, though some at the rear leaned against the encircling trees so as to better see the various speakers.

"You could always say you heard me escaping and you all came after me, knowing it would take the entire squadron to recapture me."

Chip's suggestion was at least as sensible as some others, although less seriously meant.

"There's no—" another Ranger began and then stopped sharply as a low, rippling whistle sounded from the trees.

The signal was from one of the sentries, warning of someone approaching. In an instant, the whole camp was at the ready, but before any action could be taken, a second whistle sounded, this one with a rising note. The code sign by which one Ranger identified her position to another.

"What are they playing at?" Chip muttered in confusion, her hand moving to the hilt of her sword. Surely the Guards could not have traced them? And why were the sentries signaling to each other?

A sudden cry of alarm issued from the sentry, but even as swords were whipped free of their scabbards, the yell turned to an unmistakable whoop of delight. The Rangers around the fire looked at each other uncertainly, wondering what was happening. At Chip's signal, they spread out so as not to present a solid target, and archers slipped to positions at the edge, from where they could get a clear line of sight. All were facing the direction of the sounds when the sentry herself emerged from the bushes accompanied by a woman it took everyone a few disbelieving seconds to identify.

Kim walked forward into the firelight, a broad grin on her face, and finally broke the stunned silence. "You know, Chip, I hate to use clichés, but you look like you've seen a ghost."

"Kim?" Chip's voice was hushed. "You fell into that river. We saw you."

Kim shrugged her shoulders nonchalantly. "I can swim."

There was no chance to say more. With tears in her eyes, Chip launched herself forward, flinging her arms around her friend, and threatening to unbalance them both. Kim laughed and said light-heartedly, "Hey, steady on, you don't want to make Katryn jealous."

Not that any risk of that existed, as within an instant, Katryn was also there, wrapping them both in an embrace, followed by as many of the others as could get close enough to pat Kim's back or rub her head. It was not in any of the books of standard military procedures, but no one was bothered.

❖

It was some time before all the recounting of events was completed, but in the end, the decision was very straightforward, a unanimous vote that the Rangers would join with the heretics. Although many were unsure or unhappy about the atheist beliefs, it seemed to offer a fair and free life, and the squadron had no other honorable option. With over sixty dead Guards to avenge and the predictable contents of Rozek's report laying part of the blame on the Rangers, there was no hope of the squadron being accepted back.

The meeting was about to disperse when Chip stood up one last time, holding out her hands for attention. The murmuring around the camp stilled. "Okay. So we're all deserters and have seen our last pay packet. But can I take it we still want to function as a squadron, and I'm still your lieutenant?" A loud succession of cheers and whistles left no doubt that this was agreed. Once the noise quieted, Chip went on, "Well, a squadron needs a captain, and since we won't be getting one from Fort Krowe, we'll have to make our own arrangements and vote for a leader. I would like to start by nominating ex-Lieutenant Kimberly Ramon."

The second burst of applause was if anything, louder than the first. No other nominees were put forward, and the final vote was also unanimous.

CHAPTER SIXTEEN—A DREAM FOR THE FUTURE

Kim was not sure exactly what she had been expecting of the heretics' farm. Gina had warned her that it was little more than a collection of temporary huts, and she had accordingly overlaid the image of hovels onto a memory of her parents' farm. What she had not been ready for was something the size of a village, comprised of fifty to sixty round huts, the home to nearly two hundred women, plus their cows, sheep, pigs, chickens, and horses. The buildings were arranged around a central square. They all had conical, turf-covered roofs, and dry stone walls, about a meter high, the cracks filled with mud and grass. Judging by the trails of smoke seeping from the apex of the roofs, the ones in the middle provided dwellings for the inhabitants. The outer huts were slightly more variable in size, and were doubtless storehouses and animal byres.

The place gave the overwhelming impression of poverty, which Kim found hard to pin down. After all, many farm laborers in the Homelands lived in conditions that were equally basic, if not worse. The heretics themselves all looked well fed and clothed, and the farmlands were clearly fertile. Fields golden with ripening corn were interspersed with rows of beans, cabbages, and other vegetables. Thriving herds dotted the surrounding hills.

Only when she had dismounted in the open space at the center of the village and looked around did Kim finally put her finger on the discrepancy. It was the uniformity of the community. In a place of a similar size in the homelands, a few, the poorest, at the fringes, would have been living in an even worse state, but there would have been others in fine homes of dressed stone, with tiled roofs and under-floor heating. The village would have had a welcoming tavern, a public bathhouse, and a council hall, the main civic building, which would have functioned as school, law court, meeting room, and church at the appropriate times. There would have been gardens. And without these, the place seemed uncivilized, crude, and shoddy.

Word of the Rangers' arrival had spread, and a fair number of heretics had left their work to watch the column of green and gray clad women ride in. As she ran her eyes over the gathering, another difference to the homelands struck Kim. Many elderly faces were dotted among the crowd, but the range of ages hit a sharp cutoff at the other end. There were no young girls abandoning their lessons to run behind the Rangers, or toddlers peering from behind their mothers' legs, and Kim found their absence far more unsettling than she would have believed.

Kim did not have long to dwell on her first impressions. Gina was waiting at the head of a small group of elders who welcomed the Rangers to the village. The welcome was noticeable both in its informality and in the speed with which it turned to practical matters: which huts had been cleared for barracks, where the horses should go, who could allocate food. Kim managed to restrain a broad grin. It was anyone's guess how the two groups, the Rangers and the heretics, would get on, but it was evident they both started with a common disregard for time-wasting ceremonies.

Later that night, when everyone had settled, Kim had a chance to talk things over with the heretic leader. They sat outside the hut where Gina lived with her partner and three other couples in communal domestic arrangements that seemed to exist in a permanent state of happy, although noisy, chaos.

"Have any of your Rangers begun to regret their decision to join us?" Gina asked.

"Not that I've heard. How are your people feeling?"

Gina pursed her lips and waggled a hand horizontally in answer.

"What don't they like?"

"Not all are convinced of the wisdom of admitting a large group of armed soldiers when you don't share our religious beliefs."

"Shouldn't that be lack of religious beliefs?"

Gina smiled. "Maybe."

"They aren't worried at us eating our way through your food stores?"

"I shouldn't think so. It looks like it will be a good harvest. There will be plenty to see us all through winter, and food has never been a problem so far. However, now that the Guards know we're here, we'll have to move. Rozek won't get back to Landfall for well over a month, and they won't have time to assemble another company before winter makes the mission impossible, but we must not still be here come spring." Gina looked rueful. "It will be the third time we've been forced to move. I can guarantee that everyone will be extremely grateful for thirty capable, robust women to help rebuild the settlement. You're going to work for your keep, believe me."

Kim looked at the glittering array of stars that hung above them, her thoughts adding things together. "So it's the need to keep moving that stops you from building better homes?"

The implied low opinion of the village had not been intended as criticism, but Gina hung her head. Eventually she said, "Yes. When we first fled here we...I had hopes. At the first site, we began to lay out a proper settlement. We had nearly completed the bathhouse when we had to run again. The work we put into it...we've never had the enthusiasm to make a real start again. But I feel so guilty. These people listened to me, and look where it's gotten them."

"You could move farther west. So far that the Guards would never find you. You've got the whole planet to hide in."

"We still have a lot of adherents in the homelands, and their numbers are slowly growing, despite the efforts of the Guards to identify them. We can't desert them. They must have somewhere they can escape to if they get discovered. And also there are certain essential items we can't make ourselves, so we have to send people back from time to time to procure things."

Kim was silent for so long, eventually Gina turned and asked, "What are you thinking?"

"A compromise, of sorts."

"Which is?"

"Once you've finished moving the village, it doesn't strike me that you're going to need the Rangers much to help with the farming, except maybe at harvest time," Kim said.

"True."

"Which means we can be freed to do what we've been trained for: patrolling large areas of wilderness, and fighting. The village could move another thirty days west of here, a distance that would strain the supplies of anyone who came looking for it. We Rangers could patrol this region, meeting any escaping refugees, and harrying any Guards.

We could pick a strong defensive site for the village and fortify it, because now you've got a proper fighting force to garrison it. And once you're safe from attack, you could rebuild your bathhouse."

Gina's face was thoughtful. "I'm not sure. I'd have to talk it over with the rest. But...maybe."

"I know, it's typical. You've been here years, and then a new girl comes in and wants to change everything around." Kim's tones were self-derogatory.

"Some might see it like that. But..." Gina paused. "You can find a safe site for a permanent settlement." It was a statement rather than a question.

"Yes," Kim said in confirmation.

"Go and find it. Once we have a definite proposal, I'm sure we can talk the doubters around."

❖

The long line of cliffs soared nearly two hundred meters, a sheer precipice of rock, overhanging the broad flood plain below. The only break for several kilometers was a hanging valley, looking for all the world as if the Goddess had placed a gigantic finger atop the escarpment and pressed halfway down. A river issued from the mouth and cascaded the remaining distance to the lowlands in plumes of white spray.

Kim and Chip stood at the top of the waterfall and took in the view. The climb up was not easy, but a little judicious work with a pickax and it would be possible to make a path that animals could be herded along in single file. The mouth of the valley was narrow, little more than fifty meters wide. With a strong wall across and a dozen archers behind it, that same path up would be suicide for any enemy force foolish enough to try attacking.

The Rangers turned their back on the low-lying plain and walked a short way along the valley to the point where the vertical sides started to draw apart. On both sides, the tops of the cliffs became ever higher, until they joined with an encircling ring of mountains. From two days of surveying, they knew the valley before them was over four kilometers long, broadening out to nearly a kilometer at its widest point. It held a small lake, good grazing, and an abundant stock of timber. Apart from the mouth, there were two, or possibly three, ways into the valley. All were treacherous and all were easily defended. The site was a little closer to the Sisters' homelands than had originally been intended for the new village but was, all in all, far too good to be dismissed. It even opened south, so as to be sheltered from the worst of the cold northerly wind.

Chip's expression made her approval evident as she said, "So, what do you think?"

"I think that with a squadron of Rangers and a strong barricade, we could hold out here against a thousand Guards."

"And their friends. If they had any."

Kim nodded, her eyes taking in the white-capped peaks, the sunlight sparkling on the lake, and the dense green forest of firs. The terrain could not have been better if had it been sculpted for their needs. That it was also beautiful was a bonus. A contented smile touched Kim's face; there were far worse places to live.

❖

The bright day in early February held the promise of spring. A crisp blue sky arched over the valley, and sunshine painted the world in sharp, rich colors. Overnight, a thaw had cleared patches of snow, although a cold pinch in the air warned that a change in the wind could easily bring it back. The first signs of buds were already appearing on the trees.

Kim and Gina walked though the building site that was the beginnings of the village. The work of preparing for the arrival of people had progressed all through winter, whenever the weather allowed. The first year would be hard, just to do enough to establish themselves while still ensuring the fields were cleared, plowed, sown, tended, and harvested. Yet morale among the women was sky-high. Already, the site had been chosen for the bathhouse and meeting rooms, and plans had been made for stone-built houses, with proper heating and sanitation. It would not all come at once. Many years would pass before everyone would be able to move from the temporary round huts, with their damp floors and cold drafts. But it would come; the women had a dream for the future. Over the winter, a mutual regard had grown between the Rangers and the heretics. This aspect of the previous few months was the topic that Kim and Gina were discussing.

"I think it comes down to Rangers being intrinsic non-conformists," Gina said.

"What makes you say that?"

"The way you all seem quite content to toss the rule book out."

Kim pursed her lips. "It depends on what the rule is. Our discipline is very tight where it counts. But sometimes, as a Ranger, you have to choose between following the rules and staying alive. It works pretty well at whittling out the people who prefer the first option."

"Perhaps," Gina conceded. "I've only got my experience with the temple Guard to compare you with."

"Oh well, compared to the Guards, we're all raving subversives. As I'm sure Rozek would tell you, if she were here."

Gina laughed. "I've noted none of you tried quoting the book of the Elder-Ones at me."

"I doubt if many of us could remember the relevant quotes, though it may not mean that all are convinced by your arguments."

"That's hardly surprising, as I don't think you're fully convinced yourself."

Kim shrugged. "I'm trying to cultivate an open mind."

"I won't hold it against you. We heretics are too much in your debt as it is."

"Pardon?" Kim asked, confused as much by the earnestness of Gina's tone as her words.

"You brought us hope. After ten years living in crude huts, we'd given up everything apart from the aim of surviving from day to day. Well, that and feeling smug because, although we might be wet and cold, at least we knew the truth."

Kim nodded her head. "It's not been a one-way exchange. I think we Rangers are just starting to see what we've gained. The authorities like to keep Rangers flexible, so they make a point of moving us around, and they disapprove of close personal ties. We have to choose between family and the call of the wide-open spaces. Now some of us are realizing we can have them both."

"And some have realized it quicker than others."

Kim matched Gina's grin, aware that over the winter, quite a few relationships had sprung up between Rangers and heretics, but she missed the thoughtful gaze Gina directed in her direction.

After a few minutes of walking, their footsteps took them to the high wooden barricade across the mouth of the valley. From the fortified gateway, they could look down on the women with pickaxes who were modifying the path up, cutting a route which pack animals could manage, but one that would not allow more than two women to walk abreast, and one that would be exposed to arrows from above every step of the way. It was urgent work, as the entire move from the old site had to be completed inside two months at most, and much had to be transported up to the site of the new settlement.

"You know. We're going to have to think of a name for the place. Otherwise it will end up as New Village or something equally banal," Gina said.

"Too late. I've already heard people start to refer to it as Westernfort."

Gina wrinkled her nose. "Could be worse."

From their vantage point, they had a panoramic view of the broad, snow-covered lowlands. Even when work on the path to the upper valley was complete, the animals would normally be kept down there on the rich water meadows, only retreating to the safe fields behind the wall when danger was near. Currently, a herd of sheep was scattered beside the riverbank and cattle congregated under the shelter of trees, where bales of hay had been put down to supplement what other food might be found. A few rough sheds and hay barns had been built and stocked the previous autumn, the first work to be undertaken at the new farm. Of necessity, the herds had been moved before winter set in, since by now they were all heavy with young. If they had been left at the old site until spring, the presence of new lambs, calves, and piglets would have delayed the long trek until well after the time when the Guards might return to the mountains. And whatever the Rangers might feel about the tracking skills of the Guards, it did no harm that several months would have passed to cover all traces of the passage of hundreds of hooves.

As her gaze took in the animals below, a new, worried frown creased Gina's forehead.

"Is something wrong?" Kim asked.

"I was thinking about the herds."

"What about them? They seem okay."

"Oh, they are. But all the work going on here has reminded me that I need to plan slightly further ahead than I've been used to, and I'm not sure of the herds' future."

"Why not?"

"Lilian is not as young as she used to be," Gina said simply.

"Oh," Kim said in sudden understanding. "Is her health failing?"

"No. She's in very good condition for her age, but..." Gina did not need to say more.

Lilian was the heretics' Cloner, an ancient, shrunken woman who was a familiar sight, tottering around the animal pens. It was her skill with the healer sense that had called into existence the new generation of farm animals that were bulging the sides of the creatures below. Without her, there would be no others to follow. Yet, since Lilian must be well into her eighties, it was unreasonable to expect the new farm would be able to employ her services for many more years.

Gina shook her head slightly and said, "Still, it's not fair to write Lilian off too soon. She's a tough old thing and could outlive us all. And there is nothing much we can do in the way of useful planning. Except maybe a little research into a few vegetarian dishes."

"We might get a new Cloner."

"Possible, although not too likely, when you think of how rare Cloners are. For a community as small as ours, we were very lucky to get Lilian to start with."

"We could be a bit more enterprising and deliberately set out to recruit a Cloner."

Gina laughed aloud and pointed a finger at Kim. "Now that's what the Rangers bring to us—a more positive way of looking at things."

"Standard military procedure. Always plan ahead to secure your resources." Kim's voice was heavy with self-parody.

"An interesting idea." Gina bit a corner of her lip. "But it will need some thought as to how we identify a suitable convert."

Kim turned away sharply and stared out toward the row of mountains on the far horizon.

"Kim?" Gina had to ask three times before she got an answer.

"I think I might know of someone already."

"A Cloner?" Gina's voice reflected a little surprise.

"No, an Imprinter. Imprinters can clone as well, can't they?"

"Of course..." Gina paused. "I imagine you're referring to the subject of your indiscretion in the stable?" Over the winter, the full story had been recounted on many occasions.

"Yes...Lynn. She told me how much she hated being held in the temple, and she loves mountains. She might be persuaded to come here. Also, she took the full blame for everything that happened in

Petersmine, which saved my life. The least I owe her is to find out whether she's safe and happy, even if she doesn't want to join us. But if we had an Imprinter, then we could have children, and that really would give us a future."

Gina studied Kim's profile thoughtfully. "You would also have slightly more personal reasons for wanting her here?"

"Well...I'm...possibly not," Kim mumbled. Her eyes slipped from the horizon and finished up somewhere much closer to her feet.

"Not?"

Kim shrugged. "I don't think it was terribly seriously meant, certainly not on her side. I mean the words she used—*adolescent crush*—don't point to anything heavy, and it's coming on a year since we last met. I think she'd enjoyed the freedom of the mountain fort. We'd been friends, and she was upset at parting and not thinking too clearly. Otherwise, surely she'd have made things obvious before, rather than blurting it out after the time when she was supposed to have left."

Gina's face held a slightly skeptical look, although all she said was, "And how about you?"

"Oh...I was mainly caught by surprise. Yes...I liked her, but I'm a Ranger." Kim pulled a wry face. "It's almost part of the job to try your luck with half the women you meet." She sighed heavily, then shook her head. "For this settlement to have a long-term future, we need an Imprinter, and Imprinters have to be celibate."

Gina looked as if she was about to say something and then changed her mind, although she continued to watch Kim thoughtfully. After a long pause she said, "Getting an Imprinter out of a temple won't be easy. We need to carefully evaluate the risks and benefits."

"Of course," Kim agreed.

"If we do decide to go for it, it would be better if the attempt was made as soon as possible, before Rozek starts crawling around the mountains again."

"That's no problem. I'm quite used to traveling during winter. I could leave within days."

"You're assuming you'll be the one to go?" Gina's voice was lightly amused.

"Try and talk me out of it."

❖

"I want to go as well." Chip's voice was quietly adamant, but Kim shook her head.

"One of us has to be left here in command."

"So why don't you stay? I'd have said that I was far more expendable than you."

Kim looked at her friend in slight confusion. "Why are you so eager?"

"I've already said. Because I think I owe her. Owe you both. Remember, it was me who put my foot in it."

"That's hardly a recommendation for a tricky mission."

Chip sank her head into her hands and then raised it again to look out over the small lake. Evening was falling on Westernfort, and work was stopping for the night. A moon was glimmering in the darkening sky and reflected on the ice-bound water. That afternoon it had been agreed that Kim would go after Lynn, leaving before the middle of the month. The only thing remaining was to work out who else would be in the party. Chip chewed on her lip as she tried to think of more arguments for her own inclusion, but nothing came to mind.

"Chip? There's more to it than feeling guilty, isn't there?" Kim asked softly.

Chip shrugged one shoulder. "Are you still interested in her?"

"What's that got to do with it?"

"It might affect whether she's still an Imprinter when she gets here." Chip could not bring herself to meet Kim's eyes, but carried on in a rush. "I know it's not a fair thing for me to put on you, but Katryn and I wanted kids. Well, at least one, and joining the heretics, we thought we had to forget it, but if Lynn comes here and she's still an Imprinter, even for a short while, then..." The trail of words ground to a halt.

Kim put her arm around Chip's shoulder. "So you wanted to come along and make sure we were never left alone together?"

"Oh, nothing that crass. I was just going to let you know what it meant to me, and then stand around looking pathetically miserable any time the pair of you seemed to be getting along too well. I'm not proud. I don't mind stooping to emotional blackmail."

Kim laughed. "How would I tell your pathetically miserable look from your normal one?"

"I'd make suitable hand signals." Chip turned and faced Kim.

"But forgetting the jokes, Lynn coming here would mean so much to Katryn and me. I want to come and help on the mission because it's so important."

Kim's expression became serious. "That's all right. But you've got nothing to worry about. I'm going to do everything possible to get her here safely, and I'm going to do it because the village needs an Imprinter, with all that implies, and not because I like my chances with her. In fact, I don't even expect Lynn to still be interested in me. What happened in the stable was a mistake, on both sides. She was feeling lonely and miserable, and I...Well, you know my record with women."

"Record is the right word, and that's partly what worries me," Chip said forlornly, and then took a deep breath. "Although I'll admit you've slowed down a little over the years."

"It's called growing up." Kim punched her friend's arm gently. "Don't worry. I promise you, I'll get her here and she'll still be an Imprinter when she arrives."

❧❦

Part Three

Westernfort

CHAPTER SEVENTEEN—IN CLOTHES LIKE THESE

Sometimes in the temple you had good days, and sometimes you had bad days, and usually you could not be bothered to spot the difference between the two. Lynn stood in the imprinting chapel, feeling not so much exhausted as drained. Drained of all energy and enthusiasm, drained of the ability to take pleasure in the smiling faces of the young couple before her, drained of life. Surely the most ironic state for an Imprinter to reach, yet one they all got to in the end. Being told of Kim's death had simply pushed Lynn into it a bit sooner than expected. She was still one of the better Imprinters in the temple, but she no longer stood out as exceptional.

The change had Sister Dunsin both peeved and confused. Showing Lynn the dispatch from the Rangers should have improved the cynical Imprinter's respect for the will of the Goddess and should have enhanced her discipline, making her better able to do Celaeno's work. That it had not was obviously Lynn's fault in some way that the dogmatic Sister had yet to pinpoint, beyond a general confirmation that sins of lust were as damaging to an Imprinter's talent as the teachings of Himoti warned. Lynn could sometimes reach an odd, dispassionate sympathy for the woman. Dunsin was not particularly malicious or stupid; she was just hampered by her beliefs, which insisted on providing her with answers before she had the chance to start thinking.

In the chapel, the couplets of the litany of thanks stumbled on. Keeping up required no concentration. Lynn latched onto the rhythm, and the words were so familiar she could recite them in her sleep. From the advance of shadows across the wall, Lynn estimated she had been in the imprinting trance for nearly three hours, pretty much average for her over the past few months. With the nearest thing she had felt to pleasure all day, Lynn realized it was now too late for her to be introduced to another couple of prospective parents. She had only to finish the family prayers, offer her private thanks in Himoti's oratory, and then she would be free until the evening meal. Unless Dunsin caught her first.

The escort of Guards fell into place around her as she left the chapel, clearing a way through the crowds of worshipers and bystanders who always wanted to congregate in the most awkward of places. Most sidestepped quickly, but those too lost in religious awe to shift in time were roughly elbowed aside by the Guardswoman in the lead. None should hinder an Imprinter, the chosen of the Goddess, the woman in blue, whose aloof, glazed stare seemed oblivious of the ordinary folk and the circle of reverence that surrounded her.

In truth, Lynn was so tired she was scarcely aware of the flow of people in the temple—the march of the Guards, the shuffling of the public, or the purposeful, yet sedate, progress of the occasional white-robed Sister across the great hall, but her eyes did fix on the open exit and the brief flash of daylight beyond. Then it was gone, and in its place loomed the entrance to the sanctum. Lynn passed through the hanging curtains alone, into the corridors of the quiet inner sanctum, the preserve of the initiates.

Himoti's oratory was deserted when she entered. The only movement was the flicker of candlelight. The flames danced in the draft as Lynn closed the door. She knelt before the small shrine, her eyes fixed on the traditional carved fresco. She was supposed to be offering thanks for the gift of life, yet no words rose in her heart. The festival of Landfall had been celebrated only a few weeks before, sharpening the memories of the same time the previous year at the mountain fort. How could she give thanks when life was so unfair, so devoid of hope? It would not help even if she could believe Dunsin's constant preaching: that Kim had ensnared her using cheap, sordid tricks; that Kim had wanted to harm her, violate her; and that the Goddess had inflicted a just punishment on the sinful Ranger. Because if she believed that, then life would be devoid of any value, any beauty, any thing worth caring about.

Dunsin was probably consulting her books at that very moment, devising new lectures to bombast her protégé back into the full grace of the Goddess. Even as the thought occurred to Lynn, the door opened and a tall Sister stepped into the oratory. Lynn's spirits sank still lower, if that were possible, but a quick sideways glance showed it was not her mentor. The masked figure was too lightly built for the thickset Dunsin.

The unknown Sister knelt beside her at the shrine, and for a few seconds there was silence before the new arrival said quietly, "Please don't shout or run away, but I need to talk to you."

"Pardon?" Lynn said in total bewilderment. The line was hardly a conventional opening for a Sister to use.

"I need to talk to you. And for starters, is it okay for me to be here? I followed you from the great hall, but I don't know whether a Sister is supposed to come into this room."

Lynn froze, unable to accept that she recognized the voice. She turned her head and met the level pair of eyes above the mask. "Kim?" The name was mimed more than spoken.

"Yes."

"They said you were dead."

"Not quite, but not for the lack of them trying."

Lynn's gaze darted back to the shrine as she concentrated on breathing, on reassuring herself she was not dreaming or hallucinating.

"Lynn? Are you all right?"

"I...I think so."

"Is it okay for me to be here? I can't risk attracting attention."

Lynn tried to pull herself together. "Er...yes...It...it would not be unusual...certainly not enough to...er...concern anyone."

"Good. I'm sorry to just appear like this, but there was no way to warn you first."

"That's all right, I was..." Lynn's words halted. "You are...really here, aren't you?"

Kim laughed softly. "If ever I come back as a ghost, I promise I won't do it in clothes like these."

"Right." A confusion of emotions chased across Lynn's face and she could feel her eyes were dangerously close to filling with tears. She concentrated on the carving of the shrine while her mind tried to come to terms with what was happening.

The robed figure beside her glanced toward the door and then began talking quickly. "Now please, listen. I don't want to be here too long. I wanted to talk to you about...well, two things really. First, I wanted to be sure that you're all right."

"Me?" Lynn looked back at the disguised Ranger, fighting with the sense of unreality that was threatening to run away with her.

"Yes. Your confession was read out at the court-martial. It saved my life, but I've been really worried about what might have happened to you because of it."

"Oh...um..." Lynn struggled for words. "As I told Coppelli, the Sisters weren't going to risk harming me. You needn't have worried. I wasn't in any danger, not like..." She stopped again. "You. Are *you* all right? I saw what happened to you. I...I'm sorry. It was my fault. I didn't—"

Kim cut her off. "I'm fine. Honestly. As long as you're all right, the rest doesn't matter, and we haven't got time to talk about it now because there is a lot I need to tell you. It's hard to know where to start. Did you hear that the whole 23rd Squadron deserted last autumn, me included?"

"Deserted?" Lynn said, confused. "No, there's been nothing said about it."

"I'm not surprised. The Sisters are probably quite anxious to keep it quiet." Kim's voice sounded amused. "We've joined up with a group of heretics. They've got a small farming community way out in the western mountains, beyond the reach of the Sisters and the Guards. It's a bit basic there at the moment, but we've got plans for the future. That's the other reason why I've come to see you. At the moment, we have a Cloner at the farm, but she's very old. We need someone younger who can take over the work, and when we were talking about recruiting another Cloner, it occurred to me that an Imprinter would be better, because then we could have children at the village. I know it's a big step to take, but you'd said you didn't like living in the temple, so I'm here to see if you might be willing to come and— "

"Yes."

"...join us at..." Kim trailed off, in obvious surprise at being answered so quickly. "Are you sure?"

"Yes." Lynn felt not a trace of doubt.

"It's not very comfy there at the moment. We're virtually living in mud huts."

"I don't care."

"There's no proper heating. We may not finish the bathhouse for a couple of years."

Lynn fixed Kim with an ironic frown. "Aren't you supposed to be trying to talk me into it?"

Kim shrugged. "They always said I'd never earn my living as a shopkeeper, but I don't want you to commit yourself before you know what the score is."

"You said it was in the mountains?"

"Yes."

"And I'd be allowed to stand outside from time to time and look at them?"

"Of course. Whenever you wanted," Kim answered, although she sounded uncertain as to whether Lynn's question had been meant seriously.

"Then that beats anything the Sisters have ever offered me."

"But isn't there anything else you want me to tell you?"

"That I'm not dreaming."

"No, you're not." Kim gave a soft laugh. "I hadn't expected you to agree quite so quickly."

"Did you really think my answer was in doubt?"

"I...er...I didn't know quite what to think." She drew a deep breath. "Okay. So the tricky part is how to get you out of the temple."

"Can you bring me another set of Sister's robes? Then I could just walk out with you."

Kim shook her head. "It was hard enough getting these."

"The trouble is that every time I leave the sanctum I get a little entourage of Guards, and even when I'm inside, I'm not supposed to just wander about. Sisters, on the other hand, are allowed to come and go pretty much as they please."

"Is there no other way out of the sanctum? A high window or something? I could leave you the clothes and climb down."

"No. There are Guards on every possible exit, and if they see you leave the sanctum not disguised as a Sister..." Lynn did not bother to finish the sentence.

"You don't have access to anywhere else?"

"At night, when the main doors to the temple are locked, I'm allowed to go into the central hall to pray. If I get permission first."

"The Guards search the temple before the doors are closed. I know because our first idea of getting to see you was to hide in there until after dark. We can't meet you that way."

"But you don't have to," Lynn said in sudden eagerness. "I think I know how to work it out..."

❖

Nobody paid any attention to Kim in her borrowed robes as she walked through the gardens on the south side of the temple. Dusk was falling, and most people had already left the temple grounds in search of a hot meal and a warm bed for the night. Only a few dawdlers still wandered the maze of gravel paths amid the trees and bushes.

At one corner of the garden was a narrow alleyway running between the wall of the temple and the back of an outlying building. Kim walked toward it at a dignified and unhurried pace. The heretic, Mirle, stood by the entrance, as if idly viewing the scene while waiting for someone. She nodded respectfully to the bogus Sister but made no other attempt to move. The far end of the passage was guarded by Carma, the squadron's healer, also in the costume of an ordinary bystander.

Kim walked sedately along the alley until she reached the halfway point, where a blocked doorway stood at the back of a deep recess in one wall. Both sentries signaled the all clear. Kim ducked inside, already reaching to draw the white robe up over her head. The swift action also removed the cowl and mask and revealed the normal civilian clothes underneath. It took seconds to lay the robe flat on the ground and roll it into a neat bundle, by which time the sound of footsteps told of Carma's arrival. The other Ranger handed a small rucksack to Kim, who pulled out her jacket, put it on, and shoved the white robe into the pack. Then the two Rangers strolled casually back up the alley, to make a show of being reunited with their friend Mirle before heading off to the town, talking quietly among themselves.

"Did you find her?" Carma asked.

"Yes," Kim said.

"And?"

"She wants to come."

"Great," Mirle said. "Did she have any idea of how we could get her out?"

Kim smiled. "Yes, in fact, she did."

❖

The central hall of the temple was a different place after dark when the crowds had left, and it was peaceful enough to draw on the beauty of the images that adorned the shrines and altars. Lynn knelt and set her basket down, then raised her eyes to the painting above her in the alcove, shimmering in the light of a dozen candles. The serene faces of five Elder-Ones looked down on her, with their multi-colored hair and skin.

The representation was taken from the book: *Their skins were diverse in tone, and their hair was yellow and red and black, and all the shades between.* Artists and theologians had spent centuries arguing over the exact interpretation, but whatever the true appearance of the Elder-Ones, Lynn had a liking for this particular picture. The central figure reminded her of a talisman her grandmother had of the patron of livestock breeders, Simon Hunt, with her deep brown skin and flowing green hair. This shrine had been the first to come to mind.

In the basket was an offering, a garland of spring flowers to adorn the shrine. Lynn removed the cloth cover and lifted out the gift, then reached forward and arranged it around the low altar, weaving it between the candles. She moved slowly, methodically, letting her actions camouflage her inspection of her surroundings. No one else was nearby. Two Sisters were deep in conversation before the main altar to Himoti, and a group of Guards stood at attention by the entrance to the sanctum, but no one was looking in her direction. Lynn slipped her hand under the mantle draped over the altar and found the tightly rolled bundle of white fabric hidden beneath. Still trying to keep her actions smooth and innocent, she transferred it to the basket and pulled the cover across.

Lynn settled back on her heels and looked again at the painting. Her strong urge was to leave as quickly as possible, now that she had what she came for. However, a hurried departure might cause comment, and all things considered, this might be a very good time to pray. Lynn bowed her head and began to softly recite the mantra of supplication.

❖

Lynn's heart was pounding as she closed the door of the meditation room. All it needed was for Sister Dunsin to decide that another lecture was due, and the game would be over, but it was a chance she had to take. That morning was Lynn's turn to be released from duties in the imprinting chapels to spend a few hours in private meditation and revitalize her spiritual energies. Lynn suspected that many of her fellow Imprinters used their meditation time to catch up on sleep or to daydream, but of course no one would admit it, and the use she was going to put the time to was even more unorthodox. It was her opportunity to escape.

Lynn tugged her blue tunic free of her belt. Carefully wrapped around her body was the set of Sister's clothing. She wondered if any at breakfast had noticed her apparent overnight weight gain, although fortunately the Imprinter's tunic was loose enough to conceal a suspicious outline. Her lips pursed thoughtfully as she shook out the robe. The hem had been raised, allowing for the difference in height between Kim and herself. She hoped that the modification had been correctly estimated, but there was only one way to find out.

Lynn pulled the gown on, dropping it over her suit and then looking down. The length was not too bad, maybe a couple of centimeters short, but acceptable. Her soft leather sandals would show, but that did not matter since they were the same style as those worn by the Sisters. What would be dangerous was if a flash of blue should show at her ankles as she walked. Lynn bent down and rolled up her leggings until they were above her knees, then she tied the mask about her face and pulled the cowl over her head.

A mirror for her to check her appearance would have been comforting, but such vanities were hardly the thing for a meditation room. Instead, Lynn stood for a short while, adjusting the way the robe hung from her shoulders and the lie of the mask over her nose. But this was merely a way of delaying her exit from the room, when the disguise would be put to the test, and Lynn knew she did not have time to waste.

It took an effort to pull the door open confidently, rather than edge it ajar and peer out first, but her escape relied on bluff, not caution. Lynn was so tense that it was an anti-climax when she found the corridor outside the meditation room empty, although the absence of people was hardly surprising. Most Sisters would still be at their prayers after breakfast. The temple day had not yet begun. The exit of the sanctum was in sight before Lynn encountered anyone else. All her willpower went into maintaining the stately tread of a Sister, confident and dignified, but she could hardly believe it when the other white-clad figure walked past with only a polite nod of acknowledgment.

The curtains shielding the sanctum from the view of the public hung in heavy folds across the exit. Lynn pushed them aside and stepped through. The eyes of the row of Guards on either side flicked in her direction before returning to their forward stare. The curtain dropped back into place and Lynn proceeded across the main hall of the temple. Few people were in sight, just some devout citizens stopping off to pray before beginning their day's work, three junior Sisters removing dead flowers from the altars, and one nervous family, so worried by the risk of being late for their appointment in the imprinting chapel that they had turned up far too early.

At the doors of the temple, Lynn stopped, temporarily overwhelmed to have the sky above her head once more. The time was just before sunrise. Bands of pink cloud lay on the eastern horizon, the air was chill and fresh, and birds screeched their song from the rooftops. The gates of the wall around the temple complex were less than fifty meters away, and through them the whole city of Landfall lay stretched before her. However, her route did not lead in that direction, not yet. Lynn walked down the steps and followed the path to the side.

Kim's directions had been explicit. Soon she was in the deserted gardens, and ahead of her was the entrance to the narrow alleyway. A young woman stood idly at one side. The unfamiliar civilian clothes meant that only as she was walking past did Lynn recognize Carma, one of the Rangers she had known at the mountain fort. The walls on either side of the passage enclosed her. The blank faces of stone seemed to stretch out, devoid of feature from one end to the other, but midway along, in the space of a few steps, a shadow on the right hand wall split open and revealed itself as a deep recess.

"Everything okay?" Kim had been waiting inside.

"Yes."

Lynn slipped into the alcove, ripping the mask off her face. With Kim's help, the white robe followed, pulled up and over her head. Then, while Lynn undid the buttons at the neck of her blue tunic, Kim knelt by two rucksacks on the floor and produced shirt and trousers in neutral homespun colors, a sheepskin jacket, and finally a sturdy pair of boots.

"We had to make a guess at what size your feet were."

Lynn's tunic was off and she had both arms in the shirt as she spared the boots a quick glance. "They look about right."

Kim was about to toss the discarded Sister's robes into a corner, but Lynn stopped her.

"Don't leave them. When the Sisters find I'm missing, they'll start by searching the grounds. If they find my clothes, they'll know I had help and will look further afield."

Even before Lynn had finished speaking, Kim had nodded and was folding the white robes and Imprinter's suit so they would fit in the rucksacks. The pair finished their tasks almost simultaneously, Lynn tying her laces as Kim pulled the drawstring on the second rucksack.

"How do they feel?" Kim asked, pointing to the boots.

"A bit loose," Lynn said after an experimental waggle of one foot.

"Not a bad thing."

"True. When we have more time, I'll take some strips from the robe to make padding. It will save blisters."

Lynn stood up straight, and for the first time, took a serious look at Kim's appearance. Seeing the Ranger in civilian clothes was more than a little strange, and her hair was even more disconcerting. It was still short, but instead of the close military crop, it had been allowed to grow into a fringe, and a parting was discernible. *I can probably get to like it,* Lynn reflected to herself, a little amused by her own reaction. Kim was also treating her to a quizzical stare.

"Do I look sufficiently ordinary?" Lynn asked.

Kim gave a wry smile. "So so. But we must do something about your hair." She pulled a long knife from her belt. "Turn around. I'm afraid this will be rather untidy. Something else to sort out when we have more time."

Lynn gritted her teeth as the knife snagged once or twice, but within seconds, she had been shorn of her heavy braid. She twisted her head from side to side, feeling the strange absence of weight, while the twisted plait of hair was also stuffed into a rucksack, then Kim helped comb Lynn's hair forward with her fingers.

"How does it look?" Lynn asked.

Kim grinned. "Like a Ranger has hacked at your hair with her trail knife. You can borrow Mirle's hat to cover the worst of it. It will do, and it changes the shape of your face quite a bit."

The entire transformation had taken less than three minutes. Kim picked up the two rucksacks, swung one over her own shoulder and held the other out for Lynn. Then they stepped out of the alcove and walked back up the alley toward the garden, falling into an unhurried stroll. As they got close to the end of the passageway, Lynn heard faster footsteps catching up behind, and a few seconds after reaching Carma, they were joined by a fourth woman.

Kim gestured to the newcomer. "Lynn, this is Mirle, one of the heretics. She volunteered for the mission since she knows the safe houses in the homelands. And I think you probably remember Carma."

Lynn nodded and said earnestly, "Yes. And I don't know how to start thanking you all."

Carma's lips twitched down at the corners. "I'm enough of a healer to know that you saved my life back in the mountains. If we all get home safe, we can call it even."

"Make that *when*, not *if*," Kim interrupted. "But the polite exchanges can wait until later. First we need to get to the horses, and also, Mirle, I think Lynn should borrow your hat."

The heretic smiled and handed it over, then the four of them strolled through the gardens to the temple gates. By now the traffic in and out had increased to a steady flow. Three Guardswomen stood stiffly at attention on either side of the arch over the road. Lynn was terrified that she would be recognized without the mask, but the glazed expressions of the Guards were oblivious to the people going by, and no challenge was issued as she passed the iron-bound doors and emerged onto the street outside.

"They didn't even look at us," Lynn whispered.

"Why should they? How would anyone dare to make off with an Imprinter when they are on duty and their uniforms look so pretty?" Kim's voice was full of amused irony.

The temple gates opened onto a wide thoroughfare lined with well-stocked shops, already busy with the commerce of a new day. Not far away, a young street urchin held the reins of four horses. She looked at them with a hopeful expression and gave a yelp of thanks as she caught the coin Kim flipped in her direction, then turned and scampered off, disappearing into the jumble of activity on the road.

The sight of the horses gave Lynn another moment of panic. Such a long time had passed since she had ridden seriously; the two brief occasions at the mountain fort had been only a game. But it was not the sort of thing you forgot how to do. The second her foot touched the stirrup, her body took over, remembering the actions as she swung into the saddle. Her horse fell in line with those of the other three women, winding through the early morning traffic that filled the streets of Landfall. By the time they reached the edge of town, the sun had cleared the horizon and its rays fell on their backs as they headed west.

CHAPTER EIGHTEEN—THE RULES OF THE GAME

They did not stop until midmorning, when Landfall was many kilometers behind and long lost from sight in the gently rolling farmlands. Some time earlier, they had abandoned the main road in favor of a lesser used sidetrack. This route followed the path of a sluggish river through freshly plowed fields and small strips of woodland. Kim finally called a halt on a deserted stretch of grassy embankment and set her horse off to graze. It was a break to rest the animals, and a chance for the women to eat a light meal and to make a final decision on the route they would take back to the mountains.

"How long before you'll be missed?" Kim asked, once they were all seated or sprawled on the grass.

The question was one that Lynn had already given some thought to. "With extreme bad luck, they'll be after me already, but I was due to be meditating all morning, so I shouldn't be missed until I don't show up at lunch time. And they probably won't begin a major search until the meal is over. Then they'll start by turning the sanctum upside down before moving on to the rest of the temple." Lynn shrugged. "It could well be late afternoon before they know I've definitely gone."

Mirle looked thoughtful. "That's not too bad."

"But as Lynn said at the beginning, we can't rely on it," Kim said.

The heretic pursed her lips. "True. And whenever the chase starts, we still have the same basic choice: either we go hell for leather and try to outrun them, or we go slowly and try to blend into the scenery."

"This part of the journey is your specialty. What do you recommend?"

Mirle had no hesitation. "Slow and steady. They may well suspect that we've got Lynn and are taking her to Westernfort. When you think about it, there's nowhere else for her to go, so they'll be looking west.

We could drop down toward Alderwood and take the roundabout route by Southwater. There are some good safe houses that way."

"Fair enough. Do you two have anything to add?" Kim looked at the others as she spoke.

"Only to agree with Mirle." The chunk of bread in Carma's hand was waved in the heretic's general direction as she spoke. "If the Guards are changing their horses at way stations, we'll never be able to keep ahead of them."

"True. Any thoughts, Lynn?" Kim's eyes moved on.

"Er...I...no." Lynn could think of nothing sensible to say and her voice sounded, to her ears, nearly as weak and unsure as she felt, but no one else seemed to notice her confusion.

Carma and Mirle were both looking to Kim as leader, waiting for her to make the final decision. She looked thoughtful for a minute and then nodded. "Okay, Mirle, we'll follow your lead. Where should we aim to stay tonight?"

The conversation moved on to routes, distances, and provisions, a detailed debate about places Lynn had never heard of. She sat to one side, trying to follow the intricacies of the plan, but suddenly she was feeling completely out of her depth. She did not know how far a horse could travel in a day, how much it cost for a room at an inn, or whether you could ford the river Wade in April. The dull security of an Imprinter's life had gone, and Lynn had no experience relevant to the new situation. In fact, apart from the journey to Landfall, she had no experience of adult life outside the temple at all. Lynn fixed her eyes on the trees overhanging the river, hoping to take comfort in their beauty, but at the moment, it all seemed frighteningly alien.

At last, the other three concluded their planning and began to get ready for the return to the road. As she went to stand, Lynn's legs felt a little wobbly from the unaccustomed strain of riding, and the sharp sting on her left heel reminded her of the intention to pad her new boots. She hesitated. She should have thought of it sooner; now it would mean delaying the others. Yet it would be foolish to get blisters if it could be avoided. Surely a few minutes extra wait would not matter?

Lynn sat down again and pulled off her boots. "Can you pass me the Sister's robe?" she asked, feeling embarrassed to be wasting everyone's time.

However, Kim was by her side in an instant, her voice concerned rather than critical. "Oh yes, your feet. How are they?"

"No blisters yet, but..."

Lynn did not need to finish the sentence. Already Kim had pulled the robe from a rucksack and began tearing off strips to pass to her.

Carma watched with melodramatic mock horror. "Oh no, after all I went through to get that."

Kim and Mirle laughed. The acquisition of the robes was obviously a shared joke, and a subject that had given Lynn cause to wonder. It could not have been easy. She paused her wrapping to ask. "Just how did you get a set of clothes from a Sister?"

The laughter became even louder, but eventually Mirle controlled herself enough to answer. "It was as heroic an example of self-sacrifice as you could ask for from a Ranger. Carma slept with the woman who runs the temple laundry."

Kim handed the last strip of cloth to Lynn before adding her own comments. "Yes, it was courage up to and beyond the call of duty. I didn't even need to order her. I just suggested it vaguely, and straight away, she volunteered. And if you'd seen the woman, I tell you, there was no guarantee Carma was going to get out of there in one piece."

"I must admit I was impressed by the valiant way she threw herself into the action." Mirle feigned seriousness.

Kim matched her tone. "You tend to get a lot of practice at it in the Rangers. Carma more than most."

"She's got a healthy running tally?"

"I don't know about running, I think the count galloped into the distance years ago."

At which point, the gibes became too much for Carma to resist some good-natured retaliation. She directed a long, hard stare at Kim. "Now that's a bit much, coming from you, Ramon. I can remember Captain LeCoup threatening to put a sentry outside the door to your room to keep the line in order."

Lynn concentrated on wrapping the padding around her feet and putting her boots back on while the laughter and teasing continued between the other three. It was all said in jest, Lynn realized, but it was based on events and an experience of life that was even more unknown to her than the planning of a dangerous journey. Now it was too late to question exactly what she had agreed to with Kim. In fact, Lynn was not certain what the right questions were, or what she wanted the answers to be. Some of Sister Dunsin's warnings echoed in her mind, and even Dunsin could not be totally wrong about everything. And then Lynn remembered the hopeless, deadening slavery of the temple. Surely nothing could be worse than that? *But whatever happens,* Lynn told herself, *I've made my choice and I'll stick with it.*

❖

The skies remained clear for the rest of the day, but the weather was cold, even for early April. As the sun drew near to the horizon, the temperature dropped still further. Fortunately, the party was well equipped, and in addition to her jacket, Lynn had a riding cloak over her shoulders. Although she was warm enough, Lynn knew she was trembling, but she knew it in a vague, detached way.

Shortly after the midmorning break, Lynn had become aware that the unfamiliar exercise was making heavy demands on her body, but she could not afford to let it impede the rest of the party. She knew all the warnings about using the healer sense to overcome physical limitations, but the situation did not allow her any other options. They had to escape. All their lives depended on getting away, so she had exerted her skill to block out the pain of overworked muscles and chafed skin. At first, it had been only the gentlest of interventions, but by the time sunset approached, she was totally absorbed in the healer-trance. The rift between mind and body was so great that she failed to notice the change in surroundings when they finally rode into the enclosed courtyard of a crossroads inn.

The innkeeper, a plump, middle-aged woman with a flour-covered apron, came out to greet her guests. "Welcome, travelers, what can I do for you?"

Mirle slipped from her horse and stepped forward. "We'd like a quiet room for the night."

A slight hesitation and flicker of recognition crossed the innkeeper's face, but the woman's voice was unchanged as she said, "We're short on private rooms. Would the hayloft over the stables do?"

Kim and Carma caught each other's eye with approving looks, knowing that if necessary, the hayloft would provide the quickest escape from the inn without drawing the attention of others. Mirle and the innkeeper walked a little to one side and spoke in low voices, giving the charade of agreeing on a price, although the information being exchanged was undoubtedly far more significant. The two Rangers dismounted and caught their horses' reins. However, Lynn remained in the saddle.

Kim walked to her side. "Lynn. Are you all right?" But as the Ranger looked more closely, she could see Lynn swaying slightly and the pallor of her face. Kim reached out to put her hand on the Imprinter's arm. At the touch, Lynn appeared to jerk awake. She shook her head slightly and then swung her leg over the rump of her horse and dropped to the ground. Quite literally. As her feet hit the cobblestones, her knees buckled, and if Kim had not caught her, she would have fallen.

"Carma, get over here." But there was no need for Kim to speak. Already the Ranger healer was at her shoulder. "What's wrong with her?" Kim asked in alarm.

Carma's eyes unfocused as she put her hand on Lynn's forehead for a few seconds before replying. "Nothing too serious. It's mainly strained muscles. She's overdone things and has been holding herself together with the healer sense."

The innkeeper had also stepped up close and now hissed. "If she's the one you don't want people to notice, then get her out of sight at once."

The advice was very good. Lynn felt herself being picked up and carried, and for a while the world pitched and swung about her. When the whirling stopped, she was set down on a fresh bed of straw with a thick cloak laid over her as a blanket. She opened her eyes to see the sloping rafters of the hayloft and Kim kneeling at one side with the other two standing behind.

"When did you last ride a horse?" Kim demanded to know.

"You saw me, back in the fort," Lynn managed to reply.

"A year ago! And when was the last time before that?"

"When I was twelve."

"Damn it. Why didn't you say before?" Kim sounded angry.

"I'm sorry. You'd planned out your route. I didn't want to slow you down." Lynn felt her eyes filling with tears.

Kim sighed loudly and lowered her head, then put her hand on Lynn's shoulder. "No, I'm the one who should say sorry. I should have thought. I'd seen you ride, but it should have been obvious you wouldn't get to practice at the temple." She looked over her shoulder. "Carma, can you do anything for her?"

"A little." Carma's voice was softly regretful. "Unfortunately, it's been a long day for me as well. Once I've had a rest and something to eat, I should be of more use. At least enough to make sure she gets a good night's sleep. By tomorrow, she'll be able to look after herself, but I doubt she'll be ready to move on."

Kim pursed her lips. "Mirle, will the innkeeper mind us staying?"

"She'd probably rather we didn't, but she'll cover for us as long as we need."

"Okay. Carma, if you do what you can now, then you and Mirle can go over to the common room and get supper. I'll stay here and keep an eye on her for a while," Kim said and moved back to let the other Ranger take her place.

Lynn closed her eyes as Carma's hand rested on her forehead, and slowly the worst of the pain slipped away, while the exhaustion softened to a bearable level. She still felt as if she had been through a mangle, and her hips and thighs throbbed, but her thoughts were back in the present and clear enough for her to know the risks she had taken that day. Only when she had released herself from the cocoon of the healer sense had she found that she had pushed herself much, much too far.

"Do you feel any better?" Carma asked eventually.

"Yes. Thank you."

"That's okay." Carma looked over to Kim. "Mirle and I will be off in search of supper, then."

"Right. I might be along later."

"If not, we'll bring something back for you."

"Thanks."

There was the sound of the Ranger and heretic climbing down from the hayloft, and then Lynn was aware that she was alone with Kim. All her doubts from the morning returned in a rush. Was Sister Dunsin right? Would Kim be looking simply to notch up another conquest? Some sort of competition? But Lynn did not know the rules of the game. She hunted desperately for something to say.

"I've been stupid. You're right. I should have spoken earlier."

"We all do mad things sometimes. And it allowed us to get safely to this inn." Kim spoke quietly.

Lynn turned her head and looked around. A third of the hayloft was taken up with a mound of loose straw. An oil lantern hung from a rafter, casting oblique shadows across the sloping roof that came down almost to the floor. At one end of the loft, a bay jutted out, presumably overhanging the road outside. The tall loading hatch at the back was bolted and shuttered. A ladder stuck up through a trapdoor in the middle of the floor. Lynn frowned. She had no memory of how she had been carried up it, but obviously it had been managed somehow. And then, sitting on the straw less than a meter away and watching her intently, was Kim.

Something approaching panic clawed at Lynn. Try as she might, she could not push away the memory of Sister Dunsin's preaching, the words that echoed in her head. *She would have taken what she wanted from you, and I can guarantee it would have been more than you wanted to give.* And what did she want to give? Lynn's eyes closed as she felt fresh tears rising. At the moment, the answer was definitely nothing. Her whole body ached from head to toe, the burning in her groin was the effect of the saddle, not lust. Dunsin had derided her for childish romanticism, had promised that reality would be both crude and unpleasant. In the security of the temple, it had been so very easy to dismiss the words as religious ranting, but now?

Lynn fought back sobs. In her current state, anything that happened was likely to be far worse than Dunsin's most dire warning. And what was Kim going to want? Lynn remembered the conversation from that morning, the jokes about a Ranger's running tally. Then another memory came to mind, the parade ground at Landfall, and what had happened to Kim there. Lynn set her jaw. That had been her fault, her ill-planned actions that had resulted in the flogging, and she owed Kim something by way of repayment. Lynn was still frightened, still unsure of what she had bought into, and the time and place were not those she would have chosen, but she was not going to start complaining. Whatever Kim wanted, she could have.

"Lynn?" Kim's voice was soft. "Are you all right to talk?"

"Yes," Lynn said. Talking was not the issue. Kim reached out a hand as if to touch her, and despite her resolve, Lynn felt herself flinch away and freeze.

Kim's hand dropped and she said, "There's something we need to sort out."

"I'm listening."

Kim hesitated for a moment and then began talking, but her sentences limped along in untidy chunks. "I...er...I came to the temple to ask you to join us because...when we were thinking about the need for a new Cloner...you came to mind...since you'd told me how unhappy you were at the temple, and I thought...perhaps, you'd be willing to join us. It wasn't that I was hoping..." And finally, the erratic speech died. Kim hesitated for the space of several breaths before continuing. "I know I'm sounding disjointed. Basically, what I want to say is...what happened in the stable in Petersmine...I haven't been putting any...expectations on it. I'll understand if it was just that you didn't want to go to Landfall, and got a bit overwrought, and didn't mean what you said to me, and you only kissed me because you were unhappy." Kim's words paused for the longest gap of all. Lynn waited in silence, unsure of quite where the awkward monologue was going, but at last Kim picked up again in a rush. "Because I didn't seriously feel that way about you, it was just the situation. And I'm not hoping or wanting for us to become lovers now, in fact, quite the opposite. Westernfort needs an Imprinter, and I know celibacy is part of the job. So we can just chalk up Petersmine as one of those stupid things that happen sometimes. And we can be friends. Okay?"

Lynn felt as if she had been thrown a lifeline. She grabbed at it eagerly. "Yes. Of course."

"Right." Kim took a deep breath. "As long as that's sorted. Now, do you want me to stay with you, or would you prefer to be left alone to rest?"

"No. You go and get something to eat."

"You're sure? Do you want me to bring you over something to eat yourself?"

"I'm sure, and I'd better wait until Carma is around before I try eating."

Kim got to her feet a little uncertainly and walked over to the trapdoor. She stopped once as if about to say something else, but then climbed down without a word. Lynn watched her go, her relief turning rapidly to a perverse and irrational disappointment.

❖

After stepping off the foot of the ladder, Kim walked to the stable door and looked out on the darkened courtyard. Night had fallen while she had been in the hayloft; one crescent moon hung low in the sky. The gusting breeze was icy cold. From the entrance to the inn's taproom came the hubbub of cheery voices, laughter, and the clunk of beer tankards on tables. The promise of warmth and food. The sound was normally enticing, but Kim was not quite ready for company. She pressed a palm against her forehead and closed her eyes. Before she faced the other two members of the group, she wanted to have her expression fully under control. Carma certainly would have questions, whether or not they were voiced aloud.

Kim leaned a shoulder against the doorpost, berating herself for her own stupidity. She realized she had managed to persuade herself that she did not want Lynn as a lover, that the kiss had been a mistake, that she had come on the mission solely for the benefit of the community at Westernfort. And her self-deception had worked perfectly. Right up to the second she had set eyes on Lynn again in the great hall of the temple. But in that second, Kim had known she was more hopelessly serious about Lynn than she had ever been about any woman before, and that in proposing to take the Imprinter back to Westernfort, she was just possibly making the biggest mistake of her life.

But the stupidity and self-deception had not ended there. Kim fought to restrain a groan at the realization. Somewhere in the previous few days, she had let herself start to hope, that maybe Lynn might...

Kim cut off the thought. There was no mistaking the way Lynn had shied away from her hand, the blank expression with which Lynn had avoided the chance to reaffirm her words in Petersmine, the eagerness with which Lynn had agreed that they should stick with friendship. Kim's hand dropped and she fixed her eyes on the stars. Never had she been so disappointed to have someone agree with what she said, but it had been a foolish dream to hope that Lynn would admit to still loving her.

Kim drew another sharp breath and finally gave vent to her feelings. "Oh, shit, shit, shit."

❖

In the middle of the night, Kim was awakened by the sound of pounding hooves. Instantly, she had slipped out of the bedding and was standing by the loading hatch. Through the lattice of the shutters, she saw half a dozen Guards charge by, their route going directly underneath where she stood, pushing their horses to a reckless gallop in the moonlight. And then they were gone, racing down the silver ribbon of road, heading away from Landfall.

Carma had also been awakened by the noise. She stood at Kim's shoulder while the hoofbeats faded into the distance and the quiet sounds of the night returned. Then she said softly so as not to wake the other two, "They'll be carrying the news about Lynn."

"Probably."

"So now the fun starts in earnest. They're in front of us."

CHAPTER NINETEEN—
A PIG FARMER'S DAUGHTER

The alert had gone out to every town Militia. Over the following two weeks, the group lost count of how many roadblocks they passed, but after the first two or three, the barricades ceased to hold any anxiety for them. The Militia was clearly hampered by their preconceptions of the person they were looking for. Initially, when the soldiers in their black uniforms waved the four women by without a second glance, Lynn wondered if they were still naively expecting an Imprinter in blue with a long braid of hair, but it became apparent that their ideas were stuck in a different rut.

Riding the horse was what confused them and provided the best disguise. Although it slowed the group down at first, while Lynn hardened to the exercise, it was their passport across the country. The most difficult part was hiding the amusement as they rode in single file around a cart that was being emptied and searched by the earnest Militiawomen. It was still a question of debate whether the emphasis on wheeled transport was because the authorities thought an Imprinter too spiritual a creature to sit astride a horse, or if the Militia were unable to grasp the idea that an Imprinter might willingly leave a temple and they were therefore looking for a prisoner, bound and gagged. Whatever the reason, evading the pursuit was beginning to seem almost too easy.

The peaks of the western mountains were lining the horizon as they reached the last major obstacle before they left the lands controlled by the Sisters—the river Coldwater. The four women rode over the brow of a hill and looked down on the valley. Below them, a six-arch bridge spanned the winding river and a small town lay amid a patchwork of farmland. The sun was low on the horizon, but even with the glaring light in their eyes, they could see the huddle of black-clad Militia on the distant bridge and the line of traffic waiting to pass. It was an irritation. The day had been a long one, and the group was all looking forward to finding a tavern and a meal with as little delay as possible. However, one more checkpoint was not a cause for concern.

Only when they were in the line and the barrier no more than twenty meters away did they notice the woman in red and gold standing in the middle of the crowd of Militia and scanning every face that went by. The presence of the temple Guard was worrying, but turning around and going back was unsafe. Such an action would have been far too blatantly guilty not to attract attention.

Kim nudged her horse closer to Lynn's and whispered, "Do you recognize her? Is she from Landfall?"

"I don't know. She's a bit far away at the moment, and all Guards tend to look the same to me anyhow."

"I know what you mean. If it weren't for Himoti's ban, I'd swear someone was cloning them somewhere. Uniforms have that effect." Kim gave a reassuring smile. "And the same applies for you, so don't worry. The blue suit is what people notice, not the face. The Guard would need to be very familiar with you to recognize you in everyday clothes with your haircut. What she'll mainly be looking out for is an expression of panic."

The corners of Lynn's mouth turned down. "She may well get to see one."

The group moved slowly up the line. After a long wait, while every sack of flour on the wagon ahead was shifted, prodded, and then pushed back into place again, their turn came to ride onto the bridge. Lynn tried to keep her concentration on the back of Kim, riding in front of her. She felt she was running a gauntlet and could hardly believe it when there was no challenge. Out of the corner of her eye, she could see the Militia already turning to the cartload of apples that was next in the line. Then, just as it was starting to seem that this roadblock would be like all the rest, the Guard stepped out and held up her hand for Lynn to stop. Immediately the Militia switched their attention from the cart and formed a circle around the group of four women.

The Guard's eyes were locked on Lynn's face, but a degree of doubt lurked there. She was not sure of the identification. Long seconds of silence dragged out and then the Guard asked, "Would you mind telling me where you're heading?"

"To Longhill, ma'am." Lynn spoke confidently, repeating the story the group had prepared.

"And where are you coming from?"

"Well...Longhill originally. I've just been up to Southwater and back with my friends. We've been..." Lynn let her voice trail off as she tried to seem innocently confused.

"So. You're from Longhill?" the Guard snapped.

"Yes, ma'am."

"And what do you do there?"

"I work on a farm."

"Doing what?"

"Whatever the boss tells me."

Lynn's reply raised a faint chuckle from the back of the ring of assembled Militia, but the Guard was not amused. She scowled and said, "Get down off the horse."

Lynn's stomach was a twisted knot of fear as she obeyed the order. When the Guard was able to better judge her height and build, the suspicions would increase, and little could be done about it. Posture might help, though not too flagrant a stoop. Lynn stood on the cobbles of the bridge in a defensive, inelegant, round-shouldered slouch, and was rewarded by seeing the frown on her interrogator's face deepen. The stance was not what you would expect from one chosen by the Goddess. Lynn could sense the anxious concern of her companions, but dared not raise her eyes to them. Instead, she tried to force herself into the role she must adopt—the bewildered farm worker, stopped on her journey home.

"It's a nice horse." The Guard's tone made it clear that flattery was not her purpose.

"Yes, ma'am."

"Is it yours?"

"No. The boss said I could borrow it because—" Lynn was about to launch into their prepared story, but the Guard cut her off.

"This farm you work on, it's near Longhill?"

"Yes, ma'am."

"What's on it?" The Guard's question had moved beyond the scope planned for, forcing Lynn into the realm of improvisation.

"Er...pigs."

"How many?"

"Two hundred saddlebacks and fifty dwarf short tails...and th-there's a few chickens as well. The b-boss likes her eggs." With the aggression of the rapid questions, Lynn did not have to worry that acting frightened would seem out of character.

The Guard paused in her interrogation and looked at Lynn thoughtfully, then she glanced across at one of the Militia, a sour-faced woman with a sergeant's badge on her black jerkin. "Weren't you telling me that your mother used to keep pigs?" the Guard asked deliberately.

The sergeant looked startled for a moment but then nodded and said slowly, "Yes, she did. She even had a couple of the dwarf short tails, but she lost them to a dose of colic from eating border weed."

Lynn did not wait to be asked before speaking. "Dwarf short tails with colic? Are you sure? The whole reason you keep the short tails is they don't mind the coarse stuff, else you wouldn't bother, 'cause there's sod-all meat on them."

The Militia sergeant pursed her lips. "Maybe they weren't short tails, then. They were those short dark ones with the long snout."

"Sicross blacks? They'd have to eat a lot of border weed to get sick, and anyway, they're finicky eaters. I'm surprised they'd touch the weed. It's the saddlebacks that are the hungry buggers with no sense and weak stomachs."

"Is that right?" the Guard said slowly, re-entering the interrogation, while her eyes shifted between Lynn and the sergeant in black.

The Militiawoman had a sneer on her face that was probably intended as a confident smile. "Oh yes. She works on a pig farm. Unless, of course, Imprinters spend their spare time reading up on how to care for different breeds of pig."

The Guard frowned. Her eyes locked on Lynn's face, but then she stood back and jerked her thumb toward the horse. "Okay. You can go."

"Yes, ma'am."

Lynn put her foot in the stirrup and hopped up into her saddle. The four set off in a line, the horses' hooves clattering loudly on the cobblestones. Each second, Lynn expected to be called back, but the shout never came. Only when they were over the bridge and heading on toward the town did she dare glance over her shoulder. The soldiers had moved to the applecart. A Militiawoman was standing on the tailboard, poking about with a long pole. Even the Guard in red and gold was no longer giving them any attention.

The four rode in silence for a while, but at last Kim cleared her throat and said, "You did well."

"Thank you." Lynn drew a deep breath.

Suddenly, the tension seemed to break for everyone at the same time. Lynn had to fight back the urge to giggle like a child. It had been a close thing, but it was over. Ahead of her, Mirle was leaning forward, shaking her head in amused disbelief. Carma started whistling a song that Lynn was fairly certain had the chorus of "Off and Over the Hills."

Kim spoke again, although this time in a tone of dry humor. "Er... Lynn. Do Imprinters spend their spare time reading up on how to care for different breeds of pig?"

Lynn shrugged. "Well, I can't speak for the rest, but I never needed to. I'm a pig farmer's daughter. I spent the first twelve years of my life looking after them."

Kim's shoulders shook with subdued laughter. "Right. I should have guessed."

"Oh, so you know a bit about pigs, then?" Mirle sniffed, making a play of banal gossip. "You might be even more useful on the farm than we expected."

"You've got pigs there?" Lynn sounded thrilled.

"Yes, lots of them. You mean Kim didn't tell you?" Carma joined in.

"No."

Carma shook her head in mock censure. "Honestly, Captain. That's the last time we send you to try and talk an Imprinter into joining us. You left the best part out."

❖

They arrived at Westernfort in the middle of June. There had been a few further encounters with the Militia, but nothing to match the bridge over the Coldwater, and once they were in the mountains, the fear of pursuit was gone completely. Even so, the Rangers set a fast pace through the wildlands. Over four months would have passed by the time they returned, and Kim was eager to know how things had progressed with the valley defenses.

The hard riding was no longer a problem for Lynn, and the mountain scenery was beautiful enough to bring tears to her eyes.

Sometimes, lying wrapped in her blankets at night waiting for sleep to overtake her, she was overwhelmed by a wave of disbelief. She had actually escaped; the sense of freedom was too much to comprehend. She would never again be swallowed by the gloom, the repetition, the hopelessness of the temple. It was quite literally true that she would rather die than go back.

Lynn would have declared herself utterly happy, were it not for an awareness that with each passing day, Kim was becoming more distant. The Ranger captain was still friendly and supportive, still fun to talk to, but this only made it worse as it became apparent that Kim would much rather be talking to someone else. The closer they got to Westernfort, the more common it was for Kim to be riding beside Mirle or Carma, joking and chatting with them. In such a small group, the shift in preferred company was painfully obvious, and all the more painful as Lynn felt her attraction to the tall Ranger growing ever stronger. She no longer had any doubts about how much she wanted to give, merely despair at knowing Kim did not want to take it. The daily close contact of the journey made it unbearable. Lynn felt relief when the party finally reached the brow of a hill and a distant barricade across the entrance to a hanging valley was pointed out to her—the walls of Westernfort.

The work on the path to the high village was complete. An easy climb, but so narrow that they were forced to dismount and go in single file. As they walked up, Lynn tilted her head back. The stout timbers of the wall were hanging directly above her. Friendly faces peered over the parapet; scouts had already carried advance news of their arrival. Yet a shiver ran down Lynn's spine as she imagined what it would be like to fight her way up that path with arrows rather than smiles raining down from above. She pitied any Guard who was ordered to storm the valley—and surely one day an attack on Westernfort would come, and many brave women would die on the very path she was now walking. Lynn's eyes dropped to the ground. For a second, the rocks beneath her feet seemed red with blood, then Lynn shook her head to dispel the image. She was an Imprinter, not a fortuneteller.

At the top of the climb, they passed under the gateway and saw a boisterous throng of heretics and Rangers standing inside the wall to welcome them. The instant they were through, Kim, Carma, and Mirle were swept away to be greeted enthusiastically by a string of women. However, Lynn sensed the familiar, reserved circle of awe start to grow around her. Once again, she was isolated, on the edge, and then an elderly woman limped over and gave a crooked smile.

"I take it that you're Lynn?"

"Er...yes. And you must be Gina."

During the journey, Mirle had spoken much about the elderly ex-Sister, ex-Imprinter, recounting tales of her life, her discoveries, her beliefs. Lynn still was not sure what to make of the stories, except for an innate respect for anyone who would so utterly outrage Sister Dunsin.

The heretic leader gave a snort of amusement. "I won't bother asking how you recognized me. I do hope you're going to be happy here, because if not, you've got a hell of a long walk back."

Lynn stopped short and then dropped her head as a smile spread over her face. The brusque humor held more real welcome than any polite formula. Suddenly, she felt part of the gathering, a feeling that increased as Gina linked an arm through hers for the short walk to the village.

At the point where the valley walls broadened out, they paused for Lynn to take in the view; the unbroken sweep of high mountains surrounding the valley, the cliff faces running down to the forest of dark fir trees lining the lake, and the newly cleared fields, planted with grain. The village was close by. It was mainly a collection of crude round huts, but there was one stone-built construction with a slate-tiled roof and heating flues. Gina pointed to this building.

"We've managed to complete our first real house. It's not too wonderful, but it has a proper floor and roof. And you'll be pleased to hear that both you and I have been voted a room in there." Gina paused briefly. "Captain Ramon has as well, but I doubt they'll wheedle her out of the barrack hut with the other Rangers."

As if hearing her name, Kim appeared at their side. The Ranger seemed less confident than normal. She took in the village and farm with an uncertain frown and said, "I did warn you it wasn't luxurious. We're working on it, and one day it will be...well, a proper village. I hope you don't think I misled you..."

Lynn smiled. "I'm not disappointed with it."

"You're not?" Kim sounded surprised. "It's not quite as civilized as you're used to."

"It's not quite as much like a prison as I'm used to," Lynn corrected. She turned through a complete circle to take in the whole panorama.

"It's got mountains and pigs. What more could I want?" But silently she answered herself. *You.*

❖

The stone house had six small private rooms opening onto a communal space. Proper furniture was non-existent, but Lynn and Gina had improvised two chairs in the shared area, and they sat talking together quietly. The morning sunlight streamed in through the open doorway, carrying with it the fresh smell of the fir trees and the sounds of people congregating outside. Sounds that left Lynn feeling unaccountably nervous. Four days had passed since she had reached Westernfort, enough for her to rest after the journey. Now it was time to begin her work. But she was in no hurry to go outside. In fact, she was feeling the childish urge to hide.

The door to her own bedroom was temptingly close at hand. The remaining five rooms had gone to Gina and other elderly heretics since, as anticipated, Kim had chosen to share the rough living conditions of the other Rangers. Lynn was embarrassed to be singled out for privileged treatment, especially as there were many frail old women still in the primitive round huts, but she had less success than Kim in declining the honor. The heretics may well have rejected the idea of a Goddess who had chosen Lynn for her own, but that did not mean that they thought an Imprinter should be treated as an ordinary person.

"Just as long as I can still imprint." Lynn spoke her fears aloud.

"Do you have any reason to doubt it?" Gina asked.

"In myself, no. But"—Lynn paused and looked down at her clasped hands—"before now, I've always had the support and sanctity of the temple behind me. Sisters telling me what to do."

"The Sisters' advice was helpful?" Gina said ironically.

"Well, no, not in the detail. But it meant I didn't have to take responsibility for..." Lynn's words trailed away as she reached the core of her uncertainty, facing it fully for the first time. She continued speaking. "I guess that's it. The Sisters always made sure I knew it wasn't really me creating a new life, a new soul. I was just a conduit for the Goddess. But now I have to ask myself whether I, personally, have the right to create a new human being."

"But the doing has always been in your hands, and yours alone.

Celaeno isn't a Goddess. I admit I don't know all the things that go into a starship, but I'm damned certain there isn't a piece of machinery up there that bestows moral prerogatives."

Lynn sighed deeply. "In my head I've a strong suspicion you may be right. But in my heart..."

Gina reached over and squeezed her shoulder. "Then follow your heart, trust your own feelings. Stop looking for absolute values and focus on the practical facts."

"How do you mean?"

"Do you have any doubts about whether Chip and Katryn will make good parents?"

"Of course not."

"And you know how much they want a child?"

"Yes."

"So why are you sitting in here when you could be doing something about it?"

Gina had a talent for reducing complex ethical questions to the breathtakingly simple. Sometimes Lynn felt dizzy trying to keep up. Sometimes she just had to take things on trust. She shook her head in bemusement and then said, "You're probably right."

"Of course I'm right. I'm always right. It's one of the best things about me. Now come on. I can guarantee Chip and Katryn are even more nervous than you, so don't keep them waiting." Gina got to her feet and started for the door. "Have they decided who's going to carry the baby?"

Lynn caught up at her side. "Yes, Chip."

"Really? I've been told it gives a fascinating insight into a relationship which one chooses to bear the first child." Gina frowned. "But I haven't a blessed clue what it's supposed to mean."

It was against all precedent to perform an imprinting in the open air, but there was no room that would hold the numbers who wanted to be present. In fact, every Ranger and heretic, without exception, had gathered in the open space outside the stone house. They all knew there would be little to see, but that was not the point. They would be witnessing the start of their future.

Lynn looked up at the clear unblemished blue of the sky. For a second, her doubts resurfaced, and then they were utterly swept away. Lynn took a deep breath of the sweet fresh air. She understood the truth of what Gina had said; regardless of whether Celaeno was a Goddess or a spacecraft, imprinting was something in which she should follow her own heart. She stepped into the center of the open space and beckoned Chip and Katryn out to meet her. As Gina had predicted, both looked uncharacteristically nervous, shuffling from foot to foot. Lynn gave her most encouraging smile. "Are you ready?" she asked.

They both nodded. Katryn swallowed and asked, "What do you want us to do?" while Chip looked too tense to speak.

It was a good question. The traditional arrangement was undoubtedly symbolic of something, but there was no altar for Chip to lie on, and Lynn had never been comfortable with the sacrifice-like overtones. She smiled. There was no need to try to replicate the temple procedures. All that was necessary was that there be physical contact between them. The new life was something they three were going to create together as a shared act, and her heart told her exactly how she wanted to do things.

"We should sit in a circle and take each other's hand."

At first the two Rangers seemed surprised, but then they matched her smile.

The ground felt reassuringly right beneath Lynn as she sat down. Her earlier doubts seemed laughable. She was an Imprinter, and the temple was not a tribute to life. It was a prison where the Sisters tried to keep captive the source of their power, but life was meant to be free.

She took their hands and gave her last few instructions, "I'm afraid this might be a bit boring for you. It will probably take a couple of hours. But while I'm in the trance, you can talk. It won't disturb me. Just don't let go of my hands. Okay?"

Chip and Katryn nodded, then their heads turned slightly and they met each other's eyes in a deep, searching gaze. The look Lynn had seen so many couples exchange before. For a second, her concentration slipped, but she restrained the urge to search the crowd to see if she could spot Kim. The heart was not always a reliable guide. Instead, she focused on the feel of the two hands she held, the texture, the warmth, the life within them. Waves of energy began to flow around the circle, carrying her away and sweeping her effortlessly into the imprinting trance.

CHAPTER TWENTY—OVER THE EDGE

The sun beat down mercilessly on the vegetable patch at the edge of the village. Lynn paused to wipe the sweat from her eyes, then stood back leaning on the hoe, and contemplated the long line of weeds that still stretched in front of her. It was backbreaking, thirsty work, but it was not supposed to be a race. No one would criticize her if she took a short break. In fact, no one would criticize her if she did not lift a finger at all around the farm, which was part of the reason why she tended to push herself so hard. For too much of her life, she had been an abstract object of veneration. Now she was going to insist on being treated like everyone else. But it was not necessary to kill herself from thirst. Lynn speared the hoe into the ground and walked back down the row of tomato plants to where the goatskin water flask lay beside the road.

She had just settled on the grass bank and uncorked the flask when a shadow fell across her.

"How's the weeding going?" a voice asked.

Lynn looked up. Chip was standing above her. "Slowly."

"You don't have to do it, you know."

"Yes, I do. It's for the good of my soul."

"But I thought you were guaranteed a place in heaven as one of Celaeno's chosen," Chip said lightly.

"And even as we speak, the Chief Consultant is probably trying to talk the Goddess into reconsidering my status."

"Does that worry you?" Chip sounded genuinely curious.

"Not too much."

"Do you think Gina's right about Celaeno and the Elder-Ones?"

Lynn wrinkled her nose. "She might be. But even if she isn't and I die and get sent to hell, at least I won't have to spend all eternity listening to Sister Dunsin."

Chip laughed and sat down beside her. "You know, you're nothing like how I thought an Imprinter would be."

That's what Kim once said to me, Lynn thought, but did not voice the words aloud. She passed the water flask to Chip. "I'm sorry to be a disappointment."

"Oh no. You certainly haven't been that," Chip said, looking meaningfully at her own stomach, although it would be a few months yet before there was any noticeable sign of her pregnancy.

"But I'm feeling a bit superfluous at the moment, now that I've run out of people who want children."

"You still have a fair amount of work to do, monitoring us and the babies."

"That's hardly a full-time job, and Gina or Lilian would be quite capable of looking after you. Even Carma could, as long as there were no complications. I only do it because"—Lynn paused, looking wistful—"because I've never had the chance to see the babies develop before."

"Really?"

"Yes. Normally a couple only gets the one appointment with the Imprinter. But what I'm most looking forward to is when the babies are born and I get to see them and hold them."

"I think Katryn and I are quite looking forward to that part ourselves." For once, Chip's voice was quietly serious.

Lynn smiled at her. "Anyway, I've fulfilled my commitments as an Imprinter, and I'm not needed as a doctor or a vet, so I might as well be useful as a weeder."

Chip looked solemn. "Well, I don't quite know how to tell you this, but..." She pointed to a tiny green shoot. "You've missed one."

"Thank you." Lynn barged the Ranger with her shoulder. "So what's your excuse for sitting here, doing nothing?"

"I'm waiting for Kim. We're making some more cover points for archers up on the sides of the wall. She wants us to go and check out the angles." Chip looked sideways at Lynn. "I don't suppose you've seen Kim recently?"

"No. I hardly get to see her at all these days." Lynn fought to keep her voice neutral.

"Don't you two—" Chip broke off guiltily and then glanced toward the village. Whatever she might have been about to ask was abandoned at the sight of Kim walking along the road to where they sat. "Ah, here she comes now." Chip scrambled to her feet, brushing dead grass from her clothes. "What kept you?" she called out.

"Nothing worth mentioning. I'm sorry," Kim replied as she drew close and then tagged on the end, "Good morning, Lynn."

"Good morning."

"Right, shall we go and see about the archers?" Kim's attention was immediately back with Chip. The two Rangers headed off on the short walk to the wall.

Lynn sat and watched them go. Then her head sank and she pinched the bridge of her nose between finger and thumb, fighting back the tears. That last exchange was the nearest thing to a conversation she'd had with Kim for days. The Ranger captain was definitely avoiding her, but sitting and crying about it was going to achieve nothing. Lynn marched up the line of tomatoes, seized the hoe, and re-attacked the weeds with the force of her despair.

❖

The end of the row of plants was getting close, and Lynn's thoughts were shifting on to the subject of lunch. Suddenly a desperate cry rang out over the fields, coming from the direction of the wall. The scream was all the more ominous for being cut off abruptly. Work across the valley stopped as people looked toward the source of the sound. Lynn also stared at the wall, shielding her eyes from the sun. She could see people moving to one end, where a massive, weathered cliff face overshadowed the mouth of the valley. Lynn knew a stairway was being cut into this crag to give access to higher viewpoints. Women were gathering around the bottom of the steps, and then one broke away, racing frantically back to the village.

"What's up?" Lynn called as the runner approached.

"Renie's fallen. I'm getting a rope," the woman replied, gasping but not breaking stride as she shot past.

Lynn tossed her hoe aside and began running to the wall. By the time she got there, clusters of people were blocking the steps. Lynn began to squeeze her way through, but at that moment, Kim's voice shouted from above. "If you don't have a reason to be here, then back off. Sergeant Horte, get these people off the steps and don't let anyone up without permission. Gomez, Akmar, we're going to need a stretcher. See to it."

People shuffled back, needing only the slightest urging from the sergeant, while the two named Rangers immediately began hunting for items to use in improvising a stretcher, but Lynn carried on undeterred. Horte looked at her uncomfortably, clearly unwilling to stand in the way of an Imprinter, despite her captain's orders. "Um...I'm not supposed..." she began.

"It's okay. I've got a reason. It sounds like a healer is needed."

The Ranger sergeant still looked unsure, but Lynn had already pushed past and was on the steps. The path followed the route of an eroded crevice in the cliff face, in places climbing as steeply as a stepladder. The final few meters had been hacked into the side of a vertical buttress before leveling out. Lynn clambered up, using her hands as well as her feet, and emerged onto the end of a wide platform of rock. On one side, the cliffs continued up, but the other side ended abruptly in a crumbling edge with a panoramic view over the flood plain below the valley.

It was easy to see why the effort had been made to open the way up. At that point, the cliff projected beyond the mouth of the valley. The ledge presented a clear view across the front of the wall, allowing the entire area to be subjected to crossfire. Anyone trying to climb the barricade was likely to get an arrow in the back. Judging from the piles of rubble, work to level the platform and provide cover for archers was currently in progress.

Kim, Chip, and two other Rangers were already there, standing back from the precipice and talking quietly. They all glanced around as Lynn arrived. "Someone is injured?" she asked before anyone else had the chance to speak.

"Yes. Renie. She's..." Kim pointed vaguely. Clearly, Lynn's unexpected appearance had caught her by surprise, but she recovered quickly when the Imprinter stepped to the edge. Kim grabbed Lynn's arm and pulled her back. "Watch what you're doing. We don't want two of you down there."

Lynn looked at the restraining hand with irritation and then raised her eyes to Kim's. "I'm not stupid. I'll take care. But someone with medical knowledge should look at her."

For once, Kim seemed unsure of what to say. Lynn shook her

arm free, then knelt down beside the edge and peered over. The cliff dropped for more than a hundred meters until it reached the level where smashed boulders littered the ground between fir trees. A sudden onset of vertigo threatened to overwhelm Lynn, and the difference between up and down was lost, but she managed to tear her eyes from the distance and refocus closer at hand. At most points, little stood in the way of a body plunging to certain death, but Renie had been lucky and her fall had been stopped by a narrow cleft in the rock, scarcely five meters below the platform. The woman was still alive, that much was certain. However, she had a broken leg with other possible injuries, and her state of consciousness was open to question.

The sound of feet on the steps announced the runner's return with a long coil of rope. Kim took it off the Ranger and said, "Any volunteers to go over?"

"Me," Lynn said immediately.

"No." Kim's rebuttal was equally swift.

"Yes." Lynn shifted back from the edge and stood up. "Renie should be examined before she's moved, and since it has to be someone adept with the healer sense, you've got the choice of me, Gina, or Lilian. Unless you think Renie should lie there until Carma gets back from patrol. I think she's due in tomorrow."

Kim's face set in a frown. Neither the crippled heretic leader nor the eighty-year-old Cloner was a feasible candidate for the job, but she was obviously unhappy with the idea of Lynn going over the edge. "You're too valuable to risk."

"Then don't drop me."

They stared at each other in confrontation while the others on the platform shifted uneasily. In the end, Kim gave way, although she insisted in personally tying the rope around Lynn and double-checking the knot.

A small flutter of panic unsettled Lynn's stomach when she turned around and stepped back off the ledge, but she fixed her eyes on her feet and refused to look down, refused to even think about the drop beneath her. Soon she had reached the spot where Renie lay. Lynn called out to those above to stop letting out the line. The crevice was too narrow for her to get a proper foothold, so she was forced to semi-dangle as she made the examination. At the touch of Lynn's hands, the injured woman's eyelids quivered open, and with the return to consciousness, her face contorted in pain.

"It's all right, you're going to be fine," Lynn said.

Hardly surprisingly, Renie looked dazed and unable to reply. Lynn placed a hand on her forehead and gently pushed her back into a deep sleep before continuing to investigate the injuries. The fall had left the woman severely bruised, her right leg was broken, one shoulder was dislocated, and she had a potentially worrying blow to the head, but no other injury that had to be dealt with before she was moved. After an awkward struggle, Lynn removed the belt from Renie's waist and bound her two legs together in a temporary splint. Performing the task was tricky while hanging half-suspended. The most difficult part of all was getting enough slack in the rope to put two loops under Renie's arms, but finally the injured woman was secure and Lynn called out to be hauled up.

The ascent was worse than the way down. Lynn had no control over where she was going. It took all her effort, plus a few knocks and scrapes, to fend her comatose patient away from the jagged cliff face. Fortunately, the distance was not great and soon they reached the platform. Hands reached down and dragged them both to safety. The same hands also assisted Lynn to her feet and continued to clasp her, even after she had regained her balance and was well away from the edge.

With some surprise, Lynn realized that Kim was the one holding her, hugging her close—unexpected, though possibly not unnecessary, since her legs were feeling slightly wobbly now that she was standing on firm ground again, with time to think about what she had just done. She tried to remind herself that she had a patient who needed attention, but it was so tempting to spend a few seconds more, leaning against Kim and feeling Kim's arms around her.

"Are you all right?" Kim asked softly.

"Yes, it was Renie who fell." Lynn tried to sound nonchalant, but her legs were still wobbly, and she was no longer sure if this was due only to the memory of dangling over the long drop. She looked up and felt her pulse leap as her eyes met Kim's.

But then, in the space of a heartbeat it changed. The Ranger's face became blank, her eyes broke from the contact, and her arms fell away. As if on cue, a voice called out from beside them on the ledge, asking for advice about arranging the injured woman on the stretcher. Feeling half dazed, Lynn turned to the group around Renie and tried to immerse herself in the task of supervising the stretcher's departure down the steep flight of steps—an awkward maneuver because the stairway had not been cut with the current situation in mind. Plenty of willing hands were available though, and soon Lynn and her patient had left the ledge.

❖

The sounds of the stretcher bearers faded, leaving only the two officers behind. Kim sighed and leaned back against the rock wall behind her, her eyes fixed on the distant mountains on the other side of the flood plain. Chip stood a little way off, studying her friend thoughtfully.

"So just how do things stand between Lynn and you?" Chip asked at last.

"How do you mean?"

"Oh, come on, Kim. You know exactly what I mean."

"We're friends."

"And you weren't in a total panic every second that Lynn was dangling in midair." Chip was at her most sarcastic.

"Of course I was. She's our only Imprinter, and I like her."

"That's all you feel for her?"

Kim stopped and took a few deep breaths. When she spoke again, her voice was quieter. "It doesn't matter what I feel for her. She doesn't want me. I told you about that."

"You told me that on the first night after she escaped from the temple, when she was tired, confused, and in pain, you gave her a three-second chance to disagree when *you* told *her* that she didn't want you. And now you're totally determined to take that as the final answer."

Kim's face hardened. "Do you see her chasing after me now?"

"You're running away from her so fast I doubt she'd catch you."

"When have you ever known me to run away from an attractive woman?"

"Well, since you're asking, once or twice."

"Oh, be serious."

"I am." And in truth, there was not a trace of humor in Chip's voice.

"So what are you getting at?" For her part, Kim was starting to sound angry.

"What I'm getting at is that you seem to be going out of your way to make yourself miserable."

"Why would I do that?"

"Because of your parents."

"How do they come into this?" Kim snapped back.

Chip was silent for a few seconds, looking at the ground. "Guilt." She raised her eyes to meet Kim's. "I remember when you first joined the squadron. You were like an over-wound spring. And I remember your face as you stood over the body of the first bandit you'd killed and you realized that revenge wasn't really what you wanted. I've seen the way you raced through women as if it was some sort of competition, until you worked out that a never-ending stream of one-night stands wasn't what you wanted either."

"Oh stop—" Kim began, but Chip cut her off.

"No. Let me finish. What you really want is a new family, but you feel guilty that you survived when your parents didn't. You feel guilty that revenge isn't enough for you, and most of all, you feel guilty at the merest hint that a relationship is becoming serious. As if you might be accused of trying to replace your parents and sisters with someone else." Chip sighed. "And I don't think I'm telling you anything you haven't already worked out for yourself."

"If you think I already know it, why are you bothering to tell me?"

"Because I'm your friend, and it's painful to watch you at the moment. I think what you want is Lynn, and I think you're frightened at how much you want her. You're feeling disloyal to your parents, but if they could see you now, do you think they'd be happy to watch you avoiding Lynn, to know you'd renounced any attempt to rebuild a family for yourself? Is that what they'd have wanted for you?"

Kim's anger had faded to a sullen resistance. "But like I said before, Lynn is our only Imprinter. And for anyone to have a family, it means that things are going to have to stay exactly as they are." She pushed herself away from the rock wall and began to head for the steps down, but Chip caught her arm.

"Okay. I'm pregnant at the moment, so maybe it's easy for me to say this, but everyone here chose to leave the Sisters' lands for one reason or another. Until you went back for Lynn, none of us thought we had any chance of having children. But now everyone who wants a baby is expecting one, and I don't see that anybody has the right to ask you and Lynn to sacrifice the rest of your lives on the off chance that they might want more at some stage in the future."

Kim stopped for a second, looking at Chip's earnest face, then freed her arm and walked on down the steps without a word.

CHAPTER TWENTY-ONE—
A LEGACY FROM THE ELDER-ONES

Nothing else under the Goddess's wide skies could complain with the same frantic desperation as a piglet. From the succession of agonized squeals, anyone would have assumed that Lynn was trying to tear it limb from limb. However, the sounds stopped the instant the small creature was put back in the pen, and were replaced by happy grunts as it charged into its sisters, in a piglet's distinctive impersonation of a small round battering ram on legs. The sow was completely unmoved by it all.

Lynn grinned at the antics and then turned back to Gina and Lilian. They were at the pigpens in the lowlands, checking the state of the young animals and making plans for the cloning work that would soon be beginning on the adults. The tour had concluded with Lynn insisting on lavishing some completely unreciprocated affection on a piglet.

"It's a shame we don't have a couple of the sicross blacks; this valley would suit them perfectly," Lynn said, her thoughts turning again to the practical needs of the community.

Lilian disagreed. "They'd do all right for food, but they wouldn't like the winters. We'd have to put them all up in shelters, and we'd still probably lose a few. The old grays are a lot hardier."

The debate continued. Gina listened with a thoughtful expression, and at last joined in. "It seems as if what we want is something combining the best traits of the sicross and the grays?"

"Ideally, yes," Lynn agreed.

"So why don't you do it?"

Lynn stopped, stunned. "You mean imprint from one breed onto another?"

"Why not?" Gina asked innocently, although she surely knew

what the answer would be.

"Because they'd be unique, so they'd have a soul. And you can't eat something with a soul."

"You're right, you can't. You'd be much better off with a knife and fork."

Both Gina and Lilian chuckled at Lynn's confusion as she stood, hands on hips, looking between the elderly pair and trying to work out just how much of what Gina had said was intended as a joke. She had still not found her voice by the time they separated, Lilian going to take a final look at some sheep she was concerned about, while Gina headed toward the path up to Westernfort. Lynn hurried to catch up with the heretic leader.

"You're going to tell me that it's not true the Elder-Ones forbade us to eat anything that hadn't been cloned. It was just something the Sisters made up?" Lynn's voice was halfway between irony and astonishment.

"The Sisters may seem dull and narrow-minded, but you should never underestimate their imagination," Gina joked, and then spoke more seriously. "And they had a basis to work on. The Elder-Ones did tell us not to eat anything that reproduces sexually, but they said it more in the way of practical rather than religious advice. It's an easy way of picking out the native fauna of the planet, all of which is poisonous to us. They also knew that Imprinters would be so rare they'd have a full-time job keeping up with the needs of the human population. Hence they arrived at only having cloned animals for food. What the Sisters made up was all the nonsense about unique individuals having a soul and cloned ones not."

"But..." Lynn started to say something and then stopped. Her head was still twisting the ideas around when they reached the bottom of the path to the upper valley and began the climb.

The trouble was that Gina made far more sense than the Sisters ever had. An Imprinter's training included reading from the Elder-Ones' books. It was essential to do her work. The Sisters did not like it; they would rather have given a censored version, but they did not understand what was involved well enough to know which sections of the books could be abridged safely. They settled for providing convoluted theological rationalizations for all the inconvenient parts of the books, parts such as mention of Y-chromosomes. Gina's explanation was far more coherent. Even so, the moral step of imprinting animals for food was hard to contemplate.

"Are you still thinking?" Gina asked cheerfully.

"Yes. And I'm not convinced."

"I could tell that from your face." Gina stopped and pointed down at the various herds that were spread across the plain below. "Think about it. All of these animals are descended from gene stock the Elder-Ones brought from the home planet, where they had been bred for human use. Originally they reproduced sexually, just like the indigenous fauna here, so for maybe," Gina shrugged, "thousands of years, our ancestors were quite happily eating unique creatures."

"Then why is cloning humans banned?"

"In part, that's a very easy question to answer. The Sisters get all their money from imprinting fees. They also get most of their power from having a monopoly on human reproduction. They'd be happier if they could keep the Cloners in the temples as well, but it's not practical to have all the farm animals brought to them, so they have to let the Cloners travel freely. Their biggest threat is from a group like us, who move off into the wildlands with a Cloner, but the rebels would only last for one generation, as long as the Sisters impress on people that you must never, never, never clone a human. That's why they drum the idea into people so hard. And very successful they are at it." Gina gave a wry smile. "Even we heretics couldn't quite bring ourselves to take the step, though we did discuss it a lot."

"Didn't the Elder-Ones ban human cloning?"

"Not entirely, although they thought it should only be done as a last resort."

"Why?"

"Ah. Now we get to much trickier ground, and to be honest I don't fully understand it. I don't think any of us now can," Gina said as she turned to continue walking up the slope. "But I've given it a lot of thought."

"And...?"

Gina said nothing for a dozen steps and then she asked, "Have you ever wondered why we only imprint couples who are partners? Why a prospective mother doesn't just choose the most intelligent or healthiest woman she knows and ask her to donate a few DNA sequences?"

"Er...no." Lynn frowned, realizing that the idea had never even occurred to her before.

"Human beings are a pair-bonding species. In theory, that means a male and a female form a long-term bond that holds the couple together until the offspring produced by the union reach adulthood. In practice, it was never that straightforward. This planet is evidence that the human need to form pair bonds is completely unaffected by the absence of one sex. Pair bonding is the reason for the link between procreation and relationships; it's a legacy from the Elder-Ones, though I'm not sure whether it's cultural or innate. Whichever it is, I don't think it's possible for us to grasp all the"—Gina waved her hands—"symbolic importance our ancestors attached to their own sexual behavior. Just imagine, by the simple act of making love with your partner, you could produce a child. They combined all the irrationality of love with the mysticism of the creation of life." Gina sighed. "All of which is a long, roundabout way of explaining why, when it got to human reproduction, the Elder-Ones could be arbitrary, illogical, and occasionally, totally inane. Cloning humans is a good example."

"Which is your roundabout way of explaining why you don't know the answer," Lynn teased.

"Well, I did come across worries about rich egotists creating thousands of copies of themselves, but to be honest, it all read like the rationalizing of the Sisters. I think the reason for the ban was more of a gut feeling a child with only one genetic parent would be an attack on the sanctity of their dual-sex relationships."

They reached the top of the path and passed under the gateway in the wall. Before them, the buildings of Westernfort nestled in the well-tended farmlands. Evening was close at hand and work was stopping for the day. People were drifting back from the distant fields. The light was softening to a golden glow, and the peacefulness of the scene carried Lynn's thoughts along as she mulled over what Gina had said, trying to resolve the conflicts between logic and ethics.

They were halfway between wall and village when the crunching of gravel alerted them to someone overtaking them on the road. Lynn glanced over her shoulder, and her mood of tranquil reflection evaporated. At first, it seemed as if Kim would walk past with only a word of acknowledgment, then she appeared to change her mind and slowed down to match Gina's limping gait. Lynn averted her face and fixed her eyes on the distant ranks of fir trees, while she made sure her expression was under control. She was certain it was not mere chance that Kim had tagged on beside Gina rather than her when joining them to walk three abreast.

"You've been looking at the animals?" Kim asked in the rigid tones of someone straining to be casual.

Gina glanced at Lynn before answering. "Yes. We were down there talking to Lilian."

"You'll be starting cloning soon?"

"In a couple of months."

Again Lynn had ignored the chance to answer, and an awkward silence fell on the group. She was aware of Gina glancing in her direction, as if waiting for her to speak. But eventually the elderly heretic carried on. "In fact, I was talking to Lynn about imprinting the animals rather than cloning. It's our chance to improve the livestock. What do you think people would feel about it?"

"You can answer for the heretics better than me. But some of the Rangers wouldn't be at all happy. I don't think I'd be totally easy myself," Kim said after a little thought.

"And that still goes for you, Lynn?" Gina's head turned to the other side.

"Er...Yes."

"So how about horses? Do you think you could ride something with a soul?" Gina was clearly fighting to keep the conversation going, but no one spoke until Gina elbowed Kim to get a reply.

"Um...maybe...probably. Most Rangers credit their horses with human personalities as it is."

"And Lynn, you'd be happy doing the imprinting?"

"Yes, well...happier."

The silence returned, worse than before, but to Lynn's relief, they reached the first of the buildings and Kim turned off toward the hut she shared with nine other Rangers. The two other women walked across the central square of the village and entered the stone house. Inside the common room, the two residents whose turn it was to cook supper were busy at the hearth. Lynn gave a hasty wave of greeting and headed for her own room, but Gina caught her arm.

"Have you got time to talk?"

Gina's question was verging on the rhetorical. Lynn shrugged by way of answer but made no other comment as she was guided into the room Gina shared with her partner. In recognition of her status as leader and the difficulty she had getting up from the floor, the village carpenters had made Gina a raised bed. It was the only item of private furniture to be found in Westernfort. Gina took a seat on the edge then pulled Lynn down beside her and said, "You know, it's really hard work keeping a conversation going between three people when two of them won't talk to each other."

"I'm sorry. I had my mind on other things." Lynn made the uninspired excuse.

"Obviously."

Lynn stared morosely at the floor, although she could feel Gina's eyes on her. The silence dragged on for such a long time that Lynn jumped when Gina spoke again. "The Elder-Ones' attitude toward relationships has implications for more than just cloning."

"Oh, does it?" Lynn tried to sound interested.

"Even when there were two sexes, people didn't always take someone from the other sex as a partner. When you start thinking it through, the whole thing becomes very confusing, and the Elder-Ones were just as confused as me, although in totally different ways and about completely different things. As I said, it's impossible for us to fully understand their viewpoint. For us, it makes no sense to even start asking whether relationships between women are legitimate, but for the Elder-Ones, it was an issue. Some thought it morally wrong, and at times during the history of the home planet, two people of the same sex who were lovers could be executed for it."

"Executed!" Despite herself, Lynn's attention was caught.

"It was an extreme response. Usually people were a tad more easygoing."

"But when they planned this world, didn't they..." Lynn's voice trailed off in bewilderment.

"Think?" Gina laughed as she finished the sentence for her. "Some did and some didn't. And at the time the Elder-Ones left the home planet, society was far more tolerant. Even between the Elder-Ones, attitudes differed. It's one of the things Peter McKay talks about in his diary. He thought same-sex relationships were all perfectly okay and normal, whereas others thought them slightly undesirable, and some were even less happy than that. I'm afraid Himoti herself was in the last group. Peter McKay admitted he was baffled by her, but there's evidence in his diary that the imposition of celibacy on her followers was due solely to Himoti's personal dislike of same-sex pairings." Gina looked soberly at Lynn. "Which is another very roundabout way of saying that I don't think there is any reason for you not to have a lover."

"Oh." Lynn's eyes returned to the floor, while a miserable frown creased her face.

Gina sat back and considered her for a while. "Now I admit, I didn't expect you to shout 'whoopee,' charge out the door, and fling yourself on the first woman you met, but I did expect a bit more of a reaction from you."

"Well... partly, what you say, I've half suspected myself, though I wasn't completely certain." Lynn's voice was flat.

"Oh, I'm not completely certain. Peter McKay wasn't a geneticist. There may be some valid reasons for Himoti's standpoint that he wasn't aware of. But I'd say it wasn't an unreasonable risk to take. If you wanted to."

Lynn took a deep breath and sighed. "That's the other part. Wanting. There's only..." Her voice died and her eyes squeezed shut in an agonized grimace.

"Kim," Gina suggested quietly.

Lynn needed several more strained breaths before she could go on. "I'm that obvious?"

"About as obvious as she is over you."

Lynn shook her head in denial. "She doesn't want me."

"How do you know?"

"She told me so."

"Did she, now?" Gina said in mock surprise. "Well, I wouldn't pay any attention to that. If I were you, I'd take her somewhere private and have a few words with her."

"Oh no," Lynn said swiftly. "Not after the last time I did that, in the stable." Her head sank even lower. "You heard about what they did to her?"

"The flogging?"

Lynn nodded. "Sister Dunsin made me watch. It was..." Lynn stopped, hunting for words. "It was awful and it was all my fault. And Kim...it's not surprising if she doesn't want anything to do with me. Sometimes I'm amazed she is even willing to wish me a good morning." Lynn buried her face in her hands.

Gina shifted over and put an arm around Lynn's shoulders. "I'm probably not the best person to get advice from. I came to the whole game a bit late in life myself. But I think it's like imprinting. You need to follow your heart."

Lynn nodded and slowly got to her feet. "I don't know. It's..."

"It's probably best if I mind my own business," Gina said in self-mockery. "I'm sure the pair of you will sort things out in the end."

"What's the point in having a leader who minds her own business?" The corner of Lynn's mouth twitched in a sad smile. "And I'm not sure if there's anything to sort out, but thanks for trying to help." She turned and left the room, leaving Gina still sitting, looking in despair at the closed door.

CHAPTER TWENTY-TWO—
THE FESTIVAL OF THE FIRSTBORN

The eleventh of August was the festival of the firstborn. At the temple in Landfall, the occasion would have been marked with great solemnity. The Sisters would have spent the day in fasting and prayer, and the Chief Consultant herself would have read to the assembled faithful from the book of the Elder-Ones. Streams of worshipers would have entered the temple to lay offerings at the various shrines, amid sweet, thick clouds of incense.

At Westernfort, the heretics decided to hold a party. They might not have seen the birth of the first children on the planet as an act of divine benevolence, but they did concede that it was an important historical date, and by the following year, they would have their own firstborn to celebrate.

The day was hot and sticky, an added incentive to quit the fields early, so that by midafternoon all work in the valley had ceased, except for the heroic chefs who braved the heat of the cooking fires to prepare food. By the time the sun was dropping behind the mountains, groups of women were congregating all around the village square, laughing and shouting to their friends. In one corner, a band with pipes and drums were engaged in a last practice before their skills would be called on to entertain their comrades.

Lynn sat with the players, adding her clear voice to their music. At the prompting of a couple of the Rangers, she even sang a few of the traditional hymns for the day, songs in praise of Celaeno. Some heretics frowned disapprovingly, but Gina only looked at her from the far side of the square, smiling and shaking her head. It was not a day to get dogmatic.

The light began to fade and a gentle evening breeze eased the temperature toward more bearable levels, enough for dancing to become an attractive idea. Soon the glow from the burning torches around the square fell on rows of couples, swirling in time to the music. Pots and baskets of food were set out on blankets at one side, drawing lines, and flagons of beer were passed from woman to woman.

When her singing was not required, Lynn wandered around the edge of the gathering, entranced. The scene called back memories of her childhood: the village celebrations, scuffling with her friends, eating honey cakes, and watching her parents dancing in the moonlight. She looked up. The sky was turning deepest blue, and the shining orb of Hardie hung overhead, a full moon, like a sign of blessing upon the exuberant revelers. Lynn was struck by the thought that there was more true gratitude for the gifts they had received in the wild cavorting before her than in all the ceremonies at the temple. The goddess who did not prefer the heretics' celebration of life to the Sisters' dead chants was not worth worshipping.

However, Lynn's pleasure in the party was not unqualified. She was not sure if she was avoiding Kim, or if Kim was avoiding her, but they always managed to be where the other one was not. An awareness started to nag at her, that a loosely defined and variable part of the square was out of bounds, and a worry that she would be the one to make a false step and cause an embarrassing encounter. Singing became a refuge, since her position was fixed at the front of the band, and it was therefore Kim's responsibility to maintain her distance.

By the time true dark had fallen, the strain had begun to tell, and the smile on Lynn's face was forced. Her dejection was not helped by the increasingly common sight of couples kissing in the shadows that thickened around the edges of the square. Singing would not provide an escape for much longer. Her voice was starting to fail, and the music was progressing to more riotous tunes that were not suited to vocal accompaniment.

Lynn felt as if a cloak of misery had wrapped itself around her, isolating her from the rest of the village. She was detached. A lone, pathetic observer on the sidelines.

❖

Lynn never got near enough to Kim to see that she was also

unhappy and taking only the most desultory part in the festivities, but others were watching them both and passing comments.

Chip stood at the side of the square with Katryn, their arms around each other's waist. They talked together quietly during a lull in the music, while their eyes moved between Kim and Lynn. At last, Chip gave her considered opinion. "I can't stand watching them any longer."

"But what can you do?"

"I'll think of something."

"You're more likely to put your foot in it," Katryn warned, but her partner only grinned.

"Of course. That's what I do best."

Chip disentangled herself, but Katryn caught her hand before she could go. "I'm serious. You're not going to get thanks from either of them if you make things worse."

"Can it get worse?"

"Of course it can. Just think things through first."

The music began again. Chip tilted her head to one side. "I've thought." She turned and walked off through the crowd, heading toward Lynn's last spotted location. She found the Imprinter standing alone and well to the back of the audience. Lynn's face held an expression of poorly concealed misery that changed to a half-hearted smile of greeting when she saw Chip approaching.

"How are you doing?" the Ranger asked.

"Okay," Lynn replied, although her tone would have implied otherwise.

"You're not dancing."

"I don't know how."

"What!"

The surprise in Chip's voice drew the first genuine smile from Lynn. "The last time I was at a party like this, I was eleven. I did dance with one of my friends, but I'm afraid it degenerated into a battle to stamp on each other's toes, and I've not had the chance to improve my technique since then. The Sisters don't encourage dancing."

"Come on, then. There's someone I want you to meet."

Chip did not allow any chance to protest. She slipped an arm through Lynn's and dragged her off around the square. After the first couple of forced steps, Lynn came along willingly enough, although

Chip suspected that she would rather have been left alone, and if she was hoping for something to distract her from brooding about Kim, she was going to be disappointed. The challenge would be to get Lynn to their destination before she knew where they were headed.

To Chip's satisfaction, the shadows and the interposing bodies did the trick. Triumphantly, she pulled Lynn to a stop in front of Kim and gave a mock bow. "Lynn, allow me to present Captain Ramon, who, I'm sure, will be more than happy to dance with you. She is without question the worst dancer in the whole squadron. So no matter how rusty your own skills might be, you can rest assured that you will have a partner who is in no position to offer criticism."

Chip had not been counting on immediate smiles and harmony, but the result fell short of her most pessimistic fears. For a few agonizing seconds, Kim and Lynn stared at each other, confusion becoming dismay, and in Kim's case, anger.

Her friend turned a furious face on Chip. "You can be a complete pain sometimes. If I'd wanted to dance with Lynn, I'd have asked her myself. I don't need you dumping people on me."

Kim's raised voice had heads swiveling in their direction. Lynn took a step back. Her words were blurted out. "I'm sorry. Please don't think I put her up to this. I wouldn't dream of imposing myself on you. I don't..." Lynn's voice choked, then she whirled around and dived off through the crowds.

"No, Lynn, wait. I didn't mean..." Kim called after her, presumably realizing too late how her angry words would have sounded, but Lynn kept going, her pace not slacking as she left the square and disappeared down the pathway between two of the surrounding buildings.

"Look what you've done." Kim turned on Chip again.

"*I've* done!"

"Yes, you."

"I merely suggested that the two of you might like to dance together. It was you who gave the impression you thought dancing with her had the general appeal of a shit sandwich."

Kim's eyes fixed on the point where Lynn had vanished. "Oh... Himoti's tits. What do I do now?"

"How about going after her and explaining what you really meant?"

"I can't do that."

Chip fixed her friend with a long, hard stare. "You know, Kim, for a brave woman, you can be a hell of a coward sometimes." Then she also turned and left the distraught Ranger captain alone.

❖

The sounds of the party faded behind Lynn as she headed out of the village and up the hillside beyond, walking with no particular goal in mind, just a wish to find somewhere where she could cry in solitude. Soon the cultivated fields ended, and she reached the narrow band of rough pasture below the tree-covered upper slopes. By now, the music from the village was no more than a distant rumble. Water gurgled nearby. Lynn followed the gentle sound, still climbing, until she reached the banks of a small stream cascading down the hillside.

The moonlight was bright enough to glitter on the spray and light the scene in silver-white and blue-black shadows. The air was soft and warm. A faint breeze stirred in the treetops and carried the rich scents of the firs. Lynn stopped walking at the point where the forest began and leaned her back against the trunk of a tree, watching the leaping stream and giving herself over to grief. Yet despite her expectation, tears did not come, just a numbing wave of hopelessness. For a while, she stood listening to the senseless babbling of the water, then she heard another sound, the rustle of someone approaching, following her trail through the knee-high grass.

"Lynn?" The voice was Kim's.

Lynn hesitated. What she most wanted to do was hide, but it was hardly an adult way to behave. She forced herself to answer. "I'm here."

Lynn folded her arms in front of herself, waiting defensively, as Kim joined her beside the stream, although the Ranger elected to maintain a few meters distance between them.

"Lynn? Are you all right?"

"Oh, of course," Lynn joked with mirthless irony.

"I...I wanted to say I'm sorry. I didn't mean that I didn't want to dance with you. I was just angry at Chip for playing the fool."

"That's okay."

Seconds passed while Kim stood watching her uncertainly. "Will you come back to the village with me?"

"No," Lynn said sharply, but then relented at little and added, "No. You go back. I'll be fine."

"I can't just leave you alone here."

Lynn could not force out an answer. She raised one hand to cover her eyes as a dry sob shook her body.

Kim took a few steps forward until she was within arm's reach. "Lynn. What's wrong?"

"You told me we could be friends." Lynn's voice was raw with pain.

"Aren't we?"

"This is the most we've spoken together for weeks." Lynn's hand dropped from her face and she stared, unseeing, at the ground in front of her feet.

"I...Yes, well...I'm sorry. I've been busy and..." Kim's disordered mumbling died.

"It seems more like you've been avoiding me."

"It's not that I don't want to be your friend."

"Simply that you don't like being anywhere near me?" Lynn suggested bitterly.

"No!"

"It's all right if you don't want anything to do with me. You don't have to pretend."

"It's not that, Lynn. Honestly it's not." Kim sounded desperate. She lifted her hand to touch Lynn's arm, but then let it fall, the gesture unfinished. "If you want to see more of me, I'll make time for you. I promise. I'll do whatever you want. Anything."

Lynn's face twisted in a grimace. "You should be more careful about what you promise."

"I mean it."

"Do you?"

"Yes."

"Because at the moment, I really desperately want to kiss you again." Lynn did not dare to look up, dreading to see either anger or dismay on Kim's face.

The silence dragged on until Kim said quietly, "You're an Imprinter."

"So?"

"You have to be celibate."

"Gina thinks that's just a superstition the Sisters made up."

"And what do you think?"

"I don't know. I don't care. I love you." Lynn's eyes were fixed on the ground. "But I guess it's my problem. I'm sure I'll get over it in the end. You don't have to feel responsible or anything, and if you say good night and rush away, I'll understand."

Deliberately, Kim stepped forward to stand in front of Lynn, blocking her field of vision; then both of Kim's hands moved to rest on Lynn's shoulders, holding her gently but firmly. For a while neither moved, but at last Lynn raised her chin so their eyes met.

"Why would I want to rush away?" Kim asked softly.

"Because of what happened last time. You've got every right to want to avoid me. I didn't give you a chance back in Petersmine. It wasn't what you wanted, but I threw myself at you, and you suffered for it."

"Do you think I don't know how to sidestep if a woman throws herself at me and I don't want to catch her?" Kim paused. "I love you too. I fell in love with you at the mountain fort, and I still love you. I wanted you in the stable and I want you now."

"But you said..."

Lynn did not get to finish her sentence. Kim's hands slipped behind her back, pulling her away from the tree, enfolding her. Lynn's breath became ragged as she felt what it was like to be held by Kim again, and then to feel the firmness of Kim's body filling her own arms. She gave herself totally to the embrace. Kim's cheek pressed against her forehead, tilting her face back, and then Kim's mouth met hers. The kiss claimed her entire being. Nothing else had ever been so real. Lynn could no longer feel the ground beneath her feet. She was adrift and floating, anchored only by the soft touch of Kim's lips.

By the time they broke from the kiss, they were both shaking. Lynn's legs were weak, unable to support her, and her head was spinning. Kim looked at the ground, but it was Lynn who made the decision, sinking down and drawing Kim after her. The grass rustled beneath her and a few stray blades tickled her cheek, but then Kim was lying beside her and kissing her again and driving away all other awareness. The wandering kiss moved from Lynn's mouth to her eyes and then down her neck to the base of her throat. Lynn lifted her hands, running her fingers over Kim's back and through Kim's hair.

Kim tugged Lynn's shirt free of her waistband. At the touch of Kim's hand on her skin, Lynn gasped. The sound arrested Kim's actions. She raised herself on one elbow and looked down at Lynn, her face showing her uncertainty.

"Don't stop," Lynn said quickly.

"Are you sure?"

"I love you."

"But are you sure this is what you want?" Kim asked gently.

"Of course I'm not sure, but I can't bear not to."

Kim's hand moved to the ties on Lynn's shirt, loosening them one by one, until the two sides fell open, exposing Lynn's bare skin to the warm night air. Again, Kim lowered her mouth, her tongue investigating the line of Lynn's shoulder, and then further down. Her lips nuzzled Lynn's breasts and finally opened around a nipple, sucking gently. A high-pitched sound, like the cry of a newborn puppy, escaped from the back of Lynn's throat. She felt Kim's tongue working on her ever more ardently. Lynn tugged on Kim's clothing, attempting, without success, to pull her shirt off. Thankfully, Kim felt what she was trying to do and sat up. In a few deft movements, Kim had loosened the fastening at her neck, caught hold of the hem, and drawn it over her head.

Lynn reached out to touch the softness of Kim's skin, trying to draw her back, but Kim stretched down to untie her own shoelaces. After a few deep breaths, Lynn managed to sit up as well, slipping her arms free of her open shirt. She tried to copy Kim's actions, but her fingers had lost their dexterity and she needed Kim's help to complete the task. Kim then pressed her back to lie on the grass before moving her attention to the fastening at Lynn's waist. Her eyes met Lynn's in an appeal for assistance. Lynn braced her shoulders and heels on the ground, lifting her hips and allowing Kim to remove the last of her clothing.

Lynn faltered briefly, looking down and seeing her own body lying naked in the moonlight. But then Kim was back with her, also naked, driving away any doubts with the touch of skin on skin and taking her to unimagined levels of arousal. Her own mouth was moving over Kim's neck and shoulders, tracing the edge of Kim's jaw, and returning time and again to Kim's mouth. Kim's hands became ever more eager, cupping her breasts, running over her stomach, down her hips, and along the outside of her leg. The gentle stroking awoke every nerve in Lynn's body in tingling ripples. Passion swelled with each minute until it seemed impossible for it to get more intense, but finally, in a deliberate move, Kim's hand slipped over the knee and onto the soft skin of Lynn's inner thigh.

The breath stopped in Lynn's throat. Her body froze in the shock that swept through her, and then slowly Kim's hand began to travel higher, getting closer to the center of the paralyzing response. Tremors seized Lynn, shaking her in small convulsions while the sensation grew stronger, until Kim's hand finished its journey. Lynn heard her own voice whimpering, but she no longer had control over herself. All she could feel was Kim's fingers, stroking, exploring, delving in the folds between her legs, until finally they entered her.

Lynn's body arched, her arms clinging around Kim's shoulders, but the support was withdrawn as Kim slid away. Lynn reached after her, feebly trying to pull her back, but Kim moved with sure intent, her mouth fixing over its goal. Lynn felt the soft, wet warmth of Kim's tongue imposing a new rhythm on her waves of arousal, sweeping her along until nothing existed except the ever-growing ecstasy.

Abruptly, there was a moment of emptiness as the tongue left her, but Kim's hand maintained the rhythm. Lynn opened her eyes and looked up to see Kim's face above her, staring down into her eyes. Suddenly, everything bound together: the fingers inside her, the pressure outside, and Kim's face. The surge of orgasm crashed and burst over her. Lynn heard a voice cry into the dark and knew it was her own. A ball of pure pleasure erupted inside her, racing down her legs, up her spine. Kim's face became one with the night sky, while the ground under Lynn's shoulders fell away, twisted inside out, and flowed back.

And then the world dropped back into place and she was lying, gasping in the grass, with Kim beside her, holding her tightly. Lynn's limbs were heavy with the weight of the release.

Kim's mouth twitched into a smile as she asked, "Are you all right?"

This was such a silly question that Lynn was seized by a fit of giggles.

"Can I take that as a yes?"

Lynn's heartbeat was returning to normal. She looked up at Kim and then raised her hand to stroke Kim's cheek. Kim twisted her head, kissing Lynn's fingers, eyes closed. Lynn studied Kim's face, the tautness around her mouth, the faint lines across her forehead. Despite her own feeling of peace, no sensitivity was required to see the tension that still held Kim, or to know what was needed to dispel it.

Lynn shifted her hand to Kim's shoulder and pressed her back until Kim was lying on the grass and Lynn was the one raised on an elbow. Lynn looked down the length of Kim's body, taking in the clean lines of Kim's legs, the dark triangle of hair, the soft curves of Kim's hips and stomach, the arch of ribs, and Kim's round breasts. Finally, Lynn's gaze came to rest on Kim's face and the watchful expression there.

One corner of Lynn's mouth twitched down in a faintly apologetic look as she said, "I'm afraid, my love, that I'm not going to be very good at this. It's your own fault for picking a novice. I'll try my best." Lynn felt a grin growing on her lips. "But I may need to practice quite a lot."

Lynn placed her forefinger on the hollow at the base of Kim's throat, and then very slowly, she began to trace a line down.

❖

It was a long time later when Lynn stirred herself. The night was growing cold, picking at exposed skin, although the parts that were pressed against Kim were still hot. Lynn shifted around slightly, making space. Kim nuzzled back against her, drowsy in the languor that had followed their lovemaking. A soft smile crossed Lynn's face, but they could not stay there all night. She ran her hand over Kim's shoulder.

"Do you think we should be going back?"

"Mmm, probably," Kim murmured, though she made no attempt to move. But eventually, she roused herself and sat up. Hardie had traveled across the sky and the crescent of Laurel was just rising. Kim stared at the moons while her expression shifted through a range of emotions, then she looked back down at Lynn and asked. "How do you feel?"

"Wonderful."

Kim grinned, but then her face became serious. "I meant with regard to..."

Lynn finished the sentence for her. "Imprinting?"

Kim gave a quick nod.

Lynn shrugged. "I don't know. I'm not sure how it would feel not to be an Imprinter, and I probably won't know until I put it to the test. But..."

"But?"

Lynn sat up and leaned against Kim. "No matter how it works out, I've got no regrets." She raised her head and stared in the direction of the village.

"You're looking thoughtful."

"I'm wondering if there's any food left."

Kim laughed. "With a whole squadron of Rangers down there? No chance."

The walk back down the hillside was a minor revelation to Lynn. Of course, she knew there were going to be adjustments to her life, new complexities to deal with. What she had not considered was that even mundane things like walking would be affected, but she became aware of it rapidly, once they set off and Kim put an arm around her waist in the way of lovers. Lynn had watched women walking like that, even dreamed of strolling with Kim's arm around her. What she had not expected was how much it upset her balance, and the need to adjust her stride to the woman beside her. It was worth persevering with, of that Lynn was sure, but how much else would she have to relearn?

The village square was much quieter than when they had left. The music and dancing had stopped long ago, and most women had gone to their beds, although a few were still gathered, talking quietly. Midnight was not far off, and folk would be rising for the next day's work in under five hours. The cows would not take account of the festival in their demands for milking.

They separated at the edge of the square, with Kim suggesting, "If you can find some food, I'll see if there's anything left to drink."

As predicted, most of the food containers were empty, but Lynn found a pot with a few centimeters of spicy sauce at the bottom and half a loaf of bread to scoop it out. She was working her way through the other bowls when her attention was diverted from the food by a figure who came and crouched beside her.

Chip reached out and squeezed her shoulder. "It's okay. You don't have to say anything, just nod if I'm forgiven for dropping you in it again."

"I'm not sure." Lynn's voice was lightly teasing.

"You're not sure," the Ranger repeated skeptically. She nodded toward the bread in Lynn's hand and said, "It gives you an appetite, doesn't it?"

From the grin on Chip's face, there was no mistaking her meaning. Lynn felt a faint blush rise on her cheeks and averted her face. She then turned back to the Ranger and began, "What makes you..." But she felt laughter rising and could not finish the question. Over Chip's shoulder, she saw Kim returning.

Chip's grin became even broader as she followed the direction of Lynn's eyes. She answered Lynn's unfinished question. "What makes me leap to conclusions? It's easy. There's only one known activity that puts a smile on a woman's face like the ones you and Kim have got."

CHAPTER TWENTY-THREE—TROUBLE

L ynn, what is your last name?" Katryn asked in idle curiosity.
Lynn looked across at the Ranger, who was lying on the grass with her head cushioned on Chip's legs and a half-eaten apple in her hand. "It should be was, not is. And the answer is that I don't remember."

"You don't?" This time, Kim was speaker.

Lynn had to twist her neck to look at Kim. Her lover was currently sitting behind her, serving as a backrest. The four women were by the banks of the river, taking a light lunch and sheltering from the midday sun in the shade of a tree. It was the sort of gathering that had become a common event in the month since the festival. It was also a display of the adjustments in Lynn's everyday life—the inclusion as part of a couple, the casual sharing of physical space with Kim, and the intangible sense of being seen as slightly less different from everyone else. The subject of her family background had probably never occurred to Katryn before.

Lynn explained, "I think I knew what my last name was when I was a child, but it wasn't very important to me. I came from a small community where everyone recognized me and knew who my parents were. Anyway, the name of the farm was more useful in identifying me. Then, after I went to the temple, it was never mentioned again, and I just forgot."

"If you want, we could invent a new name for you, like Gina's," Chip offered mischievously.

"No, thank you," Lynn said and then looked over to the Ranger as an old question occurred to her. "While we're on the subject of names, why are you called Chip, and what's your real name?"

At the question, Katryn gave a yelp of laughter and Kim said dryly, "Careful, my love, you're on dangerous ground. Her first name is not something to be thrown about lightly. All you need to know is that she answers to Chip when she's in a good mood, Coppelli when she's being a proper Ranger, and when you hear her rank thrown in as well, you know it means trouble."

"But what's wrong with her name?" Lynn was undeterred.

Chip sighed in resignation. "My name is one of the many things I hold against my parents. They wanted me to join the Sisterhood. Not because they were particularly religious; they had ulterior motives."

Lynn stared at her for a second and then curled forward, laughing at the thought of Chip in a Sister's white robes, and the impact her blunt honesty would have on the intrigues of a temple sanctum.

"Why does everyone start cackling like a lunatic when I tell them that?" Chip feigned surprise. "Anyway, my parents decided to give me a shove in the right direction with what they thought of as a suitable name—Piety. And before you start getting ideas, I'll warn you, I've thumped people in the past for calling me it." Chip scowled, but her tone removed any threat from her words. "They sent me to a school at the temple. Like many children, I loved chips and a Sister made one of those daft comments along the lines of"—she adopted a high-pitched whine—"*If you eat any more, we'll have to start calling you chip.*" She dropped back to her normal voice. "I said that I'd rather be called Chip than Piety. The other kids overheard me and I got my wish."

"It was a good thing her favorite food wasn't tarts," Katryn cut in, teasing her partner, who responded by poking her in the ribs.

Lynn watched the resulting hand-wrestling match with a happy grin. She was more content than at any time she could remember, and for more reasons than the obvious one. *Mind you,* she thought, snuggling back against Kim, *the obvious one is pretty damned good.* Then her eyes shifted to the vegetable patch and she sighed. Not everything could be perfect. It was time to get back to work. She was about to twist around and tell Kim, when a shout came from the general direction of the wall.

"Captain Ramon, Lieutenant Coppelli!"

A Ranger was running toward them, a recently returned scout by the look of her, still dressed in full field kit with a scabbard swinging at her side. In her haste, the woman stumbled recklessly along the uneven footpath, racing on legs that seemed none too steady. She was clearly pushing her body to its limits.

"And this is trouble." Katryn gave her judgment even before the Ranger was close enough to recognize.

Kim was on her feet in an instant and advancing to meet the scout. "What is it?"

"Captain Ramon. Rozek is back with more Guards." The Ranger skidded to a halt, speaking between gasps.

"How many?"

"Two hundred or so."

"Where?"

"When I left, they were still a day's ride east of the old farm. Sergeant O'Neil and I were supposed to be meeting a family of heretics who've had to flee the Sisters, but when we saw the Guards, I came straight back here. The sergeant is staying to keep an eye on them and to see if she can find the heretics before Rozek does."

Kim nodded as she considered the information. Sergeant O'Neil was one of the oldest women in the squadron, a very experienced and competent Ranger who would have no trouble avoiding capture, but she could not be left to deal with Rozek on her own.

Kim looked back to the scout. "How long ago was this?"

"Seven days. I had O'Neil's horse as well."

Lynn looked at the woman with respect and more than a little concern. It was scarcely surprising the scout looked so exhausted. She must have punished herself getting back so quickly, and even with switching mounts, the horses would be in a worse state.

Kim's thoughts had moved on. "So by now they will have gotten to the site of the old farm and discovered we're not there. I guess it's too much to hope they'll have given up and gone back." She looked at Chip. "Let's find Gina. We need to make plans."

❖

The still night air carried the cry of a hunting bird to Lynn, a high note overlaying the distant murmur of the river. Weak moonlight edged between the window shutters, just sufficient to pick out the pile of clothes on the floor and Kim's motionless outline in the bed beside her. Lynn sighed and rolled onto her back.

"Can't you sleep?" Kim whispered.

"No. Can't you either?"

"Well, not with you tossing and turning every five minutes."

"I'm sorry."

"Are you worrying?"

"I can't help it." Lynn stared at the ceiling, making sure she had full control of her voice before adding, "When you ride out tomorrow, promise me you'll be careful."

Kim put an arm around her and held her tight. "I'll be careful, I promise. I'm not going to gamble with the lives of half the squadron."

"I guess that's partly it. There's going to be you and two patrols. Seventeen Rangers, against two hundred Guards."

"Most of us would say it was pretty even odds." Kim tried to joke, but Lynn was not amused.

"No, it's not."

Kim stroked the hair back from Lynn's face. "Don't worry. I'm not going to engage Rozek head-on. If there's a suitable opportunity, I'll make things unpleasant for her and her Guards, so they'll think twice in the future before coming into the mountains. But I won't take risks, because there's no need. They don't know where Westernfort is, and even if they did, it would take more than two hundred Guards to force their way through the wall."

"And Rozek?"

"What about her?"

Lynn paused, trying to put her fears into words. "She had you beaten and flogged. And when she couldn't rig it that you were hung by the court-martial, she deliberately tried to murder you. I'm scared you're going to want revenge, and you might not think things through clearly."

Kim leaned forward and kissed Lynn gently on the lips. "No, my love. Revenge is just a way of sacrificing your future to your past, and I'm not going to play that game. Believe me, I know what I'm talking about."

❖

The Guards' encampment at the site of the old village was the highly disciplined shambles the Rangers had come to expect. Kim studied it from a concealed hilltop vantage point and shook her head, bemused that any soldier would value straight lines over making use of the land's topography. The sentries were evenly spaced out, regardless of their field of view or any other sensible consideration. Even the decision to occupy the village was questionable. There was no spot from where a commander could observe the whole site, and the heretics had arranged the village for domestic rather than military purposes, yet without thinking things through, the Guards had placed their supplies in the old barns at the edge of the site, where they were exposed to attack, as well as being a long way from the nearest source of water.

"Doesn't it just scream 'Raid me, raid me'?" Sergeant O'Neil was equally impressed.

"Possibly," Kim said.

"Are we going to?"

"I must admit it's tempting to see what a fire in the stores would do."

Sergeant O'Neil chuckled. "Give them a hungry journey home."

Kim continued her appraisal of the site. When Rozek had not shown up by the beginning of August, she had assumed the Guards were not coming that year. Otherwise the old farm would never have been chosen as the rendezvous for the family of heretics. It was still anyone's guess why the Guards had bothered coming so late in the year. September was passing rapidly, and Rozek's troops would have to start their return journey very soon if they did not wish to be overtaken by winter. Possibly the turmoil caused by Lynn's escape had delayed the Guards. The absence of Rangers in the company might also have caused delays. A smile crossed Kim's face as she wondered how many times Rozek had gotten lost trying to retrace her steps from the previous year. Maybe she had even been forced to return for more supplies. Presumably, Rangers were no longer trusted after the desertion by the 23rd Squadron.

But all of that was speculation. What was certain was that the Guards posed no threat to Westernfort. They clearly had no idea of where the village had moved to and no way of finding out. It was hard to see what purpose they thought they were serving by staying at the site. Evading their scouting parties was absurdly easy. Their red uniforms showed up like beacons.

Kim sighed and turned back to Sergeant O'Neil with her decision. "Tempting, but not worth the risk. I think we should settle for ambushing a few of them when they leave the village."

The two Rangers were about to slip away through the covering vegetation and rejoin the others when a minor disturbance erupted on the far side of the camp. The Guards seemed excited, although at first the reason was not apparent. But then Kim saw six bound prisoners being dragged into the village, one of them a child of less than ten.

"Damn. It's the family of heretics," Sergeant O'Neil said, horrified.

"How did Rozek find them before us?" Kim was angry, largely at herself, knowing she had been a touch too complacent. "I guess this changes things."

"We'll try to rescue them?"

"We have to. We can't let them be taken back for execution. If they live that long."

"You think Rozek will kill them here?"

"Maybe not intentionally, but she's never going to believe them when they say they don't know where the village has moved to." Kim's face was stern, remembering Rozek's style of conducting an interview. Her eyes returned to the encampment, and she studied the cover and contours of the land, noting the exact position of sentries and making her plans.

❖

Midnight was very close. One lone moon hung low in the sky, Laurel as a quarter crescent. Its feeble light was only the faintest wash of blue over the occupied village, but from where Kim lay in the grass, the sentries showed up as sharp silhouettes against the brilliant backdrop of stars. Two were in view, standing thirty meters apart at one corner of the site, hidden from other sentries by bushes and a dip in the ground. Kim wondered whether the Guards had the faintest idea of how close at hand their enemies were, or how isolated they would be when the attack came. Both stood rigidly at attention, as if on display at the temple gates, and neither had moved a muscle for half an hour. By now, their eyes would have glazed, their brains would be numb, and their bodies stiff and slow to respond.

Kim's lips formed a circle to whistle the signal, an imitation birdcall, but then stopped, staring intently at the two silhouettes, in the abrupt awareness that this was not a raid on bandits. The Guards were guilty of no crime, were probably decent enough women, soldiers like herself who were obeying their orders. Kim bore them no personal ill will, but neither did she have any options. The Guards' helmets made it too risky to attempt to knock them out quietly. *Whatever I do, some women will die as a result. Either Guards or the family of heretics,* Kim told herself. *Asking politely won't be enough to make Major Rozek release her prisoners.*

Kim closed her eyes as she made a silent appeal to the Goddess that she no longer believed in, then looked up and gave the signal. At once, two new figures rose up silently behind the Guards. Swift, synchronized thrusts, and then the bodies of the Guards fell to the ground. The fact it was so easy only made it worse, but the guilt and regrets must wait. A job was waiting to be done.

Kim jumped up and signaled the rest of the Rangers forward. As they approached the first hut, the women split into three groups. The smallest was made up of Kim and three of the most experienced Rangers. The two slightly larger parties went left and right, on stealthy routes toward the stores and the horses, while Kim's group headed straight into the heart of the village, aiming for the hut Rozek had commandeered. The prisoners would most likely be there, but if not, Rozek would certainly know where they were. A grim smile touched Kim's face; it might be fun to ask Rozek a few questions for a change.

The feeling was strange, almost dreamlike, walking through the village that had been her home for several months, but which was now occupied by her enemies. The three Rangers followed her, slipping from shadow to shadow between the dark, silent huts, heading confidently to their goal. Rozek had been helpful in choosing to occupy a spot where the layout was so familiar to them, and even more helpful to mark her headquarters with a tall gold and red standard at the door.

The sound of quiet talking came from one round hut as they passed. If it had been Rangers or Militia inside, Kim would have suspected an illicit late-night card game. With Guards, it was more likely a prayer meeting for the overzealous. There was no sign that anyone else in the village was awake until they were within sight of Rozek's headquarters. The major had taken over one of the largest buildings that opened onto the central square. A smaller hut was next to it, with two sentries stationed outside the door. Surely a useful pointer to the place where the heretics were held.

The Rangers halted while Kim whispered her instructions, and then they set off again, silently moving around the square and finally approaching the jail from the rear. Once there, the small group split into two pairs that edged around the hut in opposite directions, so as to advance on the entrance from either side. As she crept around the dry stone wall, Kim could hear a voice from inside—Rozek's—speaking in the clear, impassive voice Kim remembered.

"Where have the traitors and heretics gone?"

The reply was a confused mumbling, spoken between sobs. Kim could not pick out the words, only the terror. Instinctively, her hand moved to the hilt of her sword.

Rozek spoke again. "Oh, come on. You know I don't believe that."

More mumbling, with the words "please" and "don't know" in it.

"So you went wandering through the mountains without any idea of where you were going, just on the off-chance you might come across your friends?" Rozek spoke in contemptuous irony.

By now, Kim was closer to the door of the hut, and the answer was spoken clearly enough to make out parts. "We've told you...were to be met...don't know...please believe us."

"I'm not that stupid." Rozek's voice sounded bored. "And I will get the truth from you in the end. I have not enjoyed the last few hours, but it is only the start of what I am prepared to do to get what I want. It can take all night, and all tomorrow, and as many days after that as are necessary. So perhaps we should start again, although with a different subject. You obviously don't care about your old mother, but perhaps the child. She—" Rozek's words were cut off by screams of anguished entreaty from more than one woman.

"No."

"Please."

"Oh. So you do care about your daughter." Rozek mimicked surprise. "Then where have the traitors and heretics gone?"

Waiting outside the hut was almost more than Kim could bear, and she could tell the other Ranger crouched beside her was feeling the same, but reckless haste would help no one. She drew her sword in readiness, gently so as not to rasp metal on metal, and settled back in the shadows under the low eaves of the hut. The waiting was agony, but then Kim heard the sound she had been listening for, the out-of-season chirp of a straw weevil.

She answered in kind and started counting silently. Eight years' experience in the Rangers carried her forward, silent, sure-footed and deadly, moving until she was less than a meter behind the sentry. All the time the numbers kept running in her head; on sixteen, her feet reached position; on nineteen, her hand tightened on the sword's hilt; on twenty, she launched herself forward, her left arm swinging around the Guard's throat to strangle any cry, and her other hand driving the short Ranger's sword up through the woman's body. She did not need to look to know that at the other side of the doorway, Sergeant O'Neil would similarly have dispatched the second sentry.

The bodies were dragged off into the dark. The golden helmets and red cloaks were stripped from the dead Guards, and within seconds, another pair of sentries stood at the door of the hut. It was not much of a disguise, but would be quite adequate for the dark night, particularly with the expected confusion ahead.

Flickering firelight escaped through the crack under the closed door. Kim dared not open it to see exactly what was happening, or how many Guards were there. Instead, her attention focused on listening, hoping for answers. Someone else was talking. Not a prisoner from the absence of fear in the voice, although the speaker was not completely at ease either.

"Excuse me, ma'am, it is late. And too much...disturbance might wake people."

"Maybe," Rozek conceded. "And perhaps a few hours to think things through might be useful for our prisoners. I'm sure I have given them a lot to think about."

Kim's stomach churned. Despite the dispassionate tone and earlier denial, Kim had no doubts that Rozek was enjoying every second. The urge to burst in and silence the sadistic voice was overwhelming, but it was wisest to wait until there was enough disruption in the camp to cover any calls for help. And surely it would not be long before the disruption started?

Kim looked in the direction of the barns. At that moment, a shower of sparks erupted into the night sky, followed by the glow of flames, growing stronger. For a full minute the fire grew, and then came the first shouts. The figures of Guards began to emerge from a dozen doorways, half stumbling and half awake, staring in confusion at the blossoming fire that was engulfing their stores. Kim and O'Neil kept to the blackest shadows, a little back from the doorway, but no one was looking in their direction. Already some of the more astute officers were starting to shout orders, calling every available Guard to help fight the raging fires. The two disguised Rangers remained at their posts, standing as still as stone. They were completely ignored as the center of the hubbub moved away from the village square.

Rozek had been talking quietly to a colleague. Now her voice snapped out, "What's all that?"

Kim kept silent on the chance that Rozek might recognize her voice and left it to O'Neil to call out, "Excuse me, ma'am. The stores are on fire."

"What! Why didn't you say before? You three...go and help."

The door of the hut opened, letting light spill across the ground. Three Guards raced out and disappeared into the darkness at the other side of the square. None of them paid the slightest attention to the two bogus sentries or seemed to notice that they did not follow.

At least one other Guard remained in the hut with Rozek. A voice asked, "Shouldn't we go as well, ma'am?"

"Yes, in a minute." Rozek was clearly torn between her duty as commanding officer and her sport with the heretics. And although her responsibilities had to come first, still she could not resist one last bout of intimidation before she left her victims. "We will be back in the morning. And be quite sure I am not just making idle threats. Your daughter will receive exactly the same attention your mother has had unless you answer my question, and it is a simple enough one. Where have the traitors and heretics gone?"

"Well, some of us are here."

The time of waiting was over. Kim stepped into the hut, her sword drawn and still red with the blood of the sentry. Her eyes scanned the inside of the hut, quickly noting the position of the prisoners at one side and the absence of any enemies apart from Rozek and one other officer. She faced the two Guards. Rozek's expression of stunned shock was everything Kim could have wished for. More unexpectedly, the second officer's face showed an emotion more like relief. This woman moved first, eagerly stripping off her sword belt and throwing it down in a gesture of surrender.

Rozek's eyes were fixed on Kim. "Ramon! I'd thought I—"

"I know. You thought you'd killed me." Kim finished the sentence for her and shrugged. "It was an easy mistake to make. I thought I'd drop by and set you straight. I've also got a message for you to pass on to the Chief Consultant. She doesn't own these mountains. We do. Our chosen leader is Gina Renamed, and any women who come into our lands without her permission do so at risk of their lives. Now we're going to take our friends and leave, but my advice to you is to pack up what's left of your things at first light tomorrow, return to the Sisters' land, and stay there."

The other three Rangers had entered the hut behind Kim. Rozek's eyes lit up at the sight of the red cloaks, only to fade again when she saw the gray and green uniforms underneath. Yet still she found the composure to quote, *"Do not let your feet stray from the path of the Goddess, for all who stand against her laws will die, and their lives shall be offered as tribute by the swords of the righteous."*

"Do you want to try to demonstrate this?" Kim asked, pointing at Rozek's sword with her own.

Despite her arrogant disdain, Rozek clearly realized she was outnumbered, particularly with her comrade's instant surrender. She treated the Rangers to an arrogant sneer but had no option other than to remove her belt and toss her sword to lie with the other one on the ground.

"Tie them both," Kim ordered, then turned to look at the family of heretics in more detail, and froze.

As she had seen from the hilltop, there were six of them. The oldest was a woman who must be over fifty; the youngest was a girl of about seven. The other four appeared to be scattered through their twenties. All were bound, including the child, and none looked as if they fully understood that a rescue had arrived. The child's eyes were wide in rigid panic; the younger women's were tear-stained and filled with the dead weight of horror. The oldest was the only one who was gagged. She was also the only one naked from the waist up, which revealed a body crisscrossed and bleeding with the livid marks of burns. In confusion, Kim's eyes searched the hut, not that the source took much finding. Despite the summer heat, a fire was burning in the central hearth, and in it lay an iron poker.

For a dozen heartbeats, Kim stared at it with disbelief. Even in her words to O'Neil, she had not quite believed the depths Rozek could plumb. Then in two steps, Kim had crossed the hut to where the major sat, her hands and legs already bound. The point of Kim's sword flew to Rozek's throat, drawing one small, round drop of blood, but Kim's arm locked. She looked into Rozek's eyes and saw fear and anger and religious certainty, and not a trace of guilt. Kim's hand on the sword hilt pressed forward a little and the drop of blood became a trickle, but she was shaking and could not strike.

"I shouldn't have given you the chance to surrender. I should have cut you down where you stood," Kim said, and it was true.

"That would have been closer to the sort of behavior I would expect from you."

"The sort of behavior *you* expect from *me*?" Kim was incredulous at Rozek's self-righteous tone. "The sort of behavior like torturing old women and children?"

"*For her glory, the faithful shall not question the acts they must do in her name.*"

The quote was more than Kim could stomach. She pulled back her sword and swung it down hard upon Rozek, hitting her across the face with the hilt. But that was as far as she could go. The world without Rozek would be a better place, and it was not fair that ordinary Guards lay dead outside while Rozek still lived, but Kim could not kill an unarmed woman, and certainly not one who was bound and helpless at her feet. As Rozek keeled over, the other Guard officer looked away, with a shame that was manifest. Small wonder that she had been so quick to surrender.

Freeing the heretics did not take long. Kim stepped to the door and peered out. The flames from the stores were, if anything, higher than before, and the square was deserted. She shook her head. Surely by now someone should have realized that the fire was deliberate and possibly a distraction. However, the Guards' inexperience was largely what the plan relied on. Kim spoke quickly, giving the last necessary instructions, and then the group filed out of the hut, with two Rangers carrying the older woman.

With the exception of the rumpus by the stores, the return journey was identical to the way in. No one saw them, no one stopped them, and soon they were beyond the boundaries of the encampment and reunited with the successful team of fire lighters. But the evening's plans were not quite finished. As they began to move away to the final rendezvous, a fresh commotion began in the distant corner of the village where the horses were stabled.

At first, a few neighs rang out, followed by wild shouts and yells, and then the rumble of pounding hooves in a frantic stampede. After several minutes of increasing chaos, the sounds faded into the distance on the far side of the village. The ploy was intended to steer any unoccupied Guards away from the women escaping on foot. It would also serve two further ends. Some horses would undoubtedly be recaptured, most would end up supplementing the resources at Westernfort, and in addition to Sergeant O'Neil's prediction of a long, hungry journey home, the Guards would be going on foot.

CHAPTER TWENTY-FOUR—
THE WORDS OF THE GODDESS

Just after dawn the next day, Kim joined the two Rangers posted as lookouts on a hilltop with a clear view over the village and examined the results of the raid. With the exception of three burned-out huts, the scene looked much the same as the day before, but the manner of the Guards had changed. Even from a distance, Kim could tell the swagger was gone from their walk and the razor-sharp edge of their discipline was blunted. Double the number of sentries guarded the perimeter, but they now seemed twitchy, as if they were no longer devoting their entire attention to standing still, and instead were wondering what was behind them. The horse paddock also looked different; a bare quarter of the animals remained. Much activity was centered around Rozek's hut; officers were arriving and messengers were departing by the minute.

"What do you think Rozek will do?" one of the Rangers asked conversationally.

"If she has any sense, she'll recover as much as she can from the remains of her stores and head back to the Sisters' homelands, but..." Kim let her sentence trail away.

"When did you hear of a Guard officer with any sense?" the Ranger finished.

"Well, Rozek is a lot more intelligent than some, but I'm not sure if she is any wiser."

"We'll take it from you that there's a distinction."

Kim grinned and continued studying the village. She felt under no pressure to commit the Rangers to any further action. Common sense said to wait until she was sure of Rozek's intentions, and a rest would do everyone good. Although a sensible idea might be to have the family of heretics sent on to Westernfort and safely out of harm's way. As long as the oldest one was in a fit state to travel. Finding out the condition of the elderly woman was Kim's next priority. She left the hilltop with the promise to send more Rangers to relieve the lookouts in an hour, and headed back through the wooded hillside.

The Rangers' camp was pitched on the far side of the hill from the village. Kim got a fair degree of amusement from knowing that Rozek had no idea how close at hand they were. With the Guards' total inexperience in the ways of the wild, the greatest danger of discovery lay in being stumbled on by accident, and Kim felt far safer knowing exactly where Rozek's troops were and what they were doing.

Back at the camp, high spirits from the success of the raid were in evidence, but the laughter and horseplay were not enough to compromise the defensive order. The sentries were all at their posts and alert, notwithstanding the broad smiles. Only in the corner by the heretics was the mood more somber. The faces were haunted by memories of the previous day. Yet they seemed resilient, strong-minded people. They would get over it eventually, and already the girl was starting to edge toward the Rangers in typical childish curiosity.

Kim knelt by where the elderly heretic lay in healing sleep, induced by Carma, who was also there, sitting cross-legged by her patient.

"How is she?" Kim asked.

"As well as can be expected." The normally light-hearted Ranger spoke in a voice that was uncharacteristically cold and grim.

"Will she be fit to travel today?"

"If we can rig a horse litter for her."

"Okay." Kim patted Carma on the shoulder. "See to it. I want you to escort the family back to Westernfort. I'll send someone else with you. Gina and Lieutenant Coppelli will appreciate the report if you get home before the rest of us."

Carma nodded and Kim rose, but as she was about to go, one of the other heretics moved in front of her.

"You should have killed Rozek." The woman's voice was ragged with hatred; the raw depths of it brought Kim to a stop. She could find no words in answer. Any assertion about not sinking to Rozek's level would have sounded trite and weak.

Carma looked up from her position on the ground, with eyes that were as hard as her voice. "I don't mean it as a criticism, ma'am, but I think she's right."

Kim averted her face and looked down at the elderly woman lying wrapped in bandages. Once again, she relived the scene that had greeted her inside the hut and remembered Rozek's arrogant self-justification. Despite her words to Lynn about the futility of revenge, Kim found herself worryingly close to agreeing.

❖

In early afternoon, not long after Carma and the family had left, word came from the Rangers on lookout that things were happening in the village. Kim trotted back up through the trees to see for herself.

"What's the situation?" she asked as she reached the hilltop.

"From what we could tell, most of them spent the morning in prayers. Then they broke for lunch. Now they seem to be a bit more focused in their activities. Nothing definite, but we thought you might like to see," one of the Rangers answered.

"Right. Thanks."

It was obvious that the lookouts were right. Rozek's troops were moving with an objective in mind, and before long two distinct groups had formed. The Guards in the larger section were collecting their gear and as much in the way of provisions as was available, and starting to muster on the eastern side of the village. Kim hoped she was not being overly optimistic in thinking that they were preparing themselves for the long walk back to the Sisters' Homelands.

The intentions of the other group of Guards were harder to be sure of. They had also gathered their possessions and were now assembled close by the remaining horses. Clearly, they were the ones selected to ride. But where? An officer was haranguing them. Kim was fairly certain it was Rozek, and she was also fairly certain that retreat was not the subject of the talk. Rozek did not appear to have quite given up yet; maybe she could not. To return twice with nothing to report but defeat and dead Guards might be a permanent block on her career.

Within the hour, both groups of Guards had completed their preparations and made their departure from the village. Those on foot marched away due east in the direction of Landfall. The others with their horses set off southwest, but not all were riding. A few fanned out wide at the front and walked with their eyes fixed on the ground, leading their mounts behind them. These women were the ones that puzzled Kim for a few seconds before understanding hit her. The Guards were searching for the hoof marks of the stolen horses from the night before.

The same conclusion had occurred to the other Rangers. "Oh, look at that. Bless their little woolly vests. They're trying to track us, hoping we'll lead them to Westernfort."

"Who says Guards have no imagination," the other Ranger agreed, laughing.

Kim also smiled. "Then we ought to give them a track to follow." She paused for a moment, thinking. "But we'd better not make it too difficult."

❖

Three days later, the chase was still in progress, pulling Rozek and her Guards far away from the route to Westernfort. Not that it had been easy, even with the herd of stolen horses to make a clear trail. On the first night, Rozek had kept going well after the light had failed and had consequently gotten lost. On another occasion, a roving herd of fenbucks had obliterated the Rangers' trail before the Guards reached it. Kim was reduced to more and more blatant tricks to keep the Guards tagging along. So far it had worked, but soon Rozek must realize she was being played with. Or was she too arrogant or too desperate to even consider the idea, and perhaps it was time to enlighten her?

Noon was approaching as the Rangers drove the herd of horses along a gorge-like valley. After the long, dust-dry summer, only a thin trickle of water flowed at the bottom, but in a few weeks' time, when the heavy autumn rains began, the gorge would hold a substantial torrent. As she rode along, Kim studied her surroundings. The seasonal floods meant the floor of the gully was devoid of trees and bore only the plants that had grown from seed during the summer months. These scarcely came to the hocks of the horses. The lower walls of the gorge on either side were sheer and unscaleable on horseback. Even a woman climbing would find them a challenge. The bare rock faces were washed clean of plants, but ten meters up, overhanging the top of the gorge, was a thick covering of bushy, shrub-like trees, ideal for shielding archers.

Sergeant O'Neil was riding beside Kim and noticed the direction of her eyes. "You're thinking it has potential for an ambush?"

"I was actually one step on from that. I'd gotten as far as wondering whether Rozek would be stupid enough to ride down here, knowing that we're ahead of her," Kim replied thoughtfully.

"Seriously?"

"Yes."

O'Neil grinned. "My money says it wouldn't even occur to her that there was a risk involved."

After another kilometer, the sides of the gorge crumbled away and they emerged into a far broader valley. Despite the drought, a respectable river was still flowing down the middle, although the water level was low and easy to ford.

Kim turned around to take a last look down the gorge, then stood in her stirrups and shouted, "Okay! We'll take an hour's break for the horses. After that, we're going to change the game a bit. So if you all gather round, I'll tell you what we're going to play next."

❖

Such gear as was necessary was made ready, and the Rangers set off again. At first, there was no change to the routine of the previous three days, but midway across the river, the Rangers divided. Three carried on, driving the riderless horses ahead of them while the rest followed Kim, riding upstream and keeping to shallow water. It would take vastly better trackers than the Guards to notice that fewer horses had left the river than entered, even if the planned ambush failed and Rozek's troops managed to escape from the gorge.

After a hundred meters, the Rangers returned to the bank and continued to ride along the valley until a bend took them out of sight of anyone following the trail of the stolen horses. They dismounted in the shelter of a straggling grove of young trees and secured their horses' reins to prevent them from straying. Then the Rangers climbed the hillside on foot and began to double back through the dense undergrowth, taking a route that eventually brought them out above the gorge, half a kilometer from its end.

Finally there was the long wait, a chance to find good locations among the trees, to check bowstrings and arrows, to finalize contingency plans, should things go wrong, and then to wonder whether Rozek had gotten lost again. But at last Kim heard the dull clopping of horses coming toward them down the barren gorge. In a second, all fidgeting and talking had ceased, the last few bows were strung, and quivers laid to hand.

The first of the riders came into view with Rozek in the lead. A double column followed her. Fifty-three Guards against a dozen Rangers. The corner of Kim's mouth twitched in a wry smile; the odds were not bad at all. She certainly would not have been happy to change places with Rozek, and not just because the major was about to be on the receiving end of an ambush. The Guards' morale was poor. They were obviously tired and dispirited. Many rode with their heads down. Maybe they suspected Rozek was leading them into danger. Only the most conceited could be unaware that they were totally outclassed against the Rangers in the wilderness. One or two were even looking anxiously at the overgrown top of the gorge, as if working out for themselves the opportunity it presented. *One good prod and they'll run*, Kim told herself.

Her eyes returned to Rozek, all previous qualms gone. The Guard major was unbound and armed, riding at the head of troops with hostile intent. Furthermore, a warning had been given, and she had chosen to ignore it. All of which, in Kim's mind, made Rozek a very fair target.

Chip's partner, Katryn, stood ready by Kim's side. She was far and away the best marksman in the squadron. Tempting though the thought was of being the one to kill Rozek, Kim did not want to risk letting the major get away. At her signal, Katryn pulled an arrow from her quiver and knocked it on the string of her bow. The line of Guards was getting closer, less than fifty meters from the ambush. Katryn pulled back, anchoring her hand under her chin and touching lips and nose to the string. She took time to set her aim straight for Rozek's heart. When the major was less than twenty meters away, Katryn loosed the arrow. Kim watched it fly straight and true to its target.

Rozek jolted back in the saddle, her arms flying wide, with the shaft of the arrow embedded in her chest. Then she pitched forward, slumping motionless over her horse's neck. Shouts rose from the Guards behind, making the startled beast skitter to one side and then break into a canter. Rozek was still on its back, but as it ran below her, Kim could see streams of blood running down the withers of the horse.

The shouts from the Guards became louder, spreading back along the column, and now they were joined by the sound of arrows whistling through the air as other Rangers began to shoot. For the space of a few seconds, the Guards appeared to be too surprised to know what to do, whether to go forward or back. A few reached for their own bows. The frantic, confused milling meant the Guards were no longer such clear targets, but arrows still found their mark. One officer made as if to set off after Rozek, but she spun about as she was hit in the shoulder, then another Guard took an arrow in the thigh. A third and fourth were injured, although they also managed to stay clinging to their saddles.

At the back of the line, Guards were starting to turn around. A junior officer called the retreat, her voice shading into panic. Then another woman was hit more seriously, knocking her from the saddle, and the retreat became a rout. The Guards spurred their horses and raced back up the valley trying to outrun the arrows, but two who were braver than the rest went to their fallen comrade's aid. They jumped to the ground, picked up the injured woman and literally tossed her over her horse, then scrambled back into their saddles and chased after the other soldiers in red and gold. However, the flight of arrows had already stopped. Regardless of how easy a target the two rescuers were, Kim had not shot at them, and neither had anyone else.

After the last Guard had disappeared from view, the Rangers hurried back to their horses. Kim picked out O'Neil and another experienced, levelheaded woman and said, "Without Rozek to lead them, I'm pretty sure the Guards won't stop running until they get back to Landfall, but I don't want to be caught out. Follow them until you are absolutely certain they're leaving the mountains. If anything unexpected happens in what's left of today, you can report to me at tonight's rendezvous. Otherwise send word straight to Westernfort."

"Yes, ma'am." Even before Kim had finished speaking, the selected Rangers were on their way to their horses and off after the fleeing Guards.

Another four Rangers were dispatched to retrieve any spent arrows they could find. Kim turned to the rest. "Right. Once they get back from the gorge, we can catch up with the horses. While we're waiting, I'll go and collect Rozek's horse and gear."

"Should I come too?" a Ranger volunteered.

"I think I'll be okay. I trust Katryn's aim. She sent the arrow through Rozek's heart—"

"Assuming she had one," someone interjected.

Kim grinned. "If I'm not back in an hour, you'll know her ghost got me."

As she collected her own horse and rode off, Kim was well aware of why she did not want company when she found Rozek's body. She had quite a few things that she wanted to say to the dead major, most of which she did not want overheard. The temptation to gloat in an unseemly fashion might be irresistible.

A line of blood was splattered on the ground at the point where the gorge met the larger valley. Kim followed the trail downstream for another kilometer as it wound in an erratic route and eventually linked with a deer track, climbing the side of the valley. After a short but steep ascent, the path leveled out on a boulder-strewn plateau. On one side stood a crumbling outcrop of rock. On the other was a sharp drop down to the river. Rozek's horse was standing close by the edge, but there was no sign of Rozek's body. Presumably, she had finally slipped from her horse and tumbled over the side.

Kim dismounted and went to peer down the steep, scree-covered slope. The red and gold of Rozek's uniform should have shown up like a flag, but nothing caught her eye, and suddenly Kim's trained instincts snapped in. The certainty that something was very wrong. She spun about, ready to run back to her horse and summon the rest of the Rangers, and found herself staring at a drawn bow with the arrowhead pointing straight at her.

Rozek had been crouching well back from the edge, hidden between the cracked boulders of the outcrop when Kim arrived. Now the major stepped out into the open. Her face was pale, her eyes were slightly glazed, and the red of her uniform was stained a duller crimson with her blood, but she was most definitely alive.

For the space of several heartbeats, they stood staring silently at each other, and then Rozek's lips twisted into a sneer. "I know. You thought you'd killed me. And what did you say next? Oh, yes. An easy mistake to make."

Rozek was swaying, clearly light-headed from the loss of blood. Her aim would not be good, but it did not need to be. A scant five meters separated her from Kim.

She continued speaking. "*The words of the Goddess shall be as a shield to the faithful.* Do you recognize the quote? They are good words, words every Guard should carry close to her heart." Rozek smiled. "I do. I always have. I carry a little copy of the book in my breast pocket. That was what your faithless arrow hit. The words of the Goddess really were a shield to me, but of course you don't believe the words, do you?"

Kim met Rozek's eyes and said, "I know that whatever truth there is in them is corrupted by your mouth."

"The corruption is only in you." Rozek was breathing heavily. The thickness of the book had not protected her fully, but it had been enough to save her from death. The arrow wound was not a minor scratch, yet neither was it fatal.

Luck pays no heed of justice, Kim told herself, but at least she would have her chance to address her words to the living woman. "No, Rozek. You are the corrupt one. You use your religion to justify your own evil. I'll bet you went through the book of the Elder-Ones just to pick out suitable quotes—anything to make it sound as if you were following the will of the Goddess rather than your own sordid desire to inflict pain on others. You use divinity to excuse inhumanity, but I have not the slightest doubt if Celaeno were here to choose between us, that she would be as sickened by you as I am."

Rozek only smiled and said, "Well, I'm going to give you the chance in the very near future to stand before Celaeno and put it to the test. So take off your sword and throw it over here."

Staring into Rozek's eyes, Kim knew herself to be a poor beginner when it came to gloating. Rozek intended to kill her but wanted to drag things out. Rozek did not have the faintest chance of holding Kim prisoner once the other Rangers discovered what had happened. Kim knew it and knew that Rozek knew it. Asking for her sword, rather than shooting her immediately, was part of the game. Its only possible purpose was to give Rozek the option of inflicting a slower death than an arrow through the heart, but it was not an option Kim was prepared to grant.

"I said take off your sword," Rozek snapped again, but her hands were shaking from the effort of holding the bow at full stretch. Soon she would be forced to loose the arrow.

Kim's hands moved to the buckle of her belt as her eyes judged distances. Despite the unsteadiness of Rozek's hands, the arrow would have too short a flight to hope it might miss a stationary target, yet Kim was going to have to take her chance. She held out her sword as if about to toss it down, but in the action of throwing, her hand grasped the hilt, shaking it with a whip-like action to free the sword from the scabbard, while at the same time hurling herself sideways. Kim heard the twang of the bowstring, the hiss of the arrow, and felt a sudden burning in her arm, but like Rozek's wound, it was far from fatal.

Kim's dive kept her moving. She hit the ground in a roll, triggering another explosion of pain in her arm, but then she was up on her feet and charging forward, sword in hand. Rozek had no time to string another arrow. The major tore her own sword free and leaped forward to meet Kim. The long, slashing Guard's sword against the short, stabbing blade of a Ranger.

The first clash of weapons was nearly the last. Kim blocked Rozek's stroke easily, but fire shot from her shoulder to her fingers. The hilt was almost wrenched from her weakened grasp as Kim managed somehow to parry the blow. She glanced down and saw the broken shaft of the arrow protruding from her arm. Adrenaline could only go so far in dulling the pain, and her sleeve was already soaked with blood. Soon it would trickle as far as her palm, making the hilt slippery. Kim jumped back from Rozek's second swipe and quickly transferred the sword to her other hand, her face set in a wry grimace; with Rozek half-dazed and Kim left-handed, this was not going to be a classic, elegant duel.

However, Rozek had the worst of the problems. Already fresh blood was staining her tunic as her wound broke open again, but she seemed unaware, and launched into a frenzy of slashes. Kim blocked them all easily, even left-handed, and a grim smile touched her lips. Signaling strikes so much in advance meant the effort was wasted on Rozek's part. It was energy she could not afford to squander and sped the loss of blood. The wild swings achieved little more than enhancing the greater length of Rozek's sword in keeping Kim at a distance and preventing her from closing for a thrust. Then suddenly, Rozek shifted to a sharper jab, almost catching Kim unawares. Kim frowned. She dared not get complacent, and Rozek had not lost all caution. Her attacks were not so impetuous as to leave her front open. Time was Kim's best ally. Before long, the major would weaken and make the error that would let Kim's sword through.

Rozek's sword flew in yet another sequence of slashes. Again, Kim shifted her balance to block and stumbled as one foot slid on the loose gravel of the scree slope. Kim realized she was on the brink of the drop down to the river. She cursed her own carelessness. How had she gotten so close to the edge? Or was it where Rozek had been driving her?

Rozek seized on the second of lost concentration. Her sword whipped across in a backhand slash. The stroke would take an awkward, cross-body effort to block, so Kim made no attempt. With her poor balance, there was little chance it would succeed. Instead, she half-ducked, half-fell to her knee and let Rozek's sword whistle over her head. Now her opponent was the one with lost balance. Rozek had expected her strike to be blocked, either by sword or by body, but instead her arm shot out wide, swinging her around and leaving her front unguarded. Kim propelled herself up from her crouch, throwing her whole weight into the attack and driving the point of her sword deep into her enemy. This time there was no mistake.

Rozek's expression froze on her face, then slipped from confusion, to surprise, and finally, disbelief that her Goddess had so unexpectedly, yet unmistakably, deserted her. Then her lifeless body tumbled back and crashed to the ground.

CHAPTER TWENTY-FIVE—
WHERE YOU'RE SUPPOSED TO BE

The Rangers returned to Westernfort on a dull, gray evening. The thick blanket of cloud served to hasten the onset of dusk, and a hint of rain was in the air. The bite of a chill northern wind warned that autumn was fast approaching. Leaves were still green but devoid of any luster. Within days, the first flushes of red would be visible. Fans of migrating birds flew down the valleys.

Kim dismounted and left her horse to the care of the grooms by the paddocks. She would willingly have joined the other Rangers in attending to her own animal, but once it was seen that her arm was in a sling, the reins were taken from her and she was pushed toward the steep path. On the way up to the gates, she paused and looked down on the shuffling herds huddled around their byres and then raised her eyes to the range of mountains at the far side of the valley, indistinct in the gloomy mist. The first drops of a light drizzle began to fall, but despite the weather, Kim felt perfectly at peace. The cold and damp only increased her contentment at the thought of a welcoming fire, a hot meal, a warm bed, and Lynn.

At the top of the climb, the path passed through the gates. Kim turned her back on the low-lying plain and paused for a moment to study the scene in front of her, from the protective ring of mountains to the neat farmlands. The fields were mainly stubble now that most of the crops were in, and the village was tranquil at the close of day. Trails of sweet wood smoke drifted from the huts. Posts marked out the foundations for more permanent buildings; work would be starting soon, now that everyone was released from the harvest and the threat of invasion. The vision of how the village would look in ten years' time rose in Kim's mind, and her expression became mesmerized. For the first time, she fully understood what it would mean to her, that Westernfort was not just another posting, it was for the rest of her life.

Kim shook her head, a little bemused by her own reaction, and began walking again. Word of the Rangers' return had spread and a few folk appeared from the huts, shouting a welcome. Kim's pace increased slightly. Then, running up the path toward her, came Lynn, and all the rest of the valley ceased to exist in Kim's eyes. She caught Lynn in a one-armed hug, and winced as Lynn grabbed her other arm before noticing the sling.

"Are you all right?" Lynn said with alarm.

"I'm fine."

"But your arm?"

"I was stupid enough to stand in the way of an arrow. I didn't—" Kim tried to joke, but the fear on Lynn's face caught the words in her throat. Now she had someone else whom she must answer to when taking risks. More soberly, she continued, "But I'm safe. And I'm home now."

The stories could wait until later, and the affectionate recriminations that would follow. She looked into Lynn's eyes and felt her life, her soul, her heart defined there. Home. That was the important word. For the first time since she was fourteen, Kim knew she had come home.

❖

The next day was spent in resting and retelling the story of the encounter with the Guards. By midafternoon, the clouds cleared and the mellow sunshine encouraged something like a party in the main square, with Lynn's singing talents called on frequently to the accompaniment of pipes. Even the odd flagon of beer made its appearance. Celebrating the death of the Guards did not seem right, with the possible exception of Rozek, yet neither was it a time to be totally serious. As sunset drew near, the temperature began to drop sharply. The night was not one for gossiping under the stars, and the eldest folk began to move indoors in search of the warmth of the hearthside.

Kim stood by the entrance to the stone house. Despite her original rejection of the honor, she now found herself living there, sharing Lynn's room. Gina was beside her, and the pair was trying to second-guess the Chief Consultant's next move.

"She won't be eager to send Guards against us again, but it doesn't look as if she trusts Rangers," Kim said.

"She won't leave us alone. She'll just keep upping the numbers." Gina's voice was gloomy.

"You think we won't be able to fight them off?"

Gina's face was solemn. "It may sound strange, but I'm frightened that we will. This world hasn't seen war yet, but the old world knew it only too well. I wish the Chief Consultant would go and read some of the books in her library. She could start where I did, with the Franco-Prussian war. It might scare her enough to start thinking. But she won't either read or think. She's too certain she has the Goddess in her pocket." Gina sighed. "I honestly never intended things to work out this way. All I wanted was the truth, but now I'm not sure if all the truth in the universe is worth one woman's life."

"Better to live in ignorance than die in wisdom?"

"Maybe. But we no longer have that option. The choice is down to our lives or theirs. It almost makes me wish I believed in the Goddess."

"Why?"

"Because then I'd have someone to pray to. I'm frightened that the Chief Consultant and I have set this world on the road to Hiroshima."

"What's at—" Kim began, but she was interrupted by Lynn, who had finally finished singing and had come to join them. Kim smiled and put her good arm around her lover, hugging her close.

"You look like you're having a painful conversation," Lynn said.

"We were thinking about the Chief Consultant."

"Oh well. If it's any consolation, I'll bet she looks even more miserable when she thinks about you two." Lynn looked thoughtful before adding, "And me."

Before anything more could be said, a fourth woman approached. She was a member of the rescued family of heretics. The condition of the oldest one had slowed them down, so that they had only arrived at Westernfort a few hours before the rest of the Rangers, and they had not had a chance to settle in properly.

Lynn, in the role of healer, had visited the elderly woman and learned her name was Nedda. The rest of the family consisted of her two daughters plus their partners. The young girl was Nedda's granddaughter, the child of the older couple. The woman who now approached was the younger of Nedda's daughters. When Lynn had been introduced before, she had seemed friendly, but now her manner was very hesitant, to the point of teetering on flight, and over her shoulder, Lynn could see her partner hanging in the rear. Lynn smiled in an encouraging fashion, although it did not seem to help the woman's awkwardness.

"Excuse me, ma'am..." the young heretic began uncertainly, her eyes darting between Lynn and Kim.

Lynn looked at the woman, confused. "Is it me you want, or the captain?"

"Er...you, ma'am."

"Oh, well. There's no need to call me ma'am. Kim neither, come to that, unless you desperately want to apply for the Rangers."

"Oh. Well, um..." The woman was inexplicably nervous. "Well. We've been told you're an Imprinter."

"Ah." Lynn suddenly understood where the conversation was going and was hit by an attack of her own anxiety. "I was. But I don't know whether I still am."

"Was...?"

"I'm no longer a virgin." Lynn indicated Kim's arm around her, and despite her unease, had to fight to keep the grin off her face. If it could possibly have been in doubt before, it definitely was not after celebrating Kim's return the previous night. "The Sisters would tell you my powers will be gone, but I've not had the chance to put it to the test yet." She bit her lip. "I take it you're not asking out of idle curiosity?"

The other young woman had come to stand beside her partner. "No. We were saving up for the imprinting fees. We nearly had enough, and then we were denounced and had to run and...we've brought what money we had with us, and it's yours if—"

"No," Lynn cut in abruptly. "If I can imprint, then I will do it for free. Anyway, there isn't much around here to spend money on."

"So...?"

Lynn was aware of both Kim and Gina watching her intently. She raised her chin and said, "No one here puts much faith in the Sisters' teachings, but maybe there is a reason for what they say about celibacy and imprinting. However, if you want, I will try for you tomorrow."

❖

Lynn was sitting alone in the common room of the stone house, staring into the cold fireplace, when Gina came to get her.

"Are you nervous?" Gina asked, seeing Lynn's sober expression.

"Not really."

"Thoughtful?"

Lynn pursed her lips and then nodded. "Yes."

"What are you thinking?"

"About being where you're supposed to be."

"Surely not in the temple?"

"Oh no. I never wanted to be there, never felt I belonged, despite what the Sisters said."

"And you feel you belong with Kim?"

Lynn smiled. "More than I've ever belonged anywhere else in my life. But I've changed so much. I'd loved Kim for ages, yet I hadn't realized that making love to her would cause me to feel so differently about..."

"About?"

"Everything. Some mornings I wake up and don't feel like the same person anymore."

"Do you think it's likely that you can't imprint?"

"I don't think so. I won't know for certain until I try, but it doesn't feel as if any of the healer sense has left me." Despite her words, Lynn looked troubled.

Gina studied her face for a while. "I was expecting you to be suffering from a recurrence of the doubts you had the first time you were called on to imprint in Westernfort."

Lynn shook her head. "Not really."

"But there's something else bouncing around at the back of your mind, I can see it on your face."

"It's..." Lynn frowned as she searched for words. "Despite being outside the temple, and you making me doubt everything about Celaeno and Himoti, I've never felt so spiritually complete in my life. And I was wondering, even if Celaeno didn't make the universe, perhaps there was a Goddess who did, who worked through Celaeno and the people who built her. Perhaps we were supposed to come here."

"I think you're playing with an extremely vague hypothesis with no useful or practical implications, and I'm a little uncertain of why you would want to bother."

"It's just, at the moment, I feel I need someone to give thanks to. If there isn't a Goddess, then there ought to be. I know you told me to follow my heart..." Lynn paused for a second. "And from the depths of my heart, I cannot keep from giving praise for life. It would be nice if someone was out there to listen."

Gina laughed. "Then I think you'll do all right."

The weather outside was bright and mild for the season. Sunshine from the previous afternoon had returned, burning off the last of the morning chill. The snow-covered peaks were crystal sharp against the blue sky, and the wind carried the soft scents of autumn. As had become customary, the entire village had gathered to watch. They stood subdued around the edge of the square, waiting for the leader of the heretics to escort the Imprinter out of the stone house. The thought occurred to Lynn that they had renounced the ceremonies of the temple only to start creating their own. In another two generations, she could see heretic-style imprinting getting as bound in ritual as anything the Sisters practiced.

The two young women were standing a little apart from the rest, looking hopefully toward the door of the stone house. Lynn walked over, took their hands, and led them out into the center of the square. She went through the limited necessary instructions and then the three of them sat down. A hush fell over the assembled crowd.

Lynn began to slip into the imprinting trance, but she was distracted as the two young women glanced across to meet each other's eyes. This time, Lynn did not resist the temptation to copy their action. She looked up and saw Kim in the crowd directly in front of her. Their eyes met also, and then without Lynn's conscious effort, the imprinting trance swept over her, but not like ever before. She was taken not inward, but outward.

She was surrounded by the world. The sense of it burst in upon her, soaking in through every pore. More solid, more unstoppable, more intense than ever before, from the ground underneath her to the arch of blue sky over her head. The mountains and the grass. The heartbeat of the world. Lynn felt herself caught up by the ecstasy of life. She could feel it, taste it, and smell it in every strand of her being. The two women whose hands she held were brilliant tapestries of dreams, spun on a double helix. The sight of the village square faded from her mind, but the image of blue sky seeped in, with the strength of mountains, the fresh scent of fir trees, and the wonder of Kim's love. Lynn knew with absolute certainty she had found her true place in the world Celaeno chose for her. She was where she was meant to be.

≈≫

Appendix

EXTRACTS FROM PETER MCKAY'S DIARY

15-May-2254: Ellen and I boarded the Celaeno today at 20:00 GMT. The shuttle ride up was pretty routine, including the twenty-minute delay on takeoff. As we got close to the ships, everyone rushed to get a good look at the seven of them floating against the backdrop of stars. It's an image I'll carry with me always. The colony ships are enormous. Nothing really prepared me for the scale of them. The closer we got the bigger they became. And to see them just floating in space. You can't put the effect into words. So many dreams are bound up with the ships, but I wasn't the only one to spare a glance back at the Earth and choke a little. How long before we'll see her again? But it's too late now to change our minds.

We've both been put on the Celaeno with the life scientists. A last-minute adjustment from UNSA, we only found out last night. Originally I'd been allocated a place on the Taygete with the other geologists and the terra-forming equipment, but the agency must have made one of its intermittent attempts to keep couples together, and there was a big swap around. A nice gesture, even though we'll be asleep for the whole journey.

I said the ships were big, but you'd never think it once we were inside. To call the passenger area cramped is to strain the meaning of the word, although of course, it isn't intended to provide living quarters. Ellen and I were some of the last to board. Most of the SA chambers are already occupied, and we'll be put under very shortly. There's certainly nothing on the ship to stay awake for, except the view.

An announcement has just gone out saying there's some delay in putting us into the SA chambers. I could have done without the wait, and not just because of the lack of space. I must admit I'm uneasy with the idea. Ellen keeps assuring me that suspended animation is safe, and biology is her field, not mine, but I'd still rather get it over and done with.

I spent a long while looking down on Earth, thinking about Mom and Dad down there. It's a shame they won't get to see their grandchildren while they are babies, but I know they understand what getting the place on the colony ship meant to Ellen and me. If all goes well, we'll be able to come back for a visit in a dozen years or so.

16-May-2254: We've just watched the Maia and Alcyone slip into X-space. Amazing to watch something so large just ripple and disappear. I'm pleased I saw it. It's been the one benefit from the delay on the SA chambers, but at last they seem to have sorted out the problem and are starting to put people under. Ellen and I are due to go within the hour. I suppose a second benefit is that, after having tried to get a couple of hours' sleep on a chair in the observation lounge, I'm now almost looking forward to being put under.

After giving up on trying to sleep, I spent some time searching the ship's data files for Greek mythology, trying to work out if there's any significance in the allocation of engineering discipline to goddess: Celaeno with biology, Taygete with geology, and so on, but I guess not. In fact, I'll bet that even the names of the Pleiades were only chosen because of the number of ships and someone high up liked the sound of them, nothing to do with mythology, or even destination. Trust the admin at the UN space agency to be strong on romanticism and weak on literature.

Time is a strange thing. When they wake us up, we will be only a few hours older, whereas 18 months will have passed on Earth, and the Celaeno will have spent over 300 years in X-space, traveling on auto systems, though I know that referring to time in X-space is a bit of an anomaly. I've seen the equations the physicists churn out, but the only way I can get my head around it is to think of time going more quickly there. Except it doesn't, since the only way people can survive in X-space is in SA, where time doesn't go at all.

I know this isn't making sense. I'm tired.

That's it. Ellen and I have just been called to the SA chambers. My next entry in this diary will be 18 months in the future and 21.5 light years from here.

??-???-????: I keep rereading the last words I wrote. I feel it's a joke, but I can't work out who is playing it on whom. It hasn't quite sunk in. I'm going to try and write down what's happened. Maybe putting it in words will make it seem more real.

Somehow, the guidance computer malfunctioned. It didn't know when to tell the ship to stop. The systems are so over-engineered that the Celaeno kept plowing on and on through X-space, until at last, one of the mechanisms entered a critical condition and the emergency override snapped in. Although even the definition of emergency is extremely cautious. One of the engineers told me the ship is still good for decades.

Under the emergency procedures, the Celaeno selected the nearest large planetary system, came out of X-space, and woke the crew. And as a final gesture, it sent a distress signal to Earth. But the procedure is based on the assumption that you're more or less where you're supposed to be, that Earth is close enough for a rescue vessel to be with you in months, and that any large planetary system will probably have some sort of installation there already. Whereas, where we are, is god knows where. The best guess I've had from the crew is 3000 light years from Earth.

The distance is hard to grasp, but it's the time that I can't take. While we've been in SA, over 200 years have passed on Earth—or so the crew thinks. We are way beyond normal comms range, and even if the SOS message reaches them, will anyone still be listening for us? And unless there have been some major leaps in technology, it will take further centuries for a rescue to get here.

Ellen's still in SA. I'm writing this sitting on the floor of the gangway beside her chamber. It's cold and the lighting is bad, but I need to be near her. I wish I could talk things over with her. Apparently, the crew woke me as the most senior geologist on board   possibly the only geologist on board. There's going to be a meeting later when they've finished waking the select few. God knows what they are going to say. What options have we got?

1 day after waking: We've had our meeting and time to think things over. Apart from the ship's crew, there are 35 other colonists awake, representing all the available expertise on board. We have three options to consider. One is to park the Celaeno in stable orbit and for us all to go back into SA and hope a rescue gets to us before the systems break down completely. Two is to patch up the ship and try and get back to Earth. The third option is to give up on any hope of ever getting home. The only stroke of luck we've had is that one of the planets in this solar system looks as if it might be habitable. Its mass is 97% of Earth's. It has an oxygen-nitrogen atmosphere and a developed biosphere. In fact, at first glance, it appears a big improvement on the world we were supposed to be colonizing. That's why the crew has woken us up. Before we can make a decision, we have to be certain that this planet is really viable.

It will still be a hard choice. Common sense says that both of the first two options mean putting our faith in machinery way past its planned working life, and we have nothing to go back to Earth for. All our families will be long dead, society and technology will have moved on, our skills will be outdated. But to give up on the rest of the human race is a big, big step to take.

I wish I could talk to Ellen.

40 days after waking: The reports are in, though I feel my own contribution was the next best thing to useless. All the geological survey equipment was on the Taygete, but maybe it made people happier for me to say that I think there are mineable mineral deposits down there. Everything else has confirmed that the planet is habitable.

Now we have to vote. The worst part is making a decision on behalf of all the others, but the living quarters aren't large enough to have more than a fraction of the passengers awake at the same time. I guess most of us must feel the same pressure, but it's worse for me as I'm really a very junior member of the colony team, way down the hierarchy. Unlike Dr. Himoti, who is Principal Geneticist, and gives the impression that she thinks the Celaeno is her own private property.

However, I think the vote is a foregone conclusion. Trying to get back to Earth is a non-starter. With the error on the navigation computer, the engineers aren't even certain which way Earth is. And the same counts against the idea of waiting in SA for rescue. The Celaeno's SOS message was probably focused in the wrong direction, giving absolutely no chance of it being picked up. We'd be gambling on the remote chance of someone stumbling across us by accident before the SA chambers became inoperable, and I can tell no one is keen on the idea. Especially after Douglas told us what would happen if the cryogenic cooling system broke down with us inside.

I've taken to talking to Ellen's SA chamber. Silly, but it helps me adjust my thoughts, like writing this diary. If the vote goes the way I think, we'll be waking the others up soon and ferrying down to the planet. It will be easier to face things with Ellen. Maybe part of the reason for me voting for the planet is that I have to be sure I'm going to see her again.

41 days after waking: It was a unanimous vote in favor of the planet. The site for landfall has been chosen on the main continent in the northern hemisphere, by the banks of a large river. The soil is fertile, and the river will provide good transport. All the resources we could identify are near at hand. The landing site is in lowlands, surrounded by mountains on three sides and the sea to the south. According to the surveys, its climate should be moderate at all times of the year. I've been studying the maps. I managed to restrain myself from showing them to Ellen's SA chamber. She'll be seeing the actual site itself soon.

49 days after waking: Ellen and I have made landfall. Ellen is still a little dazed by the news. I've spent so long talking to her SA chamber, I tend to forget she hasn't had much time to come to terms with things. But for me, after a month and a half on the Celaeno, it's wonderful to stand on green stuff that looks like grass with a blue sky over my head—even though it's cold. It is so nice to be able to stick your arms out straight without clouting somebody else around the ear.

57 days after waking: A third of the crew and colonists are down here. The shuttles are going up and down continuously. The landing site is a mess. We have the facilities to make a first-class genetics lab, yet don't really have the right machinery to build houses. They were on the Alcyone. But I'm sure we'll adapt. The northern hemisphere was chosen as it's mid-spring here at the moment, so we have plenty of time to get sorted before winter.

86 days after waking: Ellen and I have just gotten back from the vote. Even the skeleton crew on the Celaeno came down to take part in person. It was the first time all 2,000 of us had been together. And it was nice to be able to vote just for myself, instead of on behalf of others, particularly with all the implications.

Dr. Himoti formally proposed the motion to try and found a permanent ongoing colony, while Jaminda Uti led the opposition of those who think we should simply make things as comfortable as possible for ourselves, live out the rest of our natural lives, and leave the planet unchanged.

I think Jaminda knew she was arguing a lost cause. Her mood seemed one of frustrated despair, though she had a few good points to make. We don't have the resources to create a high-tech society. The factories and heavy machinery were on the other ships. Maybe Jaminda is simply the best historian, and the rest of us have rose-tinted glasses when it comes to a pre-industrial world. But I'm sure life wouldn't be quite as grim as she painted it. Life expectancy might be shorter than on Earth, but we do have true medical knowledge to pass on to our children, rather than the superstition people relied on in the past. And we ought to be able to reach the technology level of the old Roman Empire at the very least.

Anyway, the outcome of the vote was never in question. We all chose to become colonists because of a dream for the future. None of us could consider becoming a dead end in history. On the way back from the count, Ellen and I started planning names for our first child.

90 days after waking or 08-May-01: The date I've given is a bit of a compromise. I would have liked to have made day one of the new calendar the date of the first landfall, but the general feeling was to backdate the year to start on mid-winter's day. Which means that the colony on this planet officially began on 23-March-01. The days are a bit longer than on earth, a fraction over 25 hours, but there are only 337 days in a year, so the year still works out a touch shorter than on Earth. It has been decided to stick with 12 months, though they'll only have 28 days. The odd day over will be mid-winter's day, hanging about on its own. Then they'll be leap years, exceptions, and so on. Someone has worked it out with the aid of the Celaeno's computers.

For time, we're following the standard UNSA practice of botching a compromise between decimalization and divisions that feel right. There will be 20 hours in a day, 100 minutes in an hour, and 50 seconds in a minute. Frequency counters in the lab equipment will keep to GMT, which gives 45 point something seconds in a new planetary minute. Ellen's threatening to scream if she hears another joke about working long hours.

So far, no one has come up with a generally acceptable name for the planet. I guess our children will just call it the Earth.

19-May-01: Already Ellen is up to her neck in work at the genetics lab. There's enough stored food on the Celaeno to keep us going for years, but eventually we'll have to start producing our own. I've joined Cedric Martin on a project to smelt steel. I just hope I'll be able to recognize iron ore when I see it. It's brought home to me Jaminda's point about taking technology for granted—not that I'd change the way I voted.

27-August-01: Cedric and I got back to Landfall today, from surveying upriver. I brought back some samples that I think contain iron ore. Maybe. Most of the time I'm torn between frustration and amusement. Four years studying geology and I'm reduced to guesswork. I'm re-teaching myself the junior level stuff, how to spot metamorphic rock and all. If only I had a handheld T.T. scope, like one of the 90 or so they put on the Taygete. If it wasn't for the knowledge base of the Celaeno computers, we wouldn't know where to start with smelting steel.

At least Ellen has all the equipment she needs. She has been analyzing the native fauna, trying to see if any of it is potentially useful. But the answer seems to be that it isn't, certainly not as a source of food. It is just as well the Celaeno was stocked with genetic samples of every species known on Earth, from aardvarks to zebras. The indigenous animals have fat molecules that are incompatible with ours, to the point that we're mutually indigestible. They also have a cyanide-like chemical in their blood, and apparently we're nearly as poisonous to them—they can't take too much iron. Unfortunately, some of the bigger carnivores look as if they might bite our heads off before they learn this.

Some of Ellen's colleagues have been looking at the vegetation. They think the grass-like stuff will support Earth herbivores as long as they can engineer a gene for an enzyme to break down the cellular coating. Dr. Himoti is working on it, and once she's finished, they'll put six experimental sheep in the artificial wombs. On a related subject, Ellen isn't pregnant yet, but we're working on it.

03-September-01: One of Ellen's friends, Simon, was telling me that we have been really fortunate with the flora. Iron is poisonous to the native animals, and recently (in evolutionary terms) one family of plants has exploited this by concentrating iron in its leaves. The result is that these plants, with nothing to eat them, have run riot and triggered a mass extinction event in the fauna. The animal evolution was starting to catch up, but there is still a great big hole in the ecosphere ideally suited to iron-loving Earth herbivores.

15-October-01: The first attempt at smelting was not a complete success. Three of us burned our hands, and the steel was so weak it snapped when you tapped it. But we all stood around grinning like idiots and slapping each other on the backs. At least we are going forward.

At home, I think Ellen is starting to get a little worried. She's still not pregnant. But I know it can take a bit of time for things to get working after you reactivate hormonal cycles. We should give it a couple more months before going for a medical check. Anyway, Ellen has a lot of important work on at the lab. She doesn't need distractions. She's now working directly with Dr. Himoti.

01-December-01: The weather is getting much colder. We're OK inside the buildings, but when we go outside, the low temperatures are actually painful on the skin. It's frightening to feel so vulnerable. I almost wonder if Jaminda Uti might have been right. The emergency power sources should last for our lifetime and keep the heating going, but how will our children survive once the fuel runs out? Someone told me it's going to get a lot colder still in a month or so. You see the old pictures of people playing in snow, and it all looks like fun. I start to suspect that the truth was a little different. The daytime temperature at the moment is well above freezing, and it still feels as if the cold could kill you. What will it be like when it's low enough for snow to settle on the ground?

I was saying this to Natasha Krowe, who used to work as a ranger in a wildlife preserve on Earth. She cracked up laughing. She couldn't believe that I've never been exposed to sub-zero temperatures before, whereas she's quite used to living without the cushion of technology— tramping through the wilds and all. She's challenged me to what she called a snowball fight after the first snowfall, but I don't think I'll be taking her up on it.

03-January-02: It's not just Ellen. No one is pregnant. Ellen told me yesterday that a group at the lab has been formed to look into it. It was supposed to be on the quiet, but half the colony seems to know, although no one is voicing their worries aloud.

Despite the cold, the smelting group are throwing themselves into the work, keeping the furnace going. Perhaps it's for the warmth, or perhaps we just need to demonstrate our faith in the future.

09-January-02: More bad news. Two plant biologists out surveying in the mountains to the north were killed by large cat-like animals. The rescue team found the partly eaten remains. It's no comfort to know the cats will have had massive indigestion and most of their fur will have dropped out from iron poisoning.

A few of the colonists are service personnel who had originally been intended to form the colony's security team. Natasha Krowe is going to train them to work as rangers, patrolling the outskirts of the valley. Hopefully, they'll be able to prevent a similar cat-attack from happening again, or at least be able to warn people of where to stay away from.

02-February-02: We all knew something was wrong, though we tried to dismiss the doubts, but after eight months, someone should have gotten pregnant. Now the report from the lab is common knowledge, and it's worse than anyone guessed.

The plants on this planet produce pollen that plays hell with male hormones. The stuff is in the air, in the water, in us. Ellen has told me it acts a bit like estrogen, but with a whole set of extra complications. Most women aren't too badly affected, but every man has a sperm count of absolute zero. I feel as if I want to wear a mask over my face. Not that it would help. It explains why quite a lot of men have been complaining about feeling nauseous in the mornings.

Last night, some people were suggesting making isolation rooms, I guess with visions of prospective fathers sitting inside, waiting for their sperm count to recover. But Ellen said that women are so flooded with the estrogen complex that males couldn't develop in the womb. We could probably fix it so that a few boys were born, but once the high-tech resources from the Celaeno run out, there wouldn't be any way to carry on.

I can't believe Himoti didn't spot it in her original survey, but she says the estrogen complex wasn't detected, as it is not, strictly speaking, poisonous.

01-April-02: It's a beautiful day. The sun is out. The grasslands are ablaze with small red flowers and the air smells so sweet. For the first time in my life, I haven't been protected from winter, and now that spring is here, I can feel the new life about to break forth in the world. It would be exhilarating, if it weren't for the reminder that no life will ever come forth from us. Pretty much all work in the colony has stopped. I went out this morning and looked at the prototype furnace. I stood there for ages, crying. I feel so useless.

13-May-02: So now we know what Dr. Himoti has been working on for the past few months. No wonder she's been keeping it quiet. Even Ellen didn't know what she was up to. And no wonder the Earth authorities back home had kept quiet about the results of the research done by the neo-eugenicists. Himoti must have been close to the gods just to get a look at the reports. I wonder how she ever got permission to bring copies with her on the Celaeno.

I knew the neo-eugenicists had played around with bioengineering, wanting to create a race of superior beings. I'd heard they even had a few experimental fetuses in tanks when the government nailed them down. Like everyone else, I had assumed they were trying to make 2-meter tall supermen with IQs of 500 plus, but according to Himoti, their goals had been in a quite different direction. I was surprised when she started talking about the neo-eugenicists' work on genetically inducing extrasensory perception, but it just confirmed my view of them as potentially dangerous cranks. When she told us they'd succeeded, I was stunned. Even after the hours of explanations, I think a large section of the colonists still can't take it seriously. If it wasn't that Ellen was convinced, I'd probably be one of them.

Apparently, the neo-eugenicists had managed to bioengineer telepathy, telekinesis, psychic healing, and the all rest, but it's just the psychic healing that Himoti has concentrated on—the ability of one person to manipulate the bodily functions of another, using only the power of their mind. Himoti claims we could genetically engineer the potential for psychic healing into our descendants, to create a self-sustaining population for this planet. It will be an innate ability that will be passed down the generations, long after the high-tech equipment from the Celaeno has worn out. At first, I thought Himoti was suggesting some sort of magical cure for the male infertility, but her proposal was even more startling.

According to Himoti, not all the children would have the ability, and those that do, won't have it equally. I got a bit lost with the math of recessive genes, but Himoti estimates that in the population, one in a hundred would have enough psychic ability to be a highly proficient healer. Beyond this, one in a thousand would have enough of the ability to be able to mentally manipulate individual cells so as to induce women and animals to spontaneously clone themselves. At this point in the meeting, I think the audience was equally divided between those who were laughing and those whose jaws were hanging open. But Himoti went one stage further. She said that one in ten thousand would take psychic healing to its ultimate degree and be able to deconstruct genetic material in a cloned cell and imprint sections of another person's DNA onto it.

There was absolute silence in the meeting. I don't think any of us could really believe that psychic powers could achieve something it would normally take a fully equipped genetics lab to do. But Himoti sounded convinced it would work. She said we can do it, but is it right? She's given us a decision to make, and every vote that has gone before is kindergarten ethics by comparison.

16-May-02: We sat up all last night, arguing. Ellen is utterly opposed to Himoti's plan, and not because she has doubts about it working. She's seen the calculations and agrees they are scientifically correct, although not morally right. But I'm not so sure. The neo-eugenicists' work was outlawed because they wanted to create a select master race. On this planet, every baby will start with the same chance of having the ability, and without it, no one will be able to live here at all—and although I know it sounds pathetic, I want someone to use my furnace.

Of course, rational arguments don't really come into it. It's all on emotion, and there's plenty of that going around at the moment. Cedric joked with me that wherever you see two people together, you can hear four points of view. I'm not even sure whether Ellen's objections are because her training has encouraged her to think the issues over more fully, or because she is developing a marked personal dislike of Dr. Himoti.

No, I'm not being fair to Ellen, she wouldn't let her professional ethics be compromised by petty animosity.

22-May-02: The vote is over. There was a narrow but significant majority in favor of Himoti's plan. If we'd had to vote on the proposal on day one on the planet, it might have gone differently, but after months of dreaming and working for a new world, we couldn't give up. There are still a lot of issues to consider. Not the least is that it will be an all female world. Even if boys are conceived, they won't develop as male with all the estrogen complex in the environment. I know the lesbians in the colony decided as a group to abstain from the vote, but I have a feeling most other people did not notice, or misunderstood the gesture.

There are going to be some problems, but at the moment everyone seems relieved. Even Ellen isn't quite as upset as she thought she would be. She can feel that her conscience is clear, as she voted against, and I think she is a little ashamed to find herself excited by the new hope. It will be some time before Himoti finishes her experiments, but then the first embryos will be engineered in the lab.

26-November-03: Himoti's finished her initial work. The first batch of embryos are in the artificial wombs. We've been told one is going to be ours. I stood in the lab with Ellen, looking at the monitors and thinking of Himoti's predictions about the children being potentially healers, cloners, or imprinters. We've all become a bit cavalier about using the terms, but for the first time, the reality hit me. I tried to work out how I'd feel about rearing a child with psychic ability.

11-August-03: We received our daughter today. She's beautiful. Light brown skin, dark hair, dark eyes, and totally wonderful. We've named her Parnella after Ellen's mother. To get the genes she needed, Dr. Himoti has had to mix and match all the genetic material at her disposal. The DNA has been so well blended that there won't be much in the way of ethnic differences between the children, they'll all be uniform, homologous human. But Himoti has managed to make some concessions. Parnella even has a tiny section of Ellen's and my DNA in her makeup.

20-March-04: Ellen has convinced me that Himoti's behavior is becoming a concern. More and more, it feels as if Himoti, rather than Captain Dernic or the elected council, runs the place. She is definitely the one pushing the agenda. Ellen is supposed to be in charge of the gene bank, but she often finds her authority sidestepped.

20-January-05: Parnella is now running around and starting to string a few words together. Sometimes I look at her and just can't take Dr. Himoti's talk of paranormal abilities seriously. Parnella is such a wonderfully, beautifully, ordinary toddler, and her sister will be with us in under four months.

22-October-12: Himoti is becoming ever more autocratic. She's surrounded herself with an adoring clique. It takes an appointment for Ellen to see her, and lesser mortals like the elected council have no chance of getting her ear. Even Ellen's position is shaky. She has a senior post in the labs, but no real responsibility. She usually only finds out about decision-making meetings after they've happened. But at least it gives her time to spend with the girls. We've been allocated a fourth daughter, sometime next year.

01-September-17: I'm still shaking and stunned. Which is insane, given the amount of time I've had to get used to the idea of psychic healing—but to actually see it—

There was an accident in the tool room, and Cedric cut himself badly. There was blood everywhere. I was panicking and looking for the first aid kit, when Jake's eldest rushed over, put her hand on Cedric, and the bleeding stopped—just like that. Cedric said the pain vanished as if it had been switched off. Afterward there was just a nicely healing scab left on Cedric's arm that looked as if it was three days, rather than three minutes old.

I've just realized that, until now, I've never really, truly believed in Himoti's assertions.

19-July-19: Parnella is in love again. It's Cedric's daughter this time. Cedric came around to talk to me and mumbled and cleared his throat and then said, "Do you think they'll grow out of it?" I didn't know whether to laugh or what. Then suddenly a dozen or so odd conversations fell into place—the things people have said or not said over the years. I wonder what they have been thinking. I suspect some haven't been thinking at all. They can't have been assuming their daughters would be forever celibate, but perhaps they've been imagining sisterly, virtually platonic friendships. They look so surprised when their daughters start acting like love-struck adolescents.

I guess growing up with Anne gives me a different perspective. Younger siblings always get the advantage of the older ones breaking the ground for them, pushing back the boundaries of what your parents will allow. Anne did it for me with a vengeance. I know Mom and Dad never tried to criticize her, and they read all the pamphlets on how to support a gay or lesbian child, but they were so pleased I turned out straight, I could have brought home an alcoholic mud wrestler as a girlfriend and they wouldn't have minded.

As the years go by, I find myself thinking of Anne, more so than Mom and Dad. We were so close as children. I wonder what she would have made of this world. I think it might have amused her, or then again, maybe not. But one thing I got from her for certain. She never, for a second, let me get away with thinking that her relationships would be any less passionate or more sensible than my own.

12-April-24: Jean Smith came around here tonight, storming mad—not with us, she just wanted a sympathetic heterosexual ear. Dr. Himoti has accused her of corrupting the young. It seems that Himoti has been so bound up in her lab that she's only just noticed the children are forming steady relationships. One can but wonder at what she was expecting. Then apparently Himoti overheard some people saying how glad they were about there being a few lesbian couples in the colony to provide good role models.

It's the standard space agency line. Although it is no secret that heterosexuals are preferred for new colonies, the authorities do at least recognize that statistics will assert themselves in the second generation. That's why they insist on a few stable homosexual couples in every colony. But whatever the space agency might expect, it has obviously caught Himoti totally by surprise. Jean was the nearest lesbian that Himoti could lay her hands on, and she caught the full force of her anger. It occurs to me that Himoti might have more than a touch of homophobia about her, which I find incredibly ironic. Jean probably will too, when she calms down. But in fact, lesbianism doesn't come into it. People are innately sexual, and for our children there is simply no other option.

18-January-25: I'm going to be a grandfather. Parnella and Lilian have decided that after being together for two years, they are ready for children. They've got an appointment at the labs for tomorrow afternoon. They'll get one of Himoti's prepared embryos, but Parnella is going to carry the baby herself. All the artificial wombs are working flat out, but the waiting list for them is growing day by day, and having made up their minds, they don't want to wait.

But it gets me worrying again about the long-term future of the colony. There is no problem splicing DNA in the genetics lab, and it will be able to keep going for decades, but it won't last forever. I pray Himoti is right about cloners and imprinters who'll be able to create embryos without the need of scientific equipment. The population is getting big enough that some should start to show up soon—if Himoti's statistics were right. After all the work, it is unthinkable that the colony might die out.

It's a worry that must flit through most people's minds once or twice a year. But Himoti was certainly right about some of the children having the ability to heal by touch. The regular medical team is almost out of work.

01-September-25: Even if an imprinter does arrive, the lab will have to keep going for years. Dr. Himoti has been training some of the children in the necessary techniques, so they can carry on when all of us older ones have gone. It's a very sensible thing to do, but I share Ellen's concern about the cult growing up around Himoti. There's almost something of religious fervor about these young women at times.

12-August-28: Lilian's daughter was born at 5:00 this morning. Ellen and I have just gotten back from seeing the new arrival. Parnella and Lilian wanted to name the baby after me. We tried to explain that Peter wasn't a suitable name for a girl, though I'm not sure if it was worth the bother. Does it really matter? In the end, the baby was named Suzanne, after my mother.

23-February-30: Ellen has had a major argument with Himoti. Two of the young women working in the labs have been having a turbulent affair, although they've tried not to let it affect their work. But when she found out, Himoti refused to tolerate it and has thrown them out of the labs. Ellen took their side, and so she has been kicked out as well. Himoti will probably relent when she calms down, but Ellen says she doesn't want to go back. Says she can't put up with Himoti's games of omnipotence any more. I can't say I blame her. Ellen's offered to help the rangers studying the native wildlife, one last go out in the field before she gets too old.

I can't make Himoti out. She's not a classic homophobe. From what I can tell, it's not so much the physical act of making love that upsets her, but rather the emotional commitment. Although I think she'd be happier if they practiced neither, and of course, the distinction is lost on the children.

07-November-39: It's just been confirmed that little Suzie is a cloner! The tenth in the colony. It's been obvious since she was about four that she was going to be an exceptional healer, and I know Ellen has been convinced that she would be able to induce cloning, but I wasn't sure if her pride as a grandmother wasn't giving her false hopes. Of course Himoti wants to take charge of the child, but Ellen and Parnella have put up a fight. Suzie will go to the labs for lessons in genetics, but Ellen's determined she won't become one of Himoti's acolytes.

12-April-41: The mare has produced a foal. Suzie's first cloning. Back when she had initially induced the mare's pregnancy, I tried to get Suzie to describe how she did what she did and what it is she sees inside other living beings. She made an attempt to explain, but I guess it was a bit like trying to tell a deaf person about sound. I've stopped questioning all sorts of miracle healing by the laying on of hands. I'm just going to have to add psychic cloning to the list.

Suzie dragged Ellen and me along to see the foal. She is delighted at her first creation. I'm trying to work out whether this makes me a great-grandfather or not. But I guess this means that the colony is viable. Even if no one ever manages to psychically imprint DNA patterns onto an embryo, at least it will be possible to clone people once the lab wears out, although I can't help feeling it would be better to produce unique individuals.

09-July-47: I've just gotten back from Cedric's funeral. We buried him with a section of the original smelting furnace. I hope there will still be a piece left when it's my turn to go. We older ones from the Celaeno are starting to thin out slightly, but the children are doing well. Last population count was just over 18,000 people, including twenty-eight cloners and two possible imprinters.

It's strange how the eye adapts. All the children have light brown skin and dark brown hair, but I've gotten so used to it that they now seem every bit as varied as the original population from Earth. To their own eyes, the differences are probably even more marked.

03-February-48: I'm not sure whether to be amused or horrified by Himoti's disciples at the labs. They've taken to calling themselves the Sisterhood and wearing their lab masks and lab coats all the time, like a badge of office or a priestess's robes. But once the labs outgrow their usefulness and the imprinters take over, it will put an end to the nonsense.

27-October-53: Ellen was invited back to the labs to help file away Himoti's papers. I'm surprised the Sisterhood let her in, but now that Himoti is dead, Ellen is the most senior geneticist, and I think they wanted to be certain that nothing important was overlooked. Ellen says everything is very well ordered, so it shouldn't take her too long. Himoti had her hand on the rudder right up to the last, even though she was over 90.

04-November-53: Ellen has smuggled out a wad of Himoti's personal papers, those giving her private thoughts and plans. We don't know quite what to do with them. It's probably too late now to do anything sensible. We haven't shown them to anyone else, we just sit and read them, horrified.

At least we now know why Himoti insisted on creating a single racial type. She actually seems to have thought that with a single race and a single gender, she could create a sisterly utopia. One big melting pot, or something equally banal. No sexism or racism—as if people need race or gender to find an excuse to treat each other like shit. She even thought that with only women, there would be an end to possessive, manipulative relationships. Half an hour talking to my sister Anne would have set her straight—or maybe not. Himoti seemed to think that her perfectly engineered specimens would not make the mistake of getting passionately irrational about each other. Words fail me. How could someone so clever be so naive? And it's too late now to challenge Himoti, or try and modify her legacy. Already her followers talk about her as if she was semi-divine.

Now Ellen and I are asking ourselves questions about way back, when Himoti put her original proposition to us. We even wonder if she knew about the estrogen complex before we left the Celaeno. How seriously did she look into other alternatives? How much did she manipulate the colony to follow her own dreams and delusions? Why weren't we more skeptical that she could engineer psychic ability but couldn't engineer a solution to the male infertility? Why didn't we ask more questions?

28-May-61: Ellen's grave looks very peaceful. I found myself talking to it. Just like I talked to her SA chamber when I was on the Celaeno. The children have promised to bury me alongside her. It can't be that far off.

The Sisterhood is completing their plans to build a memorial over Himoti's grave. From what I can see, they're reinventing the temple, but there is no point trying to argue with them. Some young fanatics who lack the brains to join the Sisterhood have formed themselves into a sort of honor guard, styled on the rangers. They worry me.

Sometimes, they seem to treat all of the original colonists with reverence. They call us 'the elder-ones,' which is, I guess, partly our own fault for always calling them 'the children.' I think they would be quite happy if I was to claim to be a saint. I can see the graveyard being turned into a field of shrines. I trust our kids will know that neither Ellen nor I would want that. We did our best for the world. The lives our children create are the only monument we want.

Last entry in diary
Mid-winter's day-67: There's just us four original colonists left, Karin, Jade, Carma, and me. We met together to celebrate mid-winter and talked about the Celaeno. She's still up there over Landfall, parked in geo-stationary orbit. And we talked about the Earth. We wondered what it looks like now, who lives there, if our children will ever meet up with them, and what they'll make of each other.

Afterward, I got home and read back through all my diaries. When I boarded the Celaeno for a new world, I never dreamed I'd end up being the last man on the planet. It's been a long hard job, building a world. I don't know how our children will judge us, I only pray we did the right thing.

❧❧

About the Author

Jane Fletcher was born in Greenwich, London in 1956. She now lives alone in the south-west of England after the sudden, untimely death of her partner.

Her love of fantasy began at the age of seven when she encountered Greek mythology. This was compounded by a childhood spent clambering over every example of ancient masonry she could find (medieval castles, megalithic monuments, Roman villas). It was her resolute ambition to become an archaeologist when she grew up, so it was something of a surprise when she became a software engineer instead.

Jane started writing when her partner refused to listen to yet another lengthy account of 'a really good idea for a story' and insisted that she write it down. After many years of revision, the result, *Lorimal's Chalice*, was published. Jane's novels have won a GCLS award and have been short-listed for the Gaylactic Spectrum award.

Lorimal's Chalice will be re-released as Book One and Book Two of The Lyremouth Chronicles in the coming year (*Book One: The Exile and The Sorcerer, Book Two: The Traitor and The Chalice*) along with the *all new* Book Three in the series: *The Empress and The Acolyte*.

Jane is also the author of The Celaeno Series. All three books in this series are available from Bold Strokes Books in 2005 (*The Walls of Westernfort, Rangers at Roadsend*, and *The Temple at Landfall*).

Visit Jane's website at www.janefletcher.co.uk

Books Available From Bold Strokes Books

Innocent Hearts by Radclyffe. In a wild and unforgiving land, two women learn about love, passion, and the wonders of the heart. (1-933110-21-X)

The Temple at Landfall by Jane Fletcher. An imprinter, one of Celaeno's most revered servants of the Goddess, is also a prisoner to the faith—until a Ranger frees her by claiming her heart. (1-933110-27-9)

Force of Nature by Kim Baldwin. From tornados to forest fires, the forces of nature conspire to bring Gable McCoy and Erin Richards close to danger, and closer to each other. (1-933110-23-6)

In Too Deep by Ronica Black. Undercover homicide cop Erin McKenzie tracks a femme fatale who just might be a real killer…with love and danger hot on her heels. (1-933110-17-1)

Stolen Moments: *Erotic Interludes 2* by Stacia Seaman and Radclyffe, eds. Love on the run, in the office, in the shadows…Fast, furious, and almost too hot to handle. (1-933110-16-3)

Course of Action by Gun Brooke. Actress Carolyn Black desperately wants the starring role in an upcoming film produced by Annelie Peterson. Just how far will she go for the dream part of a lifetime? (1-933110-22-8)

Rangers at Roadsend by Jane Fletcher. Sergeant Chip Coppelli has learned to spot trouble coming, and that is exactly what she sees in her new recruit, Katryn Nagata. The Celaeno series. (1-933110-28-7)

Justice Served by Radclyffe. Lieutenant Rebecca Frye and her lover, Dr. Catherine Rawlings, embark on a deadly game of hide-and-seek with an underworld kingpin who traffics in human souls. (1-933110-15-5)

Distant Shores, Silent Thunder by Radclyffe. Dr. Tory King—along with the women who love her—is forced to examine the boundaries of love, friendship, and the ties that transcend time. (1-933110-08-2)

Hunter's Pursuit by Kim Baldwin. A raging blizzard, a mountain hideaway, and a killer-for-hire set a scene for disaster—or desire—when Katarzyna Demetrious rescues a beautiful stranger. (1-933110-09-0)

The Walls of Westernfort by Jane Fletcher. All Temple Guard Natasha Ionadis wants is to serve the Goddess—until she falls in love with one of the rebels she is sworn to destroy. The Celaeno series. (1-933110-24-4)

Change Of Pace: *Erotic Interludes* by Radclyffe. Twenty-five hot-wired encounters guaranteed to spark more than just your imagination. Erotica as you've always dreamed of it. (1-933110-07-4)

Honor Guards by Radclyffe. In a wild flight for their lives, the president's daughter and those who are sworn to protect her wage a desperate struggle for survival. (1-933110-01-5)

Fated Love by Radclyffe. Amidst the chaos and drama of a busy emergency room, two women must contend not only with the fragile nature of life, but also with the irresistible forces of fate. (1-933110-05-8)

Justice in the Shadows by Radclyffe. In a shadow world of secrets and lies, Detective Sergeant Rebecca Frye and her lover, Dr. Catherine Rawlings, join forces in the elusive search for justice. (1-933110-03-1)

shadowland by Radclyffe. In a world on the far edge of desire, two women are drawn together by power, passion, and dark pleasures. An erotic romance. (1-933110-11-2)

Love's Masquerade by Radclyffe. Plunged into the indistinguishable realms of fiction, fantasy, and hidden desires, Auden Frost is forced to question all she believes about the nature of love. (1-933110-14-7)

Love & Honor by Radclyffe. The president's daughter and her lover are faced with difficult choices as they battle a tangled web of Washington intrigue for...love and honor. (1-933110-10-4)

Beyond the Breakwater by Radclyffe. One Provincetown summer three women learn the true meaning of love, friendship, and family. (1-933110-06-6)

Tomorrow's Promise by Radclyffe. One timeless summer, two very different women discover the power of passion to heal and the promise of hope that only love can bestow. (1-933110-12-0)

Love's Tender Warriors by Radclyffe. Two women who have accepted loneliness as a way of life learn that love is worth fighting for and a battle they cannot afford to lose. (1-933110-02-3)

Love's Melody Lost by Radclyffe. A secretive artist with a haunted past and a young woman escaping a life that has proved to be a lie find their destinies entwined. (1-933110-00-7)

Safe Harbor by Radclyffe. A mysterious newcomer, a reclusive doctor, and a troubled gay teenager learn about love, friendship, and trust during one tumultuous summer in Provincetown. (1-933110-13-9)

Above All, Honor by Radclyffe. Secret Service Agent Cameron Roberts fights her desire for the one woman she can't have—Blair Powell, the daughter of the president of the United States. (1-933110-04-X)